$IX ON€ Z£RO

Only Other People Die

Gary NICHOLLS

Green on Blue - July 2012

The NATO Regional Training Center near Herat was one of half a dozen RTCs from which the Border Management Task Force operated. The BMTF's mission was to provide training and support for Afghan Customs and Border officers while they rebuilt government institutions in areas hostile to foreign intervention. A chain of US corporations contracted, subcontracted and sub-subcontracted the Department of Defense mission until they found me. The objective was to have a team of twelve subject matter experts at this location for the next twelve months.

The air conditioning unit's rattle and hum had my room at a chilly twenty-two degrees Celsius. Turned up to twenty-five, the noise went down. As the air flap closed, I opened my laptop. The screen prompted Gary Wilshaw to sign-in. Nineteen-twenty hours in Afghanistan made it around three in the afternoon UK time. Online, the dialogue box stated: Insufficient Bandwidth For Video.

Voice only Skype would do.

"Hello, Russell. How are you?" I said.

The sound through the Sennheiser headset was perfect. It was good to hear my son's voice.

Automatic gunfire perforated the conversation before he could reply: the distinctive sound of AK-47.

"I'll have to call you back. Something's happening here," there was no time to explain. That sound was disturbingly familiar and disconcertingly close.

"Oh. OK. What was that?" said Russell.

I didn't reply. Disconnected. Russell was over four thousand miles away in Kent, England: safe.

Body armour held up in the air and over my head by the shoulder straps. Then dropped, wriggling my arms and torso until it felt right.

Pistol: Glock 17. Round racked. Holstered.

Rifle: M6 semi-automatic. Slung around my neck. Charging handle pulled right back. Five-five-six brass gleamed in the receiver. Slide released. Pushed forward into the locked position.

Helmet on. Fastened. Ready. For something. Prepare for the worst, hope for the best.

There'd been no warning: the attack alert had sounded *after* the shooting, now it ebbed and flowed with rhythmic alarm. No mortars or rockets had impacted. No ground shaking VBIED: Vehicle Borne Improvised Explosive Device. That's how previous attacks had begun: explosive detonation at the gate to breech the perimeter, then active shooters rushing the compound.

Whatever it was didn't start at the Entry Control Point. It must be something else. Maybe it's an exercise. Sunday evening. Perfect. To ensure authenticity, I hadn't been told. It's a test. They're going to be assessing my performance. Mess this up, I'm on the next flight out of here to Kabul and then home.

That's it. It's an exercise. Remember your training. Remember Jalalabad. Remember Standard Operating Procedures.

But this is the RTC, part of a large coalition force base. If there were local SOPs I didn't know them. Come on, I'd been on the base two hours.

The important stuff, I knew, like: my room, chow hall, gym, First Aid Station and, oh yes, password for the internet. For some reason we hadn't got around to attack-drill: in hindsight, just another one of life's oversights.

What if it's not an exercise? Not an incursion?

The alarm announced: **NO DRILL! ...NO DRILL!**

No drill? They must be inside the base - NOW!

The bunker was easy to get to, it was opposite the main door where I'd just come in, behind the lads sat around enjoying their early evening cigars and cigarettes. The sandbagged concrete structures were the best places to be during indirect fire. Direct fire or active shooter was another matter.

We'd been too busy driving the US Department of Homeland Security Attaché around the city of Herat in a three vehicle convoy for a security briefing. Maybe the Border Management Task Force Team Leader assumed we all knew what to do in an emergency. There's an old saying about assume making an ass out of you and me. I'd also been told Herat was one of the safest places to work in Afghanistan but, even before this alert, I wasn't convinced.

My room was one of six in a containerised dormitory. Cautiously opening the door to the small hallway, I was ready for anything. Knowing nothing. The next door led to a larger corridor. Opening inwards, it creaked loudly, announcing my presence.

Wait.

No one was shooting at me. Looking east, a double door, ajar. It led to another part of the same accommodation. People should close doors. Deny the enemy freedom of movement. No time to fix that. Beyond the open door, another double door in the distance locked reassuringly shut. If they'd found that way in already it wouldn't be so quiet in here.

But the gun fire had come from what was now to my left. A dozen vulnerable steps took me to another internal door. The empty corridor was brightly lit, but I was in the dark. Red Alert, Green on Blue: primary colours describe events, not my panic. Not a good place to be in a gunfight when the enemy arrives with automatic weapons intent on departing for paradise.

They'll jump out from one of the side-doors to my left or right.

The attack alarm got louder. Likely to conceal the sound of enemy approaching from behind. They didn't. They're not in the building, I was pretty sure of that.

Muffled shouting, might have been English, came from outside our accommodation. No shots fired. I moved forward into the main office.

Diego, one of my team mates of just a few hours, was at the *in*secure external door, his M6 up and in the firing position - ready to kill. I shouted his name through the alarm. His head moved slightly. He'd seen me. His hand came off the M6 forward grip indicating his intentions. Diego went out the door. Moved left. Replacing him at the door, I checked left and right.

On the ground, six metres away, a young lad, mid-twenties, sat up-right holding the top of his leg. He said nothing, but his eyes screamed: HELP! He became interpreter Hamid as my brain caught up with backlogged information. A bullet had entered his buttock and passed into his upper leg which was now twice the normal size.

Hamid had the presence of mind to keep his hand pressed down on it. There wasn't much external blood but the ballooned-thigh indicated internal bleeding. I reached inside my med-pack just as a man appeared alongside us. I didn't hear him approach. Data overload. Senses stunned. Possibly malfunctioning. Dangerous.

"Are you a medic?" said an Italian accent. His dialect may have been Calabrian, Umbrian or Sicilian. It didn't matter. He was focused. I wasn't. Armed with only a huge medical kit, pads and bandages shot out onto Hamid's lap. Trousers easily parted with a rescue knife. Medic got busy.

"No, mate. I was about to use a pressure bandage." After the bandage, what? I didn't know where to go next.

"I got this. You watch out for me." He took control. I'd already wasted too much time: thinking instead of doing.

Anything that approached within 180 degrees of our position was an easy target. To my rear, the bunker. To my right, one of our Land Cruisers. *I've got this*. Where were the other attackers? They must be here. There's never just one. Please, let there be more than one. I want to end it. Stay calm. Keep the breathing right.

Lacking emotion? No.

Focused indifference? Yes.

This was actual. Not an exercise. Sights, sounds and surroundings began to make sense. My situational awareness shifted gear. The initial rush of surprise, shock and intense concentration began to level-off, but I was still at Cooper Code Condition Orange.

Border Management Task Force colleagues formed a perimeter about thirty metres away. Three people were on the ground. Three guys took turns chest-pumping one. BMTF? Medics? Maybe.

The other two bodies lay motionless. Dead? Looked that way.

One of them was in Afghan Border Police uniform. Nearby, on the ground, his AK-47. Two magazines dropped moments apart: one empty, one full. Shot while attempting to reload. Good.

Bob Stefano lay close to the Afghan. Still. Dead.

My chair from a few moments before the Skype call lay on its side, a chunk of fabric missing from the backrest. The guy who'd been sat on my right was rapidly dying despite the frantic attentions of the first responders.

There was an expectation of more than one assailant. Don't ask me where that intelligence came from but if everyone believed it, this could be trigger-happy hour. Contractor kill-zone. Looking like one of the good guys gave me a chance of avoiding injury by gung-ho comrades.

For me, the transition from UK Customs Officer to subject matter expert with two guns, using my civilian skills in a war-zone, had been a life changing event. I had no military background. I'd done a lot of shooting on the pre-deployment courses at Fort Benning, Georgia. The intensive training had been good. Then came experience, gained very quickly in Nangarhar Province. More than some of the other fellas on the program. I'd survived numerous attacks at Jalalabad. On the subject of guns, I was a new-boy but I was confident I'd be able to hit the target if the need arose.

Don't think about how you got here. That's the past. This is now. Deal with it. Stay focused.

A squad of Italian soldiers ran past my position. Only medics and people with guns were outside buildings. The alarm stopped. Silence started. Dramatic aural contrast. Some of my team members maintained defensive positions at the corners of the building or behind the reassuring solid defensive concrete of T-walls. I could hear them thinking: *Now what?*

They'd stopped chest-pumping the BMTF guy. Joe Palomo was the oldest and most experienced on the BMTF program. That's why people called him Papa Joe: US Marine, Vietnam veteran, retired US Border Patrol agent, you name it, Joe had done it. He was 71 years old and dead. No ill health and slow decline into his own mess in a retirement home for Joe. Just a few hours earlier, Joe told me Herat was a very safe deployment. I didn't know the man. What I knew about Joe came from what other people told me: a good guy, very experienced, knows his way around.

We'd spoken less than fifty words. Whatever knowledge Joe had, was gone. Wisdom, admired by many - misguided. He'd become embedded with complacency and convinced others it was a good place to be.

The Italian medic and another First Responder got Hamid to the medical center.

Four team members and an Afghan rug got Papa Joe into the office. Staggering on uneven ground, my corner of the blanket began to slip from my grasp as we carried Bob Stefano into the building. Bob, was two hundred and fifty pounds of American Indian and Hispanic muscle. Stood he was well over six feet tall. In the blanket he lay crumpled and diminished. Through the insecure door, we entered the light of the BMTF building where we laid Bob, alongside Joe. My right hand ached from squeezing my rifle.

The cool linoleum floor contrasted sharply with the hot jagged rocks of the compound, but no one took comfort here.

Blood, outside and inside, was missing from the scene. Media images of massacres always show lots of blood: sprayed up walls, pooled on the ground, buzzing with flies. Not here. Amongst the white and grey of the compound rocks none were red, just dark and darker in the early evening gloom.

Alone with the dead, half dozen names could have been called into the empty building but, I shouted: MARK. No answer.

Outside, it was quiet. The dead murderer had been given the dignity of a blanket, his remains on the ground. RTC Afghans were locked-down. Confined to their accommodation. The gate between the two areas of the base was closed and guarded. Both sides.

The emptiness of the kill-zone slowly filled with sounds crowding in on me. An unarmed stranger crunched quickly around the corner, stopping long enough to tell me a British guy and an Afghan lad had been badly wounded. He'd seen them running to the medical station. I felt relieved. Then anxious. *Badly wounded? Running?* Didn't sound right to me. I headed back inside to tell the team about Mark. A cigarette smouldered on the rocks by the door. My careless boot snuffed it out.

Our accommodation wasn't empty, just devoid of life. In my bewildered state, I tried to deny my deep intuitive sense of imminent loss.

Too long spent looking at the blanket-wrapped bundles on the floor made me question my condition. Shock - maybe. Confusion - definitely. Papa Joe's name, Palomo: Spanish for Dove, the bird of Peace. Nothing to do be done here.

Outside, chasing the urgent voice shouting from the corner of our building, I ran into someone on a gurney. Recovery position. *Mark? How could it be Mark? Why Mark? How bad? Would he - recover?*

A US army medic held two bags of saline aloft. "Hold these. Like this." Her hard stare silently conveyed: *it's bad.*

Holding the life-giving bags while the harsh ground was killing my knees, I talked to Mark: "Hey, Mark. It's Gary. Looks like you may be home in time for the Olympics."

He wasn't responsive but there were signs of life. Through narrowed lids I could see the whites of his eyes intermittently clear and bright. Pupils rolling up and down like the barrels of a slot machine spinning towards Win, or Lose. Mark's life was flashing before him. He was trying to view it all on Fast-Forward. The power might go off, plunging him into infinite darkness.

Trying to sound cheerful was for my benefit not Mark's. Reassuring me that all would be well would have been an unacceptable lie coming from someone else.

"If I'm talking too much just tell me. OK? …I reckon I could talk for England. Hey! What do you think about that? An Olympic medal for talking. We know a few that'd be in with a chance don't we? …Do you think I'd be good for gold? …Yeah! Me too!"

Utter nonsense continued to pour from my lips but you're supposed to talk to casualties: keep them awake. A HiLux reversed to within a few metres of the gurney. Men took hold of three handles. The fourth was mine. Left hand carrying Mark on the gurney, rifle slung over my back, right hand holding saline bags. Mark's eyes were still rolling as we lifted him onto the back of the pickup truck. The first responders had done a good job on my friend. There was no visible blood but the noticeable fall in the saline level shouted: massive haemorrhage. Mark's injuries were

8

deadly serious. Bleeding means a beating heart: Life. But only while it's pumping blood.

Another NATO contingent ran the neighbouring base. It had an operating theatre and our man needed to be their next patient. Four of us and Mark were in the pickup's cargo space. We left the RTC at speed. The Army medic was doing her stuff while two colleagues and I rode shotgun. The driver and passenger were also armed. It may have been a fifteen minute drive to Camp Arena, maybe ten. Adrenaline distorts time. However long, was too long.

The Spanish medical centre would fix this. We pulled up at the Entry Control Point, close to the stop-sign but still too far from help. Jumping over the side of the pickup, I moved towards the lone ECP guard. Ten yards behind him, comrades moved around behind a wall of sandbags.

"Hey guys. Urgent," the ID holder slung around my neck was held in plain sight. "We've got one of our guys here. Seriously injured. He's been shot real bad. We've phoned ahead. You're expecting us."

"STOP! No closer," the Slovak guard raised his rifle.

For the second time that evening, I stared at an AK-47.

"OK," my M6 hung by my side. "Did you hear me? Medevac. Seriously injured. You *are* expecting us."

"No, we do not expect you," his rifle held steady.

"May I come to you?" I said, desperately wanting to prove my integrity.

"Make-safe," he looked over to the row of barrels set in Hesco: cuboid blast barriers of hessian-lined wire cages filled with sand. The AK's iron sights had me in the picture.

White painted steel tubes invited weapons to be inserted and unloaded: a precaution in case of accidental discharge. The ECP Slovak tracked me with his long-gun while three colleagues eyed our vehicle suspiciously. The machine gun in the sandbagged sangar would shred everything at this range.

On my way over to the make-safe point, I removed my pistol magazine. Pointing the barrel into the tube a quick backward movement of the slide ejected a round from the chamber. Snatching a 9mm bullet from mid-air always looks cool. With the bullet thumbed back into the magazine and mag into the gun, I was at Weapons Condition 3.

My M6 magazine sprung out. The muzzle went into the tube, round ejected. As the cartridge came out of the ejection port I fumbled it. The bullet bounced erratically on the rock-strewn ground before coming to rest between the HESCO. It went in my pocket. The Slovak's condescending smirk wounded my pride.

"OK?" I said. Hostility lurked behind my smile. This may well be a life and death event for our guy in the back of the truck but for the Slovak it's just a normal day and he has SOP. Remember those? SOPs are the things that stop people getting killed.

"OK," said the Slovak ECP guard, "wait here."

Wait.

"I am waiting," he couldn't have not heard exasperation in my voice. "My friend is in the back of the pickup. Badly injured. He's British. He can't wait." My stress-level went up a few notches.

"We are on lockdown," said Slovak, "attack at other base."

Resisting the temptation to shout invectives, I adopted the British-method for conversing with foreigners: raised voice and monosyllabic short sentences delivered with an air of superiority.

I replied calmly: "Yes. Attack. At RTC. I know. We were attacked. We come here, from there. This man," I waved my left arm towards the HiLux. "Injured in attack. Please look. Please. Sir. Call J-DOC."

Every base has a Joint Defense Operations Center, J-DOC: the command and control room where they knew everything that's going on, allegedly. I moved towards the pickup in the hope that he'd follow me.

"Everyone out. Make-safe," Slovak kept it simple.

Reluctantly, but quickly, the other people carrying weapons got out of the truck and followed the make-safe procedure. The unarmed medic stayed in the back of the truck holding the two saline drips that were almost empty. Slovak shouted to a soldier in the gatehouse. Somewhere, out of sight, a lifted handset plinked a telephone bell.

"We wait," said Slovak. One of the guards took a brief look at our human cargo.

"How long we wait?" I asked urgently, "Two minutes? Ten minutes?"

"Vehicle to inspection area," Slovak indicated the gravel patch between the twelve-foot high concrete T-Walls.

Vehicle inspections for concealed Improvised Explosive Devices, IED, only take a minute but that was precious time Mark didn't have.

My voice projected desperation: "We came here from RTC, directly along the highway. We went nowhere else."

If we had been US Army in a Mine Resistant Ambush Protected vehicle, M-RAP in military argot, Slovak wouldn't have stared too long at its fifty-calibre machine gun before opening the gate. But civilians without the fire power don't make threats, inferred or actual.

The bell rang one and a half times on a pole next to the sangar. The hand of an unseen ECP soldier must have been hovering over the receiver. An unintelligible shout from somewhere behind the sandbags prompted Slovak: "Now we know you!"

His demeanour changed. His rifle pointed down. Neither of us were a threat to the other.

"Sorry about your friend," in that moment, his former aloofness receded, the distance between us reduced. He too, had seen wounded comrades.

In the vehicle examination area a soldier with the inspection mirror quickly did his job and we were soon at the casualty reception point. The military medical team waiting for Mark carried him into the building.

I didn't see Mark again.

Retreat from Herat - July 2012

Before twenty-two hundred hours we were on the road back to the RTC. The US Army medic and two of the BMTF guys stayed at the Spanish Infirmary. Alone, surrounded by a darkness blacker than the night, I sat in the open cargo space of the pickup truck. Indiscernible forms looming menacingly towards me. My mind wandered. In a war-zone, consciousness split between situational awareness and retrospection is a dangerous place to be. But there was no way for me to stop thinking about Mark and how events had led us both to this point.

If the civil service job had paid me what I knew I was worth and if Mark hadn't listened to me about the job in the Congo and if the directors of the Congo job had been honest about the project's prospects, Mark and I would not have been here. If.

It took an hour to get into the RTC because the Afghan sector was still locked-down and the connecting gates secured. We were in no hurry.

Now, there was time for the first of many moments of thoughtful tranquility.

Shock is a very personal thing. Tragedy is rationalised at different rates, sometimes never. I needed time. Peace and quiet. Sitting alone in the common room of our building with a bottle of chilled water in my left hand - always the left hand - the door that wouldn't latch swung open. My Glock hand tightened around the pistol grip as my index finger pressed the safety release. Eric McGoff entered carrying the murder weapon.

"Hey, Gary. You OK?" He said solemnly. My right hand relaxed. This was our second meeting downrange. The first time was at Jalalabad on my first deployment, it hadn't gone well but now wasn't the time to dwell on trivialities.

"I'm OK Eric, but I don't know why. I'm still coming to terms with it."

"You and me both, buddy," he said.

Eric put the AK-47 and three magazines on the table in front of me, then sat opposite. Silent inertia belied its earlier deadly exchange. It had killed people, but Mark was my pal, I wanted him to live.

As a US Customs & Border Protection Officer based in El Paso, Eric was familiar with violent death and weapons but he stared quietly at the gun before bringing his eyes up to mine.

"Gary. I just heard. Mark died."

I sat back hard on the sofa, both hands clutching the bottle. My head shook despondently at the floor.

"I knew it. Deep down, I just knew he wouldn't make it. Who stopped the Afghan?"

"Me," said Eric, emotionless.

"Fucking good shooting mate."

We both stood to shake hands and man hug.

"You saved a lot of lives this evening Eric," I said, staring into the eyes of the only true hero I'd ever met, apart from my father. He modestly shrugged his shoulders like it was all in a day's work, but we both knew it was no ordinary day.

"I just came from the Attaché," said Eric. "We're quittin' Herat. Gonna demobilise. You OK packing the gear? Deceased's especially."

"Yes. I'm OK with that. Is the mission over? The program finished?" the prospect of losing a good income hit me as hard as losing a friend.

"Not sure about the program, that'll be a decision for someone in DC. The Herat mission is done. I'll get someone to give you a hand in here."

"OK, Eric, thanks," he turned for the door. "Eric," I said. Our previous encounter, at Jalalabad, came to mind. "Last time we met was at FOB Finley Shields. We didn't get off to a good start on that occasion."

Eric grinned as he recalled the event.

I smiled back at him. "Yes, it's funny now," I said, "pales into insignificance with today. I want to apologise for having doubts about you."

Eric smiled. "Just doin' my job," he said. Then went.

As the door slammed shut then clicked open, again, I sat and recalled the first time we'd met, just over a year earlier.

First Deployment - May 2011

Zero seven-hundred hours was roll-call and daily briefing in the conference room at BMTF Kabul HQ. It was before breakfast so, there'd be no questions.

"OK, everybody, good morning," the gentle Texan accent that made everyone in the room hush-down and listen-up emanated from George 'French' Beaumont, the Program Manager, also known as, PM. He allocated the day's assignments and introduced recent arrivals.

"We have some new guys with us today. Some of you already know each other. For those that don't, y'all best work on that." There were nods and gestures back and forth between the twenty or so advisors in the room. "Looks like one of you's real keen to get started," French grinned in my direction. "I like that. Mission focus."

The only one in the room in full gear with his M6 rifle against the wall behind him, was me. More than a score of pistol carrying men and women sat around in casual clothing and smiled, at New Boy's foolishness. They'd developed a sense of security that I felt was false.

French called out names: "Len Kinder." The fella opposite with the close-cropped hair and moustache raised his hand briefly. "Pete Thatcher," the fellow Mancunian and former UK Customs officer who'd also been at Fort Benning a few days ahead of me, sat to my left. "And Gary Wilshaw," I held up my hand for those that didn't know me, which meant everyone. "You guys are heading down to J'bad in the next few days. Get with Greg after this briefing so he can go over the logistics."

Greg Samms, the US Marine, now a civilian contractor and Deputy Program Manager, was in charge of getting people to places, and a few other things. His arm pivoted at the elbow on the boardroom table.

J'Bad? I couldn't decide if that was an acronym, abbreviation or a description of the conditions, as in, Jolly Bad. If there's a J'Good somewhere, it's probably not in Afghanistan. We were deploying to Jalalabad to work with the Afghan Customs Department Director in Nangarhar Province. But first I'd have another two nights in body armour getting to understand why turtles hate being on their backs. On the fourth night the compound seemed safe enough for me to sleep in my normal

14

nightwear: nothing. On the morning of day-five in-country, we headed to Jalalabad.

The flight to J'bad was the first of many during my time with the BMTF. Light aircraft and helicopters made travel around the country relatively safe. Travel by road was time consuming and hazardous: Taliban roadside Improvised Explosive Devices, you may know them as IEDs; armed gang hijacks and kidnappings; drug-addled jingle truck drivers asleep at the wheel despite the noise from the bells and chains that adorned their vehicles. But more often just the poor road conditions took their toll on those who had no choice but to drive.

Americans have air travel in the blood. Many have been in military service. Domestic flights are an everyday form of getting around for millions of ordinary folk in the USA because of the size of the country. For me it was a novelty.

Approaching J'bad by air allowed me to appreciate just how green and fertile it is compared with the dusty-greyness of Kabul. Areas of cultivated ground, resembling English allotments, surrounded high-walled compounds providing secure housing and privacy for families. Lagoons, for rice, reminded me I may have to start my anti-malaria treatment. Doxycycline made me feel odd. In the Congo it had taken me a week to realise it hadn't done me any good. I'm now convinced taking antibiotics, in the hope that it would prevent malaria, caused more problems than it solved. In my current environment feeling disorientated and confused is not the best condition to be in carrying a gun, or two. Mosquitoes weren't a problem in Kabul. BMTF HQ sat fourteen hundred metres above sea level, a thousand metres higher than Jalalabad, part way up a mountain. There's no standing water on the side of a mountain therefore, no mosquitoes.

As the plane turned sharply on its steep descent into J'bad we passed over boys running around on a patch of sparse dusty grass. Two of the boys ran between makeshift wickets carrying cricket bats. They paid no attention to another plane loaded with foreigners heading to Jalalabad Airfield.

Our aircraft taxied to a remote part of the base. We quickly unloaded baggage onto very hot concrete.

Hurry up.

The plane had more drops to make.

The guy who was supposed to meet us, didn't.

And wait.

Engines revved higher as the aircraft moved away in a cloud of hot sand.

Team Leader, Len, finger-poked a speed-dial number on his phone. It connected with US Customs and Border Protection representative, Eric McGoff.

The far end of the conversation was inaudible, but Len's Missouri accent was crystal: "Hey Eric. How's it goin'? We've just arrived at JAF. Where are you?"

JAF is Jalalabad Airfield. Obvious when you think about it.

"Uh Huh! Err, no. I'm looking at an airstrip running north-west to south-east and eight hundred yards across the runway to the north-east I can see what might be a terminal building," Len looked disconsolately in our direction. "Nooo, we arrived by plane. Man we gotta ton of gear." Len was getting bad news. "FOB Finley Shields? ...OK. And that's where you are?... OK. Yeah. We'll get over to the terminal building somehow. Put it this way, do we have any choice? ...Thought not!" Len wiped sweat from the phone with the brown and tan chequered cotton fabric hanging from his neck; a shemagh has a multiple uses. "So, the helicopters, how does that work?" Len stared into the distance as he took in the information. "Uhh-huh! Uhh-huh. O-Kay. And how often do they fly? ... Ya don't know?" Len seemed to physically shrink as the conversation progressed. "And that's where you are now?" He gave a thumbs-down sign. "OK, well, we'll be there in a coupla hours." Call ended. "Shee-it!" Len exclaimed pacing around our kit. After a few seconds his frustration began to fade in the intense sun. "Our man in Jalalabad is on a different frickin' base," he meant Forward Operating Base Finley Shields. Len shook his head. "He can't get to us by road as the drive is through hostile territory and he don't have an armoured vehicle and no one to ride shotgun. Can

16

you believe this shee-it?" he said rhetorically. "We need to be over there." Len pointed across the runway. "From there we get a he-lo, if there's any room for all of this," he flicked a finger at the pile of kit. "Then we got a truck ride through an Afghan Army base to another FOB!" Len glanced at his watch as if seeking inspiration, "OK, it's thirteen hundred!"

Pete, shrugged as he looked across to where Len indicated. "We'll just have to walk the gear across in relay. One waits here with some of the stuff. Two carry some kit. Then one waits at the other end with the stuff we drop," Pete paused as he looked at the pile of bags and equipment. "Probably need a couple of trips but we can do it if we take turns crossing the runway. Problem solved." Pete was right.

"Pete, when we get over there," Len looked across several hundred yards of runway to the line of sheds and T-walls shimmering in the heat, "we then gotta get a Molson helicopter to the next base. Where he's waitin' for us," Len oozed exasperation and perspiration. "He don't know departure times for the helicopters. It's basically a straight up, over and down movement but it's safer than being attacked on the highway."

A Ford 350 Super Duty that had made its way across the runway pulled up near the other two contractors from the same flight. The driver looked at us and our gear. He shouted over the noise of the three matt-black Chinook CH-47s taking off: "Hey! You guys need a lift somewhere?"

Len shouted back, "Sure would appreciate that!"

"I got my own guys to take care of so can't git y'all in the ve-hicle but I can git yer heavy gear over there," he pointed across the runway, "See the staging area? I'll be just to the right of it."

I had no idea what a staging area was and even if I did, I doubt I'd be able to see it through the atmospheric haze and the sweat running into my eyes. To me the distance was a mirage but the driver was at least eight inches taller so he could most likely see over the refraction.

"Git yer boxes and big bags of gear into the cargo space," said Super Duty driver. There was no room for us. We awaited the green light signal before commencing our walk across the runway wearing body armour, carrying backpacks and rifles. The Super Duty with our gear, slowly put distance between us at the regulation five miles per hour.

After the relative cool of the off-load area, the heat from the concrete airstrip was literally breathtaking. The smothering effect of hot air you get when opening the oven door to remove your Sunday roast, comes close. Now imagine that, but without the steam.

Bottled water wet my keffiyeh. Pulled tight across my nose and mouth, it cooled the hot air burning my nostrils. Trudging across the skid-mark blackened concrete, gave me time to watch a Chinook, two Blackhawks and a drone landing some way off. Super Duty driver greeted us at the staging area.

Len acknowledged his help: "Thanks buddy, 'preciate it."

Super Duty driver had saved us two hours and a lot of sweat. Our bags baked on the limestone ballast as the pickup truck idled nearby. We shook hands with Super Duty driver before he climbed back into his air conditioned cab. Sat in the shade of the concrete T-walls, we were able to breathe cooler air.

And wait.

My body armour, ammunition pouches, Leatherman and med-pack weighed around twenty kilograms - dry. It weighed another two and half kilos with a loaded rifle attached. I wanted to get out of my personal protective equipment but it was easier to wear it than carry it. Without looking, I knew my shirt was completely drenched in sweat, but there was no cooling effect because the ceramic plates in the body armour retained heat. My internals were about to go into melt-down.

Len called Greg in the Kabul office: "Hey Greg! How's it goin'? ...Yeah, we're at JAF ... The CBP rep ain't here ...We gotta get a Molson to FOB Finley Shields, you OK with that? ...No. He ain't here.' Len emphasised. 'He's on another base ...WHAT?' Phone reception was bad. 'Greg, it ain't yure fault. I'm on my way to the Molson's office now. I'll keep y'updated." Len pressed End Call as he turned to me and Pete. "We're on our own boys," announced Len. "The CBP guy is supposed to be here not over there," Len flicked a thumb in the general direction of somewhere else. "I'm gonna find Molson Helicopters office and book us a flight. Hopefully we'll do it in one trip."

"OK Len. Want me to go with you?" I said.

"No. Should be OK. Best both of you take it turns to watch our gear," Len pointed towards an alley between two sheds, "ya might find a D-FAC or snack-shack around here someplace."

D-FAC was already in my expanding new vocabulary. I knew it meant Dining Facility, some might call it a canteen.

Len spent the best part of an hour in the Molson Helicopters office and returned looking tired. "I got us booked on a shuddle to Finley Shields at sixteen hundred hours," we had a ninety minute wait. "But, here's the thing, military personnel get preference, so we could get bumped. Guy reckons the last flight is often empty. That's at nineteen-thirty."

"Len, we have nineteen hundred pounds of payload, including us. Are they OK with that?" I'd done the sums at the check-in scales for the plane at Kabul Airbase. For the helicopter I expected it to be an issue.

"Yeah, sure. I explained all that. I told him that it should've been sent by road from Karrbul, days ago, but we got the job instead. He said it's no problem."

"So, we can get out of this gear for a few hours?" Separating my body armour from my sodden shirt felt good.

"Sure thing bro," said Len. He pulled at the Velcro fastening to release his vest.

My vest stood next to our bags so it could dry and cool for a few hours. "I'm going to find us some water." Pete and Len watched me walk away. Pete laughed.

"What?" The source of his amusement wasn't obvious to me.

"Have you seen your shirt and trousers?" Pete stared at my waist. Looking down at my two-tone shirt and pants, wet and dry were clearly delineated in the rip-stop fabric. Pulling on the shirt to unstick it and allow air to circulate didn't make me look cool, but I began to feel it.

It took me fifteen minutes to find the water stack. On the way I paused at a sign. Blue words on white background:

Welcome to FOB FENTY.
In honor of Lt. Col. Joseph J. Fenty, Commander, 3rd Squadron, 71st Cavalry
Killed in Action, 5 May 2006.

A grim reminder of the sacrifices made by the few so that the many who came later could earn six figure salaries.

The three one and a half litre bottles of a well known brand of water were guzzled to empty within twenty minutes. Pete went for more. I drank six litres of water that day as well as several cups of tea, but didn't go for a pee until nine in the evening. Twelve hours between pees. That's a pee-pee personal record.

"OK," announced Len. "It's fifteen-thurdy. Let's get the gear moved up closer to the flight-line. Gonna have to relay it."

Hurry up.

Body armour back on, not because of a threat but because it was easier to wear it than carry it. Using the method Pete suggested earlier we soon had the baggage dumped near the weigh-in point just inside the departures' marquee. Body armour off.

And wait

"I'll check with Molson," said Len. He dodged around five soldiers on his way out.

"Pete," I said quietly to get his attention, then followed the progress of the guys that had just arrived in the departure tent. Pete pursed his lips, acknowledging my observation. Len was soon back in the marquee. We didn't need to be told: the army lads will go first.

"Yup," said Len, "we're on the next one. Sixteen-thurdy."

And wait.

We weren't on the next one. Len called the CBP rep to let him know. Nor were we on the two after that, but we did get the 18:00 hours departure. Len called Eric McGoff to expect us.

My first helicopter flight: it lasted five minutes.

Our stuff got dragged from the helicopter baggage hold onto the skull-sized grey boulders of FOB Finley Shields helipad.

Hurry up.

We ducked away from the rotor-blades as three soldiers boarded the Huey. It was soon in the air again. As the he-lo cleared the pad we quickly moved our gear off the landing area. Len called Eric to let him know we'd arrived.

"No signal," Len shouted despairingly. We turned towards the sound of a car horn. A fella leaning against a Toyota pickup truck waved at us. He was a hundred yards away and appeared to be smiling. Or laughing.

"That must be him," said Len, 'I can see some sorta uniform. Looks CBP."

"Is there any likelihood of him bringing the car over?" said Pete.

"He ain't worked it out yet," replied Len as he beckoned for McGoff to come to us. Len pointed at the pile of gear.

The vehicle crunched slowly along the gravel track and stopped a few yards past the prospective load. United States Customs and Border Protection Officer, Eric McGoff extricated himself from the vehicle. He must have had a fifty inch chest even without body armour. Smiling brightly, Eric shook hands.

"Hey! Great to see you guys, I believed him. A castaway couldn't have been more welcoming, but the feeling wasn't mutual. "Get your gear in the truck and I'll get you to your quarders," he looked at the pile. "Hmm! May have to make two trips."

Eric didn't offer to help load the truck but did give advice about how to stack the gear. We got the big stuff piled up and strapped down in the cargo space. The small bags went inside the passenger compartment on our knees. I'd heard the expression compact used to describe some American vehicles but we looked more like the Beverley Hillbillies, complete with guns.

The Toyota rocked and lurched slowly along the track to Forward Operating Base Hughie. I was tired, borderline dehydrated and didn't take in too much of the surroundings but I did notice that the two Forward

Operating Bases of Finley Shields and Hughie were separated by a large Afghan National Army base.

"You're gonna love it here," insisted Eric as we drove past a herd of tethered goats lying in the shade of shrubbery. As Len looked over his shoulder at me and Pete he was clearly sceptical. "You've gotta a nice set-up. Basic but nice," said Eric.

In different circumstances, the word 'basic' would've rung a bell but I just wanted to get out of my sodden gear, have something simple to eat, shower, then sleep.

"You Customs guys will be able to really get out there at the Inland Customs Dee-po," Eric was getting more excited as he spoke.

We turned left into an alley of Hescos. The Entry Control Point was directly ahead, just in front of a large eucalyptus tree. Sandbags partly concealed the long-gun pointing outwards from the elevated guard shack. A pipe-barrier balanced with a red and white painted cube of concrete on the short end blocked the entrance. On the long end of the pipe, a soldier could hang on to a rope to pull the barrier down to the closed position.

ECPs exist to prevent bad things happening on the inside of whatever it is they are protecting. Which means if bad things are going to happen they often start at the ECP. That's why sensible people don't hang around the gates of military bases. FOB Hughie was no exception.

We got out to show our ID cards and make-safe weapons. My weapons weren't loaded as per   SOP on flights and on base, but I made-safe anyway. One of the soldiers on ECP duty used a mirror to inspect various parts of the vehicle's exterior. Then waved us through and into the base.

"It's just around the corner," said Eric. "One of yer's gonna have to ground-guide. It's next right and straight down to the end."

Len took up position in front of the pickup. It wasn't his duty as Team Leader but Pete didn't volunteer and I didn't have a clue what Eric was talking about. Pete and I walked behind. It was easier than getting back into the truck. Len covered twenty yards slowly then turned right at the enormous eucalyptus tree that provided shade to parts of the FOB throughout the day. There were a few containerised shops on the right but they'd been closed for two hours. We entered an alley of magnolia painted wooden huts on stilts. This was Zone Foxtrot. Unique marks stencilled above doors ran from F1 through to F12. A lengthways TransLine shipping container created the dead end. Hescos added two meters to the defensive structure.

Len turned throwing his ams wide and mouthed: what the fuck? Eric stopped the pickup outside F8. We'd arrived.

T-walls lined both sides of the alley to reduce the damage from explosive blasts in the event of indirect fire from mortars and rockets. The T-walls were well placed to give some protection to the occupants of the subdivisions within the huts, small gaps by the doors allowed access. A similar door to the rear opened outwards facing onto a twenty-foot high wall of Hesco and into a narrow alley with overhanging trees.

"May as well bring in some of the boxes straight away," said Eric, getting out of the truck. We grappled the larger cases into the hut.

"You're up the end here," Eric stood, arms open, indicating some gaps between plywood partitions. Setting boxes down in one of the small spaces, we took in our surroundings. There wasn't much to see. Beneath the shallow-pitched plywood roof, illuminated by four fluorescent strip lights running the length of the shed, were ten, eight feet by six feet spaces. Plywood stood on one of its short sides created walls eight feet high. Four of the cubicles were occupied by contractors employed by two other US corporations. It was obvious the remaining six spaces were ours because they didn't have doors on which to put our names. Mattresses would have benefited the bare-board bunks. No chairs, lockers or tables: *basic*.

Len sagged onto the edge of one of the bunks. Pete and I stood inertly in the corridor. Eric grinned with a sense of achievement.

"How long have you been at J'bad Eric?" said Len. I'd only known Len a few days but it was obvious his anger was simmering.

"About two months," Eric was proud of what he hadn't achieved in that time.

"And where have you been based during that time, on Fenty?"

"Yeah, Fenty. It's not Bagram or KAI-A but it has its good points," said Eric.

Kabul International Airport is abbreviated to KAI-A, pronounced *Ky yah*. Logically, it should have been KIA, but someone in the Department of Defense must have decided that associating a US military base with Killed In Action created a bad impression.

Len didn't want Eric's reassurance: "Hmm, I bet!" Len pensively looked around at our situation. "When did you fix us up with this, er, accommodation?"

"Oh, I came over on the first shuttle today and grabbed it for you. Lucky really, this was all the Mil had ta offer."

"Lucky?" Len winced as if suddenly in pain. "So, you've been here two months and just today," Len's voice went up a couple of notches on the volume scale, "you decided you'd better get yure sorry ass in gear," louder, "and find us somewhere to live and work," much louder, "because if ya didn't the CBP Attaché in Karrbul might wonder what the *fuck*," very loud, "you've been doin' down here for two months on TDY at OCONUS rates?"

I knew OCONUS meant off-continental US: overseas. It was a while before I found out that TDY meant Temporary Duty because at that moment it seemed inappropriate to ask. Eric was visibly shaken. It took him a few moments to settle.

"Hey, Len. Easy buddy. I only got told you were comin' two days ago. I can't ask the Mil for accommodation if I can't justify it."

'The Mil' is the military and he was right about making demands, but it didn't alter the fact that I was dirty, hungry and tired with nowhere to sleep. Len was doing his best as team leader to sort out the mess.

Eric could do no more: "Hey, listen guys, I have to get back to Fenty. I've gotta return this truck to the motor pool at Finley Shields first so we need to offload the rest of your gear."

"Yeah! You better go," said Len.

The grim prospect of a night in a shed with an angry Len was tempered by the five figure monthly salary.

We offloaded the truck and dragged everything into the hut. The official stuff was stashed in the three empty spaces that wouldn't become our bunk rooms. We kept our personal stuff close.

"Give me a call if you need anything. Gotta go!" Eric departed. Len waved dismissively.

"I hope he misses his flight. Assole," said Len, acrimoniously.

I had to agree, he deserved to miss his flight, but also I had an idea: "Well, I can't sleep on bare boards so I'll have a scout around the base and see if I can find anything useful."

"I better get over to the J-DOC and let 'em know we're here," said Len. He meant the Joint Defense Operations Center: the base administrative office.

Pete sat on the creaking boards of his bunk and opened his backpack. "I'll stay here and babysit the gear and weapons. Gary, please find out where the toilets and showers are and let me know A-SAP."

Len pointed to the front door. "Pete, there's a toilet cabin right next to the hut. One of those EcoLog things."

"Yeah! I know," said Pete, "that's why I want to know where the proper toilets are."

Len and I went on our missions.

The shower block was easy. J-DOC was pretty easy too. Turn left just before the shower block, past the D-FAC and next left. The D-FAC was serving evening meals for another forty-five minutes but the 24/7 buffet always had something good. **Combat Take Aways' Only** above the door compelled civilians to eat in and dared me to correct the punctuation. We were back at Hut F8 within twenty minutes.

"Pete. Showers. Turn right at the end of the alley and it's straight ahead. You can't miss it but, you might want to eat first. Main meals finish very soon."

It was dinner time. We concealed the long guns as best we could then went to eat.

On the way back to Hut F8 we each carried two cases of water, twenty-four half litre bottles, from the nearest stack. Layers of bottled water on the pallet were separated by a piece of hardboard.

I had an idea: "I'm going to collect some hardboard from the water stacks. Might be able to spread the load on the bed boards. I'll get as much as I can."

"OK mate, thanks for that. I'm off to shower," seconds later, Pete was out the door.

By the time it got dark I'd retrieved twelve pieces of 48 inch by 40 inch board from the dozen or so stacks around the base. I also added to our bottled water supply. Pushing the brown rectangles of compressed wood pulp in through the door of Hut F8, prompted Len to shout down the hallway:

"Hey what ya got there, bro?"

"Waterboards!" I grinned.

"Ain't that what we do to people we don't like?" sounded like Len had someone in mind.

"Oh, yes. Didn't think about that. So, you won't want any?"

"I'll take 'em," Len grinned, "I'm savin' one for Eric!" We laughed.

Two pieces of hardboard took the edges off the bed slats. It was warm enough to sleep under a single sheet so my two sleeping bags became a mattress. The mosquito net was easily fixed to the bed frame.

Shower.

Bed.

Rifle to my left. Pistol to my right.

C130

Herat will always be the place where my friends were murdered. We, they, had got something wrong. We, I, needed to learn how not to do it again. Easy answer: I shouldn't be here. Get the hell out of Afghanistan. An attack inside a secure base defied logic but Mark and the other BMTF lads had made themselves targets by hanging around outside in a group. Deep down I knew it could happen - would happen. Assailants attack crowds because there's a good chance of a kill. The victims' collective confusion makes random, rather than targeted shooting, effective. Then there's the lack of direct connection between killer and killed, no physical contact that might flick some moral switch that says STOP! It's not like a one-on-one knife attack instigated by a gang leader as a form of novice initiation to test allegiance and exert control. Mass casualties inflicted with an automatic weapon are about anonymous, indiscriminate revenge.

Now was the time for logic not emotion. Walk away from this job and I would be back to being broke. That didn't appeal to me, neither did being dead. The stakes had been high from the start and the risk had just gone up but I wasn't gambling my life just for me. There were people at home who needed me to be here.

Sudden violent death was preferable to a life of lingering penury. The opportunity to earn some proper money that would benefit my family far outweighed any personal risk. If that proper money was earned posthumously by means of an insurance payout, so be it. Whatever happened, I couldn't be worse off. It was a chance to make good the mess I'd made.

My attempt to establish cause and effect defied me. The Herat mission that had been running nicely for a year was over - the day I arrived. Six of the team had been victims of green on blue attack: three dead. Several so badly damaged, physically and mentally, they would not return to Afghanistan.

I'd said maybe a dozen words to Danno, now he was shot through the pelvis. It had been an hour or more before they medevaced him to the Spanish base. He sat upright and conscious the whole time. How he managed his pain I will never know.

Someone pressed a few of the digital-lock buttons on the main door before they realised it was open. My Glock cleared its holster as Alex Brogan let himself in and brushed the remnants of his ginger hair away from his face. Part of his twenty year career in Her Majesty's Customs and Excise had been as an Excise Officer at a Highland distillery which may have accounted for his ruddy complexion. His past fifteen years on the consultancy circuit as a Crown Agent and then freelance had brought him to Afghanistan via Vietnam, Bangladesh, Cameroon and numerous other messed up areas of the world. Messed up by our standards, that is.

"Gary, There y'are," his broad Scottish accent made him barely intelligible to me, how the interpreters understood what he said will remain a mystery.

"Here I am. Nearly wasn't," I said trying to make light of the event. Alex either didn't hear my Glock click into its holster, or, chose to ignore it.

"Aye. True enough."

Alex was another survivor of the failed Congo job. He'd been lucky there too. He got out before I arrived, before it went bad. He must've realised the game was up. He also got paid.

"We got the job o' packing up," he looked around the room at the rows of cupboards, lockers and Gorilla boxes, the large reinforced baggage trunks favoured by military personnel. It was a monumental task. "I was told, it's all got tae go. Pack it all."

"Are we making an inventory?"

"Nay one said anything aboot inventory, just pack. Personally, I'd rather get the fuck oota here," Alex spotted the AK-47 on the table. "Is that it?" he said cautiously.

"Yes. That's the gun that killed Mark, Joe and Bob. There's some cold water in the fridge if you want to sit a while."

"Aye, that'll be good but al nay sit tae lang as al be asleep and we have work tae dee."

"It doesn't seem possible. I've been close to a few rockets, bombs and bullets but that was the closest yet," I said.

"Well I've nay seen too many bombs nae bullets until today and that's it fa me. Am awah. Next plane to Kabul and then oot o this shite hole."

"You know, I joked with them about sitting around out there. I told them, smoking is really bad for your health. Can you believe that?" I said, stifling a cynical laugh.

"Aye, ye were feckin reet aboot that."

"Any ideas about where to start on the packing?" I said crumpling my empty bottle.

"How aboot we get the personal effects together. They're gonnee want them ASAP."

"OK. Was today your first day here too?" I said.

"Aye. And ma last. Let's get started."

It didn't take me long to pack my own gear because it hadn't been unpacked. Mark's stuff took slightly longer, not because he had more, I just took more care with his.

Papa Joe had been deployed for more than two years. He'd accumulated a number of Gorilla Boxes of gear. There was also team kit. BMTF HQ in Kabul wanted it. Alex and I got on with demobilising the BMTF Herat station. Occasionally, people passed through the office but they didn't stop to talk. A knowing gesture was the closest we came to discourse.

Opening a cupboard, I shouted: "YES!"

"What's that?" said Alex struggling to hold down the lid on a Gorilla Box.

"Fancy a beer?" Asking a Scotsman would he like a drink rarely meets with disapproval.

"Eh? Put one in front o' me and watch what happens!"

Two Heineken cracked open.

"Absent friends?" I said, hoping it sounded appropriate.

"Aye. Absent friends," we drank. Then another.

An hour later, a pile of boxes and bags had grown on the spot where Joe and Bob had laid.

"BINGO!" shouted Alex from across the room.

"Don't do that. I'm the nervous type," I said.

"Fancy a drop e Scotch?" said Alex. He knew the answer.

"I'll get two mugs," I hadn't seen any glasses.

Alex poured a very respectable measure for each of us. "Slangevar!"

"Slange!" I replied and passed him another Heineken.

"Where's ya next job?" said Alex.

"Next job?" I said, "I'm not finished with this one yet."

"Ya nae stoppin' on this program. Are ye?"

"I have nothing else in view and this is the best paid job I've ever had."

"Aye, best paid mebbe. No point bein' the richest man in the graveyard."

"Alex, do you have family in the UK?"

"Aye somewhere. Don't hear from 'em. I cut ties with the UK many years ago."

"Hmm. I have people who rely on me."

"Whatever floats ya boat," Alex topped up our drinks.

"Here's to denying the enemy access to good Scotch," I said, lifting my mug.

"Aye. Fuck 'em," said Alex. "Our lads, bless 'em, would approve of this," he smiled. "Wouldn't want it seized by some rag heed bastard," we laughed.

Packing gained pace. It was no more organised but it was happening fast. We drank and packed and drank. The small hours receded into the past as we raced towards morning. The pile of boxes and bags would fill four pickup trucks. There was still plenty to pack but we no longer had concerns about the beverages falling into the wrong hands.

Diego's head appeared around the door: "We're leaving. Now!"

Hurry up.

Alex and I got into our body armour, grabbed long-guns and baggage then stepped out into the dazzling afternoon sunshine. My eyes felt red. Exhaust fumes from the Land Cruiser made them feel redder. The Afghan hadn't moved. He was still dead. The blanket, blown clear of his left hand, revealed fingers spread wide like he'd let go of something.

Up front in our armoured Toyota, sat behind black-lensed Oakley eye-protection, two tough looking corporate security guys with beards stared, silently, straight ahead. We moved off slowly.

At the RTC exit, five burka-clad figures in various sizes, skinny and short, fat and tall were being electronically frisked with a Garret wand. Local women had no business on a military base.

There were two possible reasons for their presence; they were wearing suicide vests under the long funereal clothing, or, they were the female relatives of the dead murderer come to collect his body. Their eyes peered out through the narrow slits in the black garments. From ten metres away, despite the hijab, the range of emotion displayed by their dark eyes was clear. Most were dispassionate, but one of the women locked eyes with me for a long moment. I saw hate. Like the Afghan women who avenged the deaths of their men folk in Rudyard Kipling's, *Young British Soldier,* this one would cut up *my* remains given half a chance.

The Land Cruiser took off at speed down the highway.

Hurry up.

We reached the airfield. It may have been the place we'd arrived the previous day. Couldn't tell. Not interested. Then we sat around.

Wait.

The recurring urgent dynamism in *hurry up* and sudden inexplicable inertia in *wait* that pervades every action in a war-zone seemed inappropriate now. But we did it anyway.

Three rows of seats occupied a demountable building: the departure lounge. Bottles of chilled water appeared from somewhere. We drank. Our silence was as hard and uncomfortable as the chairs. Rumbling crescendo and engine-scream announced the arrival of a large aircraft.

And wait.

Containerised air-conditioned comfort was abandoned for a walk through late afternoon heat. A huge grey four-engined plane languished a hundred yards away across shimmering concrete. More chilled water was thrust into my hand boarding the C130. The past twenty hours had me dazed and confused. The beer and Scotch must have had some effect but it wasn't obvious to me. I was still wide awake.

Strapped into one of the seats that ran along the sides of the C130, I made sure my rifle was held firmly between my legs. Magazine out, muzzle-down. The other guys did the same. Earplugs in.

Diego's eyes hid behind Oakleys but they didn't have anti-grief. lenses. Three large rectangular aluminium boxes lay strapped in line onto the cargo deck of the plane. Each covered with a flag. Two were Stars & Stripes. The first casket was wrapped in the Union Flag of the United Kingdom.

Our C130 left behind the runway rumble as it climbed over Herat on its way to - I knew not and cared not. In the noisy cargo hold, conversation was futile. Isolated from my fellow living travellers by noise, I had time to recall what had driven me to this point.

Change Management

It was an epiphany. The 2008 financial crisis had been less than a year old, but from where I'd sat there had been no signs of it abating. On the 1970s avocado-coloured pedestal thinking about how my life was going down the toilet, I finally accepted that doing nothing was not going to clear up my financial mess. Doing something over and over again in the hope of a different result is a form of insanity. Madness had been creeping up on me for years. Staying in that job, things would just get worse. It had been affecting my health: fatigue, anxiety, anger, my life was out of my control.

Sneering at the framed certificate dated 1999, my mid-life crisis was about to end. No. Not like that. Not end it all. Just the crisis.

That damn paper insult, with its lacklustre gold lettering, had hung above the toilet door for almost a decade:

Congratulations to Gary Wishaw
25 Years Dedicated Service to HM Customs & Excise.

Maybe it impressed some people as they sat contemplating the moment, but it didn't help with my monthly mortgage repayment and as for the missing letter L, don't get me started.

As the Head of Region handed me the award at a backroom ceremony in the Customs Department's Dover Headquarters, he smiled, or smirked, difficult to say which. He'd been in post nine months. Twenty of us each got a voucher for forty quid. They weren't presented in alphabetical order. The bloke with a name like Polish vodka got called first. I was last. One pound sixty pence for every year of service, redeemable at the local branch of a well known jewellers. You know the one, just a few years earlier the Chief Executive Officer had successfully scuppered his own business by admitting the products were: 'total crap.'

The event's most memorable moment? Warm beer and cold vol au vents. Somewhere, there's a photograph of me gritting my teeth holding the certificate.

My escape plan was so simple, I'd convinced myself nothing could go wrong. There was no reason to think it would go the way of all my other plans because at some point, one of my plans must go right. This plan *would* work because I'd be with international Subject Matter Experts who obviously knew what they were doing. SMEs employed by overseas development agencies produce impressive annual reports about all the lives they've saved, environments improved and value added to the Capitalist model, while living and working in exotic locations enjoying a good life. They didn't appear to have the trappings of failure. It took me a while to work out they kept those hidden.

But here's the thing, despite the vast sums of money invested in Overseas Development, it has no quantifiable value. OD is not really a business because it doesn't create a tangible product and yet the directors of international agencies talk the business-talk to maintain their revenue stream, usually from tax payers. Despite no palpable outcome, OD, like a business, does have a bottom line: profit and loss. Profit doesn't always pay dividends. Loss isn't always just money.

I just needed to convince my wife I was about to make either the best investment or, take the biggest gamble, of my life - of our lives together.

"If you're sure you're doing the right thing, then do it," said Alice, as she lay in bed. A subcutaneous saline drip stuck in her thigh provided hydration she couldn't get from drinking. The basket of daily medications by her side was full. It would be empty by ten o'clock that night. Intestinal failure was slowly and painfully killing her. The cost of regular trips to St Mark's Hospital in north London for specialist medical treatment, had been bleeding our household to death for five years.

"No, I'm not sure, but we've talked about this off and on for almost a year. I asked the Department for help. The best the personnel officer could do was: *go part-time.*"

My anger simmered but remained contained. Alice was already dealing with too much. She didn't need more stress, that needed to stay with me.

"Part-time working means part-time money," I said. "He either wasn't paying attention or he has no real decision making capability. Either way, he's a waste of space. It's not as if we have a lavish lifestyle. Double income families just don't understand, lose an income and you really are in a right old mess pretty damn quick. All I asked for was what they gave some other people a few years back: keep paying me without me having to go to work, maybe six months. I saved that Department hundreds of millions of pounds but that personnel bloke didn't make the connection. To hell with 'em."

"It's not my fault. I didn't ask to be ill," said Alice, "I loved my job. It's not like I had a choice. The GP didn't listen to me. I told him something wasn't right. I know my own body. It went on for too long. That last lot of surgery was just that, my last. I'm inoperable. Anything else goes wrong, it's the end," Alice rolled over, away from me.

I pushed some of the day's medical debris aside and got on a narrow bit of bed to cuddle her: "Alice, I know it's not your fault. I've never said that."

She shrugged me off. "I'm in pain. Please don't touch me. Every bit of me hurts. I know you mean well but it really hurts. Even just lying here hurts. Keep still on the bed."

"I'm sorry. I can't imagine always being in pain," I said. "No one chooses to have ulcerative colitis and all the complications that go with it."

Alice interjected: "It wasn't the UC last time. It was the ovarian cyst that got stuck to everything. I should've demanded a scan. That bloody GP. I'll never trust male doctors ever again."

"When I tell people you were in hospital for ten months, they just look at me like I'm an idiot. I can see them thinking: Ten months? Can't be. He's got that wrong. No one's in hospital for ten months. Someone asked me if you'd been in a coma." Alice laughed a little. "Honestly, they really did. They don't relate that length of time to anything in their lives. They can't, because they don't need to. Think of the friends that you had, that you now don't have, because they've drifted away. Makes me think, aside from a few nights out together, what do friends actually have in common? Nothing. Is friendship just about going to the cinema or, a Pizza

Hut meal for four with a twenty percent off your next order voucher? They don't have time to care about your suffering. They have other things to worry about: their next foreign holiday, their new car, tennis lessons for Nigel." I got slowly off the bed so as not to cause her too much pain and went around to kneel the other side to look at Alice's face. Tears were rolling into the cotton sheets, but she was also laughing.

"I'm sorry I upset you. I just ..."

"You didn't. I'm in pain. I cry and rock with pain. When it gets really too much I take more painkillers and try to sleep. I dream I'll wake up and the pain is gone." Bedding muffled her amusement.

"So, what's funny?"

"Tennis lessons for Nigel," she chuckled, "we don't even know anyone with a child called Nigel."

"No. But we know a few who are *Nigels*, they just got the wrong name."

Alice laughed. "Stop. It hurts when I laugh."

"OK. Sorry. I'll try not to make you laugh ever again."

"No, don't. You can make me laugh. Just not right now. Tell me what you were about to say about work."

"I've been offered a job in the Democratic Republic of Congo. Roger Mackey's there. So's his wife. There are other ex-Customs lads out there too, with their families. Sounds really good. It's ninety-thousand a year, tax free, plus twenty-thousand expenses."

"Wee Roger the Dodger?" said Alice in her best Scottish accent. "I've not seen him for years."

I resisted the temptation to point out that we hadn't seen anyone one for years as it would imply Alice was to blame for getting ill. Although it sometimes came across like I blamed her, I didn't.

"That's why we haven't seen him. He's been out in Africa for at least four years."

"Is it dangerous out there? Is that where they have gorillas in the mist?"

"Gorillas in the mist? Yes. It was based in the Congo. Dangerous? Probably and I have thought about that, a lot. If I do nothing, we'll be forced to move into another house. It won't be set up for you like here and you're not fit enough to move. If it all goes wrong, basically, it brings forward the inevitable."

"I can't think about it. Just do what you think is best. I need to sleep," Alice moved, slowly seeking comfort on the lambs' wool mattress topper.

Thirty-five years after I'd joined the Civil Service, the Department accepted my resignation.

No offer of inducement to stay. No Exit Interview. No interest in me: in the past, now, never.

It had been a long time coming but, in August 2009, I took my first steps from comfort-zone towards war-zone.

Kandahar - July 2012

I'd slept on the plane. It felt like moments but it must have been at least an hour. The sound and jolt of wheels-down brought me back to reality. Three flag-draped boxes immediately filled my waking moments with emotion. Mark was in that middle box. It was almost me. If it had been me, Mark wouldn't be having the same feelings. It's the first time I've said this but, sadness, remorse and survivor's guilt didn't overwhelm me. Instead, a feeling of self-satisfaction from knowing I'd made the right decision. Three had made the fatal mistake of thinking they were safe, two had life changing injuries and four others had a near death experience they'd be able to tell their grandchildren if they lived to see them.

Recalling some of the near-misses, close-calls, lucky-escapes and downright good luck I'd had in my life up to this point, brought back memories of youthful reckless behaviour with no tangible benefit. A time when risk and reward weren't part of my vocabulary. But this experience made me question if luck is quantifiable like money, an abstract concept like time and how one person gets more luck than the next bloke. Maybe it's finite like atoms or infinite like numbers. If it's universal, maybe some planets have more than their fair share of luck.

Fair?

Go on, define *fair* because at that moment, I couldn't.

The aircraft taxied to a stop. Warm, dry evening air rushed in as the C130's ramp gently dropped revealing the floodlit concrete of Kandahar Airfield: Afghanistan's third largest coalition force base. To a select group of millions of people the world over it is known as KAF.

Halos formed around the airfield's flood-lights as thermals lifted talc-like desert dust into the dying twilight. A Kamikazi of locusts swarmed in and out of the pools of light, dashed themselves unconscious on the lamps then tumbled to ground where base cats binged on the twitching remains. Land Cruisers stood beyond the Yellow Line on the concrete. Lights on, engines running. They took us to the passenger check-in building. Dozens of people from Kabul BMTF HQ were already in the large lounge. Everyone was pleased to see the survivors. But they were mindful of what we had been through. This was genuine concern and not something I'd ever experienced from a management team. Top people who lived and worked at the US Embassy were present. Some of them I'd only heard on conference calls but they were here now and I admired them for that. It was much later that I gave any thought to the logistical difficulties they must have overcome to get all those people safely to such a dangerous place at such short notice.

Scores of people stood around in the passenger check-in area. We drank bottles of chilled water, fruit juice, cola and talked about nothing in particular. Everyone present had known at least one of the deceased. The attack wasn't a subject of discussion. It was discreetly avoided. Intercourse reduced to knowing looks and the occasional, how are you?

An American male voice announced through the public address system: "The Dignified Transfer Ceremony will commence in ten minutes on Mike-Ramp ...Ten minutes ...Mike-Ramp."

It sounded like an organised event amongst my confusion. I understood the words but had no idea what they meant. Dignified Transfers would become too common an experience on KAF. I solemnly filed back out onto the hot concrete along with around a hundred other people. A multitude had already formed up in rank and file; men and women. Mostly US military but also some Royal Air Force personnel in uniform and soldiers from other nations.

BMTF joined the congregation. We were surrounded by an infinite depth of sound. Bag-piped Amazing Grace filled the air with emotion. Beyond the intense glare of lights there appeared to be nothing. We were trapped in a bubble, a Christmas snowstorm dome where the sparkly bits had been replaced with eye-watering, nose-blocking grit. Three flag-adorned coffins carrying our fallen comrades were borne ceremonially up the ramp of a C17 by people in military uniforms. A few moments elapsed before pall-bearers disembarked and the gathering dismissed with military precision.

I'd got the idea I was going on the plane with Mark. It was confirmed by someone but don't ask me who said it. We were going to Dover. If I'd given it any thought for more than a moment I'd have realised they were talking about Dover in Delaware, USA via Ramstein, Germany. But I wasn't thinking. Climbing the gangway to the plane, I just wanted to be going somewhere. Away from here. At the door a man in green overalls checked my name. Not on the list.

"But I was told I'm going with Mark," I emphasised.

"Sorry sir," said the loading officer, sympathetically, "you're not going with us. And Mark isn't on the plane."

"But I saw him being carried on board," I began to doubt my senses.

"Err. No," replied the officer sheepishly, "that was the dignified transfer ceremony. There are only two of the deceased on board. They are US citizens."

"Oh!"

Three boxes: two full.

Oh! How feeble and limp is that expression? Define Oh: Surprise? Disappointment? Resignation? An admission of personal impotence? But what else was there to say? I was tired, disorientated and didn't understand what was going on. This was new territory.

With both of my feet firmly on concrete, the Globemaster's gangway quickly retracted into the fuselage behind me. Walking towards the small group of BMTF still hanging around on the runway, my bags began to feel heavier. George "French" Beaumont, the Program Manager was amongst the gathering. I'd only ever seen him wearing cowboy boots and Carhartt jacket with threadbare seams. Not today. Dark business suit and shoes.

"Apparently, I'm staying here." it didn't seem appropriate to mention the empty box.

"Yeah," said French. His soft Texan barely perceptible above the noise of a flight of F-16s taking off, a sound that would become a daily feature of my time spent on KAF. French, apologised. "I thought everythin' was taken care of," he was clearly upset and irritated by the debacle. "There's an issue with Mark's repatriation and I need y'all here in Kandahar to fix it."

Y'all: that's Texan for, *me.*

"We'll do whatever it takes from Karrbul but Mark will stay here till we can get him home." From his demeanour I'd say French was embarrassed by the theatrical performance in which we'd all been extras. He hinted that repatriation may not be a straightforward job.

"Y'all, gonna be my-dee busy here," French assured the group but looked at me. "Y'all, feel OK with that?" He was clearly concerned about my well being. But it also sounded like he was giving me a big responsibility.

"Yes, of course," was the correct answer. I didn't say: get me the hell out of here and you sort out this fucking mess. "It's a privilege. Mark was my pal. I'd like to take him home."

"I know you were close to Mark. He told me 'bout summatha things y'all done together. You gittin him home to his family, that's gonna mean a lot to his wife an' kids." Compassion, not obligation, in French's sincerity committed me to my task.

"Yes. I'm OK with that. Just tell me what needs to be done."

I had just accepted the most challenging mission I would ever undertake in Afghanistan. Several months later I discovered most of the other Herat advisors had gone home immediately, on the C17.

"Ricco's the lead advisor here at Kandahar, he'll get you settled in," said French. "I've gotta go. Plane's on a tight schedule. I'll be in touch."

We shook hands, then French jogged over to a small twin-engined Bombardier stood nearby.

Ricco Palermo hadn't lived in New York for going on fifty years but he'd retained the accent. His time as a US Marine Corps tank commander in Vietnam led to his job as Sky Martial in the early days of plane hijackings, then on to other government jobs.

'That was my best job ever,' he told me one Thursday evening over a very large Scotch. 'That's how I met Sally. She was an air hostess. And for forty years she's been my wife!'

He had every right to be pleased with himself. Ricco retired from a career in the US Border Patrol but couldn't resist the opportunity to go to Afghanistan. He was sixty-five years old, looked fifty and had an effervescent optimism that I've not known elsewhere. He could have been a famous comedy actor, if the fella with quick-fire banter and a cigar poking through his moustache hadn't already done it. Ricco often attributed his youthful good looks and vitality to his Italian ancestry. Occasionally he admitted he'd just been very lucky. Papa Joe might have told me he was lucky, if he hadn't run out of time.

"D'ya know Chris Darrly?" said Ricco as he introduced me to the other Kandahar team members. Ricco's Noo Yoik dialect threw me for a moment. Darrly: Doreley.

"We know each other," I smiled. "We were with Len Kinder in Jalalabad," Len had been Chris's Marine Corps Drill Sergeant.

Chris and I shook hands as he delivered his usual opening line: "'ssgoin' arn?"

He knew all too well what was going on but he said it anyway. He always did.

"I didn't expect to see you again so soon," I replied.

"Always a pleasure. Never a chore," said Chris.

"D'ya know Lynn?" Ricco turned to introduce me to Lynn Jakeman.

"Yes. I know Lynn from Camp ACCL," Lynn's Debbie Harry looks turned heads everywhere she went, especially in Afghanistan. Lynn looked early forties with the figure of a woman ten years younger. She obviously took good care of herself. We shook hands. The compound in Kabul where the private sector of BMTF had its HQ was named after the company that owned it but what the initials stood for eluded me. The advisors had a nice setup with en-suite showers and comfy beds. I recalled seeing a British flag on Lynn's wall. Her father had been a US Military Police Officer at RAF Lakenheath in the 1950s. Her mother was British but wrong era to be a GI bride. Lynn was proud of her ancestry but her accent and attitude were Texan.

Engine noise crescendo accompanied the departing Dash 8-300 until it turned-tail heading towards the runway. The program management and Embassy contingent departed for Kabul. Ricco shouted above the Pratt and Whitney turbo-props. "Hey Gary! You hungry? We should eat. The D-FAC closes soon."

Food? Definitely. I hadn't eaten for days, or was it only twenty-four hours. Ricco was already moving towards the Land Cruiser in a spritely manner as I acknowledged that it was a good idea.

"Not for me guys!" announced Lynn, "I don't do supper. See y'all at breakfast. Night, night!'"As she strode purposefully towards her vehicle I watched the seat of her pants try to conceal her feminine movement.

Chris drove our Land Cruiser through darkness on black-top for fifteen minutes. Set back from the road, anonymous buildings illuminated by aerial floodlights starkly contrasted with the nocturnal background. It's a war-zone but no blackout required.

The Land Cruiser turned left into open space. No road here. Hidden rocks made their presence felt through the plastic donuts in the run-flat tyres as we traversed undulating dust. Warehouses, reminiscent of trading estates and airports in the real-world, provided supply chain solutions to the captive market inside the wire. Several large buildings had external lights over doors and on walkways. Cling-wrapped pallets of bottled water stood in close order, glinting behind the chain-link fence of a conspicuously floodlit compound.

SUPREME was the name on many compounds, trucks and tankers, its corporate force projection was gradually being revealed. But we headed for the huge structure to the left.

A placard displayed **NorthLine** at the end of the building. From a distance it could have been a warehouse or aircraft hangar but close up it became obvious the structure was a huge tent made from vast pieces of thick plasticised tarpaulins. We entered through the double doors of an airlock. AC pressurised the space, sucking the outer door shut with a bang. At the hand wash station, thirty people could make use of the basins, soap dispensers and electric hand driers simultaneously, but right now it was just the three of us. Ricco and Chris led the way to the check-in guy and showed their ID.

As civilian contractors open display of the Common Access Card was required at all times. The CAC bestowed privileges such as access to food, drink, accommodation, shopping, entering certain military bases, fuel for vehicles, flights on planes and helicopters. I can't think of a single activity that would be possible without a CAC. Lose it and you were in for a hard time. The Indian lad on the desk looked at our CACs, then ticked some boxes on a clip board.

"Good evening sir," he seemed happy in his work. I smiled. He smiled.

"Thank you sir," I received a tray, paper plate and a cellophane wrapped plastic cutlery set complete with cream-coloured paper napkin, salt and pepper and sugar sachets. Very efficient. I turned the corner into the serving area and was struck by the vastness of this marquee. It was the size of two UK football pitches. Folding tables each with eight chairs were crammed into rectangular seating areas created by small T-Walls concealed under attractive easy-wipe, plastic drapes: an anti-blast feature. This place could cater for two thousand diners. Most of the tables were empty at this time of night and appeared to be unnecessary, even ostentatious.

"Ya should see this place on Fridays," Ricco enthused, "Surf & Turf night. Guys queue around the block ta get a seat in here. They have some of the best food on base."

"It's impressive," I couldn't say otherwise.

Resisting the cookies, cakes and fruit, I gathered materials for a ham and Cheese Like Substance toasty. Chris had introduced me to CLS at FOB Hughie. Top comfort food. Especially with fresh sliced tomatoes and a scoop of black olives. Compared to the catering at the Italian-run base in Herat this was the Savoy Grill.

Next to the bank of drinks machines, the table was unoccupied. We sat.

Chris shared some useful advice: "So, Gary, there's a few things you need to know," he rolled some sliced pastrami on his plate, then impaled it on his fork. "They got the best CLS on base here." I was glad I'd made a good choice. For emphasis Chris pointed his loaded fork in my direction. "Also, we get attacked a lot. Mostly rockets. Just follow the drill," the mouthful of pastrami was gone. "Wait till you hear the alarm," he said excitedly. "Chick's gotta Briddish accent. I wanna splooge over her."

Ricco flinched sideways. "Jesus, Darrly. Give me some warning will ya. You know how I hate those traumatic mental images of you doing, whatever it is you do."

Chris pushed more pastrami into his mouth. He grinned and chewed, his mind on splooging.

"Great," I splashed my toasty with mayonnaise, "should make me feel right at home."

"Check out the posters," said Chris.

"Splooging posters?" said Ricco nervously.

"Noo. Dude. Look. We're surrounded."

Chris was right. On the vinyl walls, steel supports, sides of refrigerated displays - posters. They'd have been coming out of the woodwork, if there'd been any. Suddenly, they were everywhere: posters of some poor bastard in contractor-khaki Five-Elevens, or maybe TruSpec trousers, wearing body armour and desert boots lying in a straight-line facedown in the baking hot dirt, hands pushing against his ears. Waiting the wait: for the mortar or RPG that would surely land within a few feet of his position, or closer. Photographic proof for military personnel and hundreds of thousands of contractors that it is possible to survive an indirect fire attack.

Follow the SOP and *wait*.

If you were out in the open when the alarm sounded, lie down on your front with your feet facing north, put your hands over your head and wait for the first impact.

Then get to a bunker before the next one: *hurry up*. Then *wait*: for the all-clear.

"They reckon most of the local missiles came from one direction," Chris waved indiscriminately. "It's possible to be uninjured even if one explodes within a coupla feet. The deadly cone of shrapnel and pressure goes upwards not outwards." Chris knew some useful stuff. The D-FAC was a good place to learn. I'd make an effort to spend more time in there.

"Hey Gary," he sounded enthusiastic about a really great idea he'd just had. Priming a roll of pastrami for loading, he said: "This is the place to get slightly mangled. It just takes a small piece of rocket and you can go home with medical insurance."

"CHRIS!" Ricco called out loudly, "slightly mangled, my ass! Whadda fuck ya sayin'?" Ricco's comedic persona was gone, he became, Sicilian mobster.

"Hey, just sayin'," replied Chris. "And remember: only other people die."

"Ahh, Jesus! Please forgive our friend here," Ricco's tone mellowed as he turned to me. "You'll find that when he's not pushing food into his mouth he's often putting his foot in it!"

I liked these two fellas. They made me smile. Great company.

"Hey man. I do plenny other things with my mouth," Chris grinned. His face lit up with an openness that belied his dark experiences.

"Really? Pleeease!" said Ricco.

"Just thinkin' about the Briddish rocket attack girl," without warning, Chris slapped his hands, palms down, on the table. Ricco and I flinched an inch off our seats. "Seriously, just sayin', one of the rocket attacks last week. A soldier gettin' on the plane to go home. He'd done six months in country, some admin job in COMKAF HQ. Gets hit in the ass by a piece of rocket. Guy's lost forty percent of his ability to sit at a desk, that's a major disability. He gets guaranteed pension for life and a Purple Heart. Lucky bastard," Chris rolled more pastrami.

His humour didn't offend me, but it also didn't seem like Chris had a viable exit strategy, "I'll pass on slightly mangled. I saw a few examples of it yesterday and it's too unpredictable."

"Aww, shit!" Chris slapped his forehead. "Whad ama sayin'?" It registered. In his excitement to share a potential earning opportunity he'd overlooked the reason for my presence at Kandahar.

Ricco shot back: "How about, the first thing that comes into your crazy mind?"

I interjected: "Hey listen, fellas, no offence taken. I know none had been intended. More than ever before, I'm very aware of the total randomness of events."

I began to tell my part in the tragedy.

Time passed.

"Chris, you won't remember the old Seventies hippy poster about what to do during a nuclear attack. Ricco might," I said. It was one of many pieces of junk advertised in the New Musical Express during the 1970s that image conscious people thought would make them appear cool. I didn't buy it. They both shrugged no knowledge. "Put yure head between yure knees and kiss yure ass goodbye!" they'd heard it before. My John Wayne accent wasn't funny either.

The D-FAC guys began wiping tables around us. Ricco suggested it was time to go.

Outside, a warm night-wind threw dust around indiscriminately. The shemagh pulled across my nose and mouth slowed down some of the filth. Squinting kept grit from my eyes. Eye-protection with smoke-grey lenses is useless at night. An audible clunk from the Land Cruiser central locking released the door catches. Indicator lights flashed through the powdery gloom. I pulled on the heavily armoured rear door, climbed into the leather seat and fastened my seat belt.

Air conditioning picked up speed as the three and half litre V8 roared.

Ricco leaned over the front seat to speak: 'We'll go the other way around the airfield so you can get an idea of the place.'

Chris searched for the tarmac road. 'Not much to see at night but it's the same distance back from here no matter which way we go.'

The vehicle suspension banged heavily as it mounted the raised road surface. Bodywork rocked hard on its anti-roll bars. Headlights of oncoming vehicles appeared abruptly through the dust storm. Visibility was poor. Most vehicles travelled at half the twelve miles per hour speed limit. Some didn't.

"Are the roads always this busy?" I said.

Convoys of trucks moving produce to warehouses around the base grumbled through the heavily laden air.

"Priddy much," said Chris, "logistics moves a lotta chilled stuff at night because it's cooler. I guess it saves fuel too."

Waves of grit sandblasted our car as they passed in the opposite direction. It took twenty minutes to get to the car park near our accommodation. I grabbed my backpack, hold-all and rifle. Chris carried my body armour. It was another two minute walk to my new home.

Building 2301.

The number stencilled onto the corner of each tin wall was the only distinguishing feature. Identical desert-tan coloured prefabricated metal buildings covered a rank and file half-mile square block of ground.

An overpowering stench made tangible by the filth-laden air, penetrated my shemagh as I held it closer. "What *is* that stink?"

"That's the Poo Pond," it didn't trouble Chris.

"Poo Pond?" I said, "Self explanatory really. Don't know why I repeated it."

"Yeah! It's the largest open cesspool in Central Asia and we live right next door to it!" Ricco's enthusiasm made it sound like a desirable feature.

"That is fucking terrible. I won't be able to stand that," I mumbled through my face cover.

"You will," said Chris as we went through the main door of the tin shed. "Six One Zero!"

He hadn't forgotten the printed sign I stuck above the door in the Jalalabad accommodation. Inside Building 2301, the smell was slightly less pervasive.

The door to Room 7 had the BMTF logo on letter paper with names of several men and their contact numbers immediately below. Ricco and Chris had the place to themselves.

"Ignore the names on the door sign," said Ricco, "that's disinformation intended to prevent the billeting office from cramping BMTF's style. We don't want non-BMTF guys in *our* room. Gives the impression of greater numbers than in actuality. Maintaining the deception involves a complex bureaucratic juggling act. Maybe I'll show you sometime."

I didn't really know, nor care, where I was. My bunk was in the far left corner away from the door. Like a child who won't admit he's tired, Chris's words: 'only other people die,' ran around in my head. They settled into a quiet-zone of my mind as I made my bed. Five minutes later, I was in it.

Pistol to my right. I slept.

Wake Up and Smell the Poo Pond

Movement in the room roused me. Then the Poo Pond stink confirmed I was awake. No noxious vapour trailed under the door. Instead, nightstand lamps and sunlight streaming through a missing bolt hole revealed swarms of dust waiting to be inhaled. But worse than that, were the invisible micro-particles of bacteria aerosolised from the septic lagoon. It was zero seven-hundred hours in Kandahar and thirty-six hours since the murders.

Ricco was making quiet noise somewhere over by the door: "Hey! You're awake. OK if I put on the main lights?"

It was OK with Chris - and me. Suddenly it was bright. The day began. We got ready.

Drinking my first cup of tea and studying the wall map of KAF got me familiar with the Area of Operation: our A-O.

Yesterday evening it had taken twenty minutes to drive to the other side of the runway for a late night snack, twenty minutes to get to our accommodation and there were still lengths of road not yet travelled. The drive around the airstrip perimeter took about three quarters of an hour, by my calculations. It was about a third of the total airbase area. The scale of the coalition force military presence in Afghanistan was slowly beginning to dawn on me.

Previous occupants of Room 7 had pasted pages of the Stars & Stripes military newspaper over small double-glazed windows. It slowed down solar gain. Yellowed paper yielded legible text as the back-light increased:

> *July 22, 2009:*
>
> *US Marines launch major offensive in southern Af-ghanistan, representing a major test for the US military's new counterinsurgency strategy.* -- [page creased and il-legible] -- *The operation focuses on restoring govern-ment services, bolstering local police forces and protect-ing civilians from Taliban incursion* -- [page creased and illegible].

The journalist reported the *new counterinsurgency strategy* around the time I came up with my own blueprint for success. Unlike the window's old news, the folds and creases in my life-changing plan weren't obvious. But, they were there, hiding the flaws in the plan not meant to be seen. I didn't look too closely, but I did get lucky, which is more than can be said for the counterinsurgency strategy.

"Breakfast in ten," Ricco announced as he checked his emails and pistol.

"Sounds good," I was ready for this.

Chris said, "Luxembourg or Cambridge?"

It seemed like an odd question to me. Maybe location codes.

"Luxembourg's always good for breakfast," said Ricco. "Chris, you got the keys?"

"Hmm. Sure," said Chris touching his trouser pocket. "I'll call Lynn. Let her know where we're goin'. I doubt she'll join us. Probably in the gym. After we eat I'll drop you and Gary at the TLS then go wash the car and fill up."

TLS? I had no idea and didn't ask. Lynn Jakeman I knew from Kabul. We'd met briefly during my short stays at Camp ACCL but never said much beyond: good morning. As a former US Border Patrol Agent, she'd been hired to teach the ladies of the Afghan Customs and police services law enforcement methods.

My body armour got pulled from under my bed and over my head.

"Goin' somewhere?" Chris grinned as he looked me up and down.

I am, we are. I ...'

"Ya won't need that. Rifle stays in the locker too," Chris's look said: *relax.*

"I'm glad you didn't try to reassure me this place is safe," I said. "The last bloke who told me that, got murdered. We didn't speak much and the only words I can actually recall him saying were, 'It's safe here,' but it's good to not have to carry it."

I grabbed my backpack and followed Chris and Ricco to the Land Cruiser.

Overnight dust got swept clear of the screen by the Land Cruiser's wiper blades before   Chris made a right turn into a gap in traffic. The blacktop was filled with vehicles, mostly pickup trucks, people going in both directions: to work, to home, to gym, to eat, to die.

My first KAF rush-hour. "Is it always this busy?"

"Priddy much," replied Ricco.

"Does this road have a name?" I asked.

"Well, if it does, I don't know it. Jesus, it's just a road on a goddam base in the middle of a frickin' desert," Ricco wasn't irritated by the question, he just didn't see any possible reason for a strip of tarmac on a military installation in the middle of nowhere to have a nom de guerre.

"All American Boulevard," said Chris.

Ricco laughed, "All American Boulevard? How'd ya come up with that one?"

Amber flashing traffic lights alerted drivers to the pedestrian crossing, its white stripes partially obscured by dust.

Chris slowed to a stop, "I didn't. Someone else did. That's what it's called."

"Oh, *really*," said Ricco unconvinced.

Three black female soldiers with athletic physiques were on the crosswalk, the last one made big eyes and waved at Chris as she crossed the road. Chris waved and smiled back.

"Ah, Jesus Darrly, don't go pretending you know her. You won't make *me* jealous," Ricco tracked her movements as she passed out of sight behind the opposite traffic.

"I do know her," Chris smiled.

"You know *her*? Well, she sure as hell don't know *you*. God, help the girl if she ever does," said Ricco.

"She works in the pass office. Goes home in six weeks. I'm meetin' her in At-lanna."

"Nooo! She's, she's …"

Chris beat Ricco to it: "Hot!"

"Yeah. She's hot. I was about to say, looks the sensitive type."

"Great body. Ya should see her work out."

"Work out? You mean in the gym?"

"So far," said Chris.

"Is she another one of those plenny o' fish broads you trawl the net for?"

It sounded like a web based dating agency to me.

"Nooo," said Chris. "Plenty o' Fish? Shit. It's full of wierdos."

Ricco laughed loudly, "Ya don't say! Hey, tell Gary, what happened with that one you hooked last time you went on leave."

"Now is not the time to discuss my personal life," said Chris.

"Oh, so you'd rather tell us after we gotta full stomach? You really are perverse. Go on. Tell Gary. I already know it."

"Later."

"Darrly, if you don't give Gary, your version of events, he'll get mine. Wanna retain some dignity? Oh no, I forgot, you don't have any. Just tell him."

"OK," his reluctance gone, the story began. "I hooked up with a girl on Plenny o' Fish."

"Note the use of the word girl, it's significant," said Ricco.

"Damn it! Shut the fuck up Ricco. I'm tellin' it as it was. I was there. Remember?"

"Yeah, yeah. I remember," Ricco watched the slow moving traffic through his tinted spectacles.

"So, we chatted a lot online. She knew where I was. I told her when I'd be home next. She was keen to meet. So was I. On camera, she looked hot, specially on video. Bandwidth was sometimes good enough for the fine detail when she got close to the camera."

"So *that's* why you spent so much time in the office at night, alone," said Ricco.

"Yeah, I did think about a threesome but you told me you weren't into that sorta thing."

"I never said that," said Ricco abruptly.

"Oh, so you *are* into that sorta thing?"

"Hell, no. Well, not with you around. Just get to the climax," said Ricco.

"I was almost there, then I got Ricco interuptus," said Chris, "We met at Starbucks in Little Rock. Broadway Street, off the Seventy B."

"The Sevenny B? What the fuck's the Sevenny B?" said Ricco.

"It's the Seventy that's turned south. Ya know, like you, seventy and gone south. Maybe the seventy-one is somewhere else, I don't know. Just listen." Chris slowed at the next pedestrian crossing to allow a line of Filipino females to cross the road on their way to work at the Boardwalk tailoring shop. "The point is, we had coffee ..."

Ricco couldn't resist. "What dya have? Lartay? I bet you're a lartay guy. All milky white and fluff. You're not an espresso sorta guy. I reckon that poor young girl from the pass office'll be espresso after she's got to know you. Black and bitter. Yeah, I can see it already. Poor girl. PTSD: Permanently Traumatised by Sex with Darrly. She ..."

Chris slammed both hands onto the steering wheel. "Ricco, shut the fuck up. I'm telling the story." Ricco zipped his lips. "So, as I was sayin', we had coffee and then head back to her place. She knew what she wanted and I was ready to give it to her. As trailers go, it was nice. Drinks and munchies. She's soon down to her bra and panties and I'm thinkin', all right, I like what I see, when, in comes her daughter. Now, she said her daughter was seventeen, but she didn't look a day over fourteen to me. Put it this way, she hadn't started shaving and she didn't need to, if you know what I mean.' Chris's mind's eye was seeing a different picture to the road in front of us 'There wasn't much of her. And she looked even less, wet from the shower. The towel didn't hide much. By this time I'm thinkin' somethin' ain't right. The daughter was a bit *too* friendly - and naked. But when some dude steps out of the bedroom wearing gym shorts, capped sleeve T shirt and a big grin, that was just too much of a good ol' Southern welcome for me. I'm outta there."

Chris had my undivided attention. "What happened next?"

"Dude! Nothing happened. I'm gone."

Ricco unzipped his mouth. "So, what was the point of that story?"

"The point was, you wannid ta hear it."

"Ah, Jeez, it ended differently last time," said Ricco looking across the roadside dirt to where an infantry platoon clambered on a line of Mine

Resistant Armour Protected vehicles, you've probably heard them called M-RAPs.

"No it didn't," said Chris, "it was a different story that ended differently and I ain't repeatin' it."

As Chris related his tale we'd passed half a mile of Hut 2301 lookalikes on the South side of All American Boulevard. Some of the thirty-thousand KAF inhabitants lived here. Opposite, the Boardwalk: an al fresco shopping, eating and leisure area with a running track, soccer pitch and basketball court, was already busy. For the soldiers out-there doing the real work, the Boardwalk made a welcome break from hostilities. It survived despite General Stanley McChrystal's attempts at eradication. He had even less success disposing of Taliban.

The crossroads at Down Town brought All American Boulevard to a shopping centre of stacked shipping containers. The NATO gym on the adjacent corner housed four million dollars worth of state of the art fitness equipment, in a rocket-resistant building. We turned left.

"Does this road have a name too?" I said.

"Bronco Road," said Chris, as he swung a right between some T-Walls.

"Bronco Road?" repeated Ricco. "How d'ya know all this stuff?"

"Know your A-O," said Chris.

The Land Cruiser settled into the uneven dirt alongside a row of portable toilets. Thirty yards away, a faded desert tan building resembled a tube stuck on its side in the dust after a fall from a great height. Machine swaged mild steel radial sections, crimped together, formed the parallel arched ridges of the curved structure. It was similar in construction to an aircraft hangar but smaller. The metal-sprayed sign welcomed diners to:

D-FAC 3 - LUXEMBOURG.

The Luxembourg turned out to be an easy five minute walk from the BMTF TLS office. Within a few days, walking to work became part of my routine because it was easier. Fifteen minutes using back alleys and cut-throughs got me there as quick as driving. There were no parking issues either, because one of the vehicles was always parked near the office. It was also good exercise.

One of the signs by the Luxembourg's entrance said:

No Bags Allowed.

"It's a precaution in case suicide bombers get past base security," said Chris. "Still happens sometimes."

"What? No way," said Ricco. "They don't get past security. Take no notice of him. He's just fuckin' with ya. It's ta stop TCNs filling their bags with chow for all the illegal residents on base."

"Illegal residents?" I said.

"Yeah. An MP told me the other day. They got around fifteen hundred TCNs over stayin' their contracts, just blending into the background. Living in overcrowded huts, in disused chews," said Ricco.

"Chews?" Wasn't a word I'd heard before.

"Yeah: Chews, it's an abbreviation: CHU. Containerised Housing Unit. Hooches."

"That's another one for my glossary of military terms," I said.

"Yeah. Get it down. There's plenny more to come," said Ricco.

"So you mean, people on base are like illegal immigrants?" I said.

"Yeah," said Ricco, "like Mexicans in Texas, Arizona, California. Shit, even in government." We laughed.

"D-FAC manager here, he's a Brit too, told me they provide eight thousand meals a day in this place. Said NorthLine produced twice as many," Ricco knew quite a bit about his A-O.

We progressed through the hand wash station and got a tray and cutlery sachet from the black lad on the check-in desk. He smiled.

"Thank you, sir," I said, checking out the name on his CAC. "Moses," his smile didn't move, neither did the queue. It was backed-up long enough for us to exchange a few words.

"Yes. Moses, sir. Thank you."

"From Nigeria?" I said. All the Nigerians I'd encountered during my time in UK Customs were criminals, usually drug smuggling or stealing hire cars for export to their home country. This lad struck me as good natured and honest.

"Yes sir. Nigeria sir," he smiled.

"Good man," I said.

The queue unjammed and we were propelled forward into the line for English Breakfasts. The ID cards worn by the catering staff showed they were mostly of British Commonwealth origin: India, Kenya, Zimbabwe. I put three slices of bread in the Continuous Toaster and put my tray on the table selected by Chris and Ricco.

"This place is phenomenal," I said. "It's like, return to the British Empire. It's staffed by former colonials."

"You include us in that?" Said Ricco, as he spooned oatmeal.

'Of course," I laughed. Then went for my toast.

When I got back to my seat, Ricco resumed our conversation: "So, the Brits get to fight the Afghans again but this time using someone else's money. Is that it?"

Chris listened to the conversation as he worked his way through an Atkins-style breakfast of bacon and sausage.

"It does look that way," I said. "On the other hand, it does look like America is employing the whole world here."

Chris stopped chewing. "Yud think there'd be kids back home in the States be grateful for a job out here. OK, so fryin' eggs is borin' as shit but, fryin' eggs tax free gotta be better than Walmart on minimum wage."

"Mebbe it's the IEDs and rocket attacks puts 'em off," said Ricco. "Rather be baggin' groceries than bagged-up into one a those Coroner's Office rubber sacks."

Chris shook his head: "There ain't been a civilian contractor killed on this base for years. Well, not by rockets. A couple got knocked off their bikes by a tanker in a sandstorm a month back and there was that guy who drowned fallin' down a drain in the rainy season, but nothin' combat related."

"So, just normal everyday deaths?" I said.

"Just like back home," said Ricco, sarcastically. "People are always drowning in drains on the Pacific West Coast."

'Really?' I said.

"No," Ricco grinned, "it ain't normal, not in Washington State and nuthins normal here.'

"This is proper British bacon," I said.

"*Proper* British bacon?" replied Ricco. "We call it country ham."

"Country ham?" I said. "Well, whatever you call it, it's better than the pink and grey strips of fat that passes for bacon in the States. We have something like that, it's called streaky."

Chris knew a thing or two about bacon: "Hey, great American bacon. It's great. Comes out of the freezer on sheets of brown paper. Fifty cloned slices to the tray. They look so alike I reckon they're mechanically reconstructed from, pigs."

"Remember the J'bad breakfasts," I said. "We used to get salmonella risk-averse easy-over solid yolks. Tetley teabags? No way. Lipton's. Here, wow! Freshly prepared fruit salad. Tinned variety available, if preferred." I stopped talking and started eating.

"Hey, Chris, you're right about kids back home," said Ricco. "These African guys must be priddy smart to land the job but they ain't gonna be smarter than some kid from Utah or Oklahoma. What gives?"

"Globalisation," I said.

"Globalisation? One word? That's the answer?" said Ricco.

"Yes," I said. "It's why we're here, spreading the gospel."

"Gospel?" said Ricco.

"Gospel according to Saint Timothy."

"Saint Timothy, didn't he save some cripple some place?"

Ricco's Catholic education had not been wasted but he didn't know I meant Timothy Geithner.

"Couldn't tell you," I said, "but I do know he's US Secretary of the Treasury, the fella that helps bankroll this campaign. But Supreme is the company that runs this place and a lot of other things on the base. I saw Supreme on the fuel tankers, too. Do you know much about Supreme Group?"

"Much?" said Ricco. "Nothin."

"Formed in 1957 by a former US soldier. Started providing food to the US army in Germany. The bottled water we use to clean our teeth and make tea is made by Supreme."

"How come you know so much about this stuff?" Said Ricco.

"Noticing things is a hobby," I said.

"Evil Genius," said Chris.

Breakfast over, mount up and drive, literally, around the corner to the TLS. Ricco and I clambered out. Sweat under my backpack lost its cooling effect as we walked down an alleyway to the large double door with a stencilled sign, faded but legible:

Welcome to COMKAF HQ.

Commander Kandahar Airfield Headquarters. More military acronymic vernacular to add to my vocabulary.

The makeshift plywood double-door of the TLS fitted into a roughly constructed plywood architrave conforming to the arched entrance. In a previous incarnation it may have been a packing case for a large piece of machinery. It was rarely closed and opened outwards revealing a large hall with a high domed brick ceiling. I'd seen fire-resistant vaults in dockside warehouses around England before being demolished to build homes of sticks, chalk, paper and plastic for the new Middle Class, quantitatively eased into a lifetime of debt.

"Hey Bruce," shouted Ricco above the sound of the Tornados taking off.

"Hey Ricco," responded Bruce. "Whassup?"

"Bruce, this is Gary. He's our FNG. He's a Brit."

I'd heard FNG used before. I knew it meant Fucking New Guy. It's not derogatory. Like being called Muzzungoo in the Congo means white man, it's a statement of fact. There was no denying it, I was FNG.

Bruce Adams and I shook hands while, nearby, Smiley the cleaner, held his mop upright in the bucket and smiled.

"A Brit, huh! Anythin' I can do for ya, just let me or Sabrina know. We're right in here." He indicated towards the window.

Sabrina leaned through the small hatch and smiled in my direction. I waved and smiled back. A beautiful woman is a welcome sight anywhere, even more so in a war zone. Anything she can do for me? Wow! Just seeing her had brightened up my day.

"I gotta be out on the flight line. Catch ya later guys!" Bruce turned and disappeared through a plywood door.

Smiley squeezed his mop through the bucket-mangle. I held out my hand. He smiled, shook his head to say no and held out a clenched fist so we could bump knuckles: the alternative to hand-shake if you have dirty hands. It makes sense in an environment where most things are contaminated by thermal-drifted particles of dust-borne faeces from a poo-pond. Also, cleaning does tend to expose a person to filth.

I laughed as we knocked fists together. "My name is Gary. What is yours?"

"My name?" He paused, maybe it had been some time since last asked. "Kamal, sir."

"Kamal," I repeated. "Tell me, sir, did you come here from Sri Lanka?"

He grinned a full set of big white teeth and did the Indian wobbly-head thing, "Yes sir. Sri Lanka sir," head-wobble.

"Excellent!" All the Sri Lankans I've ever met have always been reliable hard working people, "I'm glad you are here. Plenty of work here. See you later."

"Yes sir. Always here. TLS."

"TLS? What is that?" It seemed like a good opportunity to learn about my new workplace.

"TLS? Kamal no know. Sorry sir!" he smiled. Head wobble.

Ricco provided the explanation, "Taliban Last Stand. It's where the US Marine Corps Special Forces defeated the Taliban in 2001. Cam arn!" He set off, at pace, through an archway leading deeper into the building. "I'll show ya the hole in the roof. A five-hundred pounder blew the shidowd-ov-em!"

A dimly lit plywood corridor took us past office doors stencilled with abbreviations and acronyms, some closed, some not, where military personnel electronically fought the war on terror. Zip tied red, green, blue, black, yellow and purple ethernet cables hung around in dark alleys, contorting round corners before disappearing through hole-punched ancient brickwork. The smell of old cement dust grew stronger as we climbed a wooden staircase winding upwards towards the gaping hole in the roof and a small cluster of offices. A colony of plants surrounded the blast-hole. Gnarled roots of a small tree clung to life amongst ferns and broken cement, exploiting sunlight and shade. Or, maybe it was a tangle of sleeping sand snakes. We didn't hang around to find out.

"It must've been a hell of a blast and fireball," remarked Ricco.

"Awesome. But, a five-hundred pound bomb? I'm surprised it didn't completely obliterate the place. Must be some structure to contain that amount of energy," I said.

Ricco's silent expression said he hadn't previously questioned the veracity of the explosion story. A wooden bridge directly below the huge opening in the roof joined stairs leading down. Following the passageway brought us back to the main entrance.

In the corner, obscured from view by a brick pillar, a sight-screen covered in informative posters about heat exhaustion, charter flights to Dubai and 'Fraud, Waste & Abuse,' a door bearing the initials **B.M.T.F.** lurked in the shadow of a failing fluorescent light tube.

"Hey, that's not the normal route to the office, that was the guided tour. The main entrance we just came in is just around the corner," said Ricco, jiggling the worn lock until the handle turned.

The door opened into a space made narrower by forty or more cases of bottled water stacked along the right hand wall. We were in our office. A single switch gave power to two fluorescent light tubes hanging precariously from the plywood ceiling.

If the room hadn't been divided almost in half by a brick pillar five feet thick, it would have been sixteen feet square and not U-shaped. White flakes of paint and dust, vibrated loose from vertical surfaces by aircraft noise, dragged brick dust down to the floor where it awaited Smiley's mop. Out of view, above the plywood ceiling, the wall became an arch holding up part of the roof.

Two desks faced each other from opposite walls, gathering the dust that had failed to make it all the way to the floor. On top of a battered three-drawer metal filing cabinet a printer sat waiting to laser-jet black on to white. To its right a third desk, concealed beneath a scattering of documents, a leather holster, two empty water bottles, half a dozen 5.56 rounds, and unidentifiable bits of discarded detritus. Opposite the hidden desk, a fridge shivered noisily as the faltering compressor stopped chilling its load. The deeper the dust on horizontal surfaces, the darker the grey.

A small unopened Tetra-Pak of orange juice had leaked down the filing cabinet and onto the floor. Picking up the carton was a mistake someone had to make. Glued to the cabinet with sugary spill, the base parted company with the box. The remaining contents flowed freely on to my trousers and boots. A small serrated hole out of sight at a bottom corner was the clue to the initial leak: gnawed by a mouse. By way of confirmation, there were tiny tell-tale black Nigella seed-like turds in the congealed liquid.

Dropping the carton in the waste bin, the glue-board rodent trap in the corner of the room caught my attention. A trail of pain and death tracked across the adhesive to where a skinny mouse had come to a sticky end. During its failed attempt to extricate itself from the glutinous surface, patches of fur, skin and a rear leg, ripped from its body.

"There's wireless innernet in here, although it's a bit hit and miss," said Ricco, bringing me back to the job in hand. "It's for the passengers but we make use of it, password's on the wall," he pointed to a scrap of paper that had somehow attracted dust despite being pinned vertically to a notice board. "We'll get ya fixed up with a SniperHill account later. But why use your credit when you can steal someone else's?" He grinned. That was Ricco's Marine Corps training in action.

'Is it OK if I move the printer?' I said.

"Sure, it don't work anyway," said Ricco. "If ya get a minute, check it out. See if it's fixable."

The printer was easily moved onto the nearby table. Bundles of paper towels from a shelf over the fridge soaked up the mess I'd just caused. No plumbing within a hundred yards of the TLS meant bottled drinking water from the three-quarter full pallet outside the office got used for cleaning. After half a dozen passes, paper towels cleared the area revealing a flat metal surface. The sodden mass of tissue dripped mud as it found the bin.

My laptop soon picked up the wireless signal. A dozen or more emails had accumulated in my InBox: HQ stuff about pay claims, a new leave request form, open source intelligence bulletins from the British Embassy. Some were from French. Many were about the attack. Most of them had already been forwarded several times. Mark's wife had been informed of his death. I saved her email address and his brother's contact details. There was nothing to suggest the British Embassy had been informed. I'd take care of that.

"I've been given the job of repatriating Mark," I said.

"Saw that," said Ricco. "This'll be your base for the next day or so."

"It's around five in the morning in the UK. How long after a brutal murder is it too soon to talk to a wife about repatriating her husband's body?" I said.

"Shit brother," said Ricco. "Don't ask me. Only had one occasion to visit a widow. Never again. Ain't gonna be any easier over the phone."

"I haven't trained for this but I got the job anyway. Funny the way that worked," I said. "You know, there have been hundreds of occasions where I didn't get the job I'd applied for despite having all the skills and knowledge, yet here I am doing something I didn't sign up for. No previous experience required."

"Yep, I know that one," said Ricco.

"She's probably asleep right now, so, I'll leave it till a little later, at the moment I lack conviction."

My own doubts about why we were here would show through my attempt to convince Ann that her husband had made a noble sacrifice. That Mark died doing what he enjoyed and he hadn't died in vain was too cliché for me. Maybe in a few hours it wouldn't be.

Logging into the online FedCor personnel site allowed me to view my company life insurance policy: half a million dollars to each of my two sons. I increased the premiums: a million each. Giving the boys a head start in life was my main reason for being here. People had died for less, too often for nothing. I wanted my lads to have the opportunities I didn't get. One way or another, I had to pay. So be it.

Chris returned from his chores. "Hey! 'Sgoin' arn?"

"I have internet so I'm just going through emails," I said, "I've been in touch with French and he's given me some directions. I have to make a few calls to the UK but it's a bit early for that. The British Embassy should be informed about Mark. It's just as easy for me to do that from here rather than have someone in Kabul do it. Plus, I know Mark."

Ricco and Chris listened sympathetically.

"Hey. Gary," Chris got my attention, "Ya drink corfee, right?"

"I do. Prefer tea but coffee would be good right now."

Chris pulled a filter coffee maker from a desk drawer. He blew off most of the dust then cleaned the filter-funnel with bottled water. Discarded rinse-water formed a puddle on the dusty concrete floor then slowly dispersed. Ground coffee came from the fridge where the mice couldn't get it.

"OK, man. I'll set it a makin'." Chris emptied two half litre bottles of water into the percolator tank and switched it on. Within minutes the reassuring aroma of Colombian filled the room, masking the smell of jet aircraft fumes drawn under the door by the AC.

"Help yerself when it's ready," he motioned towards the machine.

"Thanks Chris. I will."

"RICCO!" Chris called out suddenly, startling Ricco.

"JESUS Darrly! Whaat?" Ricco shouted from behind his desk.

"We gotta job to do. Sooner the better. Let's go."

"Jesus, Darrly, what's the hurry?" Ricco demanded.

"Just come on. I'll tell you in the car," Chris and Ricco closed their laptops and left the room. They weren't excluding me from anything, they had stuff planned well before I arrived so they were just going about their normal business.

I called out, "See you later lads!" But the door had already slammed shut as a turbo-prop plane taxied to a halt just outside the airside entrance to the TLS. I wasn't sure if they'd heard me.

Chris and Ricco didn't tell me they had an appointment at the morgue to identify Mark and arrange for a death certificate. It was good they didn't mention it as I may have felt compelled to go along. It spared me an unpleasant memory. A week before Mark was killed, I'd returned to Afghanistan after my mother's funeral. Although it's customary, it's not always a good idea to say goodbye to a corpse in a coffin.

Happy memories of my mum as a young woman come back to me at odd moments. Seemingly insignificant events have become treasured moments. In her forties and fifties the first signs of ageing went unnoticed by me as I lived my own life. In her sixties and seventies, dementia, but all is overshadowed by the memory of her in that box.

My mother was lucky. She died with dignity in her own home, sat in her favourite chair. I should have been there to hold her hand as it went cold, but I wasn't. I can't regret something that was beyond my control, just live with it.

Our final Skype conversation had been on a Tuesday morning around eight-twenty UK time. It was afternoon in Jalalabad. She sounded unwell but she wouldn't let me call a doctor. Mum would never have forgiven me if she'd ended her days in a hospital, or worse: one of those grand old houses saved from dereliction where the stink of urine can't wait to get out the front door as you step inside for your monthly visit. The twice weekly habit starts off with good intentions, but you know how it is.

I called mum again at ten-thirty UK time: no answer. My mum chose to die alone rather than in the company of strangers. She was a very brave woman, braver than me. By the time my friend looked through her living room window at eleven-thirty, my mum had been dead at least an hour. He knew the moment he saw her.

In the UK, police must attend all incidents of sudden death. They insisted on using the *Key* to break down the front door and wreck the frame despite the back door being glass. It's petty of me to think about that really given the circumstances, but they didn't need to be so destructive. They must have known plenty of local burglars with the skills that could have got past the lock in under two minutes, but that would've solved the issue too quickly. Always best to create more work rather than less. I guess the police need to practice in safe conditions so they can get it right for fly-on-the-wall TV.

My mum's last words were: 'I *do* love you Gary.'

'I love you too mum,' I should have said that more often.

Because I didn't see Mark on ice, my memory of him was from our time in Dover Customs and in Kinshasa on the doomed DRC project: hesitating while locating the appropriate word during conversation; twisting his irritating watch around on his wrist; brushing a flop of hair from his eyes with a comb of fingers and theatrical flick of the neck. On that Herat Sunday evening, he awkwardly held his cigarette as he became a social smoker. Mark was an entertaining bloke but not big on jokes. He had a cryptic sense of humour which eluded many people because they weren't paying attention. It came in handy when dealing with some of the Congolese Customs crooks. One of the Congolese Customs officers had asked Mark how he knew a freight agent lied about a declared consignment value. Mark replied; 'Parce que ses lèvres bougent.'

Because his lips are moving! They got it. Humour bridges many cultural divides.

The unreliable Afghan telecommunications network compelled me to Skype-call the British Embassy in Kabul. The mobile number was on the UK dot Gov website.

A gloomy little voice answered the phone: "Good morning. British Embassy."

I replied solemnly: "Good morning sir!" The line was clear. "I need to report the death of a British citizen here in Afghanistan. Can someone give me some advice, please?"

"Hold on please sir," said Mr Dismal. The line crackled. It sounded like someone looking for a favourite in a bag of Pick 'n' Mix. "I'm sorry sir. There is no one in that office right now. Please call again this afternoon."

"OK, is there a direct number I can call?"

It's always better to avoid switchboards when possible. That wasn't too difficult in Afghanistan as most of the landline telecommunications network had been destroyed during the various conflicts.

"No sir. This is the only number. Please call again at two o'clock."

"Two o'clock. OK. Who should I ask for?"

"Just call this number. The person will speak with you," Mr Dismal sounded like a twenty-something Afghan, a skinny, swarthy little chap in a shiny suit sat at a desk with a line of mobile phones in front of him. Each phone dedicated to a specific function with the appropriate script to read beneath it on a laminated card. When one rang he'd have to walk down a corridor to see if that person was on duty. On this occasion they weren't.

"OK, I will call again at two o'clock. Thank you, sir," call ended.

Sod it. This wasn't going to be straight forward. I checked my email again. Drank bottles of water. Had several cups of coffee. Then reclined in one of the leather executive office chairs: the one with the least dust and no castors because they'd all disintegrated leaving just the metal spikes. I practiced resting my boots on the edge of the filthy desk and fell asleep.

Chris and Ricco barged through the office door.

Standing up quicker than blood could get to my legs, leaning on the desk kept me upright.

"Hey! 'ssgoin' arn?" Chris smiled.

"Cor. I just dozed off," my watch said one o'clock, "sorry about that."

"Ya havin' lunch," said Ricco.

"I'm OK. I had a big breakfast so I'm OK till evening meal but I'll come and have a cuppa tea."

Ricco grinned. "A cuppa tea! How very British?" We all laughed.

"I think that calls for the Cambridge. Don't you Chris, old Chep?" said Ricco. His Dick Van Dyke impression was near perfect.

"Jolly well does," continued Chris. It was comical listening to two Americans practicing their Cockney accents. They were terribly funny.

Outside TLS, Kandahar heat desiccated everything that stood still and most things that didn't. Our Land Cruiser, originally parked in shade by the DHL depot across Screaming Eagles Boulevard, had been fully irradiated by the sun for at least an hour. A guy at the bus stop sat looking down on his sports shoes. They'd been such a bargain at Saturday's on-base bazaar. Unglued by scorching blacktop, body and sole parted company. Ground heat penetrated my Nike Special Field Boots: SFBs, but *they* weren't counterfeit.

Screaming Eagles: not only the longest continuous length of blacktop on base but a tribute to the 101st Airborne Division, whose sacrifice had made many things possible. That was back in 2001. Now, the screaming eagles were twenty-four seven jet aircraft taking off and landing, parallel to the road. It was only a five minute drive through Bronco Road dust but the car's air conditioning soon blew away my sweat.

Leaning forward through the swoosh of AC my question was for Ricco: "What are TCNs?"

"TCNs are the guys like, ... hold on, I'm thinking," a momentary pause allowed his thoughts to fall into place. "Yeah, that's it, TCNs don't represent any government, not even their own."

"So that's us," I said.

Ricco's head turned slightly as if responding to an odd sound: "No, we ain't TCNs. Well, *you* could be, I guess, technically. We're American."

"But do you represent the US government or FedCor our employers?" I said.

Chris had the answer, "Dude! Don't think about it. Just remember, Six One Zero." The rear view mirror reflected his blue-eyed grin.

Outside one of the six D-FACs on KAF, the sign on the Texas barrier by the entrance said:

Welcome to the Cambridge.

It had a distinctly British menu. Fish and chips every Friday. They also had individual steak and kidney pies that may have been Holland's: 'A Proper Lancashire Baker.' Incredible. This was Tuesday lunch and one option was Shepherd's Pie. A bowl of salad was my choice, along with lots of black olives and a cuppa Tetley tea. Chris had sliced roast beef and some chicken wings. Ricco got something from the sandwich bar made to his own specification.

"I'm supposed to call a chap at the British Embassy in Kabul at fourteen hundred," It was a verbal reminder to me but Ricco and Chris were listening.

"OK, we'll finish here then go to our other office and try from there. The phone signal's sometimes better. Don't know why," said Ricco, "also, I need to copy some documents and the printer in the TLS stopped workin' a few days ago."

"Maybe there's a mouse in it," I said.

"Hmm, mebbe," said Ricco. "Take a look at it when you get a minute."

"I'll do the vehicle checks while we're there," said Chris.

Emerging from the Cambridge into debilitating heat, sunlight reflecting off the limestone car park rocks was painful to the eyes without sunglasses. On went our ballistic eye-pro. The scorched smell of my own shower gel found my nostrils until my shemagh pulled shade over my head. It was ninety-five degrees Fahrenheit outside, the interior of the car was hotter. The AC had just about taken the edge off the heat when we arrived at our other office.

Getting out of the car, Ricco gave me the tourists' description of our location: "Welcome to the White House."

"Right. I can see why," I said. It was white. With a little imagination the rounded concrete steps and verandah resembled 1600 Pennsylvania Avenue. Beyond two concrete pillars and anti-bird mesh, four almost-white doors rattled on their hasps and staples. Paper signs stapled to the two on the right announced: **BMTF** in Bold 40, Times New Roman.

"Hey Gary!" said Chris, as we got inside the office. "This is a hardened building so there's no need to get on the floor if there's a rocket attack."

"Oh. OK. That's good," I replied. "Are those ballistic plastic?" The cracked brittle-thin orange perspex windows had very little shrapnel resistance. I knew from Jalalabad that ricochets are totally unpredictable, so the type of glazing was probably irrelevant.

"Damn!" Chris moved a tall metal bookshelf to block the window. "If that don't slow it down at least I won't see it comin'."

"Slow it down? It ain't gonna stop it," remarked Ricco.

"True," I agreed. "On FOB Hughie I heard what sounded like a very loud escape of steam passing over me in the compound. I dived to the ground and covered my head. Like you're supposed to. There was an explosive whumpf just outside the perimeter and the ground shook. I'd heard the rocket motor of an RPG. It seemed to have come from the direction of the Jalalabad highway although I never actually saw it. They're too fast and there were trees in the way. It must have passed over the neighbouring Afghan Army base so it was clearly intended for me."

"Hahaha! Clearly intended for you? Missed again," said Ricco.

"Yeah, it missed me all right. But I heard a scream from the hut diagonally opposite to ours about twenty yards away so it was obviously heading in my direction. I ran over to the hut. When I got inside, one of the army interpreters had been hit. He was holding his foot. There was quite a bit of blood splattered on the wood floor. Another interpreter came through the door at the other end of the shed at the same time. It was Freddy," Chris sat upright in his chair.

"Hey Freddy, he's a great guy," Chris knew Farooq Samiullah. "How's he doin'?"

"Oh, I have quite a story about Freddy. I'll get to that later."

"Quite a story? Quite a few," said Ricco.

"We got Mustapha to stand while he kept pressure on the wound. Then Freddy and I linked arms so Mustapha could sit on them. We ran like hell to the medical centre. Mustapha's feet, literally, did not touch the ground. That's the first arterial spurt I've seen in real life. Freddy and I got him to the medics and they took control. A couple of stitches closed the hole in Mustapha's artery and the next time I saw him he was back on his bunk with his lower leg completely encased in bandage." From the dusty stack by the door a bottle of water quenched my thirst. "The crazy thing about that incident is that when Mustapha heard the RPG pass overhead he was lying on his bunk, doing whatever Afghan interpreters do when they're not dodging bullets. When he heard the impact he sat up and put his feet in his sandals. It was at that moment that the base-plate from a 120 mm rocket of Chinese origin, arced over the wall of the base, hit several branches on a well established eucalyptus tree, glanced off the handrail of his hut, passed through the hut wall, splintered a bookcase, holed his holdall and just nicked the top of his foot thereby clipping a hole in the artery. Random chance in action. *Again!*"

"Shit man, that's a hell of a chunk a metal. That could take yure head clean off," Chris looked over his shoulder as he shifted his chair away from the bookshelf.

"All that happened 'cause he put his feet in sandals?" said Ricco. "Fuck flip-flops. Always said, they're dangerous."

It must've been the salad, maybe the olives or possibly the disrupted routine over the previous few days, but I felt movement down below.

"Where's the nearest toilet?" I said.

"PortaPotty over by the wall," Chris gestured in the general direction.

To me they were Green Meanies because they were green and often unpleasant. Most of the time I avoided them, but occasionally necessity will override style.

The SOP for using a Green Meanie was written in 2011, by me after my brand new, twenty dollar, Foster Grant's fell into the septic tank of my first Green Meanie. Fortunately, on that occasion, the tank was quite full so I didn't have to reach in too far. The mass of toilet paper and solids prevented the sunglasses from sinking into the unspeakable mess. A surgical rubber glove, kept for emergency use, made plucking them from the surface easy. It took a full bottle of water to rinse away the faecal matter.

Green Meanie [GM] SOP:

- when entering a GM DO NOT try to look cool by placing your eye-wear above your hairline because when you bend forward to lift the toilet lid, they slide off
- DO a pre-dump check [PDC] for adequate supplies of toilet paper and hand sanitising gel
- DO PDC for spiders, scorpions and snakes. Bites can result in painful injuries in difficult to access areas of the body
- after dark DO carry a torch/flashlight. ALWAYS PDC overhead for spiders and mosquitos
- GM frequented by TCNs or Local Nationals [LN] may be damaged and or dirty as a result of improper use such as 'perching' on the seat and closet.
- Perchers frequently leave part-used bottles of water in GM following ablutions. Do NOT drink.
- Avoid GM, or, use with caution.

Walking briskly across the courtyard rocks got me to the two Green Meanies. Peering into the one on the left and keeping a safe distance from the smell, my pre-dump check revealed: no toilet paper. The first door slammed shut as the second door opened. Paper and sterilising hand gel in place: all good. It was also quite clean although the afternoon heat was beginning to raise an obnoxious vapour from the waste tank directly below the seat.

I'd just finished my magnum opus and was about to start the paperwork when the wail of the rocket attack alarm wound-up, accompanied by :

Rocket attack. ...Rocket Attack. ...Rocket Attack.

"Oh Nooo! Please. Not now," no one heard me shout.

My trousers got yanked up by the gun-belt whilst clutching a roll of toilet paper, which meant my hands were full when the plastic door lock decided to resist and take off part of my thumbnail in the struggle. There was blood and pain but, being blown up by a rocket while riding a Green Meanie was something I'd never live down. I ran to the relative safety of the White House. Chris was on Page Eight of National Enquirer.

"Dude, was that you set off the alarm," said Chris. "Thought I heard something go thud!"

Breathing heavily from my exertion and the run across the yard, I rubbed antibacterial gel between my hands as Briddish girl continued to cheerfully announce: *rocket attack*.

"He's so funny, isn't he?" chipped in Ricco, as he searched the office furniture looking for anything useful. "Hey Darrly, does Jessica Rabbit know you fancy Briddish Girl?"

"She won't if you don't tell her," Chris turned a page.

"He's gotta thing for female voices," said Ricco. "Likes to hear 'em gag and beg for mercy."

Chris didn't rise to the bait.

There was a distant wumpf.

"Hey, there's number two," said Chris with a smile.

"It wasn't me," I said. "Mine was more splat than thud."

Ricco grimaced. "Nice. Thank you for sharing!"

Chris tilted his head to locate the direction of sound, "Other side of the runway."

"Ya learnt *somethin'* useful in I-raq," said Ricco.

"Yeah, got plenty of practice too," said Chris.

"Where in Iraq did you serve?" I said.

"Fallujah once. Couple other places that priddy much don't exist now," Chris flicked to another page in his magazine.

"Good," I said. "I mean, I'm glad the explosion had been nowhere near us, not, good a couple of places don't exist."

Ricco made a call. "Hey Lynn, you OK?" I could just about hear Lynn talking through the undulating alarm sound. "You're safe that's the main thing … We're at the White House. Just do what you can, when you

73

can. ... Not a problem, gorgeous!" Call ended. "She's OK, She's at the Pass Office," said Ricco, reassuringly. Then he called to Kabul HQ to let the program manager, PM, know we were all accounted for.

Ricco opened one of the dusty metal lockers. "Hey! The last guys in here must've left in a hurry. We got two cans o' nine mil here. We should book some range time."

"Saw that the other day," said Chris. "Don't like the look of that grey metal casing. Not brass. Might be Chinese shit."

"Len told me a bit about that in Jalalabad. Steel casings mean you have to clean your gun more often. Right?" I said.

"Yep, more dirt, more chance of misfire," said Chris.

"But it'll be OK to blast away on the range," said Ricco. "No way would I take that into combat."
"Has this ammo been abandoned by the army or contractors?" I said.
"Well the last guys outta here were Mil, so I guess it was army ordnance."

Ricco was too excited at the prospect of target practice to be concerned with US military effectiveness. In addition to the ammunition, the previous US army unit based in the White House had abandoned loads of useful kit: note books, legal pads, coffee maker, fridge-freezer, boxes of medals and citations. Some of the military medals got awarded to me, my teenage son and his friends.

"Have to wait for the all-clear then go to the TLS," said Ricco. "Can't get internet in here today for some reason."

"I can get to the ISP website but it won't let me log in," said Chris to his laptop's frozen browser page.

"It's two-thirty. Time I called the British Embassy again," I said, setting my computer up on a nearby shelf. "Lots of wireless internet networks in the vicinity," I counted eight on the dropdown list. One had a very strong signal but without an account it was useless. Signing up had to be done at their office, currently on lock-down. I went to my Skype account and found the British Embassy cell-phone number I'd called earlier. I tried using my mobile phone: No Service.

"Ricco, can I borrow your phone to call the British Embassy, please?"

Ricco fumbled in his pocket. "Sure, here," he held out the phone then looked at the screen. "Oh, no signal. Must be the jammers."

At fifteen thirty-eight hours the Briddish girl announced: *All clear ... All clear ...All clear.*

Time to head back to the TLS and get on the internet. A four hundred yard air conditioned drive got us to the TLS. Setting up my laptop in what was to become my usual desk space, on top of the metal filing cabinet, I tried the cell-phone again.

"Dude!" said Chris, "You won't get signal in here. The walls are eight feet thick," Chris got up from his desk. "Follow me," we went outside and stood in the passenger departure yard. "You might get a signal here. But if there's an arrival you won't be able to hear anything."

Not the best place to make an emotional phone call but, in a war-zone, where is?

Chris gestured towards the building. "Hey, here. See this?" We walked over to the sloping wall of the TLS. Chris pointed to the four inch deep gouge that ran diagonally downwards for about two feet. "That's where a rocket hit a few weeks ago. We heard it strike but it didn't explode."

"You were in the office at the time?" I said,

"Yeah!" he said, with a mixture of excitement and relief. "They found it over there, someplace," Chris jerked his head in an easterly direction. "Near the control tower."

"That was lucky," I said, lamely.

"Probably wouldn't have penetrated even if it had gone bang, but it would've shaken a few bits loose."

The British Embassy phone rang. And rang. My phone's clock showed 16:18. The Embassy had finished for the day. Call ended. We returned to the cool office.

"Got'ny larndrie?" Ricco's enunciation threw me.

"Larndrie?" I replied.

"Yeah, yer know, larndrie. Whadda you call it?"

"Oh, yes. Right. Laundry!" I said.

"Oh, so sorry, Loornderry!" Ricco grinned, "Well ya gonna need a larndrie bag. Whatcha doin' now?" Ricco seemed keen to keep me busy.

"Not much. I was hoping to get through to the British Embassy but they don't answer. I'll try later."

"It's probably arfternoon tea time." Ricco's British accent was coming along really well.

"Probably," I scoffed. "I do have a laundry bag."

"Nah, ya don't. You need a KAF larndrie bag," he grinned.

I shrugged, "OK."

"CHRIS!" shouted Ricco, over the flight of Tornados shaking dust onto everything in the room.

"DUDE!" Chris flinched an inch into the air from his seat. "Don't shout. Ya makin' me nervous."

Ricco looked from Chris, to me. "D'ya hear that? I make *him* nervous." Ricco shook his head. "He's the one that's always on about sploogin' and what's that other thing?" Ricco paused to recall another of Chris's idiosyncratic expressions. "Filthy Hose-ay, er sumpn?"

"Maan, I told ya. Durdy Sanchez!" Chris shook his head and slapped his hands palms down on the desk in mock anger. "I can't believe you forgot already."

"That's it. Durdy Sanchez," Ricco's index finger and thumb preened his moustache as he smiled.

I shrugged. "I don't know Filthy Hosay or Durdy Sanchez, but then, US citizens have more contact with Hispanics than British people."

Ricco and Chris said and did nothing to refute my statement, but their glances told me there was more to it than personal hygiene issues.

"Chris, ya gotta car?" Ricco and I were on our feet, putting an end to further remarks about the mysterious Mexican.

"Yo!" got the heavy Hilux," Chris pushed the key towards the edge of the desk.

"Good. Keep it. We'll take the Land Cruiser. Let's go."

I began packing my laptop.

Ricco shook his head: "Leave yer stuff here. It'll be fine."

Our gold Toyota stood across the street. Snorting dust from the engine compartment vents, its 3.5 litre turbo engine growled at the lesser vehicles parked alongside. Ten minutes drive along Screaming Eagles Boulevard brought us to Laundry Road.

That wasn't it's name. Laundry Road had a number not a name, but it's what we called it because it made sense. There weren't many things here that did make sense but Laundry Road was one of them. The laundry was at the other end of Laundry Road which was actually a two minute walk across All American Boulevard from our room in Hut 2301. Either one of two basic routes would get you to Laundry Road and Hut 2301 from TLS. We took Screaming Eagles because there were no pedestrian crossings on it, which meant no stop-start driving. With hindsight we should've gone the stop-start route along All American Boulevard. That's the thing with binary choices, they make the wrong decision so much easier.

A crane lifting a piece of heavy machinery into a compound to the west of Laundry Road held up traffic in both directions.

I said: "Looks like we're part of a traffic jam."

Some of the vehicles must've wanted to get into the NATO HQ compound opposite or maybe they were content being stationary targets. Other vehicles did three-point turns in the road. We couldn't park because of the storm drains each side of the compacted-mud and aggregate road. We couldn't abandon the vehicle because it would cause an obstruction. It didn't make sense to walk under heavy suspended objects and the MPs were there waiting to enforce KAF rules.

"Only one thing for it," said Ricco, "we gotta go round the blarck." Road network symmetry on-base confused me. Most of the roads looked the same: desert dust. As did the accommodation huts. The important things were landmarks. Ricco turned the Land Cruiser around and headed back to Screaming Eagles Boulevard, the runway came into view in front of us. He made a right turn and then took the next right.

"Here's the PX," said Ricco, as we rolled carefully by the biggest shop on base at eight kilometres per hour. The **EXIT** door discharged uniformed personnel faster than a raiding party of Texas Fire Ants leaving roadkill. Clutched purchases included: plastic chests of drawers; big tubs of PumpIt - The **whey** to get bigger and cartons of Chesterfields under armpits.

"That's the Niagara," Ricco pointed left to another D-FAC. Inline soldiers and civilians shuffled patiently forward through dust to door. It was evening meal time. We turned right onto All American Boulevard. A couple of hundred yards further on, a left turn brought us to the dirt track adjacent to Hut 2301. "It's just across the road," said Ricco, "Come arn. You just need your CAC card."

The Poo Pond miasma had us surrounded. Surrender was not an option. Fight through to the other side - of the road. From the traffic jam to our hut we had driven maybe half a mile. Then walked fifty yards across the road. Along with *hurry up* and *wait*, three steps forward two steps back was to become another recurring theme.

The rocket attack had disrupted activities. Many soldiers who had been about to drop off their laundry had sought shelter in the bunkers nearby, until the all clear. Ricco led the way. Because that's what team leaders do.

The laundry shed had two doors. Over one, a sign indicated: **IN.** Over the other: **OUT.** Inside was a counter about twenty feet long. Two signs: **Drop Off. Collect**. Very efficient. TCNs ran the place like clockwork.

Ricco handed over a cloakroom ticket to one of the guys at the collect counter who promptly rushed off into the room on our right. Another laundryman immediately took his place at the counter. They popped up faster than fairground targets.

Ricco greeted a laundryman with Mediterranean features: "Good evenin', sir. Can this guy get a larndrie bag?" His thumb pointed me out.

"Certainly, sir," two words spoke of his Balkan origin. The CAC on his armband said Macedonian. Handing me a clipboard from under the counter he said: "Please. Your name, Social Security number and CAC." I completed the form and handed back the clipboard and immediately received a brand-new laundry bag. Still in its wrapper.

"Thank you very much, sir," I said, picking up my KAF laundry bag.

"You're welcome, sir," his half smile conveyed sincerity.

I was genuinely pleased. It was almost five-thirty and although there were many important things left undone, I felt I'd achieved something.

Lynn joined us at the Cambridge for our evening meal.

Towards the end of our after dinner conversation Chris had a question: "Hey, Lynn."

Lynn eyed him suspiciously, she had a sixth sense for mischief, especially when it involved Chris Doreley. "What?"

"We were talking earlier, but these guys had to rush off. You know Durdy Sanchez, right?"

Lynn glared at Chris through narrowed eyes: "Not personally. And if you're offering to introduce me, forgettaboud it." Her Texan inflection left no doubt she had no interest in the subject.

Chris became more playful: "No. No, it's just that Gary doesn't know Durdy Sanchez. Thought you might help him with that."

Lynn polygraphed me with her intense stare. "Is that right? Ya don't know Durdy Sanchez?" I shrugged: no knowledge. "Well, good for you. And you ...," her red-painted index finger nail pointed menacingly not far from Chris's nose. "You, can explain it after I'm gone. I got more important things ta do than git with you on your favourite subject."

Lynn stood, smoothed her blouse and pulled the clip-on holstered Glock around to the sweet-spot on her hip. We went.

Tuning left out of the car park, Lynn's Prado turned heads of pedestrians away from the dust cloud.

In the back seat of the Land Cruiser, curiosity overwhelmed my patience: 'OK. Will someone, please tell me about Dirty Sanchez?'

Chris eyed me through the rear view mirror: "Dude, I can't believe ya never heard of ..."

Ricco's suddenly raised hand could have been mistaken for an Apostolic Blessing until he annunciated: "STOP! ... I will explain using words that our erudite friend here will understand. You, just drive the fucking truck!" Chris grinned. Ricco took a deep breath: "Durdy Sanchez is a   sexual practice between a man and a woman …" Ricco looked at Chris. "It is usually between a man and a woman, right?"

Chris flicked the wiper stalk to clear dust from the screen: "It is when I do it," he checked my reaction in the rear view mirror. I was with it so far.

Ricco continued: "Hmm. That's reassuring. Where was I? Oh yes. Between a man and a woman, usually. Now don't go confusin' usual with normal, coz it ain't. It's anythin' *but* normal."

Chris laughed: "Hey! Nice pun."

"What?" Ricco squinted at Chris. "Whaddafuck? Pun? Do you even know what a pun is?"

"Yeah! You just made one: *butt normal*. Yeah?" Chris's infantile remark made me chuckle.

Ricco shook his head in the way people do when they've just stood in something unpleasant. "Anyway, as I was sayin', this particularly disgusting practice occurs just as the woman is about to orgasm, which in Darrly's case must be a rare occurrence."
Chris irreverently raised the middle finger on his right hand close to Ricco's face.

Ricco quickly regretted slapped it away: "Oh no! Oh god. I touched it. Argh! Where's the hand cleanser?" He fumbled around in the glove box one handed and pulled out the bottle of antibacterial gel. Rubbing his hands together, he resumed his explanation: "As I was sayin', the woman is about to climax, so the man, and I use that term extremely loosely in Darrly's case, quickly rams his finger up her ass then, after withdrawal, wipes it along her top lip," Chris was enjoying watching my face involuntarily screw into a mask of revulsion. "Apparently it leaves a residue closely resembling a muss-dash," said Ricco. "And that, my friend, is Durdy Sanchez."

Ricco turned in his seat to see me stunned into silence: eyebrows raised, open-mouthed, stunned, somewhere between shock and awe.

Room 7 of Hut 2301 was just for sleeping, most of the next few days were spent in the cool confines of the TLS arranging Mark's repatriation.

Occasionally, I ventured out into the heat to make phone calls and gaze across the runway at the distant mountains changing colour with the passing hours. Aircraft and helicopter movements frequently distracted me from the spectacular view. Tornados taking off meant fingers in ears. At night, while contemplating my presence in Afghanistan, blue afterburners disappeared into the dark like receding gas-rings on a camp stove.

My mission was Six One Zero. It was not to try and figure out the purpose of all this surreal unsustainable activity in the middle of an Asian desert. Somewhere, amongst the millions of people deployed, directly and indirectly, on Operation Enduring Freedom - Afghanistan, someone must have already known the answer but, for me, there was more chance of sudden death than gradual enlightenment.

Just over a year ago, my life had been very different.

Freelance - 2010

Scam: a dishonest scheme, a fraud.

Is my simplest description of the Congo job for anyone who asks, few do. Sanctimony and acrimony polarised the views of the handful of former colleagues who took the trouble to speak. People are either jealous of success and seek to be part of it, or, quick to criticise failure from which they rapidly disassociate. My predicament served as a warning for many: stick with what you have. Be grateful for your job in a government department that will keep you until retirement, when the futility of your lifetime's work is suddenly revealed to you in the form of a carriage clock or a Wowcher.

What set me apart was that I knew the Department's *Investors in People* policy was nothing more than a human resources buzzword and that the ones still in the institution hadn't yet worked it out. Up until the FedCor call desperation might have driven me back to the safety of UK Border Agency, given the chance. Fortunately, there were no vacancies.

Necessity is often described as the mother of invention, but let me tell you, desperation is a bitch.

My Pay As You Go credit was low so I'd make the call quick. "Mark, what do you have going on tomorrow?"

"Hmm, let me see, where's my calendar," unemployment hadn't dulled Mark's wit. "Oh, I appear to be free tomorrow."

"Fancy a day out in France?"

"Nice idea but the funds are a bit low for a jolly," he said.

"It's all paid for," I said.

"Sounds better. What's it about? Have we turned into Baccy Runners?"

The Cross Channel tobacco smuggling racket between Belgium and England was still going strong but it was of no interest to either of us.

"No, nothing like that. A pal of mine in the truck rental business has a tractor unit at French Customs in Calais. He wants a hand getting it back. Free breakfast, lunch, beers, plus a hundred and fifty quid each. What do you think?"

"Count me in. What do I need to do?"

"I'll text in an hour. Standby."

"Standing," he replied. End Call.

An hour later, following a telephone conversation with my pal, a text to Mark confirmed our mission: Pick you up 07:00 tomorrow. Breakfast @07:30 Premier Inn Eastern Docks, Dover. EuroTunnel shuttle@09:30. Meeting @Douane Custom House Calais @11:00 local. Work on your French! BeSeeingYou!

Mark replied: 'Oui mon ami à bientôt!'

My pal's brand new Audi A6 Avant 3.0TDI Le Mans Tiptronic Quattro, five door estate, outside Mark's gate brought a smile to his face. "I take it all back, we're not Baccy Runners, we're drug barons," Mark got in.

"I hope it doesn't come to that. I wouldn't like the company I'd have to keep."

"Fair comment," said Mark. "Funny that, I was just looking at some old work photos. Do you recall that cannabis case a few years ago? Two hundred and fifty kilos, the one where the Dutch bloke got off?"

"Vermeen? Spelt V E R M I N," I said. "Bit of an unfortunate surname. I interviewed his mother. I mean, who takes their old mum on a drug run? No, don't know what you're talking about."

"That's the bloke. Well, his barrister did a good job. OK he was remanded in custody for four months until the hearing but at the end of it he walked free. He was grinning from ear to ear when he came to collect his bag of property. We shook hands. No hard feelings. He offered to take me for a pint. I would've gone, there's no harm done drinking with an innocent man. But, I was picking my daughter up from a school trip. Even he couldn't believe he'd got away with it. I said: try it again, see what happens."

"Hmm, sounds like a nice bloke. Did he promise to never do it again?"

"Funny that, he did. And he won't, someone made sure of that," said Mark.

"I recall doing some foreign enquiries on that case," I said. "The Dutch Customs and Police were brilliant. Even got me a trip around the Heineken brewery. How do you know he won't?"

"Yes, you did. I remember your witness statement. More to the point, I remember part of the Public-interest Immunity hearing as a result of your trip to Amsterdam. The Dutch had a lot of information on his connections, we helped them join some of the dots. They actually nailed the boss of that particular group of associates. They'd been after him for some time. Name was Van der, something or other," said Mark.

"Valk?" I guessed, "Dutch detective. 1970s TV series."

"That's it," said Mark with a smile. "Never watched it myself, bit before my time, but I remember my mum watched it. I think she quite liked the main actor."

"Oi! Steady. I'm not your dad! Actually, I got a long email from the Police Commissaris, that's like our Chief Superintendent, about that. His officers sent five people to jail as a result of what we started," I said.

"Nice. But, do you know what happened to Vermin?" said Mark.

"Something bad?" I said speculatively.

"As bad as it gets. He was found in a dike with a bullet in his head."

"Dike? As in, a flood control feature usually associated with the Netherlands," I said.

"Yes. You were hoping I meant one of those close-cropped bleached-blonde lesbians in sawn-off jeans and leather jacket sat astride a large chopper, weren't you? So was I when I first heard about it," said Mark.

"Will you stop doing that?" I said.

"Reading your mind?"

"I said stop doing that."

"No, you didn't, you only thought you said it," said Mark.

We both laughed.

"What was the story behind dead in a dike? Obviously drug related," I said.

"Well, according to the Dutch, the *woord op straat* was because Vermin got off at Canterbury Crown Court. The *management* back in

Holland got sent down for that and several other offences. His associates must have thought Vermin was a rat."

"Oh, very good. I wish I'd said that," I said.

"You were about too," said Mark. We laughed. "It was all down to good detective work by the Dutch. You know, when the Canterbury jury came back with their unanimous Not Guilty verdict, even the judge expressed surprise in his final remarks. He said to the Foreman: and is that the decision you *each* have come to?"

"Judge Crowe?"

"That's the one. Hanging Judge Crowe, he did like Customs cases," said Mark.

"Do you think the jury just liked the bloke?" I said.

"I'm sure they did. I liked him. He wasn't a dangerous fella. He was entertaining. He expected to do time, so he could have been an arsehole but it wasn't in his nature. You know, some of 'em, when you see them up there in the dock, you know they're in the right place. Vermin wasn't one of them."

"So, great British justice sets the bloke free to receive Dutch *injustice* at the hands of his friends," I said.

"It really is as simple as that. If he'd got six years in UK nick, he'd have been out in three and probably still be alive. I felt like writing to the jury members and telling them about the final outcome of their decision to ignore the evidence. But, it would have got me into Unsatisfactory Performance and Behaviour proceedings. At the time, when I thought I had a future in the Department, I didn't want a UPB on my file," said Mark

"Yes. UPBs are, were, best avoided. But, it would've been nice to make the jury members feel guilty about their innocent verdict," I smiled.

"There's an irony in that, don't you think? The unintended consequences of ignoring the evidence and information and just going with your own personal prejudices? That sometimes makes me hesitate with decisions," said Mark.

I told him: "That's intuition. Your feminine side, don't ignore it."

"Oh no, you're not getting me back on the subject of dikes," we laughed.

Jubilee Way's sweeping elevated section of A2 takes the south coast end of the road from London out over the Port of Dover. Back-lit by sunshine, English Channel clouds display their individual characteristics on the turquoise ocean with a random camouflage effect: dark grey shadows for heavily rain-laden, through green to almost blue. On the horizon, Calais looked deceptively close. At the bottom of the hill we turned left at the roundabout then into the car park of the newest hotel in Dover. Breakfast time with my pal, Patrick Black.

By eleven-hundred hours, we were in the French Custom House in Calais. Mark's conversational French was better than mine so he did the introductions.

"Bonjour monsieur. Ça va?"

"Oui, monsieur. Ça va?" said Michel Caron.

The French Douane officer held a document file in his left hand and a Gitanes between his lips. He was about the same age as Mark but with a smoker's complexion. We shook hands.

"Très bien jusqu'ici," very well, so far, said Mark with a smile.

Michel didn't sound particularly French when he said: "Monsieur, if you prefer to speak Engleesh, it eeze OK."

"Mon français, est si mauvais?" said Mark feigning disappointment.

"No monsieur, your French it eeze very good. It has an unfamiliar accent but, it eeze very good. If you please, I like to improve my Engleesh," said Michel.

"Gary and I spent some time working on a Customs project in the Democratic Republic of Congo. That may explain the strange accent," said Mark.

"The *Congo!*" said Michel. His eyes widened with the emphasis and surprise of genuine curiosity. "Did you meet Tintin?" We all laughed.

"No monsieur, Tintin was kicked out with the rest of the Belgians a long time before we got there. But, I do have a poster of the book cover."

"Ahh. Where Tintin is in the driving seat of zee car?" said Michel.

"Oui monsieur. But, when we were in the Congo, we had local drivers. It was easier for them to deal with the police who always looked for handouts."

"Ah, yes. The white man is no longer in the driving seat. And what a wonderful journey they are all having," Michel tapped ash from his cigarette. "You have a car?"

"Oui monsieur. Nous allons?" said Mark.

"We go," said Michel.

Outside, Michel was about to light another cigarette, then he saw the Audi. "Ah, monsieur, nice car. It will be no smoking," he slid the Gitanes back into its packet.

"Merci, monsieur," replied Mark.

Michel sat up front with Patrick for the short drive through the tired looking commercial district, over railway tracks and along the quayside to a warehouse.

Inside, surrounded by dozens of vehicles, Patrick's tractor unit awaited collection. It had been washed. The others hadn't. Chronic detritus marked the ones that had been inactive longest. Pigeon guano consumed paintwork because squadrons of flies couldn't eat it quick enough.

The tractor unit had been seized over a year earlier so my pal anticipated starting issues. He got jump leads out of the Audi.

"Non, monsieur, it is fine. We had it running earlier. It will start," said Michel.

Looking over at some British registered trucks along the opposite wall of the warehouse, Patrick said: "So, tell me, Michel, the other trucks here, are they all seized?"

"Oui, monsieur. Some have been here more than one year. Most, less than one year."

"Is it a problem having to keep them here?" said Patrick.

"Of course. Space is exponseeve. It is a problem when we seize the truck from the driver, we give him paperwork for the owner but maybe the owner does not receive the paperwork," said Michel.

"So, if someone were able to contact the actual owners of the trucks, that might help you?" said Patrick. He glanced in my direction.

"Of course. Eet would be very 'elpful. There is no obliga-cion to research for owners of foreign vehicles. We review cases every six months. When no one claims it, we make a decis-cion to dispose of the truck. Auction. But storage is the big cost."

Time for my impromptu sales pitch: "That is a service we can provide. No expense for your Department."

"Monsieur, we have many British camion, but if your company can also find Spanish and Dutch owners, it would be very 'elpful," ignoring the No Smoking signs, Michel lit a Gitanes.

"We can do that. Can you give us a list of the vehicles here and their registration numbers, along with the name of the man who received the paperwork?"

"Of course. It is too easy. It will take maybe one hour."

"OK, would you like to go for lunch before or after?" I said.

"Lunch? No, thank you. It is very unusual for a Frenchman to not eat lunch but, my diet does not allow it," he slapped his belly. "Also, I have the thirst of a Legionnaire. When we return to the office, I will get the information while you eat."

"OK. Well, some other time, perhaps," I said.

Michel shrugged.

The truck started on the third turn of the key. Patrick shouted above the noise from the driver's window.

"Listen, I'm heading for the train. You lads do what you've got to do with Michel and make your way back in your own time. Bring the car to the Yard tomorrow when you're ready," his huge fist couldn't conceal the roll of banknotes he handed me. Happy days.

Mark and I waved to the rear of the truck as it turned left out of the door.

We dropped Michel outside the Custom House then made our way to a quiet little bar in Calais town centre for steak and chips and several Seize Cent Soixante Quatre.

"When you told Michel that we can provide that service, were you serious?" said Mark.

"Yes," I said, "I know a bloke who can help us with the vehicle registration searches, especially if the vehicles are on finance. He's into vehicle repossessions. Met him fifteen years ago at Dover. I'll tell you the story on the way home."

An hour and a half later, we had our list of thirty vehicles. We were in business, but not for long. A few weeks later, Mark got a call from a FedCor recruiter about a job application. Just as the business began to take off, so did Mark. Two months after our day out, he was on his way to the USA to prepare for a job in Afghanistan. We kept in touch by email.

It was Mark's recommendation that led me to Jalalabad.

Jalalabad - May 2011

"O-Kayee. Good morning. Day Four without doors on our rooms," said Len as he switched on the kettle for our first brew of the day.

"The mattresses were serendipitous," said Pete.

"I do like that word," I said. "I like the mattresses even better. Maybe one day we'll get new ones. I'm not entirely comfortable knowing about the stains under my sheets."

Len smiled. "Do they give ya nightmares?"

"No, you telling me to hang up my boots because of scorpions gives me nightmares," I said.

Len laughed. "I'm just messin'. It's the snakes ya really gotta worry about," he laughed more.

"Don't talk about snakes, please," said Pete. "I saw one the other day. The exterminator bloke had one on a sticky pad, the type they use to catch rats. It was a cobra, flapping around, getting more stuck as it tried to get off the pad. Not a pretty sight. The pad was about eighteen inches square. Pity really, because snakes eat rats."

"That's right," I said. "In the Congo, one of my interpreters took me on a visit to his uncle's farm out in the jungle, not far from the border with Zambia. Quite a place: one square kilometre of land that he'd bought off the local chief. He also married one of his daughters. Apparently it's a self-preservation thing. If you're related to the chief, there's less chance of getting murdered in your sleep. It's a small price to pay for marrying a Kronenbourg."

"A Kronenbourg? What's that, a tribe?" said Len.

"No. She looks sixteen from the back, but sixty-four from the front."

Pete laughed. "Fucking hell. Can't wait to use that one down the rugby club."

Len didn't smile, or laugh. "Explain."

"Kronenbourg. The beer. Sixteen Sixty-Four," said Pete.

"Oh, OK," said Len. He got it, but not much.

"There was no electricity either. Bonus. He didn't have to look at her face after dark," I said.

"What the fuck's that gotta do with snakes or rats or, *anythin'?*" said Len.

"The point is, a snake lived under this lad's bed. It was about four feet long but not a constrictor, so he was fairly safe. There were no rats in his house. But he did have to keep the snake away from his ducks, especially the ducklings."

"Ducks? In the Congo jungle?" said Len.

"Yes. Mallard. For eggs," I said. "also, the ducks ate the larvae out of the harvested products spread on the ground to dry. Cassava mostly. For fufu. The women pound it into a kind of tapioca flour paste that has many uses, mostly dumplings. And duck meat. Very nice. Not the same issues with salmonella as you get with poultry."

"Did you eat the local stuff?" said Pete.

"When I was out and about, yes," I said. "Sometimes I was eighty miles from the office or nearest town but on the highways there were little roadside stalls, set up by people who lived in mud hut villages just a few yards back into the jungle. Children emerged from nowhere to greet customers when they heard a vehicle stop. Often they were just a few dishes or plastic bowls, with fresh fruit for sale. Mushrooms bigger than dinner plates. Just one of them, fried with garlic, was a meal. Quite a few times, one of the villagers would offer food, pirri pirri chicken or barbecued goat. It was always better out in the countryside, they didn't use diesel to light the barbecue. I had to insist they accept my money. Then the beer would come out. Have you ever had Simba."

Pete's time in Africa had been different: "Simba? No. I worked mostly in the cities at Customs HQs, Ministry of Finance stuff. In Angola, we weren't encouraged to go out because of the landmines. Pity really," said Pete.

"Hey, get this," said Len sat in front of his laptop. "Karrbul has promised us a resupply including six mattresses."

"Six?" said Pete. "Obviously got plans for this place."

"Plans? Oh boy!" said Len. "You better believe it. Gonna be real cosy in here, especially if we git some o' those Mexican CBP types: all gung-ho, talkin' their Hispanic bullshit. Oh yeah, real cosy."

"Not that you're one to pass judgement on people from south of the border," I said.

"Ha. You wait an' see," said Len.

"Guys, I'm going to shower while the kettle boils." Pete, in his gym kit, was out the door and into the sunshine.

There was never any shortage of things to do, but none of it was mission essential.

"Len, do we have an inventory of the gear we brought with us?" I said.

"I didn't git one. Maybe it's in one of the packing cases."

"No. I've had a dig around and there's nothing obvious."

"Why d'ya need it?" said Len, from his side of the plywood.

"Well, I'd like to know what we've got here, spread out over three different rooms. Finding the kettle was lucky but there's no point looking for something if it's not here."

It was busywork really but someone had to do it.

"Makes sense. I'll call Greg," Len stepped outside to make the call from on top of a six foot high T-Wall in the alley. It was one of the few places he could get a phone signal. At first we blamed F8's corrugated tin roof for the bad reception but soon realised that wasn't the only interference factor. Ten minutes elapsed.

Dazzling sunlight framed Len in the doorway, overpowering the fluorescent lighting as he entered F8. The opening bars of the Hallelujah Chorus came into my mind. The door slammed shut. There'd be no rejoicing.

"No inventory." Len announced. "No one thought to do one so they don't have a clue what we got here." Twisting the top free from a bottle of water, Len made a management decision: "So, that's your job." He pointed at me, laughed, then chugged down half the bottle.

"We can get fifteen minutes internet access in the MWR but there's often a queue," Pete's northern accent was slightly broader despite both of us being Mancunian. He'd just returned from the Morale, Welfare and

Recreation Center. "Can't use external memory gadgets in the MWR because it's a DOD network so we can't upload files to emails. Pretty much useless really."

'Can we use it for Skype?' Using my personal mobile to call home was working out expensive. Skype was much cheaper.

Pete had already tried it. 'Looks like it but bandwidth isn't much good so, forget video. Voice often sounds like Dalek.'

The DeWalt cordless tool kit was easy to find, it was bright yellow, one of the 18 Volt batteries on charge. The power supply in Hut F8 was 110V so I expected the charge to take ages.

"The MWR internet is provided for soldiers. They get priority. It's definitely not supposed to be used for business purposes and despite its DOD connection, BMTF is a commercial set-up." The plywood corridor partition creaked as Pete leaned on it to undo his laces.

"True," agreed Len. "We should have our own internet set-up tomorrow or the next day. Guy's a comin' from Karrbul to install it."

Pete kept talking as he ducked behind his bed-sheet door. "The lady in the MWR said that we might be able to get SniperHill internet here. It's a wireless service." The sound of dirt grinding a graphics card fan bearing accompanied Pete's laptop boot-up. "Len, will Kabul pay for wireless internet? It might be the way to solve our comms issues."

"Hmm. Git me the prices. I'll call Greg."

"I'm workin' arn it!" Pete's Gregg Samms impersonation sounded like a credible American accent to me. "I can't get a signal here. I'll try outside," Pete went out the front door with his laptop. Five minutes later he was back in the shed. "Signal's weak but would probably do for email. Spoke to one of the guys across the way. He's a contractor with DynCor. Never heard of the company before just now. He's got a booster which seems to work quite well. They sell them at the PX over at Fenty. I bet the Haji shop sells them too. I'll take a walk down there soon," Pete put his laptop behind the curtain.

"OK bro," said Len. "What's the innernet charge?"

"Ten dollars a day, fifty dollars a week or a hundred and fifty dollars a calendar month."

"So, that'd be four hundred and fifty dollars a month for all of us. Plus the booster. I'll call Greg," Len pressed redial on his Nokia 1280. Nothing. 'Dy-amm! I keep forgittin' there's no point tryin' the phone in here. I wonder if it works out back?"

The climb onto the T-Wall by the front door was arduous and not without hazard so Len went out the rear door of F8 and tried from the top step. Within a few moments one end of a muffled conversation penetrated the plywood.

Starting with the DeWalt tool kit, my Excel spreadsheet gained data.

"There's no way they're gonna pay four-fifty a month for us to have internet," I remarked sceptically.

"If they want reports they will," Pete sounded confident.

"Only one thing to do at a time like this," I announced, "have a cup-pa tea." Two bottles of water, went in the kettle. A tea bag landed in each of the three mugs sat on the floor. "It's weird the way it sometimes takes ten minutes for the water to boil."

"Yes," said Pete, "generator load. D-FAC must take a lot of power at certain times. Then workshops. The military probably charge cordless kit at night."

"Economy Seven," I joked.

The rear door slammed shut as Len came in with the news. "OK. Tomorrow, we git a satellite dish and modem from Karrbul. Two guys are comin' to fix it up. They're gonna call me when they're at main gate. We gotta escort 'em to the coolin' off yard and then we get 'em visitors' passes. Somewhere!"

"Tomorrow? I'm impressed." The electric screwdriver I'd just recorded on the spreadsheet went back into the tool bag.

"Pete, you busy? We need to go to the J-DOC," Len eased back the slide on his Glock revealing a millimetre of shining brass. Chambered. Holstered.

"OK. Let's go," Pete's laptop closed. The fan-whine stopped. Sunlight blazed momentarily through the open front door as Len and Pete went to make arrangements for our visitors. Even from twenty-five feet, it was obvious Pete's Glock didn't have a magazine. The pistol grip was empty. He was gone too quick to tell him. F8 rattled as the door slammed shut. In the silence, the kettle got louder. Having double-checked the serial number on the spreadsheet against the reciprocating saw, it went in the tool bag.

An hour later, Len and Pete returned.

"Successful mission?" I asked, switching the kettle on to boil, again. They replied almost simultaneously, but Pete got in first.

"Don't ask!"

Len was more upbeat: "Yeah! Found out a few things from Sergeant First Class Mueller at the J-DOC."

"Has that kettle boiled?" Pete sounded irritated.

"It did. Had mine. Just put it on again. Shouldn't be too long this time." I replied reassuringly. Len continued his briefing.

"We meet 'em ate the cooling off yard, about two hundred yards down on the left-hand side from the ECP. Should be easy to spot as there are nearly always trucks parked up," Len opened a bottle of water. "Their vehicle has to stay out there for twenny-four hours cooling off before it's allowed on base."

"Cooling off?" I said, inquisitively.

"Yeah. Make sure there are no IEDs on board set to go off on base. So," Len gulped some water, "if we walk the guys and the equipment in it will save a day," Len gulped more water. "The guys will be Afghans so they'll need to be escorted at all times. That's our job. One on one. So, as there's two of 'em, that's you and Pete tied up till they're done. Hahahaha! You Brits are gonna come in handy after all. Not sure how long that'll take but they gotta be off base by eighteen hundred hours."

"I'm going to the gym for half an hour," Pete announced as he rummaged for his kit. He sounded frustrated by something.

"Hey Pete, before you go, can I get the serial numbers from your weapons? For the inventory."

"What? Why?"

To me, it was obvious: "In case they go missing."

"They've got the serial numbers up in Kabul. They checked 'em before we got them," Pete became more irritated.

"Yes, I know and that's the point. If the guns go missing here, the numbers in Kabul won't be much help. Also, the military might ask for them," I hadn't expected resistance and didn't ask about the missing Glock magazine.

"They're on my bed. If you can call it that! Help yourself," Pete shook his head in the direction of his open door. Padlocks would be our next acquisition.

"OK. Thanks," I spoke to his back as he went out the front door. "He doesn't seem too happy at the moment," I remarked.

"True," agreed Len. "Somethin's eatin' him. These ain't the best of conditions but I think there's more to it than that." As team leader, Len was justifiably concerned. We didn't speculate about the reasons for Pete's irritability. I got back to the inventory.

"Hey, Len! Look what I found!" I shouted, holding up a long cardboard box, "It's a mobile phone signal booster! Yippee!"

"Great!" replied Len with some reservation. "Ya gonna set it up?"

"Will do," the multi-lingual, translated from the original Chinese, instruction sheet, made it look easy enough. "Just needs a power supply. It'll have to go in the tea room. I'll find some scrap wood and make a mast for outside then fix it to the wall of the shed and feed the cable through to the base unit."

"Sounds good."

"Oh. Hang on," in the small print was the biggest problem. "There's a reference to a signal direction identifying device. They've got to be joking."

"Whassat bro?" said Len, through the plywood partition.

"It has to be pointed in the direction of a mast or satellite. Where's that?"

Len laughed. "Well, you opened the box. You figure it out!"

The antenna was easily assembled and put outside the back door. The DeWalt drill made an easy ten millimetre hole in the shed wall. Cable pushed through from the outside, connected it to the box. Several lights flashed as the power was switched on. The gadget gave the impression it was doing something but the phone reception inside the shed remained constant at zero. I'd try again the next day if the internet guys weren't in the way.

Next morning it was early breakfast followed by *wait*: for the call to meet the boys from Kabul at the cooling off yard. Lunchtime came and went. We'd heard nothing so Len called the PM at BMTF HQ. Pete and I stood nearby in the shade of a eucalyptus tree.

"But we don't have email yet. That's why we're gittin' the satellite dish," Len shook his head despairingly and silently mouthed *motherfuckers*. "So, when *will* they be here?" Len took a few steps to his left. "I'm losing you. ...Can we buy SniperHill? ... Hello. ... Hello. Gone. Signal dropped. He said sump'n 'bout email so I best get to the MWR and check it," Len was not happy.

"Might as well," I said. "Pay some bills at the same time."

"What's the problem with the internet guys?" said Pete.

"Guys got in a car wreck last night. Hit by a truck. They're OK but the car ain't and the equipment's in the car at the side of the road some-where. It's on email. Dint ya know?"

Our dependence on technology troubled me: "I'm not convinced anyone gave much thought to communications. We've been here the best part of a week and we're a long way off mission-capable."

"Hey, bro. It gets better," replied Len. "by pure chance, Pete and I met with the commander of the platoon I was told would be takin' us out to the ICD. They rotate out in three weeks and they ain't in a hurry to take on civilian missions. The end's in sight for those guys. They're on their way home and I ain't about to make demands on them. Hey-ell! It ain't my job. We gotta military liaison guy at the Embassy for that." Len made his point well. Contractors can't demand the US army do things.

"We won't be going to work for at least four weeks," said Pete. He seemed unhappy about it. I wasn't.

"What does it matter?" I said. "We're being paid. That's a damn site better than my last overseas assignment."

Sour-faced Pete turned to me. "I didn't come here to sit in a fucking shed for months. I want to do something useful."

"Pete, there's a chain of command in this ...," I searched for the adjective, "... program. And we're the last link in that chain. The bottom rung of the ladder. Not that important. You must've seen it before."

Pete responded abruptly. "No. I haven't. I've worked in Africa with Crown Agents and everything is set up for you: accommodation, office. Go out to a place. Work six months. Move on to the next location." Pete waved his arm at our surroundings. "Not like this. How long was the fucking CBP guy here? Two, three months? And he'd done fuck all. Now we have to waste time doing stuff he could've already had done. Christ! In Kabul they have an office full of support staff doing this kinda work."

"True, but we're not in Kabul," I reminded him. "We're on a small forward operating base in Talibanistan and *Clown* Agents aren't." Pete bridled at that. Maybe he didn't like my sarcastic reference to the pseudo-civil service he'd worked for where he saw himself as some sort of manager. "We were sent here because someone decided we had the ability to work things out for ourselves."

It didn't sound contentious to me.

Pete got angry: "Don't tell me I can't work stuff out! That's a fucking insult. What grade were you when you left UK Border Agency?"

Maybe no magazine in his pistol was a good thing.

"Pete, my previous pay grade is irrelevant here and you know it. No offence intended but it's a different environment. We are on our own. Didn't you notice on the way over here? Transport: *we* are last in line. You said it yourself, MWR internet, military first. And quite right too."

Pete was clearly miffed at my suggestion we were insignificant. Something was gripping his shit. Len wiped dust from his laptop screen.

Pete snatched a packet of cigarettes from off a ledge in his room and went outside.

"Len, did you hear that?" I said.

"Uh hur," said Len.

"What I wanted to say was: Oh, and by the way, I resigned from UKBA, I didn't get early retirement with a nice golden handshake, but I decided inflaming the situation wouldn't be beneficial."

"Think you're right. Pete's feelin' raw 'bout sump'n."

The Morale, Welfare and Recreation building, MWR, occupied a prefabricated concrete structure about twice as long as our hut. It looked like a leftover from the Soviet occupation but with new US electrics fitted. In a different location it could have been one of those post-war temporary dwellings that housed thousands of British families, for sixty years: Prefabs. In the overall scheme of things, two generations don't count as permanent.

Miss Rose, the Filipino MWR manager, had a desk the other side of the counter. Her tight jeans must have been a Size 3, her blouse the same as her age, not fourteen, I guessed at thirty-four. Legs swung from the seat before she launched herself from the swivel chair to greet us. Miss Rose was no taller on the floor than she was on he seat.

Working on her American accent, she grinned a full set of American Dental Association Standard pearly-whites.

"Hallo gentowmen!" her alluring oriental heritage projected towards us, as did her erect nipples. "You wanna sign in?" An ample bosom followed closely behind the clipboard she pushed in our direction. It was impossible to not notice the firmness of her breasts as they rested on the counter. "You Amellican?" she asked me, smiling optimistically.

"No. Bl ...er, British!" I replied hesitantly.

"Ohh! Pity. I look for Amellican husband. Hahaaaahaa," emitting an excruciatingly loud maniacal laugh, that made me wince, she struck me as the sort of girl who had a special way of getting what she wanted, except the elusive Amellican husband.

Resisting the urge to say breast of ruck, my hesitant advice was: "Oh. OK. Well, erm, America is probably the best place to go for one of those."

She laughed some more and reminded me of one of those really noisy primates in a rain forest somewhere, the type that screech their calls in the canopy to attract a mate.

"Last four of SSN, unit and sign," Miss Rose said authoritatively, tapping the clipboard with a red fingernail. She must have asked for thousands of Social Security Numbers. I entered 5868, BMTF and made my mark.

"You wan innernet, you put name on board next to PC number and time you start. You got fifteen minutes. No problem. Go through end door."

We each thanked Miss Rose and followed her instructions.

The door opened into a space around twenty-five feet square. Three of the walls had ten plywood booths, each with a tower PC and filthy keyboard. In my booth, accumulated grease, grime and sweat did nothing to ease the progress of the mouse across the flaking plywood. Internet service was adequate for personal use, which was good for someone like me with no interest in gaming. All four US soldiers in the computer room had long guns. Only two had headphones. Time zones influenced the number of internet users. Fifteen hundred hours in J'bad meant it was zero-six hundred New York time and a full half-day earlier on the West Coast. Some of the soldiers had to come here in the middle of the night if they wanted to talk to family.

The dial-up hand shake seemed primitive compared with always-on domestic internet but it was a welcome sound to military personnel fighting the war on terror.

Emails, bank account balance, news sites: all checked. Bills paid. My financial confidence was higher than ever. I'd never had so much cash available but it was staying in my account a bit longer before paying off some mortgage. Ten minutes was enough for me. Len was done soon after. Pete had his headphones plugged in and was on Skype. He waved: *see you later*. We left him to it.

"Relationship issue," remarked Len.

"Yes. Looks that way," I replied, "he'll not sort it out here."

"True. Anyway, we got permission to buy innernet for a week. That should cover us till we get satellite service." Len sounded pleased with himself.

"How do we get the money refunded?" I said.

"Keep the receipts and they'll pay cash whenever you're in Karrbul," said Len as we walked back to F8. "Guess they have a contingency budget."

"I doubt they'll get the satellite set up anytime soon so, I'll start with a week," I suggested.

"Me too, bro," said Len.

It took me a couple of hours to arrange two stacks of bottled water in one of the spare rooms. A gap for a chair along with a piece of scrounged plywood, duct-taped on top, formed a makeshift desk. Just right for the company laptop. We had an office. Similar water-furniture in the tea room got our brew materials off the floor. In my room, twelve cases and a piece of water pallet hardboard made a nightstand. It also meant we had an emergency water supply if deliveries were disrupted.

"Len," I called out from the office.

"Yo!"

"Some of the assets I've entered on the inventory have obviously been somewhere else before they got to us. The two company laptops are paralysed by games and superfluous programs running in the background, mostly in Dari."

Len's chair scraped the plywood. "L-As must've used 'em. Or, it could be that we'd originally been issued two working laptops and a person, or persons, unknown have swapped their old junk for our new kit."

"L-As? Can't be *our* Language Assistant. He hasn't been anywhere near them," I said.

"There's a whole bunch of 'em up in Karrbul. Don't forget, BMTF has been around since 2008."

"One is so clogged with viruses and malware that it just about starts up, then freezes. I've wasted ten hours on it so far. It's going back in the box," I said.

Len stood in the office doorway. "Sounds like a good course of action."

"The other one continually tries to download updates even though it's not connected to the internet. When we get wired internet I'll install some anti-virus software and clean it up so it's useable for training purposes."

"Yeah. Good move. If it can handle PowerPoint through a projector and be linked to a printer it'll be useful. Just don't let it have contact with your own laptop," as always, good advice from Len.

SniperHill internet made our time at J'bad a lot easier. Obtaining paper versions of documents was an issue that Miss Rose helped me resolve. She was happy to print stuff from email. Collecting the work also gave me the opportunity to look her over. Miss Rose had a great little figure.

"I see you looking!" she announced one morning.

"Looking?" denial was futile.

"Yeah! You look at *this*," Miss Rose bent over the printer to retrieve documents. Rhythmic lower-body movements focused my gaze on her callipygian charms.

"You got me!" I held my hands up submissively.

"You like?" she teased, standing to attention. Chest out, nipples out further. Her bob cut black hair swayed clear of her face.

"I do. Beautiful!" it was the truth. She was a good looking girl, but dangerous. Relationships had already got me into marital difficulties, my second Afghanistan mission objective was: avoid emotional complications.

"How old I am?" she said, then gave me the printed papers along with a quick one-two sideways movement of her hips. Looking her down then up signalled my approval. She was in very good condition.

"Thirty-five, maybe thirty-eight?" I thought that was a good guess. She had an awareness and demeanour of a more mature woman but forty would have been my top bid.

"Aah, hahahah!" she laughed. I flinched. The macaque was back. "Fifty, I'm fifty!" She shouted excitedly.

With conviction, I said: "No*oo*. I don't believe you." It was true. I didn't believe her. Smooth skin and firm muscle tone didn't come as standard on most women of her age.

"Loooook!" she leaned forward to present her credentials.

I'm easily distracted by an ID card swinging on the end of a lanyard, especially when it's moving hypnotically to and fro across the backdrop of a magnificent female front. Incontrovertible proof: she was fifty years of age.

"It's fake ID!" I joked, "I will call the MPs."

"Hahahahaha!" she laughed again. *Ouch my ears!* "I like you," her chin dropped. Asiatic eyes stared seductively upward directly into mine. She'd studied the way the local cobras hypnotise mice before swallowing them whole.

"I like you too, Miss Rose," *did I just say that?* It was true. I did like her. I'd defy any man to not like her. But I had no doubt she'd be a handful, in more ways than one. Her femininity was drawing me within striking range. My unconscionable desire to get her naked stirred the serpent.

She feigned regret: "Pity you not Amellican!"

When she laughed, it was good to be British.

The shops on FOBs Hughie and Finley Shields were very good considering where we were. But for some items FOB Fenty, the base at Jalalabad Airfield, was the only option. Len arranged a meeting with a platoon leader in the hope of hooking up with them on missions. We got a helicopter ride.

"This is the swimming pool," said Lieutenant Moore as we walked around the rectangular pit. A lagoon of sludge festered below a thin crust of mud, the diving board long gone. "Used to be a Russian base. See the bullet holes in the wall?" He pointed to the shattered tiles clinging to fractured cement at the deep-end. "Firing squads. Guess the blood got flushed down the drain."

Standing momentarily on the edge of the pool, gazing at the detritus, while Len, Pete and the LT didn't, meant I had to run to catch up.

Hurry up.

Five young soldiers shook hands with Len, Pete and me as we crammed awkwardly into the containerised platoon HQ.

"So, you're lookin' for some missions to the Customs Depot, that right?' said LT Moore.

"That's the idea LT," said Len, "but from what I see here I'm thinkin' you might be busy."

The soldiers' smiles and glances gently mocked Len's understatement.

"We had fifty missions last week. On course for the same this week. The sort of work you gentlemen do sounds interesting. These guys would love it. Anythin' to get us out of the shit we've been doin'. Captain Jones knows about BMTF, but she is pushing for numbers rather than strategic stuff. I know the way she works. She won't let BMTF burn up eight hours of platoon resources when she could get maybe three missions for the same time. Understood?"

"Yeah. I get that. And thanks for your honesty, LT. I'll get our liaison guy to push it a bit harder," said Len.

"That may be the way," said LT, "Mr Kinder, if we could do four missions a week with you instead of maybe twenty of the usual shit, that'd be great. But, Captain Jones, she's looking to make Major and we're the way she's gonna do it. BMTF is not. Ya got me?"

"I gotcha, LT. It's a numbers game. We're all playin' it. Hey, if I can get our guy at the Embassy to lean on one of your guys, maybe we'll work together. You guys take care. And thanks for the corrfee!"

"Carfee?" said LT, "Oh, haha, yeah, you're welcome." We laughed, picked our way through the jumble of kit, then fell out the door.

"Was that a Key Leader Engagement?" I said as we made our way back to the flight line.

"Sure was," said Lens "KLE. Thanks for taking notes." He'd noticed I hadn't.

"The swimming pool, firing squad thing," I said, "I'm not convinced. Why would anyone get people to stand around in a hole in the ground if you knew you'd have to drag the bodies out to dispose of them?"

"What? Do you think the LT made it up?" said Pete.

"No. I don't think he would deliberately misinform us but, think about it," I said.

Len did think about it: "Hmm. Not even the Russians are that dumb. It was probably just target practice. If I was gonna shoot a bunch of people, a Caterpillar digger'd have a hole dug in no time. Then just line 'em up and gun 'em down."

"So, you think that story about the swimming pool is bollocks?" said Pete.

"I might if I knew what bollocks is," said Len

"It means made up," I said. "Bollocks are actually testicles but it's an expression used for many different situations."

"Bollocks. Hmm, sounds good. Yup," said Len. "What ya might also call an urban myth. Bollocks, I like that. Has a kinda ring to it."

"Ah, now, put a ring through it and that is called something else," I said.

"Prince Albert," said Pete.

"Prince Albert is the nob, Hafada, is the bollocks. Only what I've heard," I said.

"What the fuck! Hafada? Bollocks? I've heard of Intifada. Stop, stop. Don't tell me anymore," said Len.

In the Fenty PX, the main shop on base, I made an impulse purchase of Sensuous Noir.

"Who ya got in mind?" said Len as I pushed the package into my cargo pants. "Not *me* I hope."

"Len, I do like you, but not that much. I thought it would make a nice gift for Miss Rose even though she's more light tan than black. She has been very helpful and some of BMTF's work couldn't have been done without her assistance," I said.

"Nice gesture. Zat all you got in mind?" Len winked.

"We'll see. It was on special offer," I said.

"Miss Rose might make you a special offer," said Len. We laughed.

Next day, after breakfast, I went to the MWR.

"Miss Rose. This is for you. Thank you for helping us. I know you didn't have to."

Snatching the small package, she tore eagerly at the wrappings.

"For ME?" she shouted. Followed by staccato laugh. "For me?"

As the bottle came out of the box she kissed it and sprayed herself all over. Perfume filled the office, but not quite enough to set off the fire alarm. It seemed I'd made a good choice.

"Thank you! Thank you! Thank you! You very nice man," Miss Rose ran to my side of the front desk. Her arms couldn't quite reach around me. Her breasts got in the way. But I was glad she tried.

"You want anything? You ask," she insisted. The cobra was in the room. "*Anything!*"

Len arranged for the satellite guys to bring an inkjet printer with them. Three weeks later they arrived. At around eleven in the morning we met them at the cooling-off yard as the temperature rose.

"Hey! Good journey?" said Len to the two Afghan lads.

"It took us six hours to come from Kabul," said Ali, "It is one hundred and twenty kilometres. The road is very bad." He looked tired.

"OK, we gotta get you guys signed in. Let's take some of the equipment with us now," said Len.

By the time we got them ID carded and their gear moved to F8, it was thirteen hundred hours. Getting them some food from the D-FAC was easy: rice mostly. Glancing up at the sign on the way out: **Combat Take Aways' Only,** the superfluous apostrophe troubled me.

Cables were soon run along nails hammered into the outside wall of the hut, but the hardest part was lining up the dish with the satellite transmission. By five in the afternoon things were looking desperate. They might have to spend a night in their new car outside the base. There's not much room in a Toyota Corolla for two skinny Afghan lads, even with the seats down.

"Hey, listen guys," said Len, "I get better phone reception if I stand on top of this T-Wall, how about we lift it up there?"

Suddenly it worked. We were online. The DeWalt tool kit came in handy - again, to cut and screw bits of old pallet into an additional bracket.

Sandbags helped secure it in place. The internet guys were off base by seventeen forty-five.

We had hardwired internet to each room, six connections. Enough for all the advisors that were expected to join the J'bad team.

Our Operations & Communications Centre just entered the twenty-first Century.

"Hey Len, Pete, look at this," I shouted.

Len and Pete stood in the doorway admiring the light show.

"Priddy cool bro," said Len.

"Impressive," said Pete.

Flashing lights from the modem, phone signal booster, power tool battery charger, Hewlett Packard printer and illuminated kettle, looked even better with the lights off.

"The phone signal booster doesn't boost signal," I said.

"Yeah, but keep it plugged in because someone in Kabul went to a lot of trouble to make sure we got it," said Len.

"It gets very hot so, it might be good to have in the winter, if we're still here," said Pete.

We shared our hut with three or four other contractors. The number of residents varied as they rotated in and out and the nature of their work meant they were often away for several days at a time. The chap in the first room on the left of the front door looked Hispanic but his accent wasn't. Outside Hut F8 smoking his first Marlboro of the day, his dishevelled demeanour told me he'd just woken from his first sleep in a few days.

"Good morning sir," I said, leaning out of the door to check the weather.

"Good morning sir. A little cooler today," he replied drawing on his cigarette.

"Yes, nice. Just making tea, would you like some?" I said.

"That would be very good. Just one sugar if you have any."

I took two mugs of tea to the front alley.

"My name is Gary," we shook hands. "I'm with the Border Management Task Force. We try to work at the Customs depot down the road."

"Suleiman Alizade. Call me Solly, everyone does. I'm an interpreter. But not like the young lads next door. I'm not Afghan. I used to be, thirty years ago."

"Really, what made you come back after all this time? Did you miss the old place?" I said with a smile.

"Not really. None of the *old* places I knew in Kabul, before we left, are still there," the hint of regret was more fond memory recalled, than sadness. "When I left with the rest of my family in nineteen seventy-nine, we thought it would be for a few months and then everything would settle down and we'd be back in our home."

"Oh, so you got out during the Soviet invasion?" I said.

"A little before, but yes. We had no choice. My father could not live as a Communist, he knew he couldn't fight it and he also knew the Soviets would invade to support fellow communists. He worked for the OIC." Solly caught my puzzled look, "The Organisation of Islamic Cooperation. It's like a Muslim UN, but even more useless. So, you see, he had too many enemies. We could not stay."

"Sounds desperate," I said.

"It was. Fortunately, my father knew people in the States and they helped us. He always encouraged his children, boys and girls, to learn languages, even Russian. My father was a very wise man."

"Did you find it difficult to live in the US?"

"Not really. Language was no barrier. Before communism, Kabul had been a cosmopolitan city. Women wore tweed suits to work. Can you believe that? We had a tram system. It was like a city in the Middle East or Turkey. Now it's struggling to stay out of the Stone Age."

"So, here you are fighting the good fight," I said.

"Oh no. I'm not here fighting for any moral high ground. I haven't set foot in a mosque for decades. I'm here because a guy I met in one of the hotels I own on the West Coast just happened to mention his company was looking for specialist interpreters for a contract over here. Said it would be for a year. That was four years ago," he smiled then sipped tea.

"Four years?" I couldn't conceal my surprise.

"If someone offered you two hundred and fifty-thousand dollars a year and all you had to do was listen and talk, wouldn't you?" Another Marlboro got lit.

"Er, yes. Specialist interpreter? I won't ask," I said.

"Oh it's OK. I transcribe intercepted Taliban radio chat and telecoms. They intercept our telephones and email and we listen in to them to make sure they've got the disinformation we sent earlier. In fact you may be able to help me."

"Really? Does it mean that after you've revealed secret information I may find myself at Guantanamo Bay?" I smiled.

"No. I won't be telling you anything," he laughed smoke, "just a few linguistic tips, that's all. Some Taliban come from the UK. They speak English but their dialects are very difficult. I speak twenty Pashto dialects but the British guys, that's something else."

"Where in the UK are they from?" I said.

"Not London," he said confidently.

"Ah, raht lad. Abb at lak tat?" I said in a broad accent.

Solly sat upright. "More."

"Appen ah maht, abbat thee sen?"

Solly laughed. "I have no idea what you just said, but it sounds very familiar. What is the accent?"

"Yorkshire, northern England. Mass migration from the Indian subcontinent started in the Fifties. Many people would have you believe that *presence* is bigger than the two or three percent in actuality."

"So, they are the children, possibly grandchildren, of people who made a better life in the UK?" Said Solly.

"Yes, but obviously they have a crisis of conscience about something," I said. "Maybe it's Capitalism, exploitation of just about everything for material gain. Maybe they've found another way to save the world."

"A lot of young men from UK are Taliban," said Solly, "any thoughts on that?"

"In my opinion, it's the environment in which they grew up. In the UK they, *we*, are taught that you are free to do pretty much as you please. Let's call it Freedom. And freedom of speech is encouraged - allegedly."

"In the US, freedom comes with responsibility, but I get your point," his Marlboro-wave meant continue.

"You know more about Islam than me, does it say something about not allowing fellow Muslims to be oppressed by Infidel?"

"Somewhere. It's a long time since I read any Koran. But it's all about interpretation."

"Here's an interesting, tenuous, connection: after Winston Churchill and Franklin D. Roosevelt signed the Atlantic Charter in 1941, they sang a song called Onward Christian Soldiers. That song was written by an English priest when he lived in Wakefield - Yorkshire. I bet some of your Taliban acquaintances are from Wakefield. How about, Forward Islamic Fighters?" I said.

Solly squinted through tobacco smoke. "I like that. Could you write down some common phrases for me? Phonetically. Then run through them with me."

"Pleasure," I said. "We don't have anything urgent to do today so, I'll crack on with it."

It was another two weeks before the new platoon arrived on base and took over from the outgoing unit. A week later we had our first mission to the Inland Customs Depot. We were about to go to work. I'd been in-country two months for which I'd been paid approximately £22,000. That was almost as much as my post-deductions final year salary as a UK civil servant. Who wouldn't be happy with that? Answer: Pete.

Mitchel 'Mitch' Aldred resided in the room opposite Solly. He was a police officer from North Carolina but shorter than the stereotypical image of a US cop. His tranquil, Gone With the Wind, accent may have had a calming influence on some of the Afghan police he trained, which might explain why he hadn't been shot to death but three of his colleagues had.

One Thursday evening we invited Mitch to watch a film in the BMTF office. Solly was at work. It was cramped with four of us in such a confined space but Mitch brought his folding camp chair so he was comfortable. Pete plugged a small projector into his laptop that could send images from an external hard drive. It produced a picture about three feet across onto the wall six feet away. A small set of speakers plugged into the headphone-jack gave sound. I hung a white sheet over the top of the partition and it worked fine as a screen.

"Anyone like cocoa?" I said. The kettle had been heating water for several minutes. Electricity was consistent during the day when most people were out working. In the evening when demand increased for air conditioning and laptops the power varied a little, which meant the kettle occasionally took longer to boil. It was hot enough for instant drinking chocolate.

"Sure ...yes please ...sounds good." Came the replies. Three cups were received through the door way before I turned off the main lights and wriggled into a corner of the office.

"What's the movie?" Mitch cradled his cocoa.

"The Great Escape," shouted Pete over the introductory music.

"What's that, some Briddish movie?"

Pete explained: "It's American. Same director as The Magnificent Seven and Gunfight at the OK Corral. It's about a bunch of guys living in a shed in enemy territory. Sound familiar?"

With breaks it's a three hour movie. When it finished at around twenty-two hundred it was early evening in the UK. Skype time.

As Pete moved his equipment back to his room to make a call he revealed something which should have been kept in the dark: "I've got to try and reassure the missus. One of the neighbours is paying her a lot of attention. She's worried."

"He's tranna fuck her!" announced Mitch candidly.

I froze. In my room the embarrassment of eye contact with Pete and Len was avoided. Mitch's analysis of the situation was faultless, but it made me cringe with empathy at the demoralising effect it would have on Pete. Undermining long distance relationships is a tactic used by an enemy during conflict, made even easier with modern methods of communication. There were enough enemies here without having more at home. Mitch was no Hanoi Hannah and I didn't want to hear about Pete's problems. He probably didn't really want me to know. Distraction required.

"Len!" I called through the partition. "Fancy some supper?" Contrivance rarely works for me but on this occasion, it did.

"Sure bro. Right with ya!" Len was soon heading towards the front door. He pulled the slide on his Glock just enough to see brass. Chambered. On the way to the D-FAC Len anticipated what I was about to say.

"Good idea givin' Pete some privacy. He don't need us knowing all his business."

"We now know what's been behind his mood," I said.

"Yep. When I think back to our meeting at the ICD, he didn't want to be there," remarked Len.

"Can't say I blame him, but that's the job," I said.

"Yeah, but, to turn down a place at the lunch table with the Regional Customs Director, that ain't a good move. Embarrassing."

"I felt uneasy too. Sitting down to eat a meal wearing body armour in the company of strangers isn't normal behaviour. But I think we made a reasonable impression despite that," I said confidently.

"I sure hope so," Len signed into the D-FAC first.

Two muffins, some sliced cheese, sliced ham, sliced tomato were enough for me. The waffle maker created my two toasties. Len had two ladles of chicken noodle soup in a paper bowl from the bain-marie.

"Something else that bothers me is, why no magazine in his pistol," the sliced ham resisted the serrated edge of my plastic knife until it snapped.

"I don't get it either. I'll speak to him about that. Puts us all in danger. I think Pete might be on his way back to Kabul before long," said Len between plastic spoonfuls, "I ain't gonna push him, but it's a damn sight easier getting home in a hurry without the additional travel from here."

Len was right about that. Weather and security issues meant flights from Jalalabad could be delayed for up to three days: not good in an emergency. We finished our supper, put our trays on the trolley by the exit and went.

Back in F8, Pete was in his bunk.

Torkham Gate - June 2011.

Len got us three missions to the ICD for the following week. Our initiatives were going well. We were to report on progress with the new security features: Entry Control Points at the gate; concrete anti-blast barriers around the Customs office; assessments and evaluations of Customs procedures; drink chai; eat lunch with Customs Director Khairfullah. Important work. It was a great achievement. Up to this point we'd struggled to do our job. Pete was still distracted by domestic issues and wasn't very happy. Len and I kept an eye on him. That's what Battle Buddies do.

Saturday morning, French called. Len hung off the steps at the rear of F8 to get better reception. The kettle noisily heated water in the Ops & Comms room which meant I couldn't hear the conversation, but some words exploded with such force, they penetrated the plywood: *fuck, CBP* and *shit*. It went quiet.

The rear door creaked open, then slammed shut as Len slumped into his room. "You made that coffee yet?"

The kettle clicked off.

I was already on my feet. "On it boss. Pete, tea?"

"Please," mumbled Pete from his room.

"You guys need to hear this," said Len, plugging his phone into the charger. We gathered around his doorway. He spoke with enthusiasm: "We have a mission to Torkham."

Torkham meant nothing to me. At first I thought it was *talk them*, as in some sort of communication thing with the Afghans: talk 'em into doing their jobs; talk 'em out of killing us. I was way off target.

Pete leaned on his door frame with his left hand and held his cup in his right. "Torkham? As in Torkham Gate in the Khyber Pass?" That saved *me* asking the question that would have shown my ignorance.

"Yep," said Len, "but wait, it gets better. It's next week."

"Hold on a minute. We have three missions next week with our own unit, here. Did you tell 'em that?" Pete's mood went down a notch.

"Hey, I'm just Team Lead, I don't tell PM, he tells me. But, yeah, I reminded him. I said, it took me weeks to get three missions arranged and

114

now I've gotta go back and tell the LT that we're off on some BS manoeuvre down on the border with Pakistan. It's gonna make BMTF look like a buncha dumbasses."

"Border with Pakistan?" I said, my anxiety barely concealed.

"Yeah, it's the main port of entry for Nangarhar Province," said Len. 'All the traffic they get at the ICD comes through Torkham. Some CBP guy thinks it's a good idea if we go down there. PM is just deploying resources at the request of some DHS hotshot."

"Who's running this show now? CBP or the contractor?" said Pete.

"Well, that's a good question," said Len. "Looks like CBP wanna show they're actually doin' sump'n over here, so they get our PM to give the order. It ain't supposed to be like that. Program overview is from Tampa. Guy called Steelman. Good guy. Marine."

"They just lost three blokes from there," said Pete.

"Lost? That's a bit careless," my remark was deliberately light-hearted as no deaths had been announced.

"Lost, as in, they went home," said Pete.

"Yeah, they went home. Two of 'em had been there a year so had money in the bank. The other'd had enough of the rocket attacks," said Len.

"Rocket attacks?" no one detected unease in my response.

"Yeah, they reckon they get 'em most days. Anyway, boys, we better pack for a week. We gotta CH-46 to catch ... tomorrow. Yee-har!"

"TOMORROW?" Pete and I shouted in unison.

"Saved that bit till last. Knew you'd like it," Len's coffee mug didn't conceal his grin.

Zero eight-thirty hours, Sunday: Len, Pete and I stood on the skull-sized boulders of Finley Shields helipad. Mitch and one of the other DynCor guys had volunteered getting us to the flight-line in an old Ford Ranger belonging to the army. Sat in the cargo space with my rifle, my role was to discourage child bandits as we passed through the Afghan Army base. We didn't have much kit, as we were only away for a week, but what we did have I intended to keep.

115

The distinctive thrub-thrub-thrub pressure wave of an approaching CH-46 preceded it swinging into view on a long arc towards the helipad. We waved farewell to Mitch and his buddy.

Earplugs pushed in, shemagh dragged across my face and Foster Grants slid up to the bridge of my nose: ready to board. Ordinary sunglasses are ineffective against helicopter dust storms. It was the hard way to learn why so many of the US military wore high-end eye-protection. The time had come for me to spend a hundred and fifty dollars at the PX on some Wyley-X antiballistic eye-pro.

The Chinook's ramp was down.

A flight officer emerged from around the other side of the helicopter.

He waved: *hurry up.*

Ducking under the rotating blades, we shuffled up the ramp with our gear. Our baggage went in the cargo net then we fastened ourselves into seats along each side of the aircraft. Taking his seat behind the cockpit, the flight officer spoke unintelligibly into the headset microphone as the CH-46's rotors gently supported its own weight. Moving in a widening circle we gained height in the relatively safe zone over the base. In less than a minute it vectored eastward and continued to climb. The speed at which the ground retreated from the open ramp was unnerving. Holding my rifle close made me feel less uneasy.

Two Hueys swung into view behind us. Escorts. Jalalabad was soon in the distance and we were over open country. Noise made conversation impossible.

Our three helicopter flight zigzagged a course above a grey-dry river bed, then gained altitude as the terrain rose up to meet us. We dodged and weaved, dipped and climbed with the contours. Jagged mountain peaks passed quickly beneath us revealing the dramatic depths of remote valleys. Tiny stone compounds clinging on to bare rock were home to isolated communities. How anyone lived here will remain a mystery: no trees for fuel, no visible water, sparse vegetation even for goats. At its best, inhospitable. At its worst, a very hostile environment. But for some, it was home. People had died for it - and still would.

Time spent evading insurgent hot-zones elevated a twenty minute flight up to three quarters of an hour. We came low over another dried up river bed, not quite a wadi, then veered to starboard above the rusting remains of a Russian tank. The turret was somewhere else, lifted off by the force of the blast that had vaporised the crew.

We passed over Highway 7, the road to Khyber Pass and Pakistan. Then over a row of T-Walls and into the airspace of a military base. On the concrete below, a white-painted circle enclosed a large white H denoting helipad. Touchdown. The flight officer gestured: offload.

Hurry up.

We grabbed our gear. As we made our way down the ramp, a ground-crew person waved to us from fifty or so yards away: come to me.

Hurry up.

Standard operating procedure to avoid decapitation by the rear rotor blades. We followed his directions until his horizontally extended right arm indicating that we should turn left. Another fifty yards and one of the two BMTF Torkham guys stood by a Toyota HiLux waiting to take us to our quarters.

"Hey, Bill!" shouted Len through the engine noise. "Howzit goin'? Shot 'ny body recently?"

Former Border Patrol agent Bill 'Don't For' Sakers, had gained his nickname after saving the lives of several colleagues during an armed confrontation with smugglers on the border with Mexico. Len knew about the event but not the details. The full story would be revealed to me by someone else in the Sign Cutters' Bar at the Duck & Cover Club, Kabul HQ. I'd have to wait to go on leave for that.

In a lugubrious tone that could have made Our Lady weep, Bill replied: "No, not for a while. Had plenny opportunities, but he went back to Karrbul."

"Yeah?"

"Yeah. Good thing too. He ain't real Border Patrol. Did somethin' in Procurement," Bill hawked phlegm.

"Hmm. I know the type," said Len.

I shouted from the back seat: "This place looks like one of those old forts you see in black and white films."

The HiLux rocked from side to side across the stones and grit of the track leading towards the crenellated compound. It would be our home and office for the duration. Grey boulder walls rose thirty feet from the hard grey earth. Hard grey cement had held everything in place for decades.

"Sure does," said Bill. "Plenty people tried to knock it down over the years but, it's still here."

On the nearby gate tower, yellow letters on the green background of a wooden shield said:

Welcome to Torkham Firebase

To the left of the solid wood gate, on a newly laid concrete pad stood the remains of a Soviet artillery piece. Thirty years earlier, it may have been a KPV-45 heavy machine gun. It was considerably lighter now, without one of its wheels and part of the breech. Passing through the archway we were into a small courtyard surrounded by wooden huts and refrigerated containers. German words written in Gothic script by previous NATO occupants faded on doors below newly fixed American-English nameplates. A sign on a pole with a downward pointing finger indicated the location of **Berbars' Shop.**

"Who is Berbar?" I said.

'Berbar? Yeah right," said Bill with a hint of sarcasm, "makes me smile too."

"What's his specialty?" said Pete, "cut-throat short back and sides?"

"Only by appointment. Best damn one-eyed barber I've ever known. Does great neck-click," said Bill.

"Neck-click, oh yes. The barber on FOB Hughie does that. It feels so good afterwards," I said.

"Couldn't get that in the UK. Health and Safety," said Pete.

Bill stopped the HiLux at the end of a single-rise building with a flat concrete roof. Half a dozen brown doors were bottom-half faded where the canopy hadn't kept them out of the sun.

"You guys got two rooms here. I guess the boss gets his own" said Bill as he handed Len a key, "our office is past the D-FAC. Look for the building with three satellite dishes on top. We're at the far end of the corridor. See ya there when you've dropped your gear."

Next door, Room 6, was for me and Pete. Our bunk had two mattresses each. Pete got the top bunk so there was plenty of head room but it was impossible to sit up straight on mine. Trying not to disturb too much dust, my top mattress got dragged into a corner of the room. It stood on end wedged upright with miscellaneous boxes of abandoned junk. Maybe it would slow down a rocket.

"Hey, Pete, do you get the impression we're not really wanted here?"

"Yes, I also get the impression that we should fuck off A-SAP."

"Hmm this is going to be fun."

The toilet and shower block was closer than at FOB Hughie, but they weren't better. Septic gas continually eluded the traps in the sewage system and made ablutions unpleasant. This was a good place to break that nasty habit of reading while on the toilet - not that I did. The D-FAC was busier and didn't have the same range, quantity and quality of food we had on Hughie. Outside of strict meal times, it was locked to prevent soldiers helping themselves to extra rations.

Convoys of food rolled by FOB Torkham every day on their way up country to Jalalabad and Kandahar. And there was the issue: they rolled right by. Once they'd arrived at a distribution center somewhere, they could be distributed and would roll right back down to Torkham, if they didn't get blown up by moped jihadis.

BMTF's Torkham office was easy to find. The three and four metre diameter satellite dishes were an excellent reference point. The building's conspicuity from the opposite mountain could have been slightly increased by a neon sign in Pashto, or Urdu, flashing: **Aim Here to Kill Infidel**, but the local tribesmen and guest para-militaries were already zeroed-in on the place. They had been for generations.

The Soviet era solid concrete construction was an addition to an existing fort. It was in the northern corner of the inner compound and ap-

119

peared to be unused apart from by BMTF. Maybe no one else wanted to live, or die, under the huge metal dishes.

The office had all the hallmarks of established routine: wall maps and charts with circles and dots in different coloured marker pen. Map pins stuck in places of interest by people who no longer had an interest, because they'd gone home. Whiteboard dates that had evaded erasure for over a year confirmed lack of management oversight, for anyone who cared to look. Untidy piles of dusty papers added to the myth of activity. The dartboard had seen plenty of action. A corridor led away from the end of the office towards four rooms belonging to BMTF advisors. They weren't out of bounds, I just never got to see them.

"Hey, Bill!" Len called to Don't For, who was over on another desk cleaning his rifle.

"Whassup, Len?"

"You got innernet here?"

Bill wasn't distracted from his work. "Sure, they are BMTF laptops but you can plug the ethernet cable into your own if you like. Makes saving files easier. I don't have a laptop. Never had the need."

"So, you got corporate innernet?" said Len.

"Sure, we gotta dish on the roof. We don't get the military networks," said Bill.

"We'd best set up our comms here. OK if we use this desk?" said Len.

"Sure, help yerself. There's only me and Haysuse."

"Hey, where is Hairsuse?" the familiarity in Len's tone suggested he knew this Herr Seuss chap.

"He's in the gym. Spends a lotta time there," Bill inspected a gun part then laid it back on the shemagh. "Works out well for both of us," Bill smiled at his own pun.

"Still the awkward cuss he was in the Border Patrol?" said Len.

Bill didn't fudge his reply. "Sure is," he slid the bolt into the top receiver of the M6.

"Great! We'll get our computers." Len's quick head-flick to me and Pete, said: let's get out of here.

Outside, Len spoke: "This is gonna be fun boys! Fucking Hairsuse Fernandez couldn't even be bothered to say hello. He's gotta routine and sticks to it. What's that tell you?"

"Herr Seuss?" I said, "Like the Green Eggs and Ham bloke? German ancestry? Nickname?"

They were reasonable questions taking into account that Bill was 'Don't For', our Texan Program Manager, was 'French' and one of the BMTF female logistics operatives, a former US Air Force officer, was known as 'Flaps Flanders.' Almost every BMTF contractor had a nickname. Maybe I'd get one.

"No, you donut!" said Pete, "It's Hispanic. For Christ sake, it's Jesus!" His frustration wasn't diluted by me laughing at his explanation.

"Oh! Jesus!" I knew enough Spanish to not need another clue but as Pete was feeling generous with his advice. I let him carry on.

"Hairsuse is the way they say Jesus in Spanish. That's his Christian name. Get it?"

"Ahh! *Christian* name. Got it. Thanks," I said.

Acknowledging Pete's superfluous linguistic explanation seemed like an easy way to lighten his mood. He was clearly not ready for my humour. Len was right: this was going to be fun.

We returned to BMTF Torkham HQ with our laptops. Len and Pete hooked up to the two available internet terminals while I read through some back numbers of Stars & Stripes, the US military's independent news source. It wasn't the gung-ho military propaganda one might have expected. It has some really well written and absorbing articles by former high ranking officers. Having survived mortal combat, they're never afraid to express opinions about government policy, because politicians don't scare them. A recurring theme was how continued US military presence in the Middle East and Central Asia contributed to the security of US citizens - or not: outstanding journalism.

Len unplugged the ethernet cable from his laptop: "Here, I've had enough."

"Thanks, Len," I got online. Checked my bank balance, paid bills. Had a five minute Skype conversation with my two lads. Scanned the news headlines. Done.

"When's our mission to the port of entry?" Len was keen to get something for the weekly report.

Bill racked the empty chamber of his M6 a couple of times to check the action then stood it on the floor to his right. "Won't be tomorrow. Our unit's on tanker escort. Don't wanna be too close to that. They don't wannus around anyway." Next was his Glock 17: the barrel, slide, frame, magazine, and recoil-spring assembly were quickly laid out neatly on an old shemagh. "Maybe Tuesday, ...or Wednesday. There's no hurry."

"HQ was in a big hurry to get us down here," said Len.

"Well, you know how it is with CBP, someone at the top has a dream about an initiative and the guys below aren't about to tell him it's a waste of time," said Bill.

"I get it: hurry up and wait," said Len.

"You betcha!" Bill laughed at the familiar expression.

"Tanker escort? They tell you what they're doing every day?" said Len, incredulously. He glanced in my direction. I didn't say it, but I thought: security risk.

"Not every day but we do have a good relationship with the military. We usually team up with the US AID guy who has somethin' going on down there. He's been monitoring the movement of some products. He's convinced there's some sorta illegal activity. We've been watchin' 'em too. Moving fertiliser in among the bags of wheat flour is a great way to get explosive precursors to the Taliban," Bill pulled a small piece of cleaning cloth through the short barrel.

"US AID? They don't have an interest in explosives," said Len.

"True. He ain't interested in that. He thinks there's somethin' else going on as well. Shit, what ain't goin' on here?" said Bill, rhetorically.

My knowledge about the use of ammonium nitrate based fertilisers in truck bombs came from Irish Republican Army activity in the UK during the 1970s and 1980s:

"It's used to make ANFO. A skill the IRA used to great effect in their campaigns. Most notably, the Bishopsgate bomb in 1993. They used a lot of fertiliser bombs. I recall reading that some of their blokes were over here as mentors, back in the 1970s. Did you know, last year, Pakistan opened the world's largest ammonia-urea production plant. I suppose they see a bright future in fertiliser production in this part of the world. It's at a place called Daharki, over by the border with India. It's quite a long haul to Peshāwar. Kandahar Province via Quetta would be direct but I guess the cover loads are better here. Maybe there are gang territorial issues."

"Bright future? More like an explosion in demand," said Len. Pete and I smiled. Bill focused on his weapon maintenance.

"Yeah, the 1996 Manchester bomb was three times bigger than Bishopsgate but it doesn't get as much attention," said Pete. "I was heading into the city centre with my, soon to be, wife when that went off. Heard the bang from eight miles away. I read about the IRA in Afghanistan in Howard Marks' book: Mr. Nice. I forget the Irish bloke's name, he hated Brits but because Marks was Welsh, they got on OK. Put it this way: Marks wasn't killed and the IRA got into drug smuggling when they realised the potential."

Len leaned backwards in his chair. "Bill you were in the military before joining CBP, right?"

"Sure was. Air Force. Retired."

"As we flew in to Torkham on the Chinook, I got all nostalgic. Thought back to my youth. The time long before BDUs and subdued chevrons. Before ceramic plates, and MOLLE attachments. How about you, miss it?"

"Hmm, different time, place, world," Bill wiped a gun part.

"That's for sure. I don't miss it a bit. I'm here, now, and in the hellish heat of Afghanistan where I'm gettin' three times as much per day, as I was receiving for half a month's military pay back in the day."

"Sounds like we're here for the same reason. Your 401K take a hit too?" Bill began to assemble his Glock.

"Hit? Wiped out."

Len turned to me. "401K is the government pension. I'll tell y'about it sometime. But, let's just say, right now I don't have a pension."

"As a consequence of the 2008 financial, crash?" I said.

"You bet," said Len.

We drank water and coffee, played Solitaire and threw darts until Bill announced: "Hey! It's dinner time. You boys hungry?" As he stood to leave, he clicked his Glock into the Tec-Lok holster.

Jesus met us at the D-FAC entrance. Flushed and freshly showered from his gym session, Jesus was ready for supper. Self-introductions and hand-shakes all round. We ate: Chicken Alfredo, mixed veg, pizza, burritos, fries. It was pretty good considering it had been produced and frozen in the USA several months earlier and had survived the journey from Karachi, through the Khyber Pass up to Jalalabad and then the run back along Highway 7 to Torkham. The air mailed salad was fresh.

"So, Hairsuse, how come you found your way on to this mission?" said Len.

"Like everyone else here. I need der marney. I got three ex-wives, and a fourth one on the way."

"Three? You have been busy!" said Len.

"Any of you guys wanna walk up to Diamond Head after dinner? It's a great view," said Bill.

"Diamond Head?" I expected this to be another nickname.

"Yeah, it's the mountain behind the compound. It's inside the perimeter. There's a lookout station there. I take a stroll up there some evenings. Watch the sun go down. Smoke a cigar. It's nice."

"Yes. I'll join you," I said.

"OK. Bring a flashlight. May not need it, but you never know."

"What about body armour and rifle?"

"It's on base. You won't need it. There are guys in the overwatch station. Anyway, if you get shot by a sniper, ceramic plates won't save you. Best just get it over with."

"OK. See you in the office in, what, twenty minutes?"

"That'll do it," said Bill.

The shale track meandered up the mountainside for several hundred metres. Sparse grass held onto dust between the larger rocks. The sedimentary strata were clearly defined in the grey cuttings where the road had been forced through by bulldozers. Parts of the English Peak District looked similar but greener and rarely thirty degrees Celsius. When we reached the top, Diamond Head, the views were breathtaking. I scanned the distant landscape for snipers. Long stares at nothing in particular, hoping to spot movement amongst the rocks several miles a way. I didn't see any snipers but that didn't mean they weren't there. It was reassuring to know that even the world's top shooter couldn't hit me first time from that distance: safe, but not complacent.

Highway 7 stretched as far as the eye could see from left to right: West to East. It paralleled the dry river bed confined by steep escarpments on the far side. Diagonal lines in exposed mountain flanks stretched from base to apex, evidence of ancient seabeds pushed upwards by irresistible force. It was slightly cooler at the top of the track. My shirt unstuck itself from my back.

Bill identified some landmarks: "See the lookout post on the top of that mountain?" He pointed to the East.

"Yes. I see it."

An indeterminable distance away, a square structure on the ridge-line was barely discernible against the sky.

"That's Pakistan. It's a military post watching the Torkham Gate border crossing. Just down the hill a few yards and it's Afghanistan. Pakistanis got the Afghans flanked," Bill shrugged out a laugh then lit his cigar. "Helluvva place, ain't it?"

"Yes," it was indisputably, a helluvva place. "Why is it called Diamond Head?"

"No idea. I know Diamond Head is some Hard Rock band. Been around for decades. Maybe that's the connection. This place is actually called Towr Kham, I guess someone decided to make it easy for us by calling it Torkham."

I made a face that said: *sounds about right* and continued to survey the landscape below. To the East, lines of trucks parked up roadside for the night, in the relative safety of the Khyber Pass. A few solitary cars pressed on towards Jalalabad through bandit country.

"You're a Customs guy, right?" said Bill.

"Yes. UK Customs. A bit different to here but, the principles are the same.'

"Principles? Hah! I've been here almost two years. I think I got the principles pretty much worked out. Stay alive is number one. That goes for most Afghans too. They don't want all this death and destruction. Doesn't take many to really screw somethin' up."

"Two years out here? It's real frontier stuff. I'm impressed," that was no lie. Quite what had been achieved remained to be seen.

"The Wild East," said Bill through a cloud of Cuban tobacco fumes. "A lotta guys don't like it out on the frontline. I do. HQ leaves us alone."

"Is the base attacked a lot?" I said.

"Seems to have gone a bit quiet the last few weeks. Had a car bomb try to run the first ECP three weeks back. Only people killed were the two in the taxi delivering the bomb. Dead before the bomb went off. Soldiers nailed 'em before they got too close. We don't get Dial-A-Pizza up here."

"Were you on base at the time?"

"Yeah. In our office. Shook the building. Covered everything in filth."

That explained the dust in the office: caused by enemy activity, not civilian inactivity. We watched the Hindu Kush change from grey-brown through pink to ominous as daylight faded.

"Hey, Gary. We should head back. Don't wanna be out here when it gets dark. We might get mistaken for the enemy by our side and theirs."

"Good advice, Bill. Gratefully accepted.'

We crunched our way back down the track to the safety of BMTF Torkham HQ. The wide corridor leading to the office was lined with stacks of boxes, hundreds of cases of water, mattresses and bookshelves. One of the books was out of line. It appeared to have taken two steps forward. The bright red cover and gold lettering announced its name, genre and

126

publisher: Catch-22. Novel. Corgi. A few days earlier, the same book caught my attention in the front window of an M-RAP parked at FOB Hughie motor pool. This book had just volunteered to be read, by me. We went to the office. Len was browsing gun sites looking for lethal bargains. Pete was text-Skyping his wife.

On the randomly opened page was some good advice:

'From now on I'm thinking only of me.'

We were in our room around ten that evening. Pete was soon asleep. Not me. It takes a few nights to settle in a strange place. Lying awake in the dark room for several hours allowed me to become situationally aware of the nocturnal environment. External lights illuminated waves of dust blown through the one inch gap under the door. I dozed until three in the morning, waking suddenly, very hot. The air conditioning had gone off. Pete's restlessness rocked the bunk. After pulling on my trousers by the gun belt I stepped into my boots, then stepped outside.

The big round wall thermometer next to the **Hydration Alert** poster pointed to 105°F. I drank a bottle of water as tiny red dots moved, slowly, silently, erratically, blinking in the darkness between the stars. Occasionally they stopped. Motionless, hovering drones. On station. Observing. Recording. Somewhere, maybe at Jalalabad or Bagram, someone was on overwatch, ensuring my security while I didn't sleep.

I went quietly back to the room, found the remote control and switched off the timer. The AC blew cool air.

I slept.

Bill was right about the Wednesday mission to the border with Pakistan. The army unit deployed to Torkham had their own security mission but found a slot for BMTF. Leonard Yaxley Junior, the sixty-plus year old US AID agent also rode along. Six of us crammed into the eight hundred thousand dollar MaxxPro Plus M-RAP. One and a quarter million dollars worth of civilian contractors' in one box. Add to that the value of four soldiers and one interpreter: we were two and half million US dollars worth of men and machine rolling towards futility.

The journey to the border was uneventful. From our M-RAP, my limited view was very similar to the few trips made to Jalalabad ICD, but hotter. The wadi, now dry, had been an unpredictable torrent in winter. Randomly discarding boulders and lumber on its way to the Indus, created bizarre sculptures in the dirt.

Our three M-RAP convoy took up defensive positions in the Customs compound.

The army had their own mission but a Specialist was deployed with us to keep an eye open for any trouble. He also had radio comms with the main group which was reassuring. We went walkabout.

The Torkham Gate border crossing between Afghanistan and Pakistan is segregated into vehicular traffic and pedestrians. One-way traffic at that time of day. Vehicles range from mopeds to forty-foot containers. In between: jingle trucks, so named because of the decorative chains, charms and trinkets that hang from just about all parts of the trucks' exterior. Every vehicle had a common denominator: by Western standards, they were overloaded. A common sight: forty foot containers overhanging the rear end of a trailer by two meters. Some had a container and loose cargo combination. Underneath, logs for firewood. Chickens in cages for eggs and barbecue.

Leonard Yaxley Junior pointed at a stalled vehicle: "See that? It's got a bonus load of two hundred bags of wheat flour or cement lashed on top of the full containers. An additional five thousand kilograms of cargo. Probably, undeclared. Trouble is unless we get the Customs guys to stop and check it against the declaration, it's on its way. That's lost revenue."

Traffic noise intensified as grinding gears, bellowing exhausts and creaking leaf springs stifled conversation. I moved closer to Leonard Yaxley Junior so he could hear me: "It's difficult for me to determine what's normal and what's abnormal here."

"Yes. I think we need to forget about what's normal by US or UK standards. Those rules don't apply here," shouted Yaxley.

An old Mercedes Atego SKN-R engine bucked against its load as the flywheel struggled to clutch driveshaft. Momentum gained, the movement through Momand Dara began, slowly. Moped riders, barely visible in their cocoon of produce, weaved between the erratic lines of bigger vehicles.

I wanted to say: this fucking heat is killing me, how about we get in a nice air conditioned office, but it got verbalised as: "Hey, Len. Any chance we can get a look at the Customs entry presentation system?"

"Sure. Bill, where's the Customs office?"

"Follow me," Bill led us at pace to a long magnolia coloured building:

AFGHAN CUSTOMS

Was stencilled in bold black letters alongside some Pashto curly script for the benefit of the traders from Pakistan who spoke English and the Afghans who didn't. Inside, the Customs office was twenty degrees cooler.

"Bill, how old are these computers?" I pointed at the black tower PCs on desks slowly turning desert tan with electro-statically coated Khyber crap.

"I've been here two years and they were three years old then. But if you ask some of these guys they'd probably tell you seven or eight years. No one really knows. They don't stay in the job long enough."

"What about the PCs that are turned off?" I said.

"Dust busted. Gets in the fans. They overheat and the chips fry. We got 'em some boxes of compressed air cans to blow the shit out of 'em. Never seen any used. Maintenance ain't their job. They stay in lane."

Leonard Yaxley Junior the skinny old fella whose body armour only just stayed on his frame, said: "What they need here is a Customs Seal System. That way they can seal up containers and trucks and do Customs examinations at J'bad. That's where you boys are from, right?"

Pete and I made affirmative head movements: we *were* from J'bad. We weren't agreeing with his absurd Customs seal idea.

Len wasn't so diplomatic: "How would a bit of plastic stop them stealing stuff? And where would you put a seal on an open top jingle truck?"

"The Customs here could seal the containers and big trucks that have tarpaulin covers. The high value stuff. Hey Bill, weren't one of your guys

129

working on a seal system," said Leonard Yaxley Junior, trying to dodge the futility of the proposal without changing the subject completely.

Pete didn't speak, but his look to me said: is this guy for real?

"Yeah. That was Fred, er, Fred. His name'll come to me," said Bill.

Bill's half-hearted attempt at recall was rendered redundant by Len: "Wilkins? Fred Wilkins?"

"That's it. He spent a lotta time on that project."

Up to this point, Jesus had been quiet: "Spent? Wasted."

"How long was he here?" said Len.

"A year maybe," said Bill. "He's been on the program since the start. He's at Kandahar now. Went there after the attack earlier this year. He don't get out much. Stays on the RTC. A bit like he did here. Best place for him, outta the way."

"Pete, this looks like ASYCUDA to me. Did you ever see it in Africa?" I said.

"Yes. Saw it. Had nothing to do with it myself. I was more practical training than administrative," Pete had just signalled: no point asking me anything about Customs data entry. His implication that my Africa experience was administrative was wrong, but I did admire the way he'd sidestepped the issue. He was off the hook. His domestic issues clearly hadn't distracted him too much. I was going to have to keep an eye on this bloke, not just in a Buddy sort of way.

"Sounds like you just volunteered to be the subject matter expert," Len laughed.

"Terrific. Just because I know what the abbreviation stands for doesn't mean I know anything about how the system works," I said.

"You heard him Bill, Pete. He knows what ASYCUDA stands for. That's a damn sight more than me. Yup! You just got to be our *go to* guy."

"I gotta ASYCUDA training CD in the office. You can have it."

"Oh thanks, Bill. Very generous of you. Sure you can spare it?" I said.

"Hahaha! I won't need it," said Bill.

Len had security concerns: "Hey, listen guys, we should get back to the BCP with our unit. Too many of the wrong people know we've been here half an hour already."

BCP, that's Border Crossing Point, where the military were providing support for the Afghan National Security Forces: making sure they were doing their jobs. We filed out of the Customs office into the searing heat.

"Bill, tell me what you know about ASYCUDA here at Torkham," as we walked across sole destroying hot concrete, half a bottle of water went down my throat while the other half went down my collar. It felt good.

"Well, as I understand it, it's modelled on European Customs procedures, but without the same level of enforcement. Most of the freight traffic is jingle trucks, as you can see. As Len pointed out, it's wide open here. They need to standardise road traffic regulations for trucks but it ain't happ'nin anytime soon. The locals don't want regulations, specially not ours."

I volunteered my subject matter expertise: "Bill, the United Nations Customs system is supposed to facilitate the expansion of Western capitalism. But, like you say, too many people here don't want it. So, it's an incomplete network. It will never *be* completed: hardware and software lifespans are too short and expensive for failed states to maintain up to date systems."

Despite Bill's apparent lack of interest in the subject, he was surprisingly clued-up: "The system leaks like a sieve and revenue flows to non-governmental entities in the Pashtun tribal areas, instead of finding its way to central government in Karrbul. The Karrbul cabal has its own elected gangsters so, I'm reluctant to call all of the different Pashtun gangs criminals. They just have a different, more basic, form of capitalism. Ya know, we, the US, think we got capitalism all sewed up. Uh, err. These guys, the Pashtuns, it's raw and pure. Unpredictable. Unmoderated. Unexploited by a State. We got a lot to learn."

"Bill, I feel the same about that. I feel like I'll learn much more here than I'll teach," I said.

Leonard Yaxley Junior recommended the local lemonade seller's product so we stopped for some refreshment. It was an opportunity for me to do a deal with the nearby scarf salesman: two shawls and two pashmina at tourist rates: dollars only.

A United Nations team was giving free poliomyelitis vaccines to babies and young children arriving from Pakistan - the polio centre of the world. One of the aid workers borrowed my pen. I said he could keep it.

At the BCP, our unit had been busy assisting with searches of people and the two-wheeled metal carts that got pushed back and forth between the two countries all day, everyday: a form of personal transport in which families move elderly and young relatives along with goods to and from market.

We watched Afghan Customs Officers push fully loaded carts through the X-Ray Pallet scanner. They'd been trying to impress us with their diligence but instead, it jammed and split the drive belt. Another piece of expensive US supplied security equipment vandalised.

Nearby, hanging underneath a forty foot trailer, chickens watched warily from their cages as we ate watermelon as wide as a man's chest. Four ancient looking Pashtun drivers wearing shemaghs and sindhi caps squatted in the vehicular shade. My body armour wouldn't allow me to adopt their posture so I knelt, which was good because shooting is easier with one knee on the ground.

The drivers wouldn't take my money for the fruit but one of them pointed at me: "Chemen."

"Chemen?" I repeated, not having a clue what he was talking about.

"Mercedes," as the only other word recognisable from his unintelligible sentence.

"Ahh, German," I replied triumphantly.

"Ho. Ho. Cheman," he looked to his fellow drivers who all obviously agreed we'd made conversational progress.

"Me, German?" the knuckles of my left hand beat my chest twice. "No," I shook my head and touched the UK flag-patch on my MOLLE.

Frantic discourse between the drivers resulted in Driver Number One reaching forward to point closely at the yellow and black Staedtler HB pencil threaded through the loops of my MOLLE. "Blistiff. Blistiff. Chemen."

"Ahh! Pencil. German. Like Mercedes. Yes. Ho. Ho," my German vocabulary was marginally greater than my Pashto of half a dozen words. Both came in handy: ho is a very useful word. The pencil came easily from the loops. Holding the huge slice of watermelon in one hand and the pencil in the other, I weighed the two objects considering their relative values. The drivers grinned widely as they watched me act out the scene. Slowly, my arm holding the watermelon extended towards Driver Number One, then before it was within his reach, I withdrew my offer and thrust the pencil towards him. It was a fair exchange. We didn't have boxes of watermelon in the office. We laughed.

"Mananna, mananna," hands on hearts.

Len spotted something was wrong: "Hey, I've been drinking water like a retard three hump camel and I'm sweatin' my big fat ass off here. That Specialist Four over there, I ain't seen him take a sip in an hour. He looks dry as a stone and red as slapped ass. Look at him. He don't look right."
Specialist Four, is the most prevalent US army rank. But just because there are lots of them, they aren't all the same. They each have special skills and roles within their platoon.

Len quickly covered the five yards between us and the young soldier, spoke a few words then led him to an M-RAP with his commanding officer. The Specialist was quickly sat in the M-RAP and fixed up to an intravenous saline drip.

Len rejoined us as we stood at the BCP trying to look like we had something real important to do. "Kid's in a bad way: severe dehydration. I don't know how he's still on his feet. He could die. I reckon this mission'll be aborted, soon. Stand by."

Five minutes later we got the order: Mount Up. We were Oscar Mike: on the move. Casualty evacuation: heat injury.

Hurry up.

Return to base.

The Specialist didn't die that day. Maybe he died another day. Hopefully he went home. Most people did. We didn't go out on Thursday.

Friday, our day off, we shuffled on to the CH-46 and returned to FOB Hughie.

Back in Hut 8 I dropped my gear in my room and three bottles of water into the kettle. Switching it on, I announced: "Well, guys, another successful mission. Result: Six One Zero."

Pete wasn't as buoyant: "Len, how are you going to write this up? We effectively gave away three mission opportunities to our own ICD for half a mission at a place to observe, what?"

"Chaos," said Len, "I gotta try and make some order out of it."

I lobbed tea bags into mugs: "And make it appear that our mission was value for money. I have some notes. Between us, we'll be able to spin some yarn. When do you need it?"

"Weekly report is tomorrow. Your job is to make up some shid I can put in it. But you gotta prioritise: make the PG Tips tea, I had enough of that Yellow Label junk."

"Yes, boss," we laughed.

An hour later I shouted out of my room to Len and Pete: "Some notes for the weekly. Check your emails." Clicking of keyboards prompted mirth.

Weekly Report W/C 2012/07/14
BMTF advisors made a fact finding visit to Torkham Gate Customs.
Subjects covered:
  1.Risk management [Targeting & Selection] of bulk cargo [wheat flour] transport, re. Interdiction of material for production of illegal explosives
  2.ECP security [vehicular & pedestrian]

3.Control of pedestrian traffic and associated baggage trolleys

4.Use of Non-Intrusive Inspection Equipment [NII] - X-Ray Pallet Scanner.

5.Automated System for Customs Data [ASYCUDA]

6.Use of Customs seals in trader compliance and enforcement.

Full report to follow.

"Did we really cover that much ground?" said Len

"Can't wait to read the full report," said Pete.

Learning Curve - October 2011.

Len used his US Marine Corps background very effectively to make connections with the military on FOB Hughie and FOB Fenty. But even that wasn't enough to get us regular missions to the ICD. The lieutenant of the unit which we'd been assigned to provide our transport and protection was apologetic. He'd fit us in when they could but would only be able to give us twenty minutes advance notice. Our routine became: zero eight-thirty hours formation in the motor pool to find they'd either already gone or they were about to go but their mission meant they couldn't take us.

Thursday evening after dinner Pete announced he was deploying to Kabul International Airport. He was on a flight Saturday morning from JAF. His mood lightened.

"Saw that. I just got the email," Len confirmed.

"I'm really sorry to leave you guys. I've been a bugger to get on with and I apologise for that," said Pete, "I'll make sure those guys up in Kabul know how challenging it is here."

"Hey, Pete, don't tell them too much. I quite like it here," I said, "I don't want you drawing attention to our lack of activity in a moment of emotional weakness."

"OK, Mate, I've got it."

"If it's so challenging that we can't do our job they'll move us. I definitely don't want that," I said. Pete smiled.

"I'll make sure they know that we've identified areas of the Customs operation that would benefit from our subject matter expertise and that with appropriate resources a number of mission objectives could be achieved. How does that sound?" Pete smiled while Len shook his head.

"You fuckin' Brits," Len chuckled. "Is it sump'n to do with the land o' Shakespeare?"

"What? Make it up as we go along?" I said.

"Tell the audience what they want to hear?" offered Pete.

"I guess it must be," said Len.

A Gator is a small all-terrain vehicle with four, or six, chubby tyres. Gators often inhabit golf courses and farms. They make a sound like your neighbour's lawn mower at zero-nine thirty hours on Sunday, when you're trying to catch up on the sleep you lost during the late night out that you can't now remember. Saturday morning we borrowed one from SFC Mueller at the J-DOC. We got Pete to the helipad at Finley Shields with time to spare. As the Molson helicopter hovered to a standstill, Len and I man hugged Pete and shook hands. Pete kept his head down on his way to the Huey. The next time I saw him was in the Sign Cutters' Bar at the Duck & Cover Club, Kabul.

Our satellite internet service was better than the wireless system on base. Windows updates were easier to deal with as the connection didn't drop quite as often. We could send and receive bigger files but still had to reduce the size of photographs. An original image of four megabytes had to be rescaled to less than 400 kilobytes or it wouldn't attach and send.

"Hey Len!" I shouted through the plywood wall.

"Yo, bro!" came his reply. I could hear the soft tapping of laptop keys.

"I did a speed-test on the SniperHill internet a week or so back and it got up to around one-eighty kilo bytes per second. For which we each paid a hundred and fifty dollars a month. I just did a speed-test on this new service and its showing three-twenty kbps. It's not significantly better. Any idea how much BMTF pays for this satellite malarkey?"

Something heavy and metallic dragged briefly across the floor in the next room. It was Len getting up from his makeshift desk. We'd found two folding chairs down the side of one of the huts. The layer of rain caked mud indicated they'd been there awhile but they cleaned up quite well.

Len leaned on my door pillar. "Not significantly better? It's almost double. Wadda yer want?"

"The three-twenty kbps was when it was just me using it. I thought we might get at least five-twelve kbps especially as they're expecting up to six people to use it." I could see Len was considering my point.

"I'll ask Greg. Are you thinkin' ya might save 'em some money? Ahh hahahaha!" Len simulated amusement at my suggestion as he set the water boiling for coffee.

"Save money? It's a thought but multiple user service will be an issue at some point."

"OK. I'll ask Greg," Len sent an email to the Deputy Program Manager.

Len's wife sent regular care packages of useful stuff such as speciality coffee. He emptied a sachet of dark roast into each of our mugs. Greg must've had a quiet moment because he'd replied by the time the kettle boiled ten minutes later.

"Ho-leee shee-it!" howled Len from his side of the partition.

"Now what?" I was just getting to the bit in my George MacDonald Fraser book where Flashman is in Afghanistan.

"Have a wild guess at how much this innernet costs. Go on. Go wiiild!" Len insisted.

I've always enjoyed mental arithmetic: "I don't know. Two guys to fit it plus equipment rental. Then monthly service charge. I'm going to say two thousand dollars set up then a thousand a month."

I was allowing for the fact that it was an Afghan company providing the service and they were expected to rip the arse out of any business with foreigners.

Len laughed derisively at my modest estimate. "Three thousand US dollars a month," he shouted then paused. Sounded like he was scrolling down the email. "Minimum twelve month contract."

I was on my feet and outside his room in an instant, Flashman went with me.

"Thirty-six thousand dollars a year for internet? That can't be right Len. It's obscene."

"Sure is bro," Len got his coffee.

"For a few reports?" I did the sums. "Hold on. One weekly report, one monthly report, that's six hundred dollars per report."

"Sure is bro. Oh, and don't forget the daily emails with irrelevant intelligence bulletins and loads of other stoopid shit."

"But Len, that's ten times the price of the local wireless service," stood in the corridor, my open-handed gesture said, *that can't be right.*

"Sure is. But is it better or worse?" he already knew the answer.

"Better, but ..." Len raised his hand to halt my reply.

"Better. Exactly. So, it's worth it," he was right. Better equates to good value.

"I don't know why I'm bothered. It's US government money, so, what the hell," I said, having considered Len's point of view.

"Sure is. And if my current salary didn't depend on the incompetence of those higher up the pay grades I might be inclined to do somethin' about it. But it don't so, as you say, what the hey-ell."

"True! And it's not like it's your money."

"Well, it is really. I'm just gettin' more of it back this way."

"No, you're not. It's not your money," I replied, 'even the dollars in your pocket aren't yours."

"They damn well are and I intend to have a whole load more of 'em before I leave this place." Len seemed pretty confident of that.

"No, seriously. The money is not yours," I could see I had his interest.

"Go arn. Yure gonna have some convalutin' explanation for this I just know it. Explain," he leaned back in his chair and eyed me suspiciously.

"All money belongs to the state that issued it. So, dollars belong to the USA. Sterling belongs to the UK. Euros belong to the Member States of the European Union, ...well, Germany actually, but you get the idea?" Len was shaking his head. He did not agree.

"No. My money is my money," he was insistent. "Right now I got my mind on my money and my money on my mind!" Len laughed raucously.

"Len, as a citizen of the United States of America you cannot produce your own money. Hey, there was a time when US citizens weren't even allowed to own gold. Can you believe that?"

Len knew it was true. From 1933 to 1974 it was illegal for Americans to own gold without a special licence that only special people could get.

"Yup! Franklin D. Roosevelt made it a legal requirement to hand in all bullion in exchange for twenny paper dollars, or go directly to jay-ell," said Len.

"That's right. FDR needed to take control of the money supply to pay for all the economic growth he had planned. He had to borrow loads of money. Of course, he never mentioned that during his election campaign. Fact is FDR got elected on what would nowadays be called an austerity ticket," Len focused on a knot in the plywood floor as he listened to my explanation. "But my point is, the state took control of the money and the asset that backed it up. Until 1933 the paper money just like the gold, belonged to the banks and people that issued and held it. But if you can't own gold then, buy extension of that tenet, you can't own money. Money couldn't have belonged to the people and still doesn't."

Len stared at me as he thought about the logical process by which I'd arrived at my conclusion. "FDR lied about that just to get elected," he sipped coffee. "Just like he lied about a lotta things to get the US into World War Two. Because he knew that the war in Europe would create jarbs at home and US industry would thrive at the expense of Britain and Germany. The guy was a genius. Think about it, dismantle two European based empires by settin' one against the other: Britain and Germany. Here's the thing, the military production of Britain and Germany was within reach of the enemy's force projection. The game changer was Britain buyin' support from the US whose industry was untouchable. 'course, the cost to Britain was loss of their second Empire. First one went down thanks to the US of A. The Founding Fathers would've been pleased about that." Len had an annoying habit of being right about things, this was no exception.

"Yes, but I'll come back to that. You don't get me off the subject that easily," I wagged my finger. Len grinned. "Money is an instrument of state and as such belongs to the State. What's that old biblical saying? Render therefore unto Caesar the things which are Caesar's ..."

"Well, that was about whether a buncha Jews should pay tax to the Romans but, go arn," said Len.

"Actually, they were Pharisees, but, it's no skin off my nose! Point well made. But back on subject. The only way you personally could issue your own money would be if A, you could back it up by force if need be, which would require an army. And B, enough people wanted to use it because it was reliable, it was beneficial to them and it was backed up by an army. There may be other reasons but that'll do for now."

"Yeah, well that was one of the problems the South had during the war of Northern Aggression," I had a feeling the US Civil War was Len's specialist subject, "and the Brits had a hand in that too," he winked. "One of the reasons Lincoln emancipated slaves was because it undermined the British slave trade and the Brits supported the South against the industrialised North. Guess the Brits saw the North as a threat to the British economy. Hey, yaah! They were right about that."

"I never thought about it like that," I admitted, "in my history lessons, President Lincoln was the nice white man who set the black man free. I'm not so sure about the British supporting the Confederacy, I thought they'd remained neutral in the hope of exploiting both?"

"Nice white man, yeah right. Support the Confederacy, they did. But when it all went south for the Confederacy, sorry couldn't resist that one, the Brits lost the slave trade and a large part of the cotton trade too. Lincoln didn't give a shidabout the slaves, hey-ell, he wannid ta ship the whole damn loddovem back t'Africa." Len sipped his coffee. "And here's another thing about slaves. They were properdy and the South knew that if the North won, all those bought and paid for assets would be worth nutten. Zip. In fact, worse than that, they'd be goddam liabilities. No homes. No jobs. No frickin use. Ya gotta keep in mind that the Southern economy was destroyed. Plantations and farms, in the same family for generations, were worth almost nuth-thing. Unworkable without black man power. Ya know, after the Second World War there were millions of refugees in Europe. Nowadays, in places like Bosnia and Iraq, they call 'em displaced persons. Well, we had 'em first. Yep, millions of displaced Southern folks. Black and white. Equality in adversity."

If he'd been able to rock back and forth on his chair, Len could have been a good ole boy on his porch dreaming of when the South will rise again.

"Len, a lot of British people think Americans have no history. How ignorant is that? I've learnt a lot in this shed. Do you think it would've been any different if we hadn't burnt the White House?"

"Hey, you wanna do us all a favour and try agin?"

"Anyway ...about money!" I reminded Len how we got onto this subject. "For the convenience of providing a reliable means to conduct legal financial transactions, the State levies a charge on the use of its money in the form of various taxes. For example, state tax on purchases."

"Texas don't have state tax. Instead they gotta border with Mexico. Know which I'd rather have. But I gotcha," he grunted disapprovingly.

"So, money is mutually beneficial to the state and the citizens but it belongs to the state. If you use it in illegal transactions, which are anti-State, then you lose it. And quite right too. I rest my case." It was time to adjourn for coffee.

"Well, we're just gonna have to agree to disagree," Len went back to his room then shouted through the partition: "So, what's your bizarre theory on the ownership of money gotta do with how much we pay for innernet?"

"Hmm. I lost my direction on that," it took me a moment to get back on track. "Oh yes, that's it, if the state is happy wasting the money that it produces and owns, why should we give a shit?"

"So, now you *don't* want to save the program manager any money?" We both laughed at the way I'd successfully undermined my own argument. "Shee-it! Don't ever want you as my lawyer."

I picked up my book: Flashman was about to kill the dwarf in the snake pit.

The DeWalt tool bag we had lugged on and off planes and helicopters proved to be worth every cent of its $2,500 purchase price. Cordless hand-tools made short work of MacGyvered furniture and other useful items from scraps of materials found around the base. But, in terms of mission accomplishment we achieved very little. The Inland Customs Depot Director had adopted some BMTF recommendations. A tangible example was an extra metre of brickwork along the top of the existing perimeter wall so that concertina wire could be fitted. It would keep unwanted people out and created a fort that could be defended in the event of an attack. Closed Circuit TV paid for by the US government was installed to improve security and maybe give advance warning of illicit activity inside the   Customs depot. It didn't work for long. There were constant problems with the recording equipment because the ABP guys on night shifts used the VCR to watch porno movies. Then someone cut some of the cables. My best guess, it was interfering with the goings-on inside the depot that it was supposed to stop. For a security system to work, it requires the acquiescence of the people it is supposed to protect. We recommended the system be abandoned. BMTF HQ agreed. Another box ticked.

To me, travelling with military escort in Jalalabad was much better than self-drive around Kabul. Military convoys are high risk from attack but have the firepower to fight back and win. Individual vehicles don't attract as much attention but two occupants are more easily outgunned and kidnapped. Given the choice, which almost never happens, mine would be for sudden death by assassination rather than slow death by incarceration.

Len liaised with our military partners every day but they didn't have the resources to help us do our job. They were only just meeting their own regional command commitments. Today was different. Len had got an agreement with the base commander and today, we were going to work.

Formation was in the motor pool. The Third Brigade Special Troops Battalion had 3BSTB stencilled on all their vehicles. Their mission: to support BMTF on its mission to J'bad ICD. That was in addition to doing their own job which meant operating in one of the most hostile environments in Afghanistan. Hostile to foreign occupation, that is.

The Taliban had considerable support in the region and frequently reminded coalition forces by use of ambushes in villages and towns where moments before, the locals had been smiling at the soldiers.

Lieutenant Antonio Corrientes's toned olive skin exuded youthfulness. He was tall and lean, with a calm and decisive manner that had already prevented the loss of several of his platoon in combat. When his guys and girls spoke of him, it was with great admiration and they often referred to him as 'LT' which sounded like El Tee. Tony is often a contraction of Antonio and I've known several Tonies referred to as T. Add to the mix my frequent misunderstanding of foreign languages and military jargon and you have a recipe for interlocutory incoherence.

We stood on the hard limestone rocks of the motor pool at the rear of Mine-Resistant Ambush Protected vehicle, number 1001. M-RAPs are fighting vehicles - mobile forts. Its rear door was down waiting for the order to mount up. A question about an operational matter arose as we talked amongst ourselves.

"Shall I ask the Tony?" I offered. The small group of soldiers closest to me shrugged their shoulders, raised eyebrows, chewed tobacco and smoked. They didn't have a clue what I was talking about. Probably because of my British accent and diction.

"The Tony?" said Specialist Smith looking at me with a quizzical expression.

"Yes, sir. The Tony," looking around at the shaking heads it clearly hadn't registered.

"You know. LT. El Tony. The Tony," I emphasised each clause. They got it. Smokers stopped drawing on their cigarettes. Some laughed out of courtesy.

"Maaaan! That's gotta be the funniest thing I've heard in a long time," said Sergeant Germaine, "LT. The Tony!"

Len looked skywards in disbelief. "You gotta be shitten me!"

"It's a colloquialism, right?" I said.

"No, man. A colloquialism is a phrase or expression used in informal conversation," said the big black Specialist with the Squad Automatic Weapon. Soldiers call it the SAW. The M249 light machine gun has a two hundred round magazine of five-five-six ammunition. It's a fearsome weapon. It looked like a toy against this lad's massive physique. "What I got here is an acronym. Which is …"

"Yeah, yeah, yeah!" piped up the diminutive soldier with the M-RAP fifty caliber machine gun balanced on his shoulder, "we all know about abbreviations and acronyms. They're what the fuckin' military puts in the food!"

SAW soldier shook his head dismissively and continued with his explanation, "...formed from the initial letters of words," he paused to decide on an example. "MRE is an abbreviation."

"See whadda mean?" said fifty-cal soldier. "MRE. Meal Ready to Eat. Edible acronyms," more laughter and some of the soldiers were trying hard to come up with witty comebacks. SAW soldier shook his head in my direction and mouthed: *abbreviation.*

I got it: "OK. So, LT is an abbreviated form of lieutenant, right?" I was supposed to know all this but, for me, there were too many inconsistencies in military vernacular to make sense of it.

"Right," Specialist Smith confirmed.

"And the lieutenant is a lieutenant colonel, right?" I felt I was making progress.

"Right!"

"So, why isn't a lieutenant colonel referred to as LC?" Is what I said. What I thought was: sounds a bit too much like Elsie.

Fifty-cal soldier shouted down from his turret: "Man! There ain't no logic to it. This is the military. Don't over think things." He closed the cover over the ammunition belt.

"What's BMTF Mr Kind-a?" Sergeant Germaine lifted his gaze from the Velcro patch on Len's Modular Lightweight Load-carrying Equipment. It's abbreviated to MOLLE, acronymised it's Molly. Hollywood call it a bulletproof vest. "Is it somethin' somethin' Motherfuckers?"

"Nooo," Len's slow and easy Missouri accent rolled into: "Although it probably should be!" If I hadn't known the answer, Len's compelling explanation would have convinced me: "It stands for, Bungling Mentors Teaching Foreigners." A few of the soldiers were clearly grateful for the clarification then, one by one, as Len's words crystallised, they started to grin. "And it's Kinder, as in the German for children, not Kind-a, as in a similarity."

"Hey Mr Kinder, what's the sight you got on your weapon there?" Len was about to discuss the merits of his M6 mounted Trijicon Ruggedized Miniature Reflex sight, but he didn't even get time to say RMR. Lieutenant Antonio Corrientes appeared from around the side of another M-RAP to give the mission briefing.

"Good mornin' guys! Sounds like you're having fun already." Instantaneous squad formation occurred. "And the fun will continue, as we have five missions today: first one being with the Border Management Task Force." LT looked over in our direction. We held up our hands by way of identification. "BMTF has business at the Customs dee-po. We will use the time to capture biometrics on the workforce to see if any of them can be linked to IED production," the briefing lasted less than two minutes.

As we climbed into the M-RAPs, one of the squad called out. "LT. Interrogative?"

"Send?" came LT's sharp reply.

"We were talkin' earlier 'bout The Tony," there was a momentary pause in activity. A few of the troopers shook their heads in mock disbelief at the guy's audacity. "What d'ya think about the Tony?"

"The what?" said LT, fastening his helmet strap. "What are you talking about? I don't know. What's the context? Is it sump'n to do with New York?" LT looked around at his troops. "Mount up!"

The Herat Mission - 22 July 2012

The flight from Kabul to Herat was full. It emptied at Bagram Airbase. We had to wait on the ground for an hour before the plane refilled. The same BMTF guys got on but the rest of the passengers were different. Mark and I sat near the rear of the cabin.

"Hey Mark, do you think you'll ever get used to getting on aircraft with a pistol and rifle?" I said.

"I've been here a bit longer than you so I'm getting used to it but when I tell people back home, they don't believe it," he said.

We buckled up and took off. A gong sounded as the seatbelt light went off. No one moved. In front of me, heads slowly lost interest in the Afghan landscape below. One by one, chins met chests. My mind began to drift around the threshold of consciousness. Floating in the sea of somnolence, thoughts formed and dissolved before crystallising into ideas: the dream-zone where everything makes perfect sense but can never be transposed on to waking moments.

The sudden change in engine noise, as the Dornier 328 banked to the left, woke me. To my left, the horizon moved upwards passing out of sight above the top edge of the window. The ground swivelled and tilted as it filled the porthole. To my right sat Mark. My elbow-nudge got his attention on the landscape. Plucking out his ear plugs, my pal leaned across to take in the view.

"I wonder if that's our place down there?" a regimented collection of tents, huts and warehouses, spread over several hectares of dry brown ground. Irrigation created green margins around a patchwork of many shades of dirt.

"Mine's the one with the Jacuzzi and spa," said Mark. We had the same dark dry humour. Engines revved higher.

"Oh yeah? Where's that?" I shouted over the change in pitch. The plane nosed down another few hundred feet.

"The one that had the big blue courtyard," Mark winked. He'd been in country a year longer than me. He'd seen enough of Afghanistan to know it was an Afghan compound painted in sky blue, the colour of swimming pools in most countries.

"I reckon if we got the concession to supply blue paint in all of Afghanistan we'd make a fortune. It probably comes from China like most of the stuff here. Even traditional Afghan carpets are imported."

"They do like blue and yet it's not on the national flag," he was right about that.

I shouted: "Do you know what the three colours of the Afghan flag represent?" the plane circled closer to the ground. Another military base came into view.

Mark shook his head. "No, but I have a feeling I'm about to find out."

"Green is for all the US dollars that have been spent here. Red is for the blood that has been spilt and black is its future!" I winked and turned back to the window.

"Sounds about right," Mark poked the plug back into his ear.

Herat city was out there somewhere. Some of the houses did have pools, gardens and a semblance of normality. It might be nice to see some of it during my time here but if not - so what? This wasn't a guided tour. I had no illusions about leaving it a better place than when I arrived. I didn't want to get caught in the overseas contractor money trap but, like everyone else - bills don't pay themselves. Make as much money as possible in as short a time as possible, then get out, in one piece. That was my mission.

Thermal current buffeted the aircraft. I momentarily gripped both armrests. Our descent to Herat Airport continued.

"Do you think that's the same place?" to me, the compound sliding out of view looked like the one we'd already passed.

Mark shook his head. "No idea. One camp looks very much like the next, just blocks of desert-tan buildings in the tan-desert," Mark leaned closer. "One thing's certain, it's definitely a military site," he was right. It would have stood out in stark contrast to the local mud-brick houses belonging to the natives if they'd been foolish enough to have lived anywhere near it, but they had more sense than that, so didn't.

Airport perimeter buildings flashed by. Wheels down.

Kit loaded into a three vehicle convoy.

Driving at high speed from the airport to the Inland Customs Depot seemed ostentatious.

Hurry up.

Someone had scheduled a meeting at the ICD with the Regional Customs Director. We were kind of in the area so it would cram more activity into the DHS Attaché's itinerary.

I'd been on very good terms with Director Khairfullah at Jalalabad but it was a surprise to see him at Herat. He must've been reassigned soon after Len and I had left J'bad. It may have been something to do with the gangsters that had been in his office during one of our visits to the ICD, or the suspicious loads of pharmaceuticals we had identified and about which we'd heard nothing further. Or, one of the hundreds of other crooked activities going on at the ICD that we didn't uncover.

Team BMTF and the DHS Attaché trooped into the Director's office. It was overkill really but everyone wanted to be part of the event and the photo-opportunity. The presence of the DHS Attaché created a formal atmosphere. It didn't last long. Everyone did the usual salaam alaikums and hands on hearts. When Director Khairfullah saw me he started to shout excitedly in Dari. Spinning on my heel and pretended to take flight, Director Khairfullah's Afghan Customs Police body guard, with his AK-47 across his body, brought me to an abrupt halt.

Director Khairfullah started to laugh. Everyone in the room looked to each other wondering what the hell was going on. I had succeeded in creating chaos amongst order. As Director Khairfullah stepped towards me, I moved quickly to shake his hand. We did the customary back-slapping man-hug. My sideways nod to Hamid our Language Assistant primed him to translate. Director Khairfullah spoke good English but I kept that to myself.

"Mr Director. Sir! I did not expect to see you again so soon," Hamid did his job. "Now, about the million dollars I owe you," Hamid glanced quickly at me, his eyebrows expressing surprise. Inclining my head towards Director Khairfullah urged Hamid to say it in Dari. "I haven't forgotten. It's just that, well, I've been very busy!" I released my grip on Director's handshake. Hamid's upturned palms made a conciliatory gesture as he completed his translation. Director Khairfullah laughed again then replied in Dari.

Hamid turned to me. "You are his friend so it is OK. He forgives you. But it would be good to have the million dollars by tomorrow," Director smiled as he continued our joke. I turned out my trouser pockets to show they were empty. We both laughed. Khairfullah took hold of my right hand as is the local custom when engaging in conversation. I've never understood the need for physical contact while chatting but I do know the gesture has no sexual connotations. We stood in front of the DHS Attaché, my team members and three local traders who were also conducting business with Director Khairfullah. It hadn't been my intention to upstage the DHS Attaché, but we hadn't been briefed on protocol and this seemed like a good moment for spontaneity. I'd apologise later, maybe.

Director Khairfullah spoke to the gathering. Hamid translated: BMTF and Mr Gary and Mr Len helped me a lot at Jalalabad. They got equipment for us. Paper for our printers. Uniforms for the Customs Police. A fire truck.' He looked at me. Hamid translated. "Where is, Mr Len?" he referred to Len Kinder, my team leader at Jalalabad.

"Mr Len, had to go home. His family needed him," I said.

Director Khairfullah empathised.

"Family is very important," Director said solemnly.

A shalwar kameez billowed around a small skinny man as he entered the room to distribute trays of mixed dried fruits and nuts to the tables. He bowed respectfully towards Director Khairfullah. Another man entered with the familiar smoked-glass tea mugs and a pot of chai. Director gestured for everyone to sit.

Mark sat next to me and whispered: "He likes you!"

I inclined my head slightly to speak quietly. "He's a nice bloke. We tried really hard to do stuff in J'bad. I'll tell you about it later."

But I didn't.

After the meeting with Director Khairfullah but before heading to our base, someone decided we should visit Camp Stone, another military base. Maybe following the Kabul conference, the DHS Attaché decided the mission needed direction, that someone needed to show some leadership and be out there. I didn't know the purpose of the grand tour then and I don't care now.

Herat city: trees regularly spaced along the main-drag stood unexploited by vendors despite offering shade. Odd? Orderly? Or, just different? Establish the normal, question the abnormal: the most important thing I learnt as a UK criminal investigator. Mix in some situational awareness and it saves lives. Homes and businesses kept a good distance back from the wide road. It made the place less intimidating than the streets of Kabul and Jalalabad where everything seemed to crowd in on me.

Streets in Kabul? Once upon a time there had been streets. Now they were mostly rutted mud tracks. The area around the international Embassy community and the route to the airport were relatively well maintained. Elsewhere, roads were in a constant battle between construction and destruction. Herat wasn't as messed up as Kabul. It looked like a nice place but I was in no hurry to sample what it had to offer.

A chap that Mark and I knew from the Congo job worked for an international development agency. He'd sent me pictures of himself looking like a regular tourist outside the Blue Mosque in Herat City. So, it must be OK, but to me our fleet of unmarked armoured Land Cruisers shouted INFIDEL louder than the local Muezzin calling the faithful to prayer for Eid Mubarak. I'm more low-profile. I don't like advertising my presence: no FaceBook, no Twitter, no narcissistic self-promotion. I'd make sure I mentioned my concerns to the Team Leader or the security advisor at the next morning briefing. Security advisor?

A phone rang in the front seat passenger's pocket. "OK. Roger that," the call ended. "Can't get into Camp Stone," said Jo Palomo. "They're on lockdown. Security alert. We're gonna have to swing it around and head back to the RTC."

Dropping onto the roadside dirt margin, our Land Cruiser stopped in the dust cloud of its own creation. The other two vehicles followed in our tracks. Phone calls between vehicles and other places were made as we sat at the side of the road. I watched my three o'clock.

"OK. We're RTB." said Jo, as our three Land Cruisers swung a big arc back onto the blacktop. We returned along the route already travelled and headed to the Regional Training Center: safety in numbers in a compound with hundreds of trained killers, most of them were on our side.

But unfamiliar surroundings are not the place to relax. Time to ramp-up my situational awareness, get to know my area of operation. An Italian NATO contingent had command of the RTC. Except for the flags, it hadn't changed much in outward appearance since inauguration. Successive NATO contingents had occupied it from 2001 along with their Afghan comrades in arms.

My vigilance remained constant as we approached the RTC: still time for things to go wrong.

Without turning to Mark, I said: "Did you know that the landlord and when I say landlord I mean former warlord, receives a rental income from the US government for the duration of occupation?" I'd read it somewhere. Our Land Cruiser entered the base. "Part of the deal is that when the coalition forces depart, the land must be returned to its original condition unless otherwise agreed by all concerned."

"Returning it to its original condition won't be much of a challenge!" Quipped Mark, "and I bet the landlord's in no hurry to bid his paying guests farewell. Conflict is good for business."

The Land Cruiser bumped us off our seats an inch as it went over a road repair. Jo Palomo gripped the overhead rail and rolled around on the front seat. His seat belt buckle clanked against the door pillar. Mark and I didn't move much. Always wear seat belts, even in a war zone. You don't get advance notice of a vehicle roll-over.

"You know, when the Soviet army quit Afghanistan they didn't have time to demolish stuff." Mark knew a lot about the Soviet invasion. "They just got in their tanks, helicopters, aircraft and trucks and headed for what was, at that time, the friendly border with one of their own Soviet Socialist Republics. What they couldn't carry they buried and what they couldn't bury, they blew-up." Mark had a copy of Brassey's Encyclopaedia of Military History and Biography, so he spoke with some authority on the matter. I maintained watch on my sector beyond the armoured glass. "That's why the Afghan army is equipped with AK-47s. The Soviets left warehouses full of 'em and a lot got into the hands of the various factions," said Mark.

The RTC showed the signs of wear and tear caused by thousands of people constantly moving heavy and bulky gear around confined spaces. I'd seen it many times: intensely purposeful activity with no long term achievement. People in the UK civil service had made careers out of it: not so much the bulky gear but the pointless movement. One old boy in Salford Custom House gave me the benefit of his long experience: 'No matter where you're going in this building, or, in your career, always carry a   folder of papers and walk with purpose. I've been doing it for twenty-five years!'

He was right. Members of Parliament must have heeded his advice because they constantly strive to get photographed carrying large bundles of documents, the theatrical props used in their trade. Occasionally, if they want to leak something to the press, they'll have confidential documents on the outside of the binder. Before digital image enhancement was invented, MPs had other ways to disclose that which should not have been disclosed.

The fact that the RTC was still standing was a testament to the skills and dedication of the US Army Corps of Engineers. The Afghans don't have an equivalent military unit, but then, who does?

In the Afghan sector, yellow sand-textured paint blistered on external damp areas of buildings. Waste-water pipes nourished algal blooms on the outside of latrine-block walls. Overflows created mosquito farms where battle-hardened warriors feared to tread. Scuffs and scratches, dents and scrapes, scattered randomly across walls: the indecipherable glyphs of a modern combat zone. Marks of transience. Maybe the maker's only mark before departing to meet his maker.

We drove slowly through the base to our accommodation. Unintelligible shouting emanated from the basketball court on our right. A squad of around twenty Afghan army soldiers limped and hopped in line around the concrete pad in what appeared to be a training exercise. They were a mixed bunch in every sense: Hazara, Uzbek, Tajik, old, young, obese, emaciated, different coloured ill-fitting uniform tops and trousers, unlaced boots, sandals. Several had pointy-toed dress-shoes with the backs trodden down like Aladdin's genie. No socks in sight. Each man threatened the back of the man in front with sticks and broom handles. One had an offensive fence-stave. Faces bore the telltale signs of Chicken Pox and other virulent diseases. Facial hair was the common denominator. It was the only thing at which they appeared to excel. At Jalalabad, Freddy had introduced me to some Afghan Special Forces soldiers. They were fearsome warriors. I didn't see any likely candidates amongst this lot.

"This must be the Afghan equivalent of Dad's Army." I remarked sarcastically as our vehicles crawled by the pitiful spectacle. Mark grinned. When he smiled he looked like an early-80s Gordon Sumner, AKA, Sting, but with more hair.

"God help them," Mark sounded sincere.

If I'd known then that He wasn't listening I'd have told Mark to pray louder.

"Hey Mark! When we worked together at Dover did you imagine that one day you'd be in Afghanistan doing something like this?"

"No way," his reply was blunt. "If that *opportunity* in the DRC hadn't presented itself I wouldn't be here."

"And me. Mark, I am so grateful to you for getting me on this contract."

The Democratic Republic of Congo Customs modernisation job was in 2009. It seemed like a good idea at the time. We worked together for a few weeks in Kinshasa but I spent most of my time in Lubumbashi and in jungle villages on the border with Zambia.

"Do you believe that story about the missing money?" I said.

"What? That someone in the DRC Ministry of Finance made off with the project funds?" He huffed nasally. "Not convinced," Mark checked his phone for messages, "I bet the directors got paid. They always do."

"That job turned out to be the most expensive unwanted holiday I've ever had. It took me to the brink of financial ruin. It wasn't funny at the

154

time but since I got to Afghanistan I've occasionally smiled about it," I said.

"Yeah, me too. But we're here making good money now, it all balances out. So, carry on!" Reminiscing made Mark pensive: "A few of our colleagues will never recover from that mess." He was right. Even if the money owed did come through, it was too late for some.

"Hmm! Colleagues are people that work *with you.*"

People I thought I knew, misled me over the viability of the Congo project. I was still bitter about that but derived no consolation from knowing that three of them were dead. They were the wrong three. Natural causes. Well, natural in the world of international development: alcoholism, malaria, obesity.

As soon as Mark and I arrived in the DRC it all began to unravel. Five months' work and I'd received six weeks' pay. They owed me over thirty-thousand pounds salary. No chance. The directors stuck to a cock and bull story about a claim against the DRC government going through some international court in Paris but I never saw any evidence of it. No witness orders, court announcements or hearing letters. Just occasional emails, usually combined with Happy Christmas greetings from somewhere in Spain, explaining how the Company's legal team were tirelessly working towards a judgement. Some of the sycophantic losers who'd never ventured out of the Kinshasa office wasted their time replying with emails of encouragement and gratitude for continuing to pursue the debt. They used email's Carbon Copy option as an opportunity to brag about their latest exotic contract.

In February 2010, thirty expatriate experts were on their way back to London. We sat in the departure lounge at N'djili Airport, with nothing but a few cases of used clothing. The contract stipulated Business Class for the long-haul flight to Brussels from Kinshasa, but my contract was worth less than the staple that held it together. Instead, we were crammed into Brussels Airlines Economy. One of the passengers passed me on the way to his seat five rows back. His stink stuck to me as he walked by. I tasted it in the air and gagged. Bromhidrosis that bad requires a major commitment to hygiene avoidance. I've never been airsick but even before we took off I

155

came close that day. After we were airborne the cabin crew walked the dis-insecting walk down the aisles with aerosols while I got the blowers on my face. The 747 began to smell less like the locker room at the Stade des Martyrs de le Pentecôste after the African Nations Championship.

Mark was the first person I knew to have got the job in Afghanistan with FedCor. Don't ask me how he did it, just a better networker than me I guess. He was also seven years younger. Mark's recommendation to the company director got me into this job and out of a black hole of debt and despair. That first day in Kabul, in the company of other lads from UK Customs and Crown Agents, it was apparent there wasn't a single significant career achievement between the lot of 'em. Not colleagues, not before, not now, never.

Mark had saved my life. It was a great feeling being back on my feet. One of our former workmates from Dover now lived in his car. Another had fallen under a train at an unmanned level crossing in a remote part of Kent, but not before transmitting an unmentionable disease to his wife during the home coming.

"Mark, in the previous twelve months I've earned more than in my last five years as a UK civil servant and I got to keep more of it. I resigned from UK Border Agency because of poor pay and the inability to earn more. You must've felt the same way." I recalled we'd got on the subject over a few beers one evening.

"I'd also had enough of incompetent people making decisions about my future," said Mark. "They didn't care that their annual assessments had a direct impact on my family. Twats!" Mark turned towards me. "You know that Band Eleven, Tim Naylor?" My expression confirmed I'd had the displeasure. "He came round one day and gave us his Change Management speech. Said a lot of people were institutionalised and needed to embrace change. Twat! Can you believe that? He was talking to the people that helped him get an OBE. And he thought *they* were institutionalised? You don't get much more institutionalised than a fucking OBE!" Mark was right about that. "Forget about institutionalised, if I hadn't got out of there I'd be in an institution now."

I laughed. "That's why they refer to the OBE as Other Buggers' Efforts!"

"Too true," Mark turned to look out his side window.

I watched our three o'clock. "During the First World War, one of my ancestors was awarded the British War Medal and the Military Medal. I have no idea what he did to get them."

"British War Medal? You just had to be there," said Mark, "but the MM, you had to do something special for that."

"Yes well, he may have been special and so must the event, but he fell on hard times and in 1921, swapped them for a pair of shoes. The government can keep their fucking medals. Give me the cash, every time," I said.

"That is so sad and yet typical of so many of those Lions," said Mark, "the system demands the best, but it's rarely rewarded."

"Yeah, it's a bit like our old job. They claimed to want people that can see the big picture and positively influence, blah, blah, blah, but it really is utter bloody nonsense." It was the wrong time to get on my soapbox, subject change required: "Do you have any plans for the big bucks you're earning?" I said.

"If you mean after I've got my two daughters through university, well, yes," Mark was prepared to go through hell for his girls. He had three, including his wife. "I've been looking at a few things. Rail freight-car rental in the US looks good. I don't want to do consulting forever. Seen too many get stuck in that rut. Institutionalised! I'm not sure how long I could maintain the superficiality, if you know what I mean? What about you? Any ideas?"

"Not really," I said. "my youngest lad is nearly done at Uni. So, that bill is almost paid. Pay off debts. Buy my ex-wife a new place to live. Job wise, I had an email from the Foreign and Commonwealth Office a few weeks back. It was a job in Kabul. Can you believe that? All that time I was out of work and could have done with a contract they weren't interested. As soon as I'm in country, they're interested. Tossers."

"Yeah. Typical British government. Whatever it is, it better be cheap. Only recruiting because the last bloke got pissed off with the BS. How much they offering? Not that I'm interested," Mark wasn't about to jump ship.

"Not enough. Even with all the travel expenses and per diem it works out at less than eighty-thousand. And it's only a twelve month contract. After that, who knows."

"Stick with what you know. I take the view that every contract could be my last," Mark looked despondently out the window. "See these guys. Paid a hundred dollars a month to learn new skills," the last trainee went out of view. "Aside from three meals a day, clean drinking water and a mattress under cover from the elements, what else do they have? Aspirations? To what?" We simultaneously shook our heads benightedly.

"Maybe an early assignation with Allah," I suggested.

Mark sighed. "Just think, in a few weeks, they'll give those guys real guns."

"Hmm," it bothered me too. That'll test their allegiance. Self, family, elder, tribe. That's about as far as it goes with most of these lads. There's a god somewhere amongst all that Sunni and Shiite nonsense. But, government? State? Huh? Forget about it," I was telling Mark what he already knew.

The Afghan force's accommodation was separated from the NATO area for cultural and security reasons. Gates could be closed to prevent movement between the two sectors if there was an emergency, such as an attack. We sat silently contemplating our new surroundings as we passed through a large opening in a wall. We'd entered the coalition forces' sector.

Our gear got dumped in hastily allocated rooms before making the short walk to the D-FAC. Time for the evening meal. Externally the building was a clone of our own accommodation and dozens of others on the base. Internally, there were no subdivisions. It could have been a school dining hall except for the three large refrigerated displays stood upright by the door. Ready to serve: cartons, cans, bottles of assorted drinks. An orderly arrangement of catering equipment formed up along the wall. In the centre of the space, tables and chairs awaited occupation. On other bases, multi-national corporations emblazoned company logos on signs and serviettes: brand force projection. Not here. It was outgunned by bland source protection. Anonymous signs concealed the caterer's identity. Modesty? Indifference? Shame?

"I'm looking forward to this," I said. Mark and the other guys were too focused on food to reply.

My expectations of culinary excellence were high. Italians are famous for creating gastronomic delights. Pasta is the foundation of many of the world's most popular dishes: spaghetti, garganelli, vermicelli. All superb with pesto, meat sauce, chopped salad.

The food counter did not inspire me. "It appears that thousands of large black flies don't share my disappointment," approaching the salad bar disturbed the resident Diptera. They momentarily retreated from their territory. I chose not to make a choice.

"Your pre-deployment vaccinations will cover you for morbilli or varicella if they're on the menu," said Mark reassuringly. That's why I got on so well with Mark, he used words very few people understood. It was great for confounding the Yanks. A bit like Cockney rhyming slang in the Stalags.

"Yeah, right, I'm not in a hurry to test their effectiveness," I moved on to the hot food.

Catfish lurked in the slime of a bain-marie. It had the aroma and appearance of something that glowed on a beach after dark. Despite the Glock at my hip I lacked the courage to disturb it. In the next tank some, let's call them burgers, drifted morbidly from lukewarm towards biohazard. It was just bad timing. We'd caught the end of the offerings. Things could only get better. Right?

Meat patty with CLS: cheese-like substance, in challenging ciabatta with extra-crispy fries, some sort of cake and Fanta made a disappointing repast.

Returning to our accommodation, I was in no mood to socialise but reluctantly sat with most of the team outside our block enjoying the late-July evening. Double-doors into the secure building flapped complacently in the warm breeze. Eight strides away from the door was the concrete bunker, the go-to place during a rocket or mortar attack. Its ambient temperature was greater than the cooling evening breeze. Thermal emanation could be felt from six feet away. The space between bunker and building had the ubiquitous coalition force regulation two-inch limestone aggregate on the ground. One of our armoured Land Cruisers, twenty feet away, partially blocked the alley to the South.

A dozen team members sat in a rough oval of folding chairs and a wooden bench. Smoking cigars and cigarettes was one way they got to know each other. I don't smoke. They were relaxed. I was uneasy. Jalalabad was my last deployment. It taught me that if you don't make yourself an easy target, you are less likely to get hit. My previous experience and the fact that it was a good time to call my family clinched it for me.

"Gentlemen," the folding camp chair rocked unsteadily on the uneven ground as I stood. "It's time to Skype my lads. But not only that, smoking is very bad for your health." My wagging finger of mock reproach made them smile. Several guys shook huge cigars at me and laughed.

OK buddy. Have a good evening. See you later! Was the collective response. Mark grinned and took a drag on his cigarette. I'd never seen Mark smoke.

"Yeah … you to … later," I replied, then went inside and tried to close the main door. The digital lock refused to catch. It drifted lazily open, again.

As the room to my door slammed shut, I shivered and reached for the AC's remote control.

Ammo Can - January 2012 to April 2012

The M-RAP, towed through the ECP, joined three slightly mangled vehicles at the back of the motor pool. A vignette of black soot framed a deadly fan of small dents caused by ball bearings. The mechanics might be able to make one full one out of the four now unserviceable.

Over the months that I'd been on the FOB I'd got to know many of the male and female soldiers of the 4th Infantry Division. They were a bright, intelligent and optimistic bunch. Their war-zone wit and wisdom would benefit a lot of civilians.

It was good to see they'd made it back to base. Waving to those that I got on with especially well, prompted polite but tired responses. Our supply of Gatorade in F8's fridge was quickly walked over to the motor pool in a PX carrier bag. The squad was already busy cleaning weapons and checking equipment ready for the next day's mission. The crew of the M-RAP that usually took Len and me out on our missions looked emotionally and physically drained. Private First Class Gonzales sat inventorying kit.

"Looks like you've been through the mangle today, mate," I said, offering him an orange rehydration drink.

"She-it man. That was some mission," he shook his head. "Hey! Thanks for this. Got any more?"

"Yes, I brought six. We didn't have anymore."

"Are they for us?" he looked expectantly at the plastic bag sweating in the heat.

"Yes, they are," I held out the bag.

He called out: "Hey dudes! Some cold Gatorade here," his comrades immediately surrounded me before liberating the contents of my bag.

A Corporal stood on the steps of the next M-RAP called over: "Hey! You guys been holdin' out on the Gay-dorade?" he looked jealously at the chilled drinks.

"No, man. We got room service!" Joked Gonzales.

The Corporal shouted along to the Lieutenant's M-RAP: "Hey! LT, how come Gonzales gets room service and we don't."

"He's connected," replied Lieutenant Corrientes, dead-pan, then continued his work undistracted.

"Dy-amn," the Corporal's contrived envy made me smile.

"The other guys got it rough," Gonzales craned his neck towards the damaged M-RAP. "Man it was a mess," he shuddered slightly as he reviewed the event. "I never seen nuttin' like that before. Not in a rush to see it again," he took a long glug of Gatorade. "Hey, wanna do somethin' useful?"

"Definitely," maybe he was about to tell me to, fuck off.

"Can you get us some cases of water from the stack?" his gaze targeted a guard-shack structure about thirty yards away. Walking briskly, the short distance across the sharp limestone chunks of the motor pool was soon covered. Two cases in each hand hanging by the cling-wrapped outer plastic were soon stacked by the side of the M-RAP. Two more runs, seventy-two litres, would be enough for the five-man crew. Sat on the stack, I drank water.

"Thanks, man. You saved me some time. We never know how much we gotta that."

"That's true. We can always get more money, but time ..." My words tailed off before I made a fool of myself. "Do you think I should do the same for the others?" I looked down the line of M-RAPs.

"Nah man. They'll git to it. Anyway, they don't get room service," his smile made me   realise how young he was. Probably wasn't even twenty-one. "Ya know ..." he looked through me as he recalled the recent memory. "There were some fuckers down the road kicking a guy's head around in the dirt," he squinted as though looking at the scene for the first time. "Reckon it was the guy with the vest. Chavez says the head always goes up in the air."

Chavez was the driver in the lead M-RAP. I'd heard about decapitation of bombers before, but this came from an eye witness.

"What about the crew in the M-RAP that got hit?" I said.

"They're OK. Headaches and shook up but they woulda been gone if Dawson's head hadn't been on a swivel. Man, Dawson was quick on the M4."

"Is he here?" I looked around for the man I didn't know.

"No, man. They're all gettin' checked out at medical and then debrief with the Major," Gonzales focused on his work.

"I better get out of your way. Glad you're here. See ya mate!" I stood as Gonzales closed the lid on the case. It was a good time to leave.

Around twenty-hundred hours that evening, Len and I were busy relaxing in our rooms when the front door creaked open and Lieutenant Corrientes shouted down our hallway: "Hey! You guys home?"

"Sure," retorted Len, "come on down LT."

Lieutenant Antonio Corrientes strode down the plywood corridor. He often came in to talk with Len. They had a lot in common. I played gooseberry. It was a chance for LT to get a non-military perspective on things. Not only was Len a good listener, his US Marine Corps history meant he was able to empathise with the young officers and soldiers of 3BSTB.

Len and I sat in the doorways of our rooms as LT accepted the folding camp chair in the Ops & Comms doorway.

"Scotch?" Len suggested. I contained my surprise at his offer.

"Ya got some?" LT was wide-eyed in anticipation and disbelief.

"Nooo!" Mocked Len. "Just fuckin' wid ya!"

"Bastard!" said deflated LT, "but, I couldn't even if you did. Tequila? Hmm. Don't!"

"Got some good corrfee. Wantsum?"

"Sure, that'd be good. Bit late for me really but I got reports to write so, it'll give me an edge."

Len squeezed past the LT and set-up the percolator, "I hear you guys had quite a day."

"Hmm. We don't need any more like that. We're goin' home, end of the month."

"Got sump'n on yure mind LT?" Len got straight to it.

"I've been thinking about the Customs and Border Protection agency. You talked about it to a few of my guys and they've been gettin' their résumés together. I figured I should probably do the same."

"You should. You got all the right skills. Fluent Spanish is essential for the southern border. That's where the money is. I'll send you some

163

stuff on email. Links to CBP information, recruitment, that sorta stuff."

LT's mood lightened. The coffee jug was half full. Len squeezed into the Ops & Comms room again and got the cups ready.

"Not for me Len, thanks. Don't want to wet my bed," I joked. LT grinned. Len passed a cup to LT and then resumed his seat in the doorway.

"Today …," LT faltered, choosing his words, "I saw some shit. I … I always knew it might happen … I've heard stuff from other guys …but," he blew steam from the top of his mug. "We were lucky. I don't know what you heard from my guys."

"Not much," replied Len, "they got discipline. They know when not to talk."

"Right. It was their discipline that saved us today," LT stared down at the floor. Rorschach patterns in the plywood got his attention. "When that guy with the vest grabbed onto the M-RAP it could very easily have been the end for the crew. He came outta nowhere. But Dawson, in the next M-RAP, took care of business. He's gettin' a citation."

"For sure," Len made it sound like a foregone conclusion.

"Ya know, the bomber …he killed women and children," LT cradled his cup. "Little hands and feet on the ground …One guy crawled away to die. It looked like someone had pushed a broom full of blood across the tiles of the shop. A dead guy at the end of the trail."

Len and I both listened intently as LT gave us an account of his day at the office.

"The bomber's face was lifted off his skull by the blast. It was on a pomegranate stall down the street. The pile of bright red fruit was perfectly intact. Just as the shop keeper intended and then there's this …mask. Like something in a Dali gallery. Lying there, gawping at me. Like he was saying: 'look what you made me do!' How fuckin' bizarre is that?" LT's and Len's eyes locked. "And ya know, we weren't even supposed to be there. A tanker convoy'd got hit and our assigned route was blocked, so Intelligence gave us an alternative route," the silence that followed seemed to go on for too long but I had nothing meaningful to say.

Len and LT shared a long unblinking moment, the prelude to shared wisdom.

"LT, there ain't no logic to any of it. You were there. Decisions made by other people led you down that road. To that place. Bad decisions. Maybe good decisions were in short supply. People in a remote location using some Blue Force Tracker gizmo got ya in the shit. But the goddam BFT didn't get you outta the shit. And it didn't get your guys outta the shit. You did that. You took control. YOU!" Len's pointing finger was inches from LT. Len's ability to succinctly explain the actuality of events is second to none.

LT relaxed in his chair. "Hey, listen guys, don't take this personal but, I'm glad you weren't with us today."

"Shee-it, LT. You and me, both," Len wasn't in a hurry to get in a gunfight. "Hey, as Cape Girardeau County Sheriff, I've been shot too many times already."

The subject changed to books, then to the Spanish language then going home. Before long it was good night LT.

I leaned on Len's door pillar. "Were we lucky today, or what?"

"Dy-amm right bro. Could a been us in that M-RAP."

"Does it get a mention in the weekly report?"

Len reclined on his chair. "Hmm, I guess tag a line onto the usual, *no mission today*, statement. Can't tell 'em too much about something we don't know. That'd just be gossip. They got plenty o' that in Karrbul already. And they gotta military liaison guy for that sorta thing. You'll think a sump'n. Remember …" Len pointed towards the door: Six One Zero! "Hey," shouted Len over the partition, "what's the difference between intelligence and gossip?"

After a few seconds thought I came up with: "Intelligence is for men and gossip is for women?"

Len laughed. "Close bro. I was thinkin', there ain't none really 'cept intelligence can get ya killed."

It was that time again: bedside lights on, overhead lights off and Skype the family.

The next morning, the local day labourers arrived on FOB to litter-pick, carry materials from one place to another and have a free lunch, as usual. Today, their mood was palpable. Watching them from various viewpoints around the base it was obvious to me, they were not happy in their work. Groups of shifty looking men seemed to lurk conspiratorially in corners, or on their haunches under trees. Churlish chimps working on a mischievous plan that wasn't going to benefit me. Their dark eyes seemed more surly than usual. There was a lot of animated Pashtun chatter from one group. I couldn't understand a word of it but the hostile cadence was unmistakable. A Private First Class acted as escort. He didn't seem to have picked up on their demeanour. Maybe he just wasn't worried because he was the one holding the Remington semi-automatic shot gun with extended magazine tube and they were wearing pyjamas.

Sergeant First Class Mueller was at the J-DOC.

"Hey! Gary, BMTF. How's it goin'?" He waved me round to his side of the front desk, but remained seated as we shook hands.

"Sir. I'm a bit concerned about some of the day labourers."

"Oh yeah," he scoffed. "Me too. Always," then hit a key on his computer keyboard. "More concerned than use-yul? Why's that?" he said while following the cursor on his monitor.

"I'm not sure what it is. But …they just seem different." Even to me, it didn't sound convincing.

"OKa-ey! D'ya think that's maybe 'cause they're a different bunch to the other days?" Asked SFC.

"Hmm. No. I don't think it's that," this needed to sound compelling. "Sir, security is your business, I know that, but I've been watching these characters today and they are definitely in a mood for something and it's not cricket!" SFC looked away from his screen and directly at me. Describing my observations got his attention.

"OK. I'll have the K9 patrol their work areas and where they congregate for work breaks. And I'll double the escorts."

My conscience eased, but not my concern.

"I'm really sorry to trouble you with this. I can't explain it. It's just that I'm …" My foolishness required justification.

"Vigilant?" offered SFC. He smiled up at me from his seat.

"Yes, vigilant," I agreed and left his office.

166

The extra patrols didn't turn anything up. Perhaps it disrupted a plot. The additional escort with the semi-auto shotgun would have easily taken care of a dozen hostiles. Long enough for more force to neutralise any resistance.

A few days later, the hut was getting me down. A change in the weather had an effect on the hut's fabric. An unpleasant aroma exuded from the plywood causing Len some respiratory issues for which he used NiQuil when he was asleep and DayQuil when he was awake. It was too nice a day to sit in the artificial light of F8 so I took my laptop to the square gazebo over by the Morale, Welfare & Recreation centre. The picnic table made a good desk.

Fobbits are people who never go off FOB. They arrive, live, work, eat, sleep and depart without ever going outside the wire. I was becoming one of them. Soldiers and fellow Fobbits paid me no attention on their way to use the recreational facilities in the MWR. I'd been there about fifteen minutes working on a report when I looked around for somewhere to discard my chewing gum.

In common with all communal areas on military bases there was a 7.62 ammunition can on the wooden table. The matt-green canister was the designated smoking materials waste disposal unit. You can call it an ashtray. The former contents may have been as deadly as the discarded material it now contained. Opening the lid to flick my gum amongst the cigarette butts, I froze in surprise and disbelief. Not only did the ammo can contain the usual dimps and stogies, it also had three fragmentation grenades nestling in the sand. I gently allowed the hinged lid to rest on the table. The matt-green balls, about two inches in diameter, had a short stalk out the top and what looked like a wire retaining pin. There was nothing attached to them that suggested they were rigged to detonate but it wasn't my job to determine their condition.

My laptop clicked shut as my Nokia 1280 speed-dialled Len. It wouldn't connect. After several failed attempts I gave up and moved away from the table. With my back against a hut about four yards away no one could approach from behind while my eye remained focused on the ammo

167

tin. Pressing the holster lock made my Glock feel reassuring. Before I'd left F8, Len reminded me to break base protocol and chamber a round.

Redial got me: *lutfan, shu mhurray* blah, blah, blah … from the recorded female voice telling me, in Pashto, that the caller was unavailable.

The grenades had to stay in situ, moving them was not down to me. They might be safe, they might not. They could be part of a security operation: a trap set to catch people on the base intent on doing harm. Carrying them over to the J-DOC and dropping them on the front desk was out of the question. SFC Mueller would know what to do. My call connected. Different phone network.

A male voice boomed: "J-DOC."

"Good morning sir. My name is Gary Wilshaw of the BMTF. Is that SFC Mueller?"

"Yes sir. Hey, Gary, BMTF howzitgoin'," SFC Mueller responded cheerfully. It sounded like he was having a good day, so far.

"Sir. Sorry to trouble you but there's something you need to see."

"O-Kayee," he didn't sound too keen, like a civilian couldn't have anything of significance to show him.

"I can't talk about it on the phone. Could you come to the gazebo by the MWR. *Now!*" I resisted the urge to say: hurry up!

"Sure!" there was curiosity in his voice. He ended the call.

Two minutes later SFC Mueller strode around the corner, a few yards from me, his expression loaded with: this better be worth it. Our handshake, a professional courtesy not a gesture of friendship, was brief.

"Sergeant," I said, pointing towards the gazebo, "you need to look in that ammo tin." His suspicious frown said: explain. "I'd been here about fifteen minutes when I just happened to look in the box," we stepped over to the table. SFC Mueller peered into the ammo can.

"Awww. Shee-it!" he exclaimed.

"At this moment only you and I know about this," I said.

"Yeah and the perps," he was referring to the guys that put them there: the perpetrators.

"Hmm. Yeah! And them. I tried to call my mate but couldn't get through. I'll have to tell him for his own safety but that's as far as it'll go on our side," I assured Mueller. I'd had time to give this some thought. He didn't say no. "If I send a report to my HQ, all hell'll break loose and they may pull us out. I don't want that."

"Absolutely," SFC Mueller was on the ball. 'I'll deal with this on my end and keep BMTF out of it.' He closed the ammo tin. Tucking it under his arm, he was about to walk.

"Sir," I said, 'I think one of the local labourers was supposed to pick them up. You know; empty the ash can, retrieve them from the waste bag, stash them somewhere. Or, immediate use.'

"Hmm. Thought had crossed my mind too," he replied. "I'll check the CCTV."

"Do you think it's too late to mount an operation? Do some obs? Surveillance observations are another of my specialisms. Maybe, catch the culprits? It's something I've done before as a Customs investigator."

"In my opinion, as soon as you sat there, their operation was compromised. If you hadn't been wearing that,' he clocked my Glock, 'they may have gone to Plan B!" his chin dropped to give me his Evil Headmaster over the spectacles stare, implying: if you know what I mean.

"OK. Sergeant. I got it," I said.

He stepped closer. "Between you and me, I don't have the resources to mount an operation like that."

"I did wonder about the number of guys you have here," I said. "If I've worked that out I'm damn sure the enemy has.'

"Huh! Tell me about it!' He replied. As he walked away he turned towards me and winked. "Stay vigilant!"

I grabbed my kit. We went our separate ways.

Pressing "Len" on speed dial got me: *Lutfan, shu mhurray* blah, blah, blah ... Call cancelled.

"Hey Len!" I shouted swinging open the front door of F8. "Is that corrfee I can smell," my fake American accent didn't seem to be improving.

"Sure is," came the reply from the far end of the shed. Len was in the eight foot by six foot cubicle on the left. An A4 piece of paper stapled to the wooden door spelled out '**Ops &Comms'**.

"Wantsum?"

"Please," I replied.

A contractor's name, contact phone number and company was on each of the first four doors. During the day, they were usually out at work. It was obvious three of them were not at home because they were padlocked on the outside but the fourth guy never used a padlock. He reckoned, for him, it would serve no purpose as he had nothing of any value and the cost of the padlock wasn't worth it. He also reckoned a hasp and staple could be used to slow down your exit. He had a point.

The dimensions of most of the FOB Hughie accommodation were determined by the size of the materials available. The sheets of eight feet by four feet, three-quarter inch plywood made construction of a hut measuring thirty-two feet by twenty-four feet relatively simple. It could provide bunk rooms for up to twenty-four men. Our shed had ten rooms with eight by four plywood creating the dividing partitions. BMTF had six of the rooms. Right now it was just me and Len.

"Corrfee's in yer cup. Just need milk and sugar, bro!" Len went back to the homemade desk in his room and began working on a BMTF document. I got my coffee and knocked on Len's open door. We maintained the courtesy of door knocking despite living almost on top of each other.

"Come on in bro," said Len, pointing to a folding chair set between his desk and bed.

"Len," I said as he typed and listened, "I had a near miss earlier," Len looked up from his laptop.

"Huuuuh?" he said, in Missourian.

"I found a cache of grenades," my voice was almost a whisper.

"Holy shee-it!" Exclaimed Len. I fanned both my hands in a downward motion indicating, shhh! I explained how I couldn't get through to him on the phone and hadn't had my camera to photograph the incident.

"Hey-ell, I haven't had a call since yesterday. Ain't called out neither." He checked his phone. Dy-ammn ! No barrs, his signal strength indicator was blank. "Gee, buddy. Sorry 'bout that."

Don't worry about it. I sorted the problem. But comms are obviously an issue here. I know sometimes it suits us to be uncontactable but maybe we should think about Walkie-talkies for non-secure stuff around the base. Anyway, I met SFC Mueller and discussed security issues.'

"Hey, Key Leader Engagement. Noted."

"Yes, KLE. He's on the case. Also, I think we need to be extra vigilant from now on. Ramp-up our situational awareness."

"Damn right, bro!" Agreed Len. "We need to secure the doors at night. We're not supposed to in case there's a fire, but hey-ell! This is serious shit brother."

"Yes. I can't help thinking about what Chris Doreley said once. Do you remember?" Len watched my expression change, recalling Doreley's remarks. "He talked about lying awake waiting for the bump, bump, bump of the grenade bouncing down the corridor in the middle of the night," I said.

"Yeah, I remember that. That's just Doreley. That's the way his mind works," said Len, reassuringly. "He's fucked up!"

"True. But he happens to be right," I sipped coffee.

"They ain't gonna like this in Karrbul that's fur shure," Len was thinking about the Significant Incident Report, the SIR, he would have to send to program management.

"Don't tell them," I said bluntly.

"Don't tell 'em?" Len didn't sound too sure.

"Len, tell them about this and they'll have us out of here tomorrow. Probably move us to FOB Finley Shields or Fenty, which to me is an even bigger risk. Or, worse."

Len anticipated my thoughts. "Worse bein' move back to Karrbul, right?"

"Yep. That's what I'm thinking," I sipped coffee and awaited Len's thoughts.

"This stays between us, bro," Len insisted.

"I've already told SFC Mueller that this will go no further than you and me and him. How he deals with it on his side, I neither know nor care," I said.

"He'll just put 'em back into stores. He's gotta be real careful how he handles it 'cause he's either gotta discipline some soldier for negligence or there's a security breach," Len thought hard about the implications. "But yer right bro, we gotta keep this to ourselves."

"We can't even mention this to the DynCor guys." The DynCor guys lived across the alley in another shed. We got on very well with them. "I feel bad about that. I really want to tell them, but if they reveal the source of the information through their chain of command and our HQ hears about it, they'll want to know why we didn't make a similar report."

"Shee-it, man! You've really thought this through already," Len tutted as he considered the dilemma. "If this finds its way upstream on a military security briefing or Intell report, so be it. SFC won't mention BMTF because that would be embarrassing for him as base security officer. If he even mentions it, it'll be down to a routine patrol." Len's logic was on target. "If this comes downstream from BMTF HQ, we know Mueller reported it and if they ship us out as a result of it, so what, it was gonna happen anyway," Len sipped coffee. "Here's the thing, our military liaison or intelligence guys are gonna have to pick this up before there's any action taken," he grinned. "It ain't happnin bro!"

Len was right, there was so much intelligence in the system that this would get missed. Even if the intelligence section knew about FOB Hughie they probably wouldn't know BMTF had advisors on station. Len and I understood each other very well. We both knew that we were here for the same reason. Money.

"So, we're agreed?" I said.

"Yup," said Len, "We do nothing! Situation normal, except ..." Len pointed at the rear entrance. "We gotta fix that goddamn door," gesturing towards the front entrance: "Don't see as there's much to be done with that one without alerting the other guys."

"We could put a curtain up across the corridor at night. In line with our office and the spare room," I said. "It won't stop a grenade going bang but it will slow it down. Maybe make it bounce back the way it came. Might stop it getting to our rooms. OK, there's gonna be shrapnel but it'll be coming from maybe eighteen feet and not two feet away. The bits are spread out more."

"Jeez-uss!" exclaimed Len, "Doreley was right. You really are an evil genius."

"I'm not proud of that idea Len. The guys near the front of the hut might die. But this is a good assignment and the risks are high everywhere. I feel we've got this place pretty well worked out. It's just a matter of surviving it."

"You've definitely got it worked out, bro!" said Len. "I reckon you do what you think's right."

"So, what yer sayin' Len? Carry on?" We both laughed.

"Carry orn old chep!" shouted Len in his best British accent.

Black Bayonet - April 2012

It was hot. I struggled with the intensity of the Afghan midday sun which is why I tried to stay out of it as much as possible. So did the locals. Generations of Pashtuns had squatted in the shade watching Farangay come and go. My boonie hat and shemagh must've saved me from first-degree burns on many occasions. Forget about Mad Dogs and Englishmen, when I moved, it was from shade to shade using the shadows of buildings, trees and vehicles to give me cover from direct sun.

Swinging open the heavy wooden door of Hut F8, I hopped over the raised step. The cool air-conditioned interior welcomed me. My perspiration-drenched Blackhawk shirt resisted removal until I'd wrestled it inside-out. Hanging it near the AC unit to dry, salt-defined tide marks on the rip-stop fabric emerged from the ebbing sweat. Dark wet stains on my tactical T-shirt faded to desert-tan as it dried on me.

Len was shouting into his Nokia 1280 so that the new US Customs and Border Protection representative could hear him. Franco was based on the US Embassy compound, seventy-four miles away. Had Len stood on the doorstep facing west, the CBP guy could probably have heard him better - without the phone. Len acknowledged my presence, then turned his voice down to loud.

"It's in the goddam weekly report!" Len emphasised. "It was in last week's. It was in the week before. It'll probably be in next week's."

From the Ops & Comms room I took two bottles of chilled water from the fridge. The sign stuck on the fridge said: **Take One Out. Put One In.** A reminder to replenish the stock. An empty fridge is an inefficient fridge: keep it full. I followed the SOP, then knocked on Len's open door. He waved me to a seat. I put one of the bottles on his desk. Len's thumbs-up said: thanks. I cracked open my bottle and sucked down half the contents instantly.

"Franco," said Len, "when was the last time you went off-base?" There was a muffled response. "And I'm not talkin' 'bout trips to the Embassy shop for yure booze!" Len shook his bottle at me. I opened it and passed it back. He sipped an inch. "Well, I guess I don't need to know what CBP are s'posed to be doin' here. Ya got no budgets to manage. Ya got no personnel reportin' responsibilities. Initiatives come down from the Embassy to our program management and that can be done by email." A voice on the other end of the call was unintelligible but angry. "We go out when we can. We depend on the military for transport and security. Eric must've briefed you on all this before he moved," Len sipped water. "No. We don't. You have been misinformed. Yussee, I know you got an armoured vehicle for gittin' around on the Embassy compound over there, but we don't. ... "The photos? Same way we get all the other information for the weekly report: Remote Monitoring." It wasn't Franco's first encounter with remote monitoring, it was mentioned in the reports. "Remote Monitoring?" said Len. "It's the same thing you do with us, except we give the LA specific instructions on what questions to ask and the photos required to back it up." The LA was BMTF Language Assistant, Mustafa, not to be confused with Mustapha the US Army interpreter who lived in the hut next door to the DynCor guys. The connection went quiet. "He's garn!' Said Len, 'I think the signal just dropped or he hung up on me. He'll think I hung up on him. Who gives a shee-it!"

"What's going on?" I knew it was the Kabul office giving Len a hard time, again.

"Well, the problem is ...," Len was interrupted by the phone. He held up his right index finger. "One moment!" then pressed the green icon, "Franco!" Len sounded polite. "I didn't, ... no, I did not." Hostility from the other end was tangible. "I don't care what *you* think," Len looked at me and rolled his eyes disdainfully. "It happens here all the time. Git used to it... No, that was not insubordination. That was a statement of fact. And anyway, how can I be insubordinate to someone who's not in my chain o' command? I could be goddam rude. Ya wantsum?" There was a brief lull in the noise coming from Kabul. "Ya had to think about that one din't ya?" Len laughed down the phone. "The M-RAPs have signal jammers. Ya know? ...To stop these bastards detonating IEDs. They're supposed to turn 'em off when they come on base but sometimes they forgit. ... 'course if you'd taken the trouble to come here you'd know all about that... Listen, the last time we went to the ICD we stumbled over an old Soviet munitions dump buried, under our feet! And ... Yes you were... Because it was in the weekly report, with full-colour photos! ... It was when they were preparing the ground for the imported cars compound. The one we recommended so that the Customs Director could manage the latest policy that came down from the Ministry of Finance... When I say we, I mean us here, Gary, Chris and I... We got the Mil to supply T-Walls for the checkpoint and the Customs office... Noo, it was *our* initiative because we identified an issue we could resolve... No, it was not a CBP initiative because your predecessor had no input into it... Hey, I'm tellin' ya man, I don't care how it looked in the CBP-DHS report you read in DC. We all know you just copy and paste stuff from our reports and claim it as all yure own work," Len took a deep breath, then exhaled: exasperation. "We couldn't go for two weeks because the local ground-works guy kept dredging up artillery shells with his excavator, ... Hello! ... Hello! ... Hello! ... He's garn agin! I don't think he got half o' that!"

Len plugged his phone into the charger. "He thinks we self-drive to the ICD and wants to know why we ain't doin' it. I told him, even if we could self-drive, the military wouldn't let us because it creates security problems for them. They don't wanna have to finish fights that contractors start. Hell, they got enough of their own fights," Len drank from his bottle. "I don't know why we bother writin' the weekly report, No one reads it," Len shifted in his chair. I shrugged an acknowledgement. Len continued: "If they'd read 'em, they wouldn't call me asking dumbass questions about stuff that was in 'em!" For Len, the obtuseness of public sector employees was a constant source of irritation.

"Maybe he has difficulty reading. Dyslexic?" I suggested.

"You may have sump'n there bro. He claims to be from Laredo," Len smirked. "Might have sump'n to ta do with it. Maybe he's really from Nuevo Laredo!"

The significance of Nuevo Laredo was lost on me at that time. I didn't know it was in Mexico.

"Laredo?' I affected a puzzled expression, 'as in the Sound of Music?"

Len turned from his laptop to face me. "Huuh?"

"Julie Andrews sang a song about it. Remember? Something about the distance to the place," I could see Len didn't have a clue what I was talking about which was, of course, my intention. Confusing each other with random thoughts and words was part of our daily routine. Len frowned and shook his head.

"You know ...So Far, Lar Ray Doh!" I grinned. Len glanced up momentarily, shook his head and continued to peck away at his keyboard. "I did wonder what a group of Alpine singers had to do with a Wild West Texan town," I said reflecting on a distant memory of the Rogers and Hammerstein film.

"Texas ain't Wild West, never has been. Deep South, now your talkin'." said Len. The pecking didn't stop. "And Laredo is in the East,"

"What? A Wild West town in the East of the Deep South?"

"How many more times? It ain't Wild West. But it is the largest inland port in the US. One of the main border crossing points for Wets. You know what a Wet is, right?"

"Yes, it's a person who has circumvented the US border controls by swimming across the Rio Grande."

"Circumvented? Yeah, that's one way o' puttin' it. Few months back they found the son of a Wet workin' in the US Border Patrol. Can you believe that? Guy shouldn't have been in the goddam country. It's fucked up bro," said Len.

"Nothing to do with the Von Trapp family's life in America after escaping Nazi persecution?"

"What?" Len looked up but he stayed hunched over the keyboard.

"The Von Trapps, ... went to Lar Ray Doh ...right? That's where they lived when they moved to America in 1939?" I awaited Len's response.

"Von Trapps? What the fuck are you talkin' about?" Len was puzzled. Mission accomplished. I just grinned. Len shook his head as an extended middle finger gestured for me to depart. "Uhhh, jeeez! Get outa here!" Len's hunched back looked painful. I went to my room. Through the plywood, Len chuckled: "Von Trapps in Laredo! That's some crazy shee-ite!"

I began to sing in my best Homer Simpson voice: "Doh! - a deer, a female deer. Ray a drop of golden sun," then stopped. "Will you call him?" I shouted over the partition.

From the tone of his voice it was apparent Len was becoming irritated, "What? Who?"

Distracting Len was one of my pastimes. "Franco …will you call him?" I repeated.

"Hey-ell no! I don't wanna talk to the guy. He's a jerk!" Len's computer mouse scraped a sound from the rough surface of his desk. I guessed he'd opened a new window on the screen. "If he's got anythin' important to say he can call me. Hey, ya know what? Even if he flies down here tomorrow from Karrbul, he'll still have to get over from JAF. Remember the difficulty we had?"

Len sounded amused now, but he hadn't been at the time. The oppressive heat, sweat, exasperation, frustration and exhaustion during the five hours waiting at Jalalabad Airfield to get to the rendezvous with the bloke that was supposed to meet us. As the crow flies, it was just two miles to FOB Hughie, but we had no ground transportation and the CBP guy that was supposed to meet us, not Franco, had been at the wrong landing strip.

Len continued with the scenario: "What's that, four, maybe five miles away by road? That'd take him, what? Maybe two hours with all the checkpoints?" Len said. "'cept, it's too damn dangerous and the Mil ain't gonna put a convoy together just to get him across the road," Len laughed out loud. "Hey! I got a joke: why'd the CBP guy cross the Jalar-labad Road?" he paused, giving me time to think of a punch-line.

"I give up," I replied, "why did the CBP guy cross the J'bad Road?"

"Because he's a jerk-off!" we both laughed briefly. It wasn't funny, but it was true.

"It's five minutes by Molson," I added, referring to the helicopter shuttle service that continually hopped between FOB Fenty and FOB Finley Shields, all day, every day.

"Exactly!" said Len, "five minutes in a Huey and we can pick him up at Finley Shields flight-line in that piece o' shit they gave us for transport," Len was referring to an old Toyota Prado stood at the end of the alley.

178

It was rumoured to have belonged to legendary US company, Blackwater. I had no way, nor need, to confirm that but what I did know for sure was that the Vehicle Identification Number, the VIN plate, on the engine-space bulkhead was not original. It had a badly riveted alloy 'dog-tag' style plate with a serial number that vaguely resembled a Toyota Corolla VIN. My guess was it had probably been stolen from across the border although I did wonder who in their right mind would steal a car from Pakistan. There were a number of things tricky about the vehicle and I'm not referring to just the electrics and the right-hand drive.

The pages of Flashman got splayed open on my bed before I stood in Len's doorway. "Do you think they might recall you to Kabul?" I was gradually beginning to understand the relationship between the US Department of Homeland Security, of which CBP is an agency and the private sector company that got the contract to provide services to the Afghan government: fractious.

Len's chair made metallic stretching noises as he leaned back. "Is Franco yure boss? 'cause he sure as hell ain't mine." Pulling the cap free from a bottle of water sent some on to the floor to dry. The 'Tear Here >' strip on a sachet of powder came away easily, sugary crystals billowed down through the water turning bright orange as he shook the mix.

"No. French is my boss," I said after a few seconds.

"Right-on bro, French is my boss too. That's what these CBP guys just don't git. They think they're runnin' the show and the fact is, they ain't," Len swigged his drink. "CBP don't pay me. FedCor pay me."

I completed the corporate mission statement: "And FedCor is a subcontractor for CACI who got the US Department of Defense contract to provide training and advice to Afghan ministries of interior and finance on matters of customs and border management." That was straight out of my contract of employment. It did seem a complicated way of doing things but someone, somewhere, must have done the sums on this.

"That's right, bro. But not only that, ground truth is: this is still officially a war-zone. The CBP guys can't do what we can do because they're not officially allowed out in some places," Len reclined on his chair enjoying his drink. "Jee-zuss! Not even we can do what we can do,

179

because the military's too damn busy *not* achievin' their own goddam objectives!" We both laughed. "That's why we, BMTF J'bad, developed Remote Monitoring with the LA! Course, it helped you bringing him that brand new laptop from the UK. He got quite emotional about that. He's a good kid and he'll do anything we ask of him, but I won't abuse his good nature."

During a conversation at the ICD one day, Mustafa had mentioned that his old laptop was crumbling and it would affect the wedding dress business he fronted for his wife. I'd kept the promise to myself that I'd help him.

"Yeah, well. You know what I say at times like this?" I said. I gave Len a couple of seconds to think about it. In concert we shouted: "Six One Zero!"

"Sheee-yit! Bro," laughed Len.

Six hundred and ten US dollars: the daily rate for the job.

We monitored all intelligence bulletins that came our way for two weeks. Emails received each morning from project management flagged-up which routes to avoid when driving in Kabul. They either didn't have any intel relevant to J'bad or they just assumed we knew that every route was dangerous. Taliban activity was steady just about everywhere albeit in a reduced capacity. The non-Taliban affiliated violent gangs carried on their criminal business as usual.

Military and para-military organisations rely on spies. Friend and foe exploit information and misinformation to achieve objectives for their cause. The deployment of spies can be traced back two and a half thousand years to an Ancient Chinese general and philosopher by the name of Sun Tzu. He wrote The Art of War. The original text is the military equivalent of the Ten Commandments. Sadly, it has been corrupted by analysis, adaptation, revision and plagiarism into the equivalent of an old and new testament of conflict. And there's the irony, just like the Good Books that allegedly have all the answers, despite studying the Art of War, modern Generals make the same old mistakes, because their political masters compel them to do so.

The contemporaries of old-school spies are referred to as human intelligence sources. HUMINT is one of several acronymic descriptors. In Afghanistan, as in many war zones, HUMINT provide information about the movement of enemy operatives and materiel. Suspect movement reports form the basis of a system that tries to create a sense of security, keep people safe, including the local population. Each agency produces its own intelligence so there's a lot of duplication. Spies always try to sell their goods to as many customers as possible, that's capitalism, right? Some spies supply intelligence for idealistic reasons but we can forget about them for now. The British Embassy in Kabul also sent me Intelligence bulletins saying pretty much the same as all the other sources. There was a lot of open-source material around but it rarely applied to our area of operation. Even now, it amuses me to think that open-source intelligence is really nothing more than what a person, or group of persons, has gleaned from, amongst other things; newspapers, magazines, Al Jazhera, CNN and BBC World Service. So, someone tucked away in a nice, safe office in Bagram, Kabul, Langley or Lambeth has been busy plagiarising media reports and reproducing them as intelligence. Most of the stuff was worse than gossip and yet a lot of people relied on this data to make logistical decisions. There were other sources of intelligence but we couldn't get access to those because we didn't have the Secret Internet Protocol Router Network, abbreviated to SIPR, phonetically, Sipper. Not being able to get Sipper email was a bonus. My three work related email accounts were already difficult to check because of the poor internet service.

The good news was, there had been no mention of grenades at FOB Hughie and SFC Mueller had said no more about it to me. That was reassuring because it meant that we would be staying at J'bad for a few more months. Chris Doreley was due to return from leave the next day. Len and I would meet Chris at Finley Shields flight-line.

"What time's Chris getting in?" I said towards the wooden wall of my room.

"Should be here around fourteen-thirty. He's on the shuddle service that goes to Bagram, Mazar-e-Sharif and a cuppla other places first," said

Len. "We've been offered some new accommodation over on Finley Shields. It sounds priddy good. We can take a look at the place."

"Are you thinking, pick up Chris, view the new place and then dinner in the Finley Shields D-FAC?" it sounded like a plan to me.

"Kinda what I had in mind."

"Another full day of opportunities ahead of us," my fist jubilantly punched the air.

"Yep, sure is," replied Len. "Good job we don't have to cancel goin' some place."

"We can fill up that piece of crap vehicle while we're over at Finley. It's either got a leak somewhere or it's a guzzler," I said, stood in Len's doorway. "I put some of those pieces of hardboard from the pallets of bottled water underneath it. I'm hoping to see some drips on it tomorrow. It's impossible on the stones."

Catching drips on hardboard was my way to detect a leak. What to do if I determined the fault, was another matter. Even if we'd had a vehicle service arrangement on the base, the cost of repair would likely be more than the value of the vehicle. But, despite being thirsty and unreliable, it was a useful truck. I just hoped it wasn't the tank that leaked.

"I'm gonna need somethin' substantial to put in this week's weekly report. Think of anythin'?" said Len.

"Yes," I said decisively, "I talked with SFC Mueller about security procedures here on the base."

Len turned on his folding chair. "Go arn."

"I didn't mention the grenades, it didn't seem appropriate, but I did ask about what happens if there's an attack. It's time we had a Standard Operating Procedure."

"OK."

"I asked about having an exercise or safety drill so that if the balloon does go up, we know what to do. We've been here how long? And we have no SOP for an attack."

"Right bro," confirmed Len. "We've bin to several meetin's with the Mil but it's never been on the agenda," Len turned and scribbled a note on his legal pad. "When we get more advisors here we're gonna have ta brief 'em on security procedures." More advisors? Len was maintaining a positive mission focus. "D'ya need anythin' from me on this one or you OK to work on it?" Len asked.

"No problem, mate. I've got this one."

"Great. Give me a paragraph for the weekly. Somethin' along the lines of 'Key Leader Engagement, KLE, with Mil at J-DOC on security procedures SOP with a view to joint operation, blah blah, blah, BS, BS, BS,' you know what I need," Len closed his laptop.

I knew exactly what he needed. He needed me to be creative.

"Anyway," Len got up from his MacGyvered desk. "I'm off to the gym for an hour. Gotta keep ma self trim. Don't ya know!" he slapped his abdominal muscles then picked up his training shoes. "Later bro!" The shed door slammed shut as he skipped down the steps.

The next day, we went about our usual business around the base: wake up cuppa tea at zero six-hundred. Cuppa tea at zero six-fifteen. Cuppa coffee at zero six-thirty. Check emails zero six-hundred to zero seven-hundred. Ablutions at zero seven-hundred, breakfast by zero eight-hundred. Back to F8: check emails, phone Mustafa, our Language Assistant, to make sure he was still alive. Mustafa was fine. He was hanging around the ICD drinking chai with his pals. He was on the payroll so it didn't matter to him if we were stuck on the base and he had nothing to do.

Around ten-hundred I went over to see SFC Mueller at the J-DOC.

"Good morning sir," I said quietly. There were several people in the office talking on phones.

"Hey, BMTF. Gur mornin', let's step outside," SFC Mueller led the way. The morning sun was already intense so we stood in the shade of a eucalyptus tree. "I've done some work on the security op. The DynCor guys are included. There's a briefing tomorrow and we'll run it maybe Sunday."

"Sounds good," I said. "One of our guys is back from leave today so there'll be three of us Sunday and the two Dyncor lads. Should be productive."

"Yeah. Great! I'll email ya later today. There won't be a subject heading. Just time and place."

A Specialist swung on the inside of the J-DOC door as it opened outwards. Something was urgent. "Sergeant. Sir?"

"I gotcha!" SFC Meuller pointed at the young soldier, then gave me the thumbs-up sign. Contractors and military never salute, gestures of mutual respect are rare events but the grenades had changed our relationship. He leapt up the steps behind the Specialist and into his domain.

During my daily constitutional around the base perimeter: on the inside, it was apparent that one of the lookout posts on the wall was unmanned. There had been a soldier, possibly two, up there the day before. I recalled a Squad Automatic Weapon deployed at that position, but not now. The tower at the corner was manned with two vigilant soldiers so, although everything was how it was supposed to be, military resources were now spread even thinner. I shouted up to the soldiers.

"Good morning, gentlemen," they waved nonchalantly. "Can I join you up there for a few minutes?"

"Sure!" came the reply. It was half a dozen or so steps up into a rectangular confined space created by Hesco. A square wooden post wedged vertically supported the plywood roof sagging under the weight of a dozen or more sandbags. The horizontal opening about four metres long and half a metre high gave a good view over the fields towards the highway and some commercial premises about half a kilometre away. The SAW was at ease on sandbags with a field of fire from left to right for around half a mile. Open farmland with small spinach-like crops made me realise how vulnerable this place could be.

"Zat a Glock?" enquired the private excitedly.

"Yes sir. Glock 17," I replied.

"What d'ya think of the nine mil?" said the soldier on the right. I smiled. A highly trained killer asking me, an inexperienced Brit for my opinion on handguns. My entire knowledge of firearms could be written on the piece of pull-through wadding he used to clean his rifle.

"It's OK," I said. "But I find it a bit inconsistent," I paused to give the impression I was thinking about the question. "I mean, it doesn't inspire me with confidence."

"I know whatcha mean," said the soldier on my left. "I have a Ruger P345 at home. Forty-five. Damn thing good as shoots itself. Tried one o' them Glocks down the gun shop and, well, it ain't for me. Guess it's what you're used ta."

"For me, this takes a lot of effort to be consistent and that's not how it should be. It does its job but, well, you know." Both soldiers did indeed know what I was talking about, even though I didn't. The SAW soldier's attention was attracted by something, he turned the SAW a few degrees to the right.

"Did you ...?" his question was answered by a huge explosion in the distance over by the commercial buildings. Energy rippled through the ground towards us. Into the blue, punched an orange fist of incandescence rapidly smothered by dense black smoke. SAW soldier must have heard the initial detonation.

"SHIT!" we shouted in unison. SAW soldier charged his weapon while the other was on the radio to J-DOC. "Looks like a tanker'er somethin' got hit."

"Gentlemen!" I said excitedly. "Can I get a few quick photos? Then I'd better get out of your way."

"Sure thing man!"

I snapped away with my Sony digital camera until the smoke plume settled to a rolling boil of dark opacity.

"Thanks gentlemen!"

You're welcome and *later* Followed me down the ladder: American courtesy in a hostile environment.

"I'll bring you a CD of the photos."

Making my way through the motor pool, soldiers were forming up for a mission. Outside F8, Len was discussing the explosion with the two DynCor guys who lived opposite.

"Hey! Did the earth move for you too, bro? Hahahaha!" Len scratched his nuts.

"Feel it? I saw it!" I replied. "Got the pictures too."

"No way," Len shook his head.

"Yep! I was in the gun position on the wall when the thing went bang. Looks like a tanker got hit."

I headed into our hut to copy the images onto a CD. Len and the two Dyncor guys followed me in to F8. They looked at the photos over my shoulder.

"Shall I call Mustafa see if he's OK?" I suggested.

"Sure. We cain't do much for him. But go ahead."

Speed-dial connected me to Mustafa. We had an agreement that if it was not safe for him to speak English at his location he would say: Nor sa hal dee? Pashto: What's happening? His phone rang.

"Good morning Mr Gary! How are you sir?" Mustafa seemed happy.

"I am very well sir. How are you, how is your family?" I asked Mustafa.

"Everything is very fine today," he said reassuringly.

"We heard the explosion. Len and I were worried about you. Is everything OK?"

"Yes sir. Everything is fine."

"Did you see the explosion?"

"Yes sir. I was meeting with my friends at the time. We were drinking chai. It was very loud."

"Were you close to it?"

"Hahaha! Not too close! But I saw it. They are saying it was a motorcycle with magnetic bomb. They stuck it to the tanker."

"Oh. Very bad," I said emphatically.

"Very, very bad Mr Gary. Five people dead. Maybe twenty with skin burnt very bad." Mustafa sounded genuinely sad for the injured people.

"Mustafa, is it safe for you to go home?"

"Yes sir. It is safe to go home. But only if I get things my wife wants from the market. If I do not get those things for her, I will not be safe," we both laughed.

"OK Mustafa. Take very good care of yourself, sir. I will call you tomorrow. Sabah!"

"Sabah Mr Gary. Sabah!"

I related Mustafa's account to Len: "Sounds like the cost of fuel may have just gone up. I'll give you a few lines about it so you can email French now and also for the weekly report."

The plywood panel creaked as Len leaned on the door frame. I quickly produced a paragraph on a Word document and pasted the text on to an email for Len. He forwarded it to French.

"If we go lock-down now, Doreley could be stuck over on Fenty till this evening," said Len.

"Do you think Molson will stop the shuttle?" I asked. Molson helicopters were the only safe way to cross from FOB Fenty to our side of the road. If they cancelled some of the day's flights, Chris might be stuck over on the neighbouring base. He might even have to find a bunk somewhere in a tent.

"Well, it's that road they have to fly over," said Len. "OK, so it's down the road a piece from the attack but it's still the same road." We all knew the topography. Len's phone rang. "French! Hey. Howzit goin' boss? ... Yeah we're good. ... We couldn't get a mission today, kinda fortunate 'cause it was on our route. ... 'You betcha!" the call ended. "Guess what he said."

"'Be safe,' is the usual advice!"

"Roger that," laughed Len. His phone rang.

"Hey! Doreley. Where are you?... No shit! ... You're early. What went right? ... "No it's down the road towards the ICD. Tanker'r sumthin"... Yeah, we'll come getcha. ... When's yer shuddle? ... O-Kayyy! ... You ready for lunch? ... Call me as you take off ... See ya bro!" Len pressed the red icon. "Doreley's flight went the other way round the loop so he's two hours early. Said he saw the explosion as they approached. The pilot thought about taking the plane somewhere else. Anyway, he's here. We better get ready."

Our two DynCor pals bid farewell and went back to Hut F9.

Len and I stepped out of F8 in our gear: body armour with three M6 double-magazine pouches and two pistol mags. Medpak. Helmet. Rifle.

Walking down the alley towards the car, we met one of the army interpreters coming the other way. He'd just returned from a mission and looked impressive in camo-gear and body armour.

"Hey! Mr Len. Mr Gary! You guys goin' out?" Freddy worked with 3BSTB. In my opinion, he was the best interpreter they had.

"We're just goin' over to the flight-line to get Doreley," said Len. Freddy looked us up and down.

"You guys going to Finley Shields?" he smiled.

"Yeah, Freddy," said Len lugubriously.

"You guys expectin' trouble?" Freddy checked out our weapons and body armour. It was less than a mile to Finley Shields and inside what was considered to be a secure perimeter, so, we did appear to be a bit overdressed but the in-country SOP applied: body armour and weapons at all times off-base. FOB Hughie was our base and FOB Finley Shields was another base so travelling between the two was off-base. It also meant driving, always driving, through the Afghan National Army base. There was a prevailing risk of Green on Blue which meant, off-base, one in the chamber of each weapon.

"Always expect trouble Freddy. Always," Len remarked.

"Hey Freddy," I said, "You've seen what we have on the wall in our office?" It was a phrase from Catch-22 that seemed relevant to my current circumstances, printed on A4 paper and stapled to the plywood along with other useful reminders.

Freddy smiled. "Yeah man! The enemy is anyone that's gonna get you killed no matter which side he's on." He sounded more American every day. Freddy's right hand flicked a V for Victory gesture in our direction. "OK. See you guys later!" Freddy kept walking.

We kept walking.

Len's phone rang. "OK buddy. We're on our way!" Call ended. "He's just takin' off."

My knees hurt from kneeling on the rocks looking for leaks underneath the car. It was also reassuring to see that the local day labourers hadn't attached any IEDs. That business with the grenades made me double-cautious. With my SureFire flashlight the dark tell-tale stain could be seen on the cardboard between the front wheels. Fuel mixed with dirt and oil had dribbled down the engine block.

"Len. I've found the leak. I'll take a closer look when we get to Finley."

"OK bro," replied Len.

It was an early 90s J70 semi-long. With the seat right back on the rails it was just possible for me to get behind the steering wheel wearing body armour. My long-gun got tucked down the side of my seat, muzzle in the dust on the floor, butt within reach. The Prado started on the third key-turn. Len was ground-guide. That is, he had to walk in front of the car until we were clear of the accommodation area. Ground-guide is army rules and reminiscent of the early days of steam locomotives and cars in the UK when a bloke with a red flag had to walk in front of them. You still see it in some US DIY stores when they're moving stock around by fork-lift. In theory, it prevents people getting run over; apart from the ground-guide walking in front who would, of course, be the first one to cop it.

Pulling the gear-shift into Drive, got the machine rocking forward on its brakes like a team of dogs in front of a sledge. Len began to walk: two and a half miles an hour. Lifting my foot off the brake allowing it to move forward on tick-over. A small parade of shops made out of old shipping containers faced onto the alley on the way to the FOB Hughie ECP.

Behind plate glass doors, salvaged from a failed business in the city, machines stitched garments in the air conditioned comfort of a tailor's shop. There's no shortage of demand for glass and windows in Afghanistan.

Haji in the DVD shop busily exchanged fake discs for genuine dollars.

Rug Man reclined on a pile of product drinking chai with his associate. Two pairs of sandals were on the ground. Rug Man's left foot rubbed on the top carpet while his associate picked skin from between the toes of his own right foot. They both smiled and waved limply as we passed.

Len walked forty or so yards then made an anarchist's clenched fist gesture: the signal to stop. He got in the car slotting his rifle down the side of the front passenger seat, mirroring mine on the other side of the auto gear-shift.

"I still don't git how the hell you guys drive with the goddamn wheel on the wrong side of the vee-hickle," laughed Len as he squeezed through the door.

"Well, it's generally OK if you don't drive on the wrong side of the goddamn road!" I quipped. We'd said it before, many times, but it was always fun. "Doors locked?"

"Doors locked," confirmed Len. He sent a text message to the program manager in Kabul to let him know we were going off-base. Within seconds: *OK. Be safe.* Replied French.

"Then we may proceed," I said.

A few yards ahead there was a sharp left turn around the biggest eucalyptus tree ever seen. One of the soldiers on ECP duty appeared from behind the tree. He made the STOP gesture. Stepping on the brake, the Prado creaked and rocked on its suspension as it came to a stop. The soldier gestured to reverse shouting: CONVOY!

"What the fuck!" Len grumbled, then got out and ground-guided the Prado as I reversed.

We'd gone around twenty yards when Len gave the anarchist salute and got back in the Prado. A moment later a convoy of six army vehicles came past us on their way to the motor pool. It was noisy and the ground shook as M-RAPs, mine sweepers and some kind of excavator painted desert-tan went passed from left to right. Each vehicle had a soldier ground guide walking ahead of it as per the on-base SOP. It had a funereal air about it which I hoped was a misconception. The soldiers looked tired and hot. Diesel fumes from the convoy began to blue the air. We rolled up the windows: sweating was preferable to suffocation. The first two military vehicles passed by unimpeded but the third stopped directly in front of us. Len sighed, looked at his watch and cracked open the bottle of iced water he'd brought from the fridge. The bottle tucked inside my body armour, intended to keep me cool, had already begun to melt. The chilled water tasted good.

"Can you believe this shit? We've driven forty yards, reversed twenny yards and now we're stuck in traffic!" Len shook his head at the scene.

:FYF-TYB!" pronounced as two words, it sounded good to me. "Forty yards forward - twenty yards back. Should be the program motto."

"Ain't that the truth."

We couldn't see from our position but the first vehicle was probably in the motor pool. Each vehicle had to wait while the preceding vehicle had parked. The important thing about a motor pool is, getting the vehicles out in as short a time as possible. That is especially important for the Quick Response Force, the QRF. Time taken positioning the vehicles after use is time saved getting them out when it really counts.

I started to think about a BMTF SOP: vehicle use. Parking SOP: the last movement should enable the next movement to be forwards.

Len's phone rang. "Hey, Doreley. Yeah we're on our way but we're stuck in traffic... Well actually, we're tryin' ta get outta Hughie." Chris could be heard on the other end of the call. Len looked at his watch. "Man, we left F8 fifteen minutes ago. I'm tellin ya, it's chaos here. ... Just stay under cover, we'll be at the RV in one-five mikes," call ended.

"Fifteen minutes?" I said questioning Len's ETA. "That's a bit optimistic!"

'Yeah well, you know me bro," said Len forlornly, "the glass is always half full."

Wait.

"Oh, and also, do we tell Chris about the grenades?" I felt he should know but Len's judgement on disclosure would be final.

A deep breath preceded Len's decision: "He needs to know. He also needs to know that Karrbul don't need to know. He'll just laugh and say sump'n like, bump, bump, bump."

Wait.

Another five minutes and the last military vehicle cleared the ECP.

The soldier on guard duty waved us on. We followed the wall

towards the blue-arched exit that would have taken us out onto the highway, but then made the sharp right turn towards Finley Shields.

A randomly constructed collection of shacks and old buildings stood decaying along one side of the dusty track. The Prado's engine noise attracted attention from the occupants. Men and children emerged to watch. Some waved.

"People live in those shit-holes?" I said.

"Yup!" said Len. "Don't acknowledge ..."

My right hand returned the gesture of friendship.

Len shook his head. "Urh! Too late. They'll be wantin' baksheesh now."

We approached some open ground that had been a park or leisure area at some point in its past. Now, it was divided into small holdings and allotments growing different crops. As we passed the irrigation ditches defining the fields the stink from human sewage filled the car. A hose snaked away from behind a run-down building with peeling blue paint. The open mouth of the flexible pipe twitched and gagged occasionally as it coughed out some solids. Mostly it just discharged a murky thin grey soup that soaked into the ground amongst the crops.

"Hey Len, they're growing crops with recycled human waste!" I said smugly.

"Uh-huh!" his lips didn't move as his head turned to face front. "And we thought *we'd* discovered organic! Hey, I don't let shit distract me." His attention was on a small group of Afghan Army soldiers about a hundred meters away. Oakleys concealed his watchful eyes. Without giving the enemy sight of his weapon, Len's long gun came to rest in his lap. The M6 lurking just below the window line would easily find targets. "Don't look at 'em, but there's four guys about fifty metres at ten o'clock that I don't like the look of. If one of those guns comes up to bear on us, I'll shout, GO. There'll be plenty of broken glass flying around. Just keep your right foot down," said Len.

"I'm not looking, but I see them," there was no mistake, we were in range. Squatting in the shade of a T-Wall wearing sandals, AK-47s and murderous expressions, the Afghan National Army soldiers eyed us suspiciously.

Tethered goats grazing amongst dumped plastic and vegetable detritus were disturbed by a group of skinny unwashed children, the progeny of Afghan soldiers, running towards our car. They weren't wearing their brightly coloured Sunday-best clothing for our benefit. Perhaps their everyday rags were in the wash. Their hands were out in the hope of alms.

"Here ya go. Whaddid I tell ya?" Len's scorn was for what appeared to be the bunch of four or five year olds alongside us, but they were probably nearer eight. "Human shields. I'm OK with that. Keep 'em alongside for as long as you can."

Some smiled, most didn't. Last time I'd seen children like this they'd been passengers on a EuroLines bus many years ago, within days of Romania joining the European Union. The coach, crammed with Romanian peasants, had to be searched by Customs: that was my job.

The Balkan Route is an established smuggling network, its principal commodity being heroin.

Amongst their bundles of rags and jars of pickles were ancient photographs of ancestors, pieces of broken jewellery and religious icons: precious reminders of lives lived in poverty and persecution. A new wave of Roma gypsies had just arrived to work as agricultural labourers on British salad farms.

The Afghan children ran perilously close to our car. One them might fall under the wheels, but we were safer with them nearby. Stones stopped bouncing off the roof as we drove out of range. The AK-47s didn't move.

"Make a note. Did not return fire," I said.

"Liddle shits," said Len.

Two hundred more yards of gravel and we made a sharp left turn, stopping at the Afghan ECP: a chain hung limply across the track between a tree and a concrete block. The Afghan army guard in sandals dangled an AK-47 in his right hand while making a show of inspecting our ID cards through the windscreen. His comrade held on to a slice of water melon in his right hand while allowing the chain to fall in the dirt. As we drove over it, the guard's surly stare followed us. Several members of his unit sat around a shiny metal canister of chai, drinking tea in the shade. The blue-labelled bottles of drinking water from the FOB, strewn around them, empty. They viewed us with suspicion.

"Anyone'd think we're the enemy," said Len.

"Mate! To them, we are." I said. "The book I'm reading at the moment is called Flashman. It's fiction in the form of a false historical document. It's made up, but the author researched it well. The main character is a British Cavalry officer in Afghanistan during the late nineteenth century. There's a lot in common with our situation, especially the absurdity." We both waved and smiled at the guard and his comrades. One of the seated guys actually managed to raise a hand in acknowledgment, before sipping his chai. Steering the car at the regulation five miles per hour brought us to the US ECP. Our IDs were checked again and the barrier raised. "I'll pass the book on to you when I'm finished with it."

"Is that why I keep hearing you laughin' when you're in your bunk?"

"Yes," I said, grinning. "It's outrageous," my description of the main character ended as we turned right at the top of the hill.

"I'll get some fuel while we're here. Could be that lost tanker might have an impact on supplies," I said.

"Sure," Len continued to take in our surroundings: four meter high Hesco barriers to the left, motor pool to the right, gravelled track down hill to the helipad and diesel station.

At the filling station, our Prado came to rest on the butyl-rubber spill-mat preventing ground contamination. Someone in US Central Command, that's CENTCOM to just about everyone in the US military, must've written an environmental strategy as a joke: *Environmental Issues in a War Zone*, but then someone took it seriously.

"I doubt it would get published today," I said, resuming my Flashman review, "although Tarantino seems to get away with similar politically incorrectness."

Fuel Guy, in his fire-resistant hood and overalls, removed the cap and hand-cranked twenty-five litres into the tank. We stayed in the vehicle with

194

the engine off and windows closed as per the fuel station SOP, until I had to sign the chit. Fuel Guy returned my CAC before we drove slowly away.

It was another seventy-five yards down the gravel road to the flight line.

Chris sat in a wooden gazebo drinking orange coloured liquid from a bottle of water: "Guys! What kept ya?"

It had been over an hour since Chris had called us. It was a mile from F8 to the flight line. I could've walked there and back twice in the time it took us to drive but walking wasn't part of the SOP.

"Traffic," said Len in an exasperated tone. "Lunch?" offered Len generously.

"Sure," said Chris as he pushed his bags, body armour and rifle behind the rear seat and climbed in. The Prado crunched a hundred yards up the hill to the D-FAC with five minutes remaining to make a cheese and ham sandwich, scoop some salad into a paper bowl and chose a sachet of ranch sauce. The mug of Lipton's tea and biscuits went down well. Len and I briefed Chris about our activities while he'd been away. It didn't take long as we'd only been off-base once during his absence.

Chris laughed at the grenade incident. "What did I tell ya? Bump, bump, bump!" Len and I smiled at each other. "Dude. Ya shoulda kept 'em. They had some down at Torkham," Chris had spent some time at the Khyber Pass. The BMTF contingent at the border, a few miles and several hours away down the road but only thirty minutes by helicopter, had a small arsenal of salvaged materiel.

A Soviet era solid concrete building housed Finley Shields D-FAC. Designed to withstand bombs. It had been built into the contour of the hill which meant the D-FAC was mostly underground. It'd be a good place to be during a rocket or mortar attack. The D-FAC guys were wiping tables and arranging chairs. It was time to go.

Returning to the car, I said: "I just want to have a closer look at this leak while we're here."

"Sure thing, bro," said Len. "We'll just hang around and shoot the shit while you do all the work. How's that sound?" we all laughed.

It took me five minutes to get the bonnet open and fifteen minutes wiping away years of accumulated oily grime to find the split return-fuel pipe. My flashlight made it easier explaining the split fuel pipe problem to Len and Chris.

"You can see it glistening. The rubber's perished," the three of us peered into the engine compartment.

"Uhhuh," Len pushed his Oakleys up the bridge of his nose, "I think I'll call our logistics guy up at Karrbul, see what he has to say 'bout it."

"Well, I was about to say that I think I spotted a pile of engine bits over by the mechanical workshop on the way round here. They may have some old fuel pipe."

"OK. Sounds good," said Len. "But let's keep those guys up there informed of our issues or they're gonna keep thinkin' everythin's fine and dandy down here an' we got nuttin' ta do." Len poked a speed-dial number on his phone.

"Hey! Greg. Howzit goin'?" ... Greg Samms, Deputy Program Manager, was in charge of everything that moves: cars, flights, that sort of thing. "Yeah, ya know, still dodgin' 'em... Doreley? Yeah he's here. I'm lookin' at him now... Well I know he sent it," Len lied, "I'll git him to check.' Len muted the phone against his thigh as he spoke to Chris. "Message from French: he didn't get your text confirming arrival here."

Chris slapped his head: he'd forgotten but quickly pulled out his phone to send a message as three M-RAPs drove by.

"Probably the jammers," said Len, returning the phone to his ear. "We might lose this connection any moment, there's a convoy approachin'... Hey listen, we got a leakin' fuel pipe on our truck. Do we take it somewhere or d'ya wannus ta fix it? ... Uhhur... Uhhur!' Len glanced towards me. 'Yeah, Gary's gotta idea. ... Hey, Greg, that's why we're here ain't it? To do somebody else's jarb!" Len started to laugh. Greg had just agreed with him. "Greg! Greg! I can't hear ya!" Len looked at the phone screen. "Signal dropped," M-RAPs came into view from around a corner of HESCOs. "Jammers," said Len.

I brought the Prado to a halt by the vehicle workshop where a M-RAP and a Humvee were in various stages of disassembly. A wire cage on a pallet outside the garage overflowed with pieces of twisted metal, wheel hubs, bits of drive-shafts and scrap from numerous vehicular casualties.

Despite the shade and fans of the garage it was as hot inside as it was outside but it felt good to be out of the skin-peeling sun. A US army specialist standing in overalls busily contemplated a mechanical issue.

"Good afternoon sir!" I said. My hand was out but he showed me his filthy palms.

"Don't worry about that." I said. We shook hands.

"Good afternoon, sir. Wassup?"

"I need a length of rubber fuel pipe for our truck," the Prado was the only vehicle in view. "I wondered if you might have some in the scrap pile."

"Sure," he replied, "got rolls of it out back."

"No, no. Thanks for the offer but I thought I saw some in the junk over there." Chris was already by the cage on a pallet.

"Help yerself, but ya can have new if ya wannit."

"That's a good offer sir," I replied. "But I don't want you to waste your time on my problem and also, I don't want to double the value of the vehicle with your new fuel-hose," we both smiled.

"OK fella," he shouted over the noise of a Huey coming into land. "Help yerself," we shook hands.

Some of the metal junk on top of the pile was too hot to handle without gloves. The cross-head screwdriver on my Leatherman liberated some fuel pipe from its Jubilee clips.

"Dude," said Chris. "D'ya need 'nythin'?"

"Have a scout around in the other cages," I pointed to the two similar pallets a few yards away. "See if you can find any screws, nuts, bolts, Jubilee clips, brackets, lengths of wire. Anything really that may be of use to us in the hut. Especially anything that could be used as a hook and eye set-up to secure a door."

"Jubilee clips?" he hadn't heard of them before.

"Yes. Metal bands that tighten around a pipe when you turn a screw."

"Oh, ya mean worm screw pipe clamp?" said Chris.

"Like I said, Jubilee clip. Why use two words when four will do?" Verbosity is one of my pet hates.

"I'm gonna call you the Scrounger from now on," said Len. "Like that guy in The Great Escape, played by whatsiss name?"

"James Garner," I recalled the character was a likeable bloke. Maybe I'd found my nickname.

"That's the guy," said Len.

"Nooo!" shouted Chris. "Gary's the Evil Genius!"

An empty cardboard box, rescued from another skip, held our collection of bits and pieces. The Specialist looked briefly at my box on the ground but continued to direct one of his guys on a some mechanical issue.

"SIR!" I shouted as the engine roared. "Is it OK if I take these?" he waved at me shouting, "take it!" Then turned back to the job in hand.

Every base has several sheds or shelters in which pallets of bottled drinking water are stowed. We figured taking water from a bigger base meant the military wouldn't have to move it to FOB Hughie. The remaining space in the Prado got loaded with cases of water. Our potable water consumption was around six litres per man per day so that was twenty-one cases per week. It sounds a lot but that includes tea and coffee making as well as brushing teeth and drinking. Signs in the shower block shouted: **Water Not Potable**. Scores of bottles of water, part consumed by people cleaning their teeth, filled the garbage cans evenings and mornings: open the bottle, mouth rinse, discard. No thought for their wasteful action, nor for the cost of production and transportation. It seemed no one considered the risks taken by anonymous logistics guys in support of profligacy. We got sixty cases, that's about two-thirds of a pallet, or, 360 litres of water. Always best to have a reserve.

"We gonna check out this new place?" suggested Len.

"New place?" asked Chris.

"Yeah, we got offered a place of our own. Won't have to share it with other guys. Be great for when we get more advisors comin' in," Len was still thinking: glass half full. It's an admirable trait but in the contracting world, planning is often futile.

We drove another hundred yards and pulled up outside a shed similar in size to F8 but with a different internal configuration. Inside, created by plywood partitions, a large communal space for an office and sitting room gathered dust, along the back wall were six rooms. The only furniture was a desk made of two plywood eight by fours. It looked like it had been used for operational planning. Cable remnants, plastic water bottles part filled with the brown juice of chewed tobacco, a Stars & Stripes, were part of the detritus abandoned by previous residents. Len was excited about it. Chris and I didn't share Len's enthusiasm but for different reasons.

"What don't ya like about it?" asked Len.

"Well, my first thoughts are: we will have to move all our bunks and other bits of furniture over here, probably in the Prado. The internet modem will have to be moved and we can't do that. It's a job for the service provider who will have to come from Kabul and that will take at least a week. It's near the motor pool ..." I shouted over the noise of six M-RAPs manoeuvring a few yards away. "... so we can expect to be disturbed at all hours of the day and night. The Jammers will disrupt our phones more here than on Hughie. We're closer to the helicopter shuttle landing strip. So, more noise."

"Shee-it!" said Len. "Stop! You're beginnin' ta put me off the place."

"But, worst of all. I don't like the position. It's made conspicuous by the absence of other huts around it. It looks important."

"OK. And?" said Len.

"Well, if it looks important, it makes it a target."

Len's disposition changed as he considered the implications.

Chris smiled in my direction. "See whadda mean Len. The guy's an evil genius!" said Chris. He almost had me convinced.

"Finally," I came to my last point, "it's too close to the wall. Over the other side is the exit road to the highway. The main road to the border with Pakistan is less than two hundred yards away with nothing between the main gate and us." Turning through ninety degrees I said: "And, there's the perimeter wall which runs parallel with the highway." A quarter of a mile away, a line of trees paralleled the highway. "To me, that's a security risk."

"Well there's the Afghan army at the gate and they're always up and down the road here." Chris was referring to the road the other side of the wall, parallel with the new hut.

"Like I said, there'd be nothing between us and the enemy coming up the road."

"Yeah. OK bro," agreed Len. "I gotta say I did have my doubts about it. You just confirmed them for me. Also, I don't think I could stand the arguments with Franco and all the other idiots about why we got no innernet for weeks."

Chris made a good point: "Man! They want us to have Nipper, Sipper and CENTRIXS but there's no cabling here and this place is even further away from the hub than F8 where we already ain't gettin' it."

The Non-classified Internet Protocol Router Network is the US Department of Defense internet system. Acronymised to NIPR, phoneticised to Nipper. It's a relatively secure internet service for use by all DOD employees worldwide who don't require a secret network. The good thing is it's free. The bad thing is it's slow, content is very restricted and it's not wireless. It requires a cable connection between a DOD provided dedicated computer and the router and then up line to the server. Personal computers cannot be plugged into Nipper and Sipper and memory devices cannot be used in DOD PCs. The Army wouldn't run cables to F8 for Nipper and CENTRIXS and as for Sipper, the secret network for classified stuff, forget it. Also, we would be further away from the toilet and shower block. So far, toilet urgency hadn't been an issue but it's always best to be prepared.

"Len, if this hut was somewhere else, it'd be perfect but it's just too …" the appropriate adjective eluded me.

"Vulnerable," said Chris. We all agreed. We would stay at FOB Hughie.

Body armour on. Mount up. We were Oscar Mike. Back to Hughie over the flaccid chain, through the rain of stones, and the fetid faecal mist. We waited at the gate for a convoy to depart. Len ground-guided the Prado up to F8. As we unloaded the water, Freddy came out of the neighbouring shed blinking bleary-eyed into the sunlight.

"Hey. Mr Gary. Whass goin' on?"

"Just stocking up with water. Want some?"

"Sure, man," said Freddy. "How many can we have?"

"Ten cases do?"

"Sure thing, Mr Gary," said Freddy gratefully. "I'll get a coupla guys to form up."

Freddy went back into F6 and quickly reappeared with two of the other army interpreters. They formed a human chain and within seconds had thrown ten cases of water from one to the next and into their hut.

"Thanks, man!" Shouted Freddy. He went back inside. After parking the Prado at the end of the alley, I returned to F8. The rug guys were still picking their feet and eating nuts, tailors stitched and the DVD pirate's sales filled his treasure chest.

"Len, I'm gonna do half an hour on the bike. Dinner around seven?" I said getting into my shorts. Wash-kit and trainers went under my arm.

"Sure thing," replied Len.

Chris relaxed on his bunk. I went to the gym.

After dinner we set up the projector and watched Generation Kill. Chris had the full series on an external hard drive. The projector had been provided for use in the training sessions with the Afghan Border Police and Customs but the opportunity had never arisen and our need was currently greater than theirs.

"OK. Who's for a tincture?" I announced, pulling a bottle of Grant's Standfast whisky from the DeWalt tool bag. It was Thursday evening and Friday was our official day off. We could relax. But not too much and we definitely could not afford to have anyone else know we had alcoholic beverages on base. That was a severe offence. All US bases are dry, the severity of the offence compounded by it being in a Muslim country. We agreed the risk of detection was slight and worth it.

"Not for me man," replied Chris. "I don't, err … It don't agree with me," he didn't go into detail.

"I'll have a small one. Just to celebrate Doreley's return." said Len. Three D-FAC Cokes from our fridge: one each. Len and I drank about a quarter of the contents then topped it up with Grants.

"Well, cheers guys!" declared Len. "The end of another successful week," we touched Coke cans and watched two episodes.

The next day was Friday, that's Muslim-Sunday. BMTF didn't work because the interpreters got the day off to fulfil their religious obligations. It was our chance to catch up on domestics: do laundry, clean our rooms and communal spaces and mop floors. It's important to disrupt the routines of the local spiders and deny scorpions access to our kit. We occasionally had to go to meetings with the military despite it being our day off but it was difficult to argue a case for doing nothing on a Friday when that's what we'd done all week. No one could say we didn't have a consistent approach to our work.

"Dudes!" shouted Chris from his compartment. "You ain't gonna believe this."

"What?" shouted Len.

"I'm goin' back to Karrbul!" Chris sounded exasperated.

"Whaddafuck?" Len's chair scraped noisily on plywood as he stood up from his desk. "Do these idiots actually have a plan?"

"I'll assume that to be a rhetorical question," I shouted over the partition to Len.

Chris stood in his doorway. "I thought there was somthin' goin' arn before they sent me back here. There was a lotta scrubbin' out of names on the white board and stuff."

"It's messed up man," said Len. "They can't keep people in the program because there's no continuity in what we're doin'."

"What's continuity got to do with it?" I was momentarily distracted from reading Flashman.

"Well, some people like to think that they're actually achieving somethin'. That they're part of somethin' bigger than them. Sump'n that's gonna make a difference," explained Len.

"People *actually* think that?" I said, cynically

"I don't know,' said Len. "Just guessin', I know I ain't here for that."

"Len, no one comes to Afghanistan for their own benefit," I reminded him.

"I gotta flight tomorrow. I'd better pack," Chris started throwing things around his room.

Len's frustration came through in his voice. "I'm gonna call French and ask him what the plan is for this mission 'cause if we don't get more than two advisors we may as well pack up too."

I didn't like the sound of that. "Careful Len, we don't want them making meaningful decisions. We might find ourselves in a place where we have to do some work. I'm happy with the set-up here at J'bad. I feel in control of the risk, but I'm not complacent. I intend to spin it out for as long as possible." Flashman went down on my bed, pages splayed open at the battle of Gandamak.

Conversation was easier for me standing in the corridor: "Len, are you here to advise them on program management?"

"Hey-ell no!" shouted Len over the sound of Chris's packing.

"OK. So, we have to exploit their incompetence and not allow them to put us at risk for pointless box-ticking objectives. Agreed?"

Len adjusted the Glock on his belt. "Hmm! Ya got somethin' there, bro. That's even more so with CBP leading from behind." Len stroked the new beard he was cultivating. "They don't have the same risk awareness as us because the consequences of their actions don't affect them."

"True," I concurred, "as long as the report looks good and they can copy and paste stuff into their own reports, nothing else matters. In five years' time none of this BMTF stuff'll be relevant here. It'll look good on a résumé somewhere down the line but no one will be able to confirm or deny the veracity of the claim." Scepticism often gets the better of me, but right now my realism had the upper hand.

"Chris!" Len called over the partition.

"Yo!" Chris's reply didn't stop the sound of packing.

"You want me to get French to keep ya here buddy?"

"Sure. But from what I saw on the white-board, the decision's made," Chris stopped packing. His door creaked open as he stepped into the corridor. "It'd be good to do some advising and training but they don't seem to have any direction." Chris went into the Ops & Comms room and emerged with a cup of coffee.

"And that was before CBP muscled in on the program," said Len.

"They got huge gaps in the advisor deployment at current areas of operation and they're talking about extending to new locations," Chris blew steam off his drink. "If either of you go on leave it means the guy left on his own can't go out unless they change policy. That ain't happenin'."

"Shee-it!" exclaimed Len. "I ain't going out there without someone watchin' my six," Len stepped into the corridor. "Any o' that corrfee left?"

"I just put on another pot. Give it a cuppla minutes," said Chris.

"The military's good for transport and security but they got their own missions. I don't expect them to babysit me. We need six advisors here with two armoured Land Cruisers. Then we could self-drive. That's what Franco's always on about." Len rinsed has coffee cup with bottled water and emptied it out the back door of the shed.

"Len," I held out my hand to accept Len's mug, it went next to the kettle with mine, "call French but don't give him more questions than answers." The Ops & Comms doorframe creaked from the weight of my chin-ups. "If Chris wants to stay here, I'll go. I'm OK with that. You two lads go back a long way. It makes sense you should work together," the coffee maker gurgled on the fifth chin-up.

"Dude! It don't matter to me," said Chris reassuringly. "You get on well with the Customs director here and you and Len already got somethin' goin' arn. My specialisation is ECPs." Chris made his point well.

Pointing to the printed sign over the back door, I said: "What it comes down to is: Six One Zero!"

"Too right, Bro," exclaimed Len. "Six One Zero. Except in my case it's Five Nine Five with paid leave!"

"Good for you mate." I said, without a hint of jealousy. He damn well earned it.

Len called French and the conversation went the way we'd discussed. Len didn't mention the leave issue because, as the program manager was on over a quarter of a million dollars a year he'd probably already worked it out. Or, he was at least, *workin' on it*!

After breakfast on Saturday, Chris loaded his gear into the Prado. We allowed ninety minutes for the journey to Finley Shields. It was only a mile away but there was always an obstacle. On this occasion, the Prado wouldn't start. There was no time to look for the problem we needed a transport solution.

Hurry up.

SFC Mueller answered my call on the fourth tone. Explaining our predicament wouldn't cover it so, I begged: "Please could I borrow one of your Gators for about two hours?"

"Well, key's on the hook so it should be right outside. Come and get it," SFC Mueller ended the call.

"OK. I'll bring the Gator here. Back in ten minutes." Stench from the ablution block septic pump-out quickened my pace.

"Roger that," replied Len, leaning into the shade of a hut.

Chris pulled a Placker from his body armour and started working it around his teeth. "A little piece of heaven," he remarked working loose a fragment of pig flesh.

Len stood with his chin on his chest contemplating the situation.

"Uh-hur!" he grunted. Perspiration had already leaked through. my skin before I began my walk.

I knocked on the door of the J-DOC and entered without awaiting a response: "Good morning Sergeant."

"Hey! BMTF. Howzit goin'?" said SFC Mueller.

"Huh! Got one of our guys moving out to Kabul in about an hour and the car won't start. Gorilla boxes and bags, you name it," the key was on the hook.

"Take it," there was nothing to sign. "Is that the guy who arrived yesterday?" he said.

"Yes. Thanks Sergeant. I'll bring it straight back. Hopefully only be an hour," he looked at me as if wishing me good luck with that.

Clutching the dog-tagged key, my search for the Gator didn't take long. It was parked round the side of the J-DOC just as SFC Mueller had said. It started on the first key-turn and soon had me back at the Prado. Chris's boxes and bags were quickly stowed in the Gator's cargo space before he reclined across it with his rifle to discourage the Afghan junior snatch-squad from stealing his stuff. I drove while Len held his long-gun. We didn't experience stone-rain and the stink of shit had subsided but the flaccid-chain gang were still drinking chai. We gave them the courtesy of salute and they waved us on without checking our ID. Maybe today we weren't the enemy. You never really knew with those guys.

We arrived at the helipad just as one was leaving but it was no big deal as they were every fifteen minutes or so. We had time to drink a bottle of water before Chris's flight arrived. Earplugs in and eye protection, on. When rotor blades whip up grit and kick it in your face, no matter how tough you think you are, it hurts. Len and I carried Chris's boxes over to the Huey as he climbed aboard. We waved as the Huey lifted off the ground, hovered, turned and then moved away from us in a gradually ascending vector.

Len and I dropped our rifles and body armour off at F8 and drove the Gator back to the J-DOC.

Hanging the keys on the hook, I thanked SFC Mueller.

"Hey, BMTF. Is this the full team?" he asked.

"Sure is," confirmed Len, "we just lost one."

"You guys still OK for the security exercise tomorrow?" asked SFC Mueller.

"Sure thing, Sergeant," said Len.

"Formation ten hundred hours, J-DOC. Full gear," SFC Mueller insisted.

"Yes, sir!" we said simultaneously. A phone rang. SFC Mueller waved us goodbye.

Next morning as Len and I emerged blinking from F8 at zero nine-thirty in full gear, two DynCor lads were outside F9 in full gear. Both drank coffee, one smoked a cigarette.

"Ga mornin' guys," Len greeted Richy and Brad. Both grunted favourably.

"Hey Len. Gary." Richy, six feet four inches of living proof that smoking does not always stunt growth. He dropped his cigarette into a plastic bottle. It sank into the two inches of nasty looking brown water along with the other morning dimps. Draining his cup, he said: "You headin' up to J-DOC?"

"Uh-hurr,' said Len. 'Comin'?"

"We ain't been invited to a military security exercise before," remarked Brad.

"Well ya got my pardner here to thank for that," said Len.

"Yeah?" Richy lit up another Marlboro. He seemed more comfortable when holding a cigarette. "How'd that happen?"

The grenades didn't get a mention but, the moody day labourers did and how in conversation with SFC Mueller the subject of base security had come up.

"Hey, yeah. I noticed that too," said Brad. "Din't think nothin' of it at the time. But, yeah ..." His remark tailed off as he realised it was a pretty dumb thing for a cop to say.

Richy drew on his cigarette. "There's definitely been more insurgent activity round these parts recently. The military's been busier," smoke drifted between his words.

The four of us walked up to the J-DOC. Some military guys were already hanging around with their comrades. We joined the assembly. SFC Mueller emerged from the J-DOC building followed by a Colonel. The soldiers formed up at sight of the Colonel but were quickly put at ease. SFC Mueller introduced Colonel Stafford who gave a brief speech about vigilance and efficiency and teamwork. He then handed over proceedings to SFC Mueller.

A lot was said in Mil-speak that meant nothing to me but Len seemed to get it which was good because he'd be writing the report. Then we got a mention: BMTF and Dyncor. An arm each went aloft although, being the only four non-Mil guys in the crowd, it was fairly obvious who we were. There were a few nods of recognition from some of 3BSTB guys. Big

SAW soldier, who on a different occasion had explained the difference between acronym and colloqialism, grinned over at me.

The gist of the briefing was that, in the event of attack, the alarm would sound accompanied by an announcement. Red Bayonet meant the enemy were attacking the perimeter of the base and that we should get our gear on and be ready for further orders. Black Bayonet meant the enemy had breached base security and were inside the base. If Black Bayonet was announced we, BMTF and Dyncor, should take up defensive positions at the four corners of the D-FAC to protect the front and rear doors. The civilian personnel, including interpreters, would already have made, or, be making their way to the safety of the D-FAC which was a mortar resistant hardened building. Civilians would be briefed later this same day about their actions in such an event. They would be told to leave all possessions. Carry nothing. Any civilian seen carrying a bag was to be considered a threat - possible IED. When we were in position at the D-FAC, further orders would be received directly from an officer with a rank of Lieutenant Colonel or above. Simple, straightforward, effective. We had a practice session without alarms. It went well. Job done. Dismissed. Back to F8.

"Len, why did Colonel Stafford order me to the rear of the D-FAC with Richy and you and Brad to the front. He knows we work together, why not keep it that way?" I said.

"Effective deployment of resources," said Len. "Think about it. We approached *him* about a security issue. So, we already have the mindset. We know what we're doing and what we may have to do. So, put one of us with one or more people who maybe don't have the same awareness or though processes. Makes sense, don't it?"

"Right. Like mentoring," I said.

"You got it. Mentoring. That's what we do."

Over the next few days Len passed several hours in heated discussions with the CBP representative who really had nothing of any value to say but insisted on saying it anyway. Monday and Tuesday my mission was fitting a new length of fuel pipe to the Prado and also fixing the starter problem. Turned out to be the High Tension terminal on the starter motor. Somehow the captive bolt in the starter motor body, the one to which the red cable is clamped, had worked loose which meant there was no connection to the battery. Using some of the washers and bits of wire scavenged from the garage on Fenty, got the terminal to stay in place. It's amazing what can be done with just a Leatherman, plastic cutlery and duct-tape. Seeing a project through from start to finish gave me a great feeling of achievement. The Afghan traders at the nearby shops enjoyed the entertainment. No doubt they would have done it differently but they did keep me supplied with chai. One of the tailors even sold me a T-shirt embroidered with a Death's-Head logo and **Taliban Hunting Club - Jalalabad** in Gothic type: *special price, sir!*

On the Wednesday we got a mission to the Customs depot with 3BSTB who were going there anyway. Len informed our program manager by phone and email. PM replied: *BE SAFE.*

After formation briefing we got in the third of the six M-RAPs. We rocked and bumped along the road to the main gate of the Afghan army base. Then stopped. The door of our M-RAP slowly clunked open. The radio operator up front pointed to me and Len and waved towards the open door.

"It's for you," he shouted over the engine noise. LT came alongside.

"Gentlemen. I'm sorry. We gotta new mission so we won't be going to the ICD," he shrugged an apology. "I'm gonna have to leave you here. I can't turn this convoy around just for you. Not that there's room to turn. Sorry!" We were at the blue arch of the main gate looking at the Jalalabad Road and already holding up traffic in and out of the base.

"No problem," shouted Len over the roar of the engines, "maybe another day."

"Sure," shouted LT. "Look forward to it!"

We shook hands before LT walked briskly back to his M-RAP. The door of our vehicle slowly dragged itself off the ground and slammed shut with a resounding clang. The engine revs increased as it inched slowly forward.

"SHIT!" I shouted, but my voice was overwhelmed by the noise from six M-RAP engines. My M6 followed the M-RAP. The loose end of my rifle strap had somehow got trapped in the door. I'd thought about cutting off the superfluous two feet of polypropylene webbing belt but was reluctant to spoil it. Too late to worry about appearances, getting dragged into Jalalabad was the immediate problem.

Instinctively swapping the rifle into my left hand while jogging alongside the M-RAP, my hand touched the Blackhawk folding knife at the corner of my pocket. It came out with my thumb on the blade's stud. The assisted-opening blade deployed. The M-RAP's speed increased over uneven ground as the strap became taught. My razor-sharp blade sliced through the webbing with ease leaving several inches of black polypropylene dangling from the door jamb.

I stopped running and started gasping. M240 turret gunner in M-RAP-four had seen it all. He knew I was a complete idiot, an overpaid, incompetent civilian contractor who didn't belong in a war-zone. But then, both his hands were giving me the thumbs-up gesture. He was impressed by my quick reaction. Leaning forward on to my knees, I gasped through my keffiyeh.

"What da fuck?" shouted Len through the noise and dust. He hadn't seen what happened.

"Don't ...ask me ...to do ... that again," that taste of blood from exertion was in my lungs. Sweat burst from my skin to flow down my back. It was between my buttocks in seconds. The weight of my body armour became suddenly oppressive.

"What the fuck happened?" shouted Len over the noise of receding M-RAPs.

"Strap... Snagged... In door," my keffiyeh stopped most of the airborne muck getting to my lungs. "I need to ... get this shit off ... and have ... a cuppa tea!" I said as my heart rate began to return to normal.

"She-it bro!" said Len. "Lose a two thousand dollar rifle and you are definitely going home."

Len and I shrugged at each other then trudged the mile to Hughie through the Afghan army camp. Never mind the SOP which required us to never walk through ANA compounds, forget about risk assessments, just avoid confrontation.

We arrived at F8 very hot and drenched in sweat. Len sent a text to French to let him know that the mission had been aborted and that we'd walked back to the base without incident. The predictable text-reply pinged a few seconds later: ROGER THAT. BE SAFE, he shouted.

Thursday evening was enjoyable thanks, once again, to Mr Grant's presence.

"This kinda reminds me of my time as a farm troop in Rhodesia," said Len.

"Farm troop? Rhodesia?" meant nothing to me.

"Yeah, that was my first contractor job. Security for South African farmers. It was a war-zone long after it wasn't if you git me," Len sipped Scotch through ice. "It'll be the same here, bro. It's too far gone to make a comeback from where it's headed. Too many people beyond compromised."

"Where's it headed?" I had a pretty good idea, but Ken might have a better one.

"One of the para-military groups here is gonna be left standing at some point. When has it ever been any different?"

"I can't think of an example."

"That's 'cause there ain't one," Len rattled almonds into his hand.

"So, what you're suggesting is that the US will be defeated."

"Not defeated. The US cannot be defeated. No one can occupy the USA. And there's that Second Amendment again, yup, good old James Madison. He should be on the ten dollar bill instead of that guy Hamilton."

"Why?"

"Because Madison was a president, Hamilton wasn't. He was a banker. You now what I think about bankers. Madison was on the five thousand dollar bill but they disappeared in the nineteen-sixties."

"Five thousand dollar bill? Nice."

"Yeah, but unusable, so, they got ditched. Even gangsters din't use 'em," Len opened a bag of Doritos - Extra Cheese.

"Gangsters didn't use five thousand dollar bills?"

"Yeah. Because they didn't want people to know they were gangsters," said Len.

"Makes sense."

"Politicians will eventually tire of this whole god damn war fiasco and walk away. That's when they'll need a good report writer. Wanna job? Hey yeah!" said Len, mid-Dorito.

"Hmm. I reckon I'm qualified by nationality for that job. The British have snatched defeat from the jaws of victory hundreds of times, but always make it read right."

"Add in some portraits of bloody conflict, you've got the full death and glory package," said Len.

"Len, I should Skype my lads," my laptop had developed the same fan motor sound as Pete's machine, dirt in the bearing, but not as bad. It settled down a few seconds after boot-up.

"Sure thing bro, get to it. Hey, don't be surprised if there's a Farm Troop set-up over here before long. International privatised warfare package. The whole deal, dee-struction to re-construction. Hey yeah, I kinda like that," said Len.

"A bit like the British East India Company," I said. "Did you know that at one point they had an armed force of two hundred and sixty-thousand? Twice the size of the regular military."

"Goddam Brits beat us to it," said. Len.

We laughed.

Friday: same as usual, not much activity. But it was the thirteenth, so we kept our heads down. Saturday was weekly reports and conference calls on an unreliable phone network and Skype via a very poor internet service.

Sunday, Len's birthday, we had nothing planned which was just as well because the Taliban had already decided to lay on something special that day. We'd had breakfast. Len was hunched over his laptop, playing solitaire. Stretched out on my bunk, Flashman was keeping me entertained as we working on the next mission plan for the ICD when the base alarm screamed at us from just outside the door of F8. It was the first time that siren had ever made a noise. Levitating off my bed and into my boots lost my page.

No Drill. No Drill, accompanied the cacophony. There had been no prelude to the attack. No advance notice. No show of force lined up on the hillside. No drums, explosions or gunfire. One moment we were at rest, the next moment we were in motion.

"Hear that Len. No drill!" my body armour dragged easily from under my bed just before the next announcement:

Red Bayonet ... Red Bayonet ... Red Bayonet.

The base was under attack by a credible force.

No Drill ... No Drill ... No Drill.

Then we heard the explosion. It wasn't big enough to shake the hut like the tanker a few days earlier and it was some way off, but still too close.

"Sheeee-it!" shouted Len. His chair scraped as he stood up. Dropping my body armour over my head, ceramic plates chilled me even through my shirt and T-shirt. Muzzle pointed at the floor, my Glock chambered a round. Holstered. My M6 racked a round.

Black Bayonet ...Black Bayonet ...Black Bayonet.

The enemy had broken through base perimeter security. There were now active shooters inside the base.

"Len. Hear that? It's Black Bayonet. They're on us! Shit! We gotta go mate!" I was out of my room and heading towards the back door.

Our SOP was use the rear exit because the front door opened into the main alleyway which would most likely be in direct line of fire from the ECP if it had been over-run. A suicide bomber at the main gate taking out the guards followed by several guys with AK-47s dispersing rapidly through a compound was the usual Taliban tactic.

"Holy shee-it! You're ready," shouted Len as he pulled his body armour tight. He grabbed his rifle, racked a round and we slipped out the back door. Making our way along the narrow alley at the rear of the huts, we reached the containerised Haji shops. Cautiously emerged from the alley, we could see the ECP was fully manned. The M-RAP stationed our side of the closed barrier had its fifty-calibre pointing towards the exit.

We walked quickly to the D-FAC. Freddy gave orders to some of the other interpreters. We were all heading in the same direction. Len and I picked up the pace. The Dyncor guys a few yards behind over my right shoulder were dressed in mixed attire. Brad was still in his shorts after returning from the gym. Richy's helmet was at a funny angle like it didn't really fit him. Maybe he'd picked up the wrong one.

Richy and I went to the double doors at the rear of the D-FAC as instructed, taking up positions behind a short T-wall at each corner. Len and Brad had similar positions at the D-FAC's main door. Around two hundred civilians were inside. From our position at the rear, we could see the plume of smoke drifting from left to right beyond the line of trees at the base perimeter. It came from the direction of the main perimeter wall over at Finley Shields, pretty close to where we'd got out of the M-RAP on the cancelled mission. A series of smaller explosions and sporadic gunfire confirmed the proximity of the action.

"That's AK-47," Richy reliably informed me. "Sounds close. Finley Shields," he lit a cigarette.

For the first hour we heard intermittent bursts of gunfire.

"M4 auto, .. AK-47," Richy's commentary continued. A long burst of rapid shots produced a different sound. "Could be M240! Must be the QRF," I was grateful for Richy's interpretation of the aural landscape. Two small helicopters flew over us on parallel vectors. "Kiowa OH-58," announced Richy. "US Army Recon helicopter. Made in Texas. My home state," he winked. His eyes became moist, it must have been smoke from the Marlboro hanging from his lip, then he smiled proudly.

"Is El Paso still in the Republic of Texas," I said.

"Sure is. Ask my wife. She's Mexican."

The enemy might pop-up in spaces between huts and vehicles at any moment. I was ready. Several loud bursts of machine gun fire punctuated the sounds of helicopters and other military hardware. This was a serious fight. The larger calibre weapons sounded closer.

"Kiowa fifty-cal," Richy grinned. The solid bam, bam, bam of the Kiowa's big gun was followed by the swooosh of a rocket motor, then an explosion. "Hydra 70, maybe," he lit another cigarette. "Someone's shit is gittin' seriously fucked up!"

It was afternoon. We'd been stood up for a couple of hours when Colonel Stafford approached us from my three o'clock. Striding down the lane between huts with his Major body-guard he was a man on a mission.

"You guys OK?" he demanded, handing us each a bottle of chilled water.

"Yes sir!" we replied in unison.

He briefed us: "The situation's under control, but it'll be a couple more hours before you can stand-down," we were OK with that. "You guys have civilian arming agreements right?" he asked as he looked at my M6.

"Yes, sir. I have it here," I began to open my ID pouch to pull out the document.

"That's OK I'll see it later," he replied. Major bodyguard smiled: *he don't care about no bit of paper!*

I stuffed it back into the pouch. "I am contractually obliged to carry these two weapons for personal protection. They cannot be used offensively. But if I'm stood here and I'm attacked I will defend myself."

Colonel Stafford turned briefly to Major bodyguard. I thought I saw a slight smile break from the corner of his mouth as he spoke. "Outstanding! Anythin' comes over that wall …" Colonel Stafford looked towards a line of trees behind the huts, just to the right of the guard tower … "Shoot it!"

That was sufficiently explicit. We acknowledged his orders. Colonel Stafford and Major bodyguard strode around the corner of the building.

The rapidly increasing engine-whine of a fast approaching Kiowa bounced around the T-Walls of our location. It passed quickly overhead and circled twice above Finley Shields. From our limited viewpoint it was impossible to say if it was a third helicopter or one of the two seen earlier. As it went out of view the distinct sound of a launched rocket was

215

followed by the gentle wumpf of obliteration. Richy looked over to me and winked.

Forty yards away directly opposite the rear of the D-FAC was a Hesco barrier which formed part of the FOB Hughie perimeter. On the other side the Hesco, young trees tall enough to create shade when the sun was low, also made you forget that the Afghan Army base was just beyond.

Sometimes the breeze moves things in mysterious ways but I couldn't equate the gentle sideways movement of the saplings with the still air around us.

Whispering to Richy: "See that?" My M6 was already up and pointing at the movement.

Richy moved to the other gap in the T-Walls, long gun up. Something moved through the trees. Coming at me. Breathing deep and even, keeping my gun aimed at the top of the Hesco, *wait*.

Seconds could have been minutes.

Hurry up.

Something needed to happen.

I saw it first: "It's a cat," the scrawny feline scratched its way on to the Hesco and sat in the middle of my sight picture.

"I see it," replied Richy.

"It might be a decoy. Shoved up there to attract our attention from somewhere else," my brain was in overthinking mode.

Richy put me at ease: "No way anyone could make that cat do anythin' it didn't have a mind ta do. If there was anyone the other side of that wall, the cat'd be gone."

He was right. The camp cats were fiercely independent. Cats aren't idealists. They don't take sides. Feral cats exploit humans to survive not for some higher ideal. The cat stood, turned to its left and moved slowly along the top of the Hesco until out of view behind the row of huts.

Guns down.

We'd been stood up for around four hours when the all-clear sounded. People emerged from huts and other safe places. The D-FAC cleared and the base slowly repopulated. Len, Richy, Brad and I returned to our huts. It would be dinner time in a couple of hours and the catering crew had been busy preparing a special evening meal whilst locked-down.

Back at F8, I extracted myself from the body armour and stripped-off my shirt and vest. It would have been drier and straight from the washing machine and smelled better. I hung everything up so the AC could extract the water before it went in the washing machine. Salt tidemarks began to creep across ripstop material.

Tip: never put sweaty wet kit into a laundry bag unless you particularly want a furry growth on your garments.

Len hunched over his laptop working on the After Action Report. I knocked on the inside of Len's open door as he sent the email to French.

"Oh, Len, I almost forgot."

"Huh?" Len looked at me with a tired expression.

"Happy Birthday!"

"Hahaha! Thanks bro!" Len smiled. "Ya know, the fireworks were a nice touch."

Len's phone pinged. SMS from French: *AAR received. Be safe.*
We both laughed.

Around five o'clock, I took my rope outside to do a few minutes skipping. At the end of the alley I could see dozens of soldiers in PT gear carrying small bags of belongings. Dozens more carried nothing. SFC Mueller talked with some of the lads in black shorts and grey Army T-shirts. Standing a discreet distance away so as not to impose on the somber gathering, I kept quiet until he turned towards me.

"Hey! Gary, how goes it?"

"Yeah, I'm fine. Are your guys OK?" some of them didn't look OK.

"Hmm. They're OK." Soldiers in gym kit stood shock-still. "These guys lost everything in the attack. Uniform, weapons, accommodation. Everything."

"Oh!" I said. I was surprised at the severity of the loss although it should've been obvious to me from the scale of the attack. "Well, erm, We could free-up some space in F8 if that would help. If we double-up and rearrange our office it would give three, maybe four rooms," SFC Mueller considered my offer.

"Thank you, sir," he replied.

"We have two bunks free so they'd need to find some more somewhere."

"Right," replied SFC Meuller. "I think we fixed it already but 'preciate the offer."

"OK," I said. "Better let you get on with stuff," we went our separate ways.

Entering F8, I called out: "Len."

"Huh?" he was hunched over his laptop.

"You should see the soldiers coming over from Finley Shields."

"Huh?"

"Because of the attack. Loads of 'em are moving over here. It must've been worse than we imagined."

"Sounds like it, bro," Len got up from his desk. "Anythin' we can do?"

"I just had a chat with SFC Meuller and ..."

Len interjected: "Key Leader Engagement - KLE!" he jotted it down on his legal pad.

"...yeah. Like I was sayin', just had a KLE with base security supremo. I offered him some of our rooms but accommodation's not an issue."

"OK. Good," said Len. I leaned on Len's door frame.

"D'ya get it? Accommodation's not an issue ..." I leaned forward for emphasis, "...because troop complement is depleted."

"Hmm, you got that right," he stroked his beard. It was coming along nicely. "Not sure how I'll report this up the line."

"You can't tell the full story," I said, bluntly. "If you, we, had secure email, you could mention troop numbers. But on Hotmail or YaHoo? No way. It's sensitive material. The enemy get enough military intelligence without us giving them more."

"Shee-it bro. You're damn right. Evil Genius," we both laughed. 'Guess we just gonna have to let HQ work it out through other channels.'

"Yes," I said. "What is it Franco keeps telling us? Stay in yure lane."

"Stay in yure lane! Yep. That's what we godda do," Len glanced up at the sign over the back door. "And what's the other important thing to remember?" I followed his gaze over to the sign above the door.

"Six One Zero," we both laughed.

The next day, at J-DOC, we were debriefed by SFC Mueller.

"Gentlemen, I recommend you stay clear of FOB Finley shields for two or three days unless you have real urgent business there. Check this out," he clicked a video file on his desktop. Mostly static CCTV video of the attack: a Toyota Corolla driving towards the outside of the perimeter wall. Five burka-clad people got out of the car. The car then rapidly accelerated into the wall where it immediately exploded. Five men ran through the gap, two of them still wearing burkas. They were all bulky and carrying AK-47s. Two had RPG launchers. They disappeared off camera.

"Got some stills here from a coupla hours afterwards," he clicked on another folder.

From the photos we could see the gap in the external perimeter wall where two large Hesco barriers had once been. The Hescos contained around eight tonnes of sand. The VBIED had distributed the contents at very high-speed over several hundred square metres. The Toyota Corolla and the steel mesh of the Hescos no longer existed but the engine block could be seen in the distance with a wheel still attached.

Photos catalogued the trail of destruction: three huts, previously accommodation for soldiers, were charred stumps and twisted steel as a result of Kiowa action because the attackers had been shooting from underneath them. A series of images showed a bloody shemagh next to a burka, discarded AK-47 magazines, a trampled copy of Stars & Stripes in the dirt, a mangled and charred M4 rifle.

One of the huts previously occupied by soldiers was a pile of charred rubble.

SFC Mueller described the scene: "Infra-red drone targeting identified an active shooter underneath. We don't put soldiers lives at risk to save a hut, blow the shid out of it and drop the burning remains on top of him. Job done."

"Hey!" shouted Len. "Is that …?" the images paused so Len could take a closer look at one of the photos. "Shee-it! It is!"

The significance of the image was just coming into focus for me as Len confirmed my theory about the accommodation on Finley Shields that we'd declined.

"Shee-it bro! You were right about that place!" It was the shed we'd viewed the day Chris returned to Hughie. There wasn't much left of it.

"Burka-boy detonated himself under there. Must've thought it was occupied," said SFC Mueller. He picked up on us glancing at each other: "Was that the place you got offered?"

"Sure was!" exclaimed Len, shaking his head in disbelief. SFC Mueller grinned.

"Looks like you guys dodged another one," SFC Mueller didn't mention the gazebo grenades when he looked at me.

The photo showed the hole in the floor caused by the suicide vest, the rest of the damage was from the subsequent fire. A few bits of charred plywood remained standing like blackened teeth in a gaping foul mouth.

"I would love to put those pictures in the weekly report but I know the reaction it'd get from management," said Len.

I suggested: "Pack yer shit?"

"Yup," said Len.

"That'd be a good thing right?" suggested SFC Mueller.

"Not really," replied Len.

"Ya mean ya'ctually like it here?" SFC Mueller was incredulous.

"Well, yer know, I've been in worse places, but the company's better here, Sarge," Len confessed. Other than his Farm Troop deployment, I knew nothing about Len's military experience so he must have meant Kabul. For me, there was no where worse. But, for Six One Zero, it was tolerable.

"Jeez! Whad is it with you contractors?" SFC Mueller pressed Escape on his keyboard.

"Well, it's a durdy jarb but someone's gotta do it," replied Len, heroically. We made our way back to F8.

SFC Mueller's words came back to me as the hut door swung shut behind us: "Whad is it with you contractors?"

Len laughed as we both shouted: "Six One Zero!"

Kabul Conference - April 2012

"OK guys," shouted George 'French' Beaumont, above the conference room hubbub, "...and gals," He made a point of acknowledging the two blonde female advisors on the team. Texan Lynn Jakeman and Billie-Lou Styles from one of the Southern states. The room became silent and the coffee cups still. "Welcome to our new base here at Camp Heath. I think you'll agree, the accommodation is an improvement on Camp ACCL." There were a few nods and grunts of agreement. "Thank y'all for joining us at this, the first, BMTF conference," French's Texan heritage could be heard in every syllable. "We gotta lot to get through over the next three days so I'm gonna step aside right now for the CBP Attaché Mr Joe Rosales." French turned to the guy on his left. The Customs and Border Protection head honcho stood to address the gathering. Spontaneous applause erupted from several of the delegates who'd been associates back in the US

"Thank you French," Joe Rosales, stood around six feet tall and the effects of too many working lunches were beginning to show. His speech was slow and clear. The gravelly voice resonated every particle of the room. His dark but greying moustache formed around his words as he spoke. Joe Rosales seemed to have a pleasant disposition, although some of the other guys wouldn't say so.

"Many of us here, already know each other from our time in the Border Patrol. For those of you that don't know me, you can call me JR or Boss, I'm OK with both." There was a ripple of mirth from some of his former colleagues. "I've been called many things in my time so either form of address are just fine by me." Smiling, he looked around at some of the unfamiliar faces. "For those of us not yet met, this is an opportunity for us to get to know each other and to that end I have arranged for a number of activities and presentations which will engage your collective talents for the duration of this conference."

JR enunciated clearly and softly with an elusive accent. The Hispanic influence in his voice was as discernible as Richard Burton's Welsh. He certainly looked impressive in his Department of Homeland Security Customs and Border Protection uniform.

"So, to get things started, we're each gonna give a one minute presentation to conference so that we have a brief idea of the resources that we can all draw on to achieve mission objectives." For emphasis he extended the index finger of his right hand. "When I say one minute I mean one minute. There are thirty-five advisors here today so this will take us up to our coffee break. Keep that in mind. Some of these guys don't like to be kept waitin' for their coffee." JR did have a sense of humour. I liked him already. He started the ball rolling.

"I am the DHS Attaché in Kabul with responsibility for the BMTF program but I am true Border Patrol," a whoop from the audience was quickly subdued by a wave of JR's hand. "I spent eight years in the field as a supervisor. Some of you will know me from El Paso and Brownsville. I've been stationed in Washington DC for the past four years where I've been very fortunate to have Diego LaPaz on my team," JR gestured to one of the lads down the table to his right. Diego raised his right arm vertically as if swearing an oath of allegiance. "I'm here for the long-run and together we will support Afghan-led initiatives to build sustainable institutions for GIRoA and the people of this country."

In the UK, a GIRO used to be the government's welfare benefits cheque paid to the needy. I couldn't help thinking that GIRO and GIRoA had a lot in common: the former is a government hand-out, the latter a government with its hand out.

A couple of JR's ardent supporters shouted 'Hooah!', which is the phonetic enunciation of the   military acronym HUA, that's: Heard, Understood and Acknowledged. I grinned till I realised they were serious, at which point I twisted my face into intensely committed.

My pal Len slowly turned his head, surveying the room. Under his breath he murmured: "Don't."

They could't possibly have appreciated the irony of the grunted hooah outburst. If they'd known it originated during one of the failed invasions of Afghanistan by the British Army in the nineteenth century, they may have tempered their enthusiasm.

Now, it was me: "My background is UK law enforcement. Principally Customs and Border Management where I was instrumental in

223

cross-border fraud strategy," my pal sat opposite, listening to my presentation. "I have considerable criminal investigation experience and like Mark, I spent some time in the Congo on a Customs modernisation project. I am the Director and Principal Consultant of a Customs consultancy in the UK. But most importantly, I'm currently deployed to Jalalabad where I have the pleasure of working with the talented Mr Len Kinder." My gesture to the fella sat to my right made Len shift uneasily in his chair, proving that the truth is often uncomfortable. Three more intros then, into the other room for coffee.

"Hey, Len," putting the squeeze on my Lipton's teabag didn't work. It had no more to give. "What's with the hoo ha?" My pronunciation made it sound more like the noun for a commotion than an acronym.

"Hey-ell summa these guys think they're Marine Corps. They ain't," said Len definitively. I should know cuz I was Master Drill Sergeant." he paused. "It's Hoo-Ah."

"Yes I know. Just kidding. Do you know the origin of the expression?"

"Heard, Understood and Acknowledged. Some say it comes from the Civil War but I reckon it goes back further'n that."

"Have you seen that picture hanging in the Camp Heath bar? It's a print of William Barnes Wollen's painting depicting the British retreat from Kabul in 1842. It's hung over the urinal in the washroom."

"Uh, huh," said Len.

"The bloke that put that there has a sense of humour," I said. "It's either an American reminder to the Brits of how the USA demolished their empire. Or, if one of the British blokes put it there, it's a warning to Yanks: it'll happen to you."

"Uh, huh. Sure thing bro. You and I just need to be out of here before it does," said Len. "How many people here d'ya think even give that a thought as they piss away their Man Love Thursday night booze?"

"Well, I expect we can discount the girls," I said.

"Most of 'em."

"I can't recall where I read it but, Hoo-Ah was used during the Afghan campaign."

224

"Yeah, I heard that too. We just gotta hope that this program ain't as fucked up as the Brits were back in the day," Len didn't sound too confident.

"Well, you've read Flashman," I said, "Afghanistan: Graveyard of empires."

"Ain't that a fact. Empire?" Len scoffed. "Wonder what the Founding Fathers would make of this shenanigans?" his head motioned disapprovingly around the room. "America was about giving all men the freedom to be themselves. Guys like Washington, Paine and Rush would have sump'n ta say about the way things turned out. It was Jefferson sent us down the empire building road."

"You mean the Louisiana Purchase?" I said.

"You gottit bro."

Coffee over, my left hand pulled a bottle of water out of the stack in the corner as we drifted back to our seats.

Next up was a strategy planning exercise.
We had to devise an operational plan to achieve an objective within our area of operation, our A-O. Len and I made some notes based on our current activity in J'bad and gambled that no one had read the weekly or monthly reports so wouldn't know we were recycling the same old material. Len suggested that as I was the Customs expert I should give the presentation. I was OK with that.

Shane, one of the two advisors recently deployed to Torkham Gate in the Khyber Pass, gave a presentation about the smuggling of wheat flour through the border crossing. He described how, in conjunction with the US Agency for International Development, BMTF would provide a strategy to assist the Afghan Customs Department in their fight against fraud and corruption. It was a very ambitious proposal. The mention of wheat flour struck a chord with me. Maybe someone had read the BMTF J'bad post-Torkham report. Bill 'Don't For' Sakers, sat impassively, not discouraging his fellow advisor's enthusiasm. Nobody realised it was unachievable. Or, maybe, like me, they just kept quiet.

Coalition forces had struggled for a decade to contain the Taliban's ideologically motivated campaign in Nangarhar. To me, it seemed that a viable proposal enabling a handful of former Customs officers to counter serious organised cross-border smuggling, was unlikely to emerge any time soon. Not only was there too much money at stake for the gangsters, but all the small bread makers in the province relied on the stability of supply and price that the gangsters ensured. Then we broke for lunch.

Len had a plate of chicken wings and salad with Ranch Dressing. "I caught that look you had on yer face when Shane was up there spouting his BS about US AID and BMTF and ya da ya da ya da!"

"It's a good job it's not a question and answer session because most of these guys would get torn up for arse paper," I had the chicken curry. Always a good bet and for some reason the Yanks didn't eat it so, there was always plenty. Low-fat too.

Len nibbled the meagre meat from tiny bones as he spoke: "I can see it already, we'll spend three days playin' at border management, come up with loads of initiatives and strategy, then JR'll turn around and say, 'OK, but this is what you *will* do.' He ain't gonna let us tell him what should be done. Din't ya hear him? He's the Barss."

"True. But someone's got to play boss. May as well be him. My concern is that some people are going to get killed because of this gung-ho, drive the business forward nonsense." The curry was damn good but I resisted a second helping. "A suicide bomber got that BMTF advisor at Kandahar ICD at the beginning of last year because he allowed himself to become a target. Maybe he got too close to something?"

"Ya mean like, the bomb? Nah, I don't think so. He just got unlucky. The family of the eleven year old kid who blew him up will have been paid more than all the men of that household could earn in a decade. Here's the thing, the kid would probably have been dead from disease before he was twenny. The kid's bedder off with Allah, than as a bed warmer to one of the village elders." Len did sometimes have a brutal way of putting things into perspective. "Ya know, the Taliban were recently offering ten thousand dollars American to anyone who killed a US soldier."

"Hmm. The Taliban certainly know value for money."

"Damn right bro, 'specially if they hit an officer. A million dollars of tax payers' money spent on education and training. Bang! Gone in an instant."

Looking around the dining area, it was clear no one was paying us any attention. "That wheat-flour thing," I said scooping some curry sauce with a piece of local flat bread. "I had a similar experience in the Congo. Massive amount of fraudulent cross-border traffic in flour, mattresses and a few other things. Not luxuries. But when I looked into it the repercussions of enforcement would have had serious social consequences for very little tax gain. For example, the human mules carrying a few bags of flour from Zambia to a truck three miles inside Congo territory. They made a few Congolese Francs a day for the effort but it was a few more Francs than they would've had if the smugglers hadn't been able to operate."

"Right." said Len. "I geddit. It's better for the little guy to get a little and feel like he's achieving something rather than have a corrupt government squeeze more out of the citizens and squander it on stoopid shit."

"Totally correct. The provincial government was getting plenty of revenue from the copper exports to China. Well, actually, the provincial governor was getting plenty, but you know what I mean. Time for pudding."

Manoeuvring around some guys loitering near the dessert counter, my dish got loaded with egg custard. Delicious.

When we returned to the conference room I volunteered to give the next presentation. Not because of any desire for self-promotion, but to avoid falling asleep.

"The Jalalabad team has put together a few slides to help you understand one of the issues we detected at the J'bad ICD. We classified the issue as urgent to maintain business continuity at the ICD and we also produced an action plan to resolve the issues."

Some of the audience were impressed by the three current DHS buzzwords all in one short paragraph: detect, classify and resolve. A series of *before* photos showed the chaos in the Customs compound with imported cars literally stacked on top of other cars. In the UK, scrap yards were better organised. Then there were some *after* photos where BMTF had engaged a local contractor to clear an area of rubble.

"Unfortunately, this delayed the project because the earth-moving uncovered some unexploded ordnance of Russian origin which the US military had to destroy on site. The photos show the pile of decrepit looking mortars, shells and bullets before destruction."

To give an idea of the size of the haul the top of the pile could be seen above the head of the Afghan digger driver as he stood morosely in front of it. Another image showed how the cars had been parked systematically to bring some order to the chaos.

"It will enable the Customs director to control the storage of vehicles pending payment of import duty. A control point under construction here," my laser pointer indicated an area on the screen, "will prevent vehicles being removed without the clearance document." Clicking forward to the next photo showed an open gate. "As you can see here, currently there is nothing to stop a vehicle being removed before payment of Customs duty. There is also the security issue of people removing car parts and just carrying them off." The next slide was of a guard shack with an ACD police officer holding an AK-47. "The Customs police guy is there for security but he's Pashtun and can't read Dari. Well, actually he can't read, period, so he has no way of knowing if the cars have permission to leave the compound." The remote's button moved a frame forward. "Here you can see one of the simple coloured-paper documents that BMTF recommended. The yellow colour indicates tax paid." A Customs Police officer inspected a crumpled document in the presence of a man in shalwar kameez who could've been anything from age forty to seventy. They were both stood by a white saloon car. Slightly out of focus in the distance, a group of men and boys stood around trying to guess why some white guy, me, surrounded by American soldiers, was taking photos of Uncle Ahmed.

But the most striking and enduring feature of the photo was the old guy's face. It was rugged and tanned and mostly obscured by beard and keffiyeh. His piercingly defiant blue eyes stared down from the screen at everyone in the conference room.

Next, a photograph of the car on its way out of the Customs depot prompted my wry comment: "And in the concluding picture you can see that the gentlemen in traditional Afghan clothing has just become the proud owner of the latest model Toyota Corolla VBIED!"

"Yee-hur. Ain't that a fact," Len got the joke. There was a ripple of amusement but most missed the punch-line. French didn't. Slowly shaking his head, he grinned: *you just had to, didn't ya!*

At breakfast the next day, Len and I were already at the table with a bunch of other guys when Billie-Lou joined us. She may have accidentally dropped her tray on the table or, deliberately made a show of slamming it down to attract attention. Either way, the outcome was the same. The room went quiet. About thirty people stopped eating and looked over at her.

Two of the lads sat closest acknowledged dolefully: "G' mornin' Billie-Lou." There was an air of amiable despondency in the verbal exchanges.

"Mornin'," she replied bluntly. But it was the tight, shiny-black, custom-made cargo pants stretched over her thighs and buttocks that got my attention, not her South Carolina accent. Black Under Armour long-sleeved open-back gym vest betrayed the absence of bra; colour-coordinated High Speed Gear drop-leg holster on her right thigh kept the Glock within easy reach. Dressed to kill.

She screeched the chair towards her then sat on it. What looked like a nervous tick turned out to be her way of tossing the blonde pony-tail over shoulders: left, then right. Tomb Raider's main character sprung to mind. Billie-Lou had pretty much got the Lara Croft look, she just needed to develop some of the character's more human qualities.

The two-inch high mound of scrambled eggs, covered with baked beans, topped with four or five strips of Great American Bacon, cascaded over the plate edge and onto her tray. She should have used a dish, or two. Or, gone back for seconds, but no. This wasn't about satisfying her appetite, it was about proving she had one.

Her food held my attention, too long. Too late: she'd spotted the micro-gestures communicating my distaste for gluttony. Like a starving bitch, she felt the need to protect her meal.

"You gotta prar-blum?" her bark would have sent a K9 running for cover, but she didn't faze my composure. Looking from the tray to her eyes, there it was. Her spilt-second involuntary exposure of vulnerability, barely concealed by bravado.

"*I* don't have a problem," she didn't bite on my insinuation. Instead, her attention turned from me to her tray as she wolfed down the food. We didn't speak again.

"She's either anorexic or bulimic. I can't remember which," said Len as we walked over to the conference room.

"That explains it. I heard they existed. But she doesn't have to prove it to everyone," I said.

"She'll be back in her room right now chuckin' it all up," Len's dour inflection had a way of emphasising the morbidity of Billie-Lou's condition.

"Probably explains why the drains are blocked in that barrack block," I recalled the plumbing issues in my room at Camp ACCL. Billie-Lou's room had been two doors downstream. "Any idea why they call people with bulimia, bulimic and not bulimians?" It was one of those questions where the answer is irrelevant. "Len, you know, bulimia is a mental illness?"

"Sure is," he said with certainty.

"And they allow people that are quite obviously nuts to carry weapons?" the practice seemed imprudent to me.

"Yup," Len grinned. "Second Amendment my friend. She'd have to be surdeefied nuts to not carry. If she's got the certificate it ain't on her résumé," he laughed.

"Len, if someone wants to model themselves on a virtual reality character, that's OK by me. But they really should download the full program."

Len laughed out loud. *"That's* who she looks like. It's been buggin' me since I got here."

"Len, we're surrounded by Zombies. We need to get out of this place A-SAP!"

"Hey! I'm a Marine. I'm supposed to be surrounded," Len winked.

It was my turn to laugh.

We took our seats in the conference room. French gave an update on the zero seven-hundred hours security briefing.

"Before we get down to business, I got somethin' here for all Karrbul-based advisors," he held a piece of paper but didn't refer to it. "Over the past few days there has been an increase in the movement into the city of Koochi tribe refugees." Len and I had seen some of them driving their camels across open country on one of our trips to J'bad ICD. The name amused me, but in Murican, coo-chie wasn't just baby talk. French ignored the sniggers. "They are a nomadic people but, those coming into Karrbul have been displaced by Taliban activity in Paktika Province. There's a camp along the Tajikan Road just past the turn-off for the airport ECP. Be advised to check your routes on the bulletin board before travel and report any sightings of refugee caravans. Any questions?"

My hand went up. French pointed at me. "Good morning, Boss. Could this be the build up to a Koochi coup?" It had been my intention to get a laugh and more than half the advisors obliged, but it was just my way of getting their attention. "No, seriously. Really, I'll tell you why I ask. I read a report a week or so back written by an Afghan professor in something or other, which said that half of the Kochi people in areas adjacent to the Durand Line had been displaced by the Taliban. So, if half of the Kochi people support the Taliban and the other half don't, which half do we have just down the road?"

French looked like he was about to say something but the Intelligence Analyst got in first.

"French, good morning, I've been working on Taliban insertion into mass displacements of indigenous people. It's shaping up into an interesting study. Hey Gary, can you send me that report, please?" said Jerry Garcia. His parents must've been Grateful Dead fans.

"I think I saved it, so, yes," I said.

Len whispered: "Ya do know that cooch is vagina, right?"

My outburst of coughing suppressed laughter. Conference resumed.

There was a lot of talk about building collaborative relationships, Afghan-led initiatives, sustainable development and a whole load of proposed projects, some of them grand, many absurd. After several hours of tedium followed by lunch we were directed into syndicates and given thirty minutes to develop an action plan for an Area of Operation other than our own. The presentations took up the rest of the day and I really can't recall any of it.

On the third day Steve Stieglitz stood up. I was in an after-lunch daze and didn't notice him at first. Maybe it was because he was only five feet two inches tall and skinny as an Afghan opium farmer. He became more animated as his presentation gathered pace. Steiglitz was a government guy, not a contractor like me and Len. His ebullient, upbeat, almost gung-ho rant about JR's leadership and commitment caught a few people by surprise, especially me.

"OK!" he shouted. His Tennessee accent flinched me back to fully awake. It was perhaps just as well because, I was at that pre-snore shallow breathing stage.

"So, the message is *numbers*. JR's a *numbers* guy. He needs *numbers* to show DC that BMTF are on message, mission focused and out there," he pointed into the audience left, right and centre, then did a little left-foot right-foot dance as if he found it all terribly exciting. Or, maybe it was to give the impression of increased stature. Dyskinesia could not be ruled out. Whatever it was, I felt myself sliding down my chair with embarrassment.

"Stats. That's what JR wants. Give him *stats* and stayduss reports. The guys in DC they need figyures. *Numbers, stats* and figyures." Steiglitz pointed at different members of the audience as if making each of those three factors someone's personal responsibility. On his command a graph flashed onto the white-wall. Several other charts and slides scrolled down the screen. "Quanny-fiables. Deliverables. Outcomes. As JR's already said," he glanced over at the top table for approval. JR didn't stop him. "Respons-*ability*, accoun-*ability*, sustain-*ability*."

All those 'billities triggered a random thought caused by neurones not focussing on something that didn't interest them. Yes, I was daydreaming. The idea that somewhere, maybe in Tennessee, there might be a *Hill Billy Tea* was eminently more interesting than this guy.

He must have spotted the audience's slow demise by PowerPoint, Steiglitz took a breath and ramped-up his delivery: "Reach-out to stakeholders," his left arm shot out too the side, "and pardners," his right arm went out. He stood, arms wide, evangelising. "Key Leader Engagements," his hands came together as if capturing the spirit of the mission right in front of us. "All in the *stats*. Keep them reports a comin'. *Metrics*. Get the *metrics* back to PM A-SAP."

His enthusiasm was wearing me down. An example of a metrics spreadsheet flashed momentarily on the screen. It was followed very quickly by the same document with blocks of colour: green, yellow, red, indicating targets achieved, work in progress and not even close. The slides came faster. He either had a lot to get through or this was an attempt at subliminal messaging.

"Detect, Classify and Resolve," shouted Stieglitz.

I didn't dare glance at Len because I knew he would be cringing at all this management-speak and that would make me laugh out loud. Instead, looking around the room, it was apparent, most of the delegates had glazed over although one or two were making notes. Maybe they were scribbling comical comments for the guy sat next to them. I saw a few smirks.

Stieglitz's performance ended as abruptly as it had begun.

My exhaling loudly into the quiet room might have sounded like a sigh of relief. It was, but no one noticed. Their ears were still ringing from the barrage.

Time to wrap up. A few final words from JR and then a few more from French and we were out the door like end of term school boys.

"Is that Stieglitz guy for real?" I asked Len, as we headed to our accommodation.

"I do believe he is," replied Len, melancholically. "Some o' these DC guys actually believe this BS."

Greg Samms maintained his pace coming in the opposite direction as we walked across the car park towards our rooms. "Hey guys. Good news!" Greg was in a buoyant mood. "Gotcha on a ro-darry flight to J'bad tomorrow mornin'. You're gonna love it. Form up at zero seven-thirty. Max and Lynn will getcha to KAI-A for a zero eight-thirty departure. It's on email." Greg didn't break step.

"Roger that Greg!" called out Len as we continued on our way. "Dy-amm!" said Len. "I was kinda hopin' we might get a few beers here tomorrow evenin'. It bein' man love Thursday an' all. Seems like someone's got other ideas."

"Yes, they are keen to get on with stuff," I agreed. "What's that expression you use?" I said rhetorically: "Hurry up and wait!"

"Yup," we agreed to meet at nineteen hundred for dinner, then parted company at Len's door.

When Len and I had arrived five days earlier, the afternoon colour of the mountains behind Camp Heath had been dusty-dry grey. Fall-out from the previous night's cool air created a definitive dew-line for thirty meters down from the peak to where a lighter shade of shale had emerged from the low cloud. The Land Cruiser's engine had been running for twenty minutes. It had just about cleared the condensation on the inside of the thick armoured front screen when Len and I bundled into the back. We sat on the fold down seats that lined the side of the truck. There were no passenger windows, so the only view was over the shoulders of Max and Lynn sat up front.

"All set in the back there?" Max shouted as he found first gear with the stick shift. The engine roared in protest at the weight of the armour plating that surrounded us.

"Yeah! Let's roll, buddy!" shouted Len.

The seat belts in the back of the truck were a Gordian knot of filthy webbing and buckles. It was futile trying to fasten mine. Instead, gripping the seat rails and pushing against the opposite seats with my legs kept me in my place. We approached the first check-point. Gurkha guards on duty smiled and saluted as they opened the gate. Our vehicle made a sharp right turn and bumped down the mountain track. Part of the seat punched me in the liver several times. Shifting position got my body armour in the way of protrusions. It gave me some protection but, sitting on the floor felt safer. Afghan National Army soldiers were on the two checkpoints before the main exit. Huddled inside their military issue jackets, heads keffiyeh-wrapped against the cold, they blinked acknowledgement as we passed through checkpoints. Like the Gurkhas, they'd been on duty through the night but they didn't look as bright and alert.

At the main ECP, ANA soldiers had vehicles and pedestrians lined up before allowing them into the base. Two of our office guys, wrapped in shawls against the cold, were being checked on their way to work. Morning gloom dissipated in response to invisible sun. Post-dawn shadows retreated up the slopes. Sinister diaphanous smog crept slowly up from the valley revealing the road amid the miasma. Cyclists wobbling along the periphery of a septic discharge cursed reckless truck drivers for the filthy deluge. Several other camps had heavy steel gates facing onto the road. Mostly owned by Afghan corporations, then rented to foreign governments, the donor money for construction often came from the same countries that provided the tenants. Good business. We passed the guard towers at the entrance to Camp Orion.

"Here's where the suicide car bomber blew up a coupla weeks back," shouted Lynn over the engine noise.

Soot and scorch marks from the VBIED blast splashed the perimeter wall. In a Western city it would have been nothing more sinister than graffiti or a black-painted attempt to conceal offensive doodling.

"Good old Alaska barriers, seven tons of twelve feet high solid concrete. They still ain't picked up all the debris. Bet the local dogs got a few treats," remarked Lynn.

Twisted bits of rusting metal, Toyota Corolla remains from the failed attempt to deliver death and destruction, were almost indistinguishable amongst the normal street detritus.

"I wonder why he didn't hit the gate?" to me it seemed odd that such a simple mission had failed just yards from its objective.

"Who knows?" Lynn shrugged. "The DynCor guy in charge of security said he viewed the CCTV. It looked like the driver just changed his mind. There was nothing between him and the gate. Maybe he didn't want to go to Allah with murder on his checklist."

Max gunned the engine through the sharp left turn and merged with the traffic. "This goddam road was bein' fixed when I got here three years ago," shouted Max. "It'd be nice if they got it done for my last drive to the airport on my way outta this shid 'ole!"

"I doubt it!" said Lynn. "There are always issues with supplies and local labourers and, of course, bribery. See those two tyre repair shops?" Lynn pointed to a row of randomly constructed buildings with their fronts open to the elements. A jumble of rusting machinery implied some form of industrious activity. The proprietor huddled in a blanket by a small brazier waiting for a pot to boil.

"Yeah," as soon as I'd acknowledged seeing them, they disappeared from view as we sped on.

Lynn continued her commentary: "They gotta steady trade while the road is in bad condition but that could change with a nice flat highway. The concrete block manufacturer opposite will be able to get trucks in and out easier so he's keen to see the work finished." The Land Cruiser bottomed-out on its bump stops as we lurched over road-ruts. Lynn wasn't fazed. "Hey, check out the lumber yard," Lynn pointed in the direction of an assortment of standing sticks and lengths of raw timber. Valuable stock corralled behind a length of chain link fence. In most other countries it might have just made firewood grade. "Then there's the blue burka brigade. Mostly female! They sit begging in the middle of the dirt road with arms extended waiting for handouts. I saw one a few months ago all twisted-up in the road. By the looks of her she'd been hit by a truck. The traffic just drove round her."

"Don't see them this morning," I remarked. "Can't say I blame them. There's no way I'd sit in this filthy mess."

"Yeah right!" said Lynn. "And they ain't gonna be gettin' much charidy from cars doing sixty miles an hour when the road's fixed."

"Hang on!" shouted Max as we bumped off the main road onto a rutted track. Our truck splashed through mud, until the smell of human waste pervaded the interior: another septic pump-out load illicitly dumped in the street. "This is the back door to the airport. There's an ECP but it's quicker than going all the way around to the main gate. That's if it's open."

"Pass me one of those cases of water back there will ya?" shouted Lynn. I did as instructed.

The Afghan soldier gestured us to halt at his checkpoint. Len and I leaned forward so he could compare our faces to the photo-IDs. He was satisfied we weren't the enemy. Lynn opened her door and spoke unintelligibly in Dari as she passed the case of water to the second guard.

"Tasha kur! Tasha kur!" said the guard. Fresh water was always gratefully accepted. As he approached to accept the gift he was surprised by the sight of a blonde female in body armour holding a rifle. He smiled. The armoured door slammed shut.

"I reckon you just made his day," shouted Max as the engine revs increased.

Len and I waved farewell to Max and Lynn then went into the Portakabin check-in area. Weapons make-safe. Stand on scales with all personal items. Move forward to departure lounge. *Wait*. Ten minutes. Out to the helipad. Hurry up. Our rotary flight was a Chinook. It belonged to one of the corporations providing logistics to the hundreds of contractor companies running the US government's war on terror in Afghanistan.

Earplugs were issued which I used in conjunction with the electronic noise cancelling hearing protectors Len had given me. He'd bought a new pair, special price for US service personnel. The APO box number on Len's address convinced the retailer he was military. Len and I strapped into seats opposite each other against the sides of the helicopter. The machine rocked gently breaking contact with the ground. Altitude increased as it moved slowly forward. I'd hoped it would lift itself vertically, just for the experience, but I guess that takes too much fuel. The rear ramp-door didn't close, adding to my sense of vulnerability. Towards the front of the Chinook, on each side of the aircraft, doors had been removed and replaced with former Australian Special Forces men, each armed with AK-47s. Secured by a lifeline to a point inside the CH-46, the muzzles of their guns were well outside the aircraft. I didn't get chance to ask them if they got much practice firing an automatic rifle from a moving helicopter. As our speed and height increased we passed over the outskirts of Kabul. Large areas of land subdivided into new compounds would eventually add to the population density of this sprawling city. Other than the high walls, which implied keep out, there was nothing but bare dirt. No financial institution would lend money to acquire stakes in such a high-risk game, they must've been cash purchases. Some people in the new Islamic Republic were doing OK.

The CH-46 curved eastwards towards J'bad. Two Hueys to the rear, dodged and weaved slightly wide of our flight-path. Both Bell UH-1Hs were with us all the way to Jalalabad as we flew through the barren grey mountain passes. No vegetation at this altitude so, no goats. No goats therefore no goat herders. No goat herders meant there was no good reason for anyone to be hanging around out here unless they were lookouts for a paramilitary group. Some of the razor sharp ridges loomed over us as we hugged the rugged contours. Good vantage points for spotters or opportunists out to kill us. To kill me. I guessed that's why we had the two guys hanging out the sides of the Chinook. Staring past Len and through the large round porthole, it was good to not see a turban with a rocket launcher on the shoulder next to it.

My view through the gaping rear hatch had been the distant horizon, but now more of the ground was visible, the horizon closer, as we approached Jalalabad Airfield. The Huey escorts dropped back, allowing distance to come between us. Two flares snaked away from the underside of our Chinook as the pilot deployed countermeasures. Then another two flares dropped away from us in a rapidly decreasing arc. I got nervous. The two guys hanging out the side doors didn't seem troubled. It was all over in seconds. We were on the ground. Another successful flight.

Thanks Greg.

The Golden Wasp of Nangarhar - May 2012

Formation was at zero eight-thirty hours in the motor pool. Len and I were early. The Third Brigade Special Troops Battalion's M-RAP engines filled the motor pool with noise and smoke. Individually and collectively, soldiers methodically checked equipment. Some found time to smoke cigarettes while they awaited further orders. Others fooled around trying to wrestle each other to the ground. I carried four cases of water to M-RAP 1001, it would be BMTF transport for the day.

The mission: visit Jalalabad Inland Customs Depot and meet with the Customs Director Khairfullah. Drink chai. Discuss development of the imported cars compound. Have lunch with Director Khairfullah and some local businessmen. Drink chai. Conduct a perimeter security review. Drink chai. Review security procedures at the Customs warehouse with the warehouse control officer, Mr Momand. Drink chai. Meanwhile, the Army would gather personal data from the hundreds of workers at the ICD using their Handheld Interagency Identity Detection Equipment. HIIDE, pronounced hide, is a device that captures iris and fingerprint images in the hope of identifying bomb makers and users. Despite the destructive energy released by a bomb, fingerprints and DNA often survive on post-blast remnants. Such evidence has been successfully used in numerous court cases and military initiatives against bomb makers.

The Department of Defense maintained a fully operational forensic laboratory somewhere in Afghanistan: another US private sector corporation offering solutions to problems caused by the US presence: the business equivalent of perpetual motion.

Mount up. Helmets on. Len climbed the M-RAP steps and sat in one of the three seats on the near side of the personnel compartment. We were crammed in next to large metal frames and cabinets containing electrical equipment with irregularly flashing lights and constant hum. No space went unused.

I sat opposite Len. Seat belts fastened. Headset on around the helmet. The step-ramp lifted, slammed shut and became a closed door. The air conditioning began to take effect but the constant white-noise from the vents was deafening even through the headset.

"Hey!" shouted Len over the roar and hiss in the enclosed space. "You got the seat next to where the Taliban put the magnetic mines on the outside! Hahahahahaha!"

Looking disdainfully at Len, my reply was dead-pan: "Hey! You got the seat they can never find after the roadside IED! Har, bloody har, har!"

The engine noise increased and drowned out Len's maniacal laughter. Len was in his element. The M-RAP rocked forward.

The view from the M-RAP's side windows was restricted not just by the thickness of the armoured glass but also because body armour made turning in the seat to look out the side windows difficult. It was possible to view the world through the opposite windows but they were about six feet from ground level so anything close to the vehicle was out of view. We passed through the blue archway of the Afghan army ECP on the main highway. The left turn out of the base and across the damaged road shook and rattled the M-RAP as it took us towards the ICD, four miles away. Forty-five miles beyond the ICD was Torkham in the Khyber Pass, then Pakistan.

Occasional glimpses through the front screen revealed dwellings and commercial enterprises lining the highway. A tyre fitter huddled next to the motorcycle repair shop next to the ...not sure, looked like a pan shop. Then, a guy working a lathe or similar machine on a bogey that could be wheeled inside at close of business. Half metre-long flat-breads hung outside the bread shop for customers while smoke from the clay oven rose lazily over the shack.

Sides of bloody meat, along with some not so bloody, hung in the dry and dusty shade of the vendor's verandah. Piles of pomegranates, the region's biggest legitimate crop, awaited juicing in some ancient mechanical press. Booths offering mobile phone credit, money-changing, printing and copying jostled for position amongst the traders of more substantial wares. Everywhere, the filth of human activity; in the air, on the ground, in the roadside water: organic and inorganic, animal, human and vehicular detritus.

Flies competed with dust particles for a place to rest undisturbed just for a moment. Scraps of cling-wrap and tissue paper danced above the throng in tune with the aerial dynamics. Throughout human history, the highway from and to the Khyber Pass has never been still. Armies throughout history advanced, fought, won, lost and retreated along the torturous route. The main artery between Jalalabad and Peshāwar had seen its share of blood, but victorious hordes always abandon Afghanistan: to itself.

M-RAP 1001 carried us past orderly fields of crops. Gradually the occurrence of buildings became more regular as we entered another built-up area. Next to a used car lot containing hundreds of vehicles, brand new bright red tractors glinted in the heat. Made in China but donated by a Western charitable organisation with a well paid management structure, brightly coloured **For Sale** signs emphasised the bargain price in US dollars.

The view from behind the M-RAP's armoured glass became chaotic. Retailers and tradesmen occupied territory alongside the ribbon of battered black-top. The road was no different to a suburban area in any other country except that it appeared to be more mayhem than marketplace. There were no orderly lines of customers queuing to leave their money at the retailer's till. No pushing and shoving to get Black Flag or Blue Crescent bargains. Just a constant erratic movement of men between stalls narrowly avoiding bumping each other as they went about their business.

Always men. In Talibanistan, men don't allow their women to market in case they are touched - by men. It's the man's duty to protect the honour and virtue of his women. To some men, a woman alone is fair game. Alone, she must be no man's property. Unowned or, dis-owned.

But there were women. Fully-clad women with nothing to trade. A blue burka sat in the roadside dirt, her work-hardened hand extended to accept passing generosity. She begged while her man waited for her, in heaven. He had all eternity. She had just a lifetime. Today, she had young mouths to feed. Without the outstretched hand, her children and those of her dead sister would die.

Within spitting distance, a small pile of shiny blue cloth rocked back and forth. Below the thin narrow palm protruded upwards for handouts, a random collection of pills: blister-packed, ones and twos in a small plastic bowl. Medication, gratefully received for a sick child. Slowly, the bowl filled.

Here, every man was in business, frantically competing for passing trade. Proximity to moving traffic determined customer volume. Men and boys in shalwar kameez hawked all manner of products amongst the crawling vehicles. Some clutched thick wads of Afghani notes. Many had bulging pockets of currency inside their waistcoats. Most wore keffiyeh, predominantly black and white chequered. A few still wore their pakol despite the heat. Like an English flat cap, but without the peak, it doesn't need to be winter to wear a pakol. Richly woven turbans gleamed in the sunlight. I tried to imagine when markets must have been this frantic in England. Dickensian London must have been this chaotic, but town planners had designed-out this sort of inefficiency decades ago. Gradual mutation from small family run shops into the rampant consumerism of retail-chains gave consumers what they really wanted: everything, cheaper.

Forty tonne trucks overtook grocers' vans as the drive to reduce labelled wares to barcodes gathered pace. Balance sheets determine what consumers get: pack size and quantity, family-sized malnutrition masquerading as sustenance; bulking agents adding value to food fraud. Advertising and supply dictating demand. Urban planners' out-of-town developments caused commercial genocide. The revenge of the corner shop came in the form of online retailers who battled the megastores for market share.

Maybe that's what the Taliban are fighting. They don't want change. Especially not change in favour of globalisation where anonymous corporate owners take refuge in tax havens. They're happy with what they have. If a man can feed his family with his honest labour, then any surplus product must be time wasted that could have been spent with family or contemplating God.

Define honest labour. It varies from culture to culture. The Silk Road is synonymous with Afghanistan but it eventually became a barely trodden track as traders grew tired of extortion. European merchants adapted: sending oriental wares to Europe by sea was more cost effective and reliable than the Marco Polo route. Perhaps Afghanistan was the birthplace of Adam Smith's Capitalism.

Our mission: the Inland Customs Depot. We were to observe the work that the Border Management Task Force had set in motion. There was a lot of activity including construction and modification of security procedures. The ICD director is responsible for managing the Customs controls at the ICD. It's a big job and not without serious risks to his personal safety. The ICD office collects lots of tax and the Government of Afghanistan relies on the income to pay for some of the regional reconstruction, allegedly. If the Taliban can disrupt tax revenue or, better still, extort money from traders, it undermines the credibility of legitimate government.

If a state claims to offer its citizens security and then consistently fails to deliver, eventually the citizens lose faith in the state and take the law into their own hands or, seek security from an alternative source. In the USA, the Italian Mafia had been prominent for decades before the State succeeded in suppressing much of its activity.

Organised crime in its various guises is raw capitalism. Rampant greed combined with unfettered exploitation of people, by any means, are the main drivers of illicit business. Where there are no laws, nothing can be illegal. Where law enforcement is weak, illegal activity is; tolerated, accepted, expected, respected but ultimately feared, in that order.

Nangarhar law is administered by local tribal elders. They represent their people through a form of democracy that has worked well for hundreds of years. They have significant influence over the state governor who answers to the President of Afghanistan, but there is another power in the province.

The Taliban has their own rules and considerable support from many people in the community. Ordinary people regard foreigners and gangsters as the agents of their misfortune. They see the Taliban taking action against them. For many people, the Taliban represents stability. For the BMTF, the Taliban were a threat the same as gangsters; some of the

Afghan security services; most Afghan drivers; Afghan women; mosquitoes; snakes; scorpions and spiders. You get the idea.

Because of the ever-present risk of attack, BMTF advisors worked alongside the US Army's ISAF contingent. The Customs Director had his own bodyguard.

Customs Director Khairfullah invited us for lunch. We took some soft drinks acquired from the D-FAC. Exotic American products, things he wouldn't normally have a chance to try. They were in a green duffle bag and included Coke, Pepsi, Cranberry Juice, Iced Tea, Shock-coffee and some of the Hi-Energy drinks such as Rip-It. There was even some alcohol-free Beck's beer, not something Afghans would normally drink as they tend to favour sweet beverages.

The office door was open so Len knocked on the inside. Director Khairfullah, stood to greet us as he conducted his business. Six men sat on various seats around the office, some wore shalwar kameez and turban, two wore suits. I don't know about you, but I always feel a little awkward walking into an office carrying a rifle, a side-arm and wearing body armour when we are supposed to be friends. I hoped to become more at ease with the people and the surroundings so that the body armour could be removed in the office. Not only does it make it easier to breathe it also looks less hostile, but that was for the future.

After lunch I needed to take a moment in the local conveniences. I didn't know the location of the nearest toilet but I definitely needed to use one. There was no way I could hold onto it during the bumpy return journey.

"Sir, could you tell me, please, is there a toilet near here I may use?" Mustafa, our interpreter, translated. The director said something in Pashto to me indicating a door to his left.

Mustafa translated. "It's the Director's own private washroom but you are welcome to use it."

"Mananna," I replied. Thank you.

I knew from previous experience how urinating whilst wearing body armour can get messy so I took it off and placed it carefully on the floor next to Len along with my rifle. I carefully opened the door of the small room and stepped inside. I was immediately confronted by a large yellow wasp flying gracefully around the room, presumably looking for a way out, or, a target of opportunity. I'd seen a similar wasp bite a chunk out of the Director's hand on a previous occasion so I knew its capability. I've also watched wasps chisel and devour wood for nest building material. I considered the situation and decided the prospect of being bitten on an important part of my anatomy was not appealing. OK, so there might be occasions when excessive swelling of that particular appendage might come in handy, but not today. I quickly turned and left the room gently closing the door behind me. There were several local people in the director's office and they all looked slightly puzzled at my quick turn-around.

Mustafa translated Mr Khairfullah's words: "Is there a problem?"

"There's a wasp in the room and I'm not sure how to deal with it." I said, pointing in the direction of the washroom as Mustafa translated. Everyone smiled. "Maybe I should have kept my body armour on?" I remarked. Mustafa continued the commentary.

The smiles got bigger. It appeared that the irony of an armed man apparently unable to defend himself against an annoying Apocrita was not lost on the Director and his associates. I felt foolish. I could easily have swatted the thing but my sense of offending cultural sensitivities got the better of me. When the wasp had bitten Mr Khairfullah, he had merely brushed it away. Mr Khairfullah smiled slightly as he pushed a button on his wireless bell-chime.

Within seconds a Customs Police Officer came in the room carrying his AK-47. Under normal conditions elsewhere that would have been regarded as a little excessive but in Afghanistan the police always carry Kalashnikovs during Vespa evictions.

The Director said a few words to the policeman who then slowly entered the washroom. Within seconds he emerged with the wasp's wings pinned behind its back and escorted it over to the Director who declined the offer. The ABP policeman turned and offered me the wasp.

Mustafa repeated the Director's words in English: "Mr Gary. Now I have a gift for you!"

I moved to accept it, "Mananna."

246

The Director spoke and the policeman escorted the intruder from the premises. The audience were quietly amused by this performance. If Len was embarrassed, he hid it well.

Mustafa turned to me and gestured towards the restroom: "Mr Gary, the director says it is now safe for you to enter."

My hand on heart conveyed thanks to Mr Khairfullah and acknowledged the other Afghan gentlemen in the office. This was clearly the best entertainment they'd had in a long time. Len dropped his chin and shook his head in dismay but continued to smile.

When I emerged from the washroom, some of the Afghan fellas resumed their smiles. I lightly blew a *phew* to confirm my relief.

We concluded our business as more people arrived to make demands on the Director's time. Mustafa took photos of our Key Leader Engagement showing hand-shakes all round. It was time to go. I put on my body armour and slung my rifle around my shoulder. I was the last one of our party to leave the office.

I was just out the door when the Director spoke, in perfect English: "Mr Gary. Did you enjoy your gift?" I leaned back into the room just sticking my head around the door. Without speaking I placed my hand on my chest, licked my lips as if enjoying a tasty snack, made a slurping noise then wiped the corners of my mouth. Everyone laughed! One of the guys wearing a turban looked down at his phone as he composed a text message.

"What was all that as we came out?" asked Len as we approached our M-RAP. I told him about my brief discourse with Director Khairfullah.

Mustafa was paying attention. He spoke: "Mr Gary, the man with the grey turban was also very entertained. I have not seen him smile before."

"Oh. You know him?"

"Yes Mr Gary, everybody knows him. He is Amadullah Dost Khan. He is the main wheat-flour smuggler in Nangarhar. A big gangster. His body guards were in the corridor to our left as we came out. Suits. You may have seen them."

"Yes. I did see them. Were they armed?"

"Maybe," Mustafa handed me my camera. "You have some very nice photos of your meeting. Especially of Mr Khan," he smiled.

We shook hands before Mustafa walked away becoming indistinguishable amongst the hundreds of shalwar clad men in the compound. Len and I climbed into our M-RAP.

It took forty minutes to return to base. The road wasn't as busy as on the outward journey which made our fifty-cal gunner uneasy. "I've never seen it this quiet. I don't like it," his voice was unusually clear through my headphones.

Our RTB was uneventful and the blue arch at the Afghan Army base ECP was a welcome sight but it was not yet time to be at ease. In F8, with my gear off, it was time to relax.

"Hey Len," I said, handing him a bottle of chilled water, "that visit had all the makings of a non-event and yet by pure chance we came away with a photo of one of the biggest gangsters in the region."

Len looked up from his laptop: "Yup. KLE and intelligence gathering mission," he grinned at the prospect of writing the weekly report. "Remember when we went to Torkham and that guy from US AID was always goin' arn about the wheat-flour smuggling gangs?"

My left hand was preoccupied feeding me water from a bottle so Len got a right-handed thumbs-up.

Len leaned back in his seat. "Well, he'd been there the best part of eighteen months and didn't know shit about any of the players in the game" Len opened his email, "And we were there what? A haff hour and we get an intelligence scoop."

"Yep, it does look like we may have actually have come away with something of value."

A sense of achievement is rare in Afghanistan but this was definitely something to write home about.

"Damn right bro. That business with the wasp was a master stroke," Len chuckled as he replayed the incident to himself.

"I hope you don't think I planned that," I remarked. "The damn thing was a monster."

"Sure was. But your reaction to it was pure comedy," Len scrolled through his emails. "Mr Khan will now grossly underestimate our capabilities. He will think we are complete fools."

"And we're not, right?" I intoned sceptically.

"Hey-ell, no! We're the smartest guys on the block. Thanks to you, Khan now thinks we're both idiots which means we're not a threat to his business so, he won't have to kill us. I feel kinda good about that," said Len.

"Yes, me too. Mr Bean and Johnny English would be proud of me." Len laughed at my analogy, but there was something we needed to keep in mind: "Len, that US AID guy down at Torkham was chasing around after wheat-flour smugglers who controlled an essential product. I can't imagine what he was hoping to achieve, but if BMTF try to persuade Khairfullah to get involved in compliance and enforcement, it'll just force up the price of a basic foodstuff, which hits the poorest hardest."

Len's chair creaked as it denied him comfort. "Uh, huh, there'd likely be a reaction to that and Khairfullah ain't about ta git hisself killed over some goddam wheat-flour. He told me that when you were on leave."

"Len, I tried something similar in the Congo. The army were one of the big players in that game. During my surveillance operations on the Zambian border I stumbled over huge dumps of product in the jungle guarded by groups of Congolese Army doing a bit of freelance work. It could have got very unpleasant but I was able to turn the encounters to my advantage." In my room, I typed *afghan wasps* into the search bar of my browser.

It took a few clicks but: "There it is," I shouted through the partition.

"What? Where?" surprise inflated in his reply.

"The Central Asian Wasp," I read from the screen.

"What another one? In here? Might be a nest somewhere?"

"Nooo! On my computer!" I laughed.

"Not in the shed?" he sounded relieved.

"No!" I quoted from the online source. "Often referred to as the Yak Killer."

"Shee-it! Yak killer? Don't need nonner them 'round here. Those yaks take some killin'!"

"True," I said. "I'm still glad I resisted the temptation to slay the Golden Wasp of Nangarhar."

Pharmaceuticals - May 2012

Formation was zero seven-thirty hours in the motor pool. LT gave mission briefing responsibility to a young female sergeant. The Velcro badge on her MOLLE said MARTINEZ.

"OK guys. 3BSTB's mission this morning is to support the BMTF at the ICD and also continue with our Hiide data capture. RTB is fourteen-hundred hours. BMTF has agreed to split their team to cover more ground so Gonzales, you will be with Mr Kinder at the ECP and the imported car compound. Daley you will be with Mr Wilshaw doing a cargo examination in the warehouse. No specific threat intel on the ICD so far, just the usual reports that confirm it's fucking dangerous out there. Expect the threat level to change once 3BSTB arrive. Stay vigilant," she looked to the LT.

"Thank you Sergeant Martinez. Mount up."

Heavy boots crunched limestone chunks as soldiers, interpreters and BMTF dispersed to our appointed M-RAPs. Seat belts fastened as the rear door lifted and slammed shut.

The four mile journey along the Jalalabad Road to the ICD took an hour. The main road to the border with Pakistan was always busy. Several checkpoints manned by Afghan security forces slowed traffic for inspection and facilitated the movement of our convoy. Without the checkpoints, our progress would have been slower. The downside of checkpoints is that the Taliban exploit them because the destructive power of a VBIED is multiplied in a crowded location. It was the fear and expectation of attacks on military convoys that motivated the Afghan security guys to get us clear of their location ASAFP.

At the ICD, 3BSTB set up security for the unit. One M-RAP stationed inside the compound with its fifty-calibre turret gun pointing towards the entrance, while another M-RAP was positioned a hundred yards away to the west by the exit gate. They had visual and radio contact and were ready to suppress any threat. The other four M-RAPs were by the Customs office facing the way out. The army guys were already out by the entrance lining up the day labourers to collect biometric data. LT, Len,

Mustafa, our interpreter, and I spent a few minutes with Customs Director Khairfullah.

We drank chai, made small talk then, acknowledging that the director was a very busy man, we went about our allotted tasks.

Mustafa walked with me and US Army Specialist Daley the few hundred yards to the UNOPS funded warehouse on the other side of the ICD.

The United Nations Office for Project Services had been busy. Work on the new warehouse had commenced at least a year before Len and I arrived at Jalalabad. Although I didn't see any work in progress, the building awaited completion. There were no outer doors but inner cages could be locked to ensure security of goods if required. Along one wall, bags were stacked five high, two deep and twenty from end-to-end. Four tonnes of unidentified material in close proximity to me that seemed out of place amongst the jumble of other goods.

"Specialist Daley, I'm going to check that stack of whatever it is over there. You might want to step outside just in case."

Specialist Daley said nothing, but from his crouching position by the door, he listened to my commentary as my hand brushed dust to reveal description and origin: "Made in Pakistan. No hand prints. No suspicious wires or packages amongst it. Nothing to indicate recent disturbance. I'm sticking my knife into one of the bags at the bottom of the pile. Cement."

I was glad it was cement but if it hadn't been, it would have made a great item for the weekly report: *'BMTF mentors assisting an Afghan-led initiative at Jalalabad ICD, during detection of cache of ammonium nitrate fertiliser explosive.'*

"Like it says on the bag. But yeah, nothing's how it should be here," said Specialist Daley.

Various government ministries and ordinary traders were busily making use of the new warehouse. I explained my mission to Mustafa and Specialist Daley.

"I want to watch a Customs cargo examination. That will give me an idea about their skill level and the capacity for raising revenue. Customs cargo checks are pretty much the same the world over. Same here as in Karachi, New York or London."

The jingle truck backed up to a loading bay. Mr Khairfullah had arranged this for me. Not what I'd hoped for, but better than nothing and it would have been bad politics to decline the offer.

"OK Mr Wilshaw. I won't be watching you. I'll be watching everyone else," Specialist Daley reassured me.

"Mr Daley, you should call me Gary. It's quicker."

"Yes sir. Gary. OK. You best call me Art. If, at any time while we're here I shout you, listen-up. It might be time to go. Got that?" Dark Oakley lenses concealed his darker eyes, but they didn't hide our mutual understanding.

"OK Art. I got that."

Mr Momand, the Customs supervisor was already at the jingle truck along with three other men. One was paying attention, two looked uninterested. We shook hands. The importer was dressed in brown shalwar kameez and dark turban like most of the Taliban that appear in news reports. I'm not saying he *was* Taliban, he just looked like Taliban.

Mustafa explained something about the truck and the importer: "Mr Gary, the importer is from Pakistan. So are all the goods. The labourers want to start unloading the cargo into the warehouse. Is it OK?"

"Mr Momand is in charge of the Customs work but it is very kind of him to ask me," I said. "How many different products are in this load?"

Mustafa relayed Mr Momand's reply: "Mr Gary, there are five different types of cargo. The biggest consignment is medicines from Pakistan pharmaceutical company in Hyderabad."

"If Mr Momand is ready, begin. Carry on. Thank you for delaying it for me," I said.

Mr Momand spoke some English but he understood my positive gestures more.

The different goods were carried into one of the cages and stacked in mixed batches of products according to who owned them. It made counting individual product quantities very difficult. The medicines formed a separate pile.

"Mr Momand, sir, could you open one of those boxes please?" the label on the end of the box was for some kind of medical cream.

Mr Momand signalled and shouted to one of the labourers who quickly responded by placing a box at our feet. My knife slit the tape. Mr Momand plucked one of the small rectangular packages out of the box and checked it against the packing list. It was as described.

Mustafa spoke: "He says it is no problem. Medicines. He has seen it many times."

"OK. How long does it usually stay here at the ICD?" Fraud seemed unlikely but supply chain integrity was of interest to me.

"Maybe a week. Sometimes longer," Mustafa and Mr Momand had reached agreement on that.

I spoke to Mr Momand: "Is it always the same exporter and importer?"

Patterns are behavioural indicators in commerce, as they are in people.

Mustafa replied: "Yes Mr Gary. He has seen this many times."

"See this?" I pointed to the storage instructions on the side of the packet:

Store in cool, dry place, below 25°C.

Rivulets of sweat on their way down my back to my crack told me it was at least 35°C and that was *inside* the warehouse. Mr Momand and Mustafa leaned over the small print on the box to take a closer look.

"Mr Momand, tell me, how long does the lorry take to get from Pakistan to here?" I said.

"Mr Gary, from Torkham Gate in Khyber it can take two days, maybe longer. But from Hyderabad to Torkham maybe a week."

In Afghanistan, distance doesn't determine the time it requires to be travelled. Journey duration is dictated by geographical and political obstacles along the way. An important factor with any planned arrival is that it may be your final departure.

"So, this medicine may be in this truck for more than a week before it gets here?" Mr Momand bowed affirmatively. "And then how long
254

before it gets to the guy who sells it?" Mustafa translated. There was a lot of shrugging and discussion before they agreed on a number.

"Mr Gary, Momand says that to Kabul from here, two days, maybe three days."

"OK. Mr Momand, is there a plan to have a chilled section in this warehouse?"

Mustafa began his explanation as Momand finished speaking: "Mr Gary. This warehouse will have a cooler. But now, UNOPS have a dispute with the contractor. So, he did not finish the work and the electrician has not been paid by the Afghan agent so there is no power."

Momand looked embarrassed by this tale of procrastination. There was no point me pursuing the issue with the Customs guys, it was way out of their lane. I made some notes, photographed labels and packing lists then shook hands with Momand. I'd seen enough. Next on the agenda was watching the off-load of some imported cars from a twenty-foot freight container. Mustafa, Art and I stepped out into the searing sun.

I shared my thoughts with Mustafa and Art: "That antibiotic cream is ruined. It's been transported from Pakistan in an open topped jingle truck through the Khyber Pass. Art, have you ever been to the Khyber Pass?"

"No sir, I haven't had that pleasure," Art's head was on a swivel. His M4 rifle ready to eliminate any threat within a thirty metre radius. I watched our six.

"Well, I was down there last year, July. It was fifty Celsius - in the shade. A hundred and thirty in your money," that was my quick conversion to US Fahrenheit equivalent. "No temperature sensitive product can survive that. I'm going to contact the manufacturer and see if they know what's going on with their products."

We approached the area of the ICD where most of the trucks parked up awaiting Customs clearance.

"Stop!" The immediacy in Art's voice left no doubt. He gestured we should stand closer to one of the trucks. And wait. He spoke into his radio: "Roger that," then turned to me. "We gotta go. *Now.*"

Hurry up.

"OK. Mustafa. The rest of the day is yours. See you again soon. Mananna," we shook hands on the move.

Mustafa disappeared down the side of another truck, becoming indistinguishable amongst hundreds of shalwar kameez clad men in the compound. Art and I emerged from the row of parked trucks and headed across twenty metres of open ground towards our M-RAP. Len was thirty yards to my right. He walked very quickly away from the ECP with two 3BSTB guys and Freddy the army interpreter.

Hurry up.

"Just received intelligence on a credible threat to military personnel at the ICD," said Art. "We're Oscar Mike."

Sat in my seat with the harness fastened felt good, but it would have been better with the M-RAP steps up and the hatch closed. I watched nearby activity through the thick armoured glass. Suddenly, every shalwar kameez clad driver and labourer were potential assassins. Even the children selling bottled water, bread and fruit appeared to be bulky around the middle. I was surrounded by suicide bombers.

Hurry up.

Len climbed the steps. The door was up and locked.

Sat in the M-RAP with the engine running the AC battled to expel heat, not only from the racks of flashing and buzzing electronic equipment, but also from the sun that was beginning to penetrate the armour.

My phone clock said 10:12 but nothing more. There was no signal strength indicator nor network ID. The M-RAP's jammers were on and soon the Afghan traders at the ICD would be complaining they couldn't make calls. If some of them were blown to bits by an IED, the survivors would blame the military for making them targets by being there. The locals didn't always regard a military presence as increased security.

The sergeant up front with the driver turned and shouted above the noise: "Just waiting for the order to move."

Len's left thumb acknowledged HUA. His right thumb was around the pistol grip of his M6. No point trying to engage in conversation, these guys may need to engage the enemy. The M-RAP passenger compartment was noisy. I'd stood next to quieter helicopters. Ear plugs in.

And wait.

Len took the bottle of water from me then held it at arm's length for the turret gunner. The young lad snatched it and gave the thumbs-up. Our driver and his sergeant gestured for theirs. I obliged.

Wait.

Our three soldiers were getting radio chatter. Driver and Comms Officer were doing stuff with the Blue Force Tracker up front. The screen content changed several times but it meant nothing to me. Engine noise increased as the M-RAP's brakes released the beast.

Turret gunner shouted down to us: "Hey, there's a can of fifty-cal ammo down there by the door. Bring it up."

This sounded serious. Len was nearest and reached the ammunition easily, then wedged it by the gunner's feet. Thumbs up came down from the turret. The engine revved.

Rocking forward to a halt behind the M-RAP in front, swayed us around in our seats.

Wait.

Going out the In Gate, made sense. The M-RAP that had been stationed by the Out Gate moved first, stopping the traffic from the direction of Jalalabad. Another M-RAP, exiting the In Gate, blocked the highway stopping traffic from Pakistan. The other four M-RAPs pulled out and formed the centre of the convoy. Len and I were now in the fourth of six M-RAPs. We were Oscar Mike to FOB Hughie.

Turret gunner was on a swivel. His big gun lingered on targets only he could see. The fifty-cal would knock big chunks off most vehicles if they got too close. A Toyota Corolla drove off the road into a ditch. It slo-mo rolled over like a compliant puppy. Wheels in the air and spinning as the big gun focused its attention elsewhere. I laughed.

"Whassup bro?" Len couldn't see it from his position. I described the scene. He laughed like he'd just got a punch-line.

"Ya saw that?" shouted turret gunner through bursts of laughter.

"Yeah I saw it!"

"That was funny as shee-it!" he was right. "The guy just lost it. All he had to do was stop."

"Dy-amm! I missed it," said Len, disappointed.

"I'll see if I can get another one to do it," turret man shouted as he turned the big gun towards the oncoming traffic. The road widened slightly by a used car sales compound. The moment for tilting cars had passed.

"Dy-amm! The ditch is this side now. Spoilt my fun. Sorry guys. You ain't gettin' another roll-over."

"Ahh, man. You promised!" shouted Len.

The traffic thinned out a little but it still took forty minutes to get to the base ECP. A jingle truck hoping to make a delivery blocked the entrance but the Afghan army soldiers soon got it shifted when they saw our convoy.

Eleven thirty-five and the door of F8 slammed shut behind me. Body armour off. Kettle on.. Combat boots off. Laptop boot-up. Salt marks emerging on drying shirt. Lying on my bed listening to the water in the kettle getting hotter.

"Len, I found something interesting during that cargo exam. It's way out of our lane but I'm going to pursue it anyway because there's not much else to do."

The other side of the plywood partition, Len was tidying his room. "Yeah? What was that?"

"A consignment of antibiotic cream from Pakistan. Looked like legit product. I'll do some background checks. But, my point is, they don't have anywhere to keep temperature sensitive cargo. The warehouse that's been funded by UNOPS is incomplete and because of some contractual dispute might never get finished."

"We cain't get involved in contractual disputes. Just fuggit about it."

"I know. And that's not my intention. I'm just interested in the supply chain aspect of this. Product integrity. For example, does the manufacturer know what's happening to the product after it's left the factory? I'm going to email the company."

"Hmm, interesting point. But does the manufacturer care? Don't see how we can use it in any reports but, yeah, why not. Won't hurt to take a look."

The kettle clicked off. We drank tea.

The email from Aldabaran Pharmaceuticals arrived three days later. Len came around to my side of the plywood to read over my shoulder.

Dear Mr Wilshaw,

Thank you for your email. I can confirm that Remedian is our product. The 50,000 units you identified represents around 0.1% of our annual production.

Remedian is an antibiotic cream used in the control of specific types of fungal infections as described in the leaflet that accompanies each package.

At Aldabaran we take great pride in the research, development and manufacture of our products. It was therefore with surprise and disappointment that we discovered, by your enquiry, that some of our partners do not share the same values.

I have checked the batch numbers you provided and can confirm that they were all manufactured at our Hyderabad facility in May 2010, as part of a 500,000 unit production run. Our products are transported in temperature controlled containers sealed at our premises to ensure product integrity.

I made enquiries to establish the supply chain is as follows:

500,000 units to our main distributor. PID Ltd of Hyderabad.

PID Ltd sold product as follows:

350,000 units to Gulf Independent Distribution, Dubai, UAE.

150,000 units to Quality Guaranteed Services, Dar es Salaam, Tanzania.

I confirmed with PID Ltd that they have a well established transport and storage partnership with Kumar Brothers of Karachi who handle exports.

We have received no reports of damaged product nor any requests for replacement.

I am not able to offer any information on further distribution of this batch. However, I can tell you that our products are available in some markets in India despite embargoes enforced by Indian Customs authority. We have long suspected that unscrupulous traders move product to India via Afghanistan to circumvent embargoes.

Aldabaran does not support or condone this activity because it jeopardises product integrity and trust in our products.

I hope you find this information helpful. On behalf of Aldabaran Pharmaceuticals I would like to thank you and BMTF for your attention to this matter.

Yours sincerely,

Milad Kermani.

CEO.

Len finished reading the message: "It didn't take 'em long to reply."

"Yes, I'm impressed. A tenth of one per cent of annual production isn't much and it can't be in their interest to mess about with small consignments like this."

Ken stroked his goatee as he spoke: "I'm thinking the stuff's either stolen or somewhere along the way, someone knows it's ruined so offloaded it."

"Could be. But I'm thinking displaced load."

"Huh? Speak Murican," said Len.

"Displaced load. It's a common way for smugglers to exploit legitimate loads." my pencil wrote numbers on the legal pad as I spoke. "OK. We counted five thousand 40 gram tubes of cream. So that's, roughly, two hundred kilos. Now, imagine if those five thousand tubes came from a fifty-thousand tube consignment. OK?"

"OK. Go on," Len was into the mental arithmetic.

"Well, that gives someone a two hundred kilo space in which to substitute legitimate cargo with something else. With me so far?" I could

260

see that he was. "Happens every day in the UK. Mostly tax free cigarettes but not always. So, whenever you see a displaced load you should look out for the rest of the legitimate cargo because the smuggled stuff will be amongst it."

"Shee-it man. That's priddy neat."

Len's remark made me smile. "It is. But here's the thing, because of delivery time slots at depots, the displaced load must be ahead of the legit consignment so that the smugglers have time to retrieve their own stuff and consolidate the original products. That way, no ones suspicions are aroused. Difference here is delivery slots aren't an issue."

"OK. Got it. So, could be that the five thousand tubes you saw could be associated with a two hundred kilo movement of Pakistani heroin?"

"That's what I'm thinking. Raw opium over the mountains to Pakistan by donkey. Refined product back to Afghanistan in a cover load of mixed cargo. Then overland through the former Soviet Republics. The Afghans who defected to the USSR have their own network in Russia, Turkmenistan maybe. Across the Caspian into Azerbaijan then into Turkey or Georgia. Destination Europe. The Armenians are well into that business."

"So, any refrigerated unit coming into Afghanistan must be worth a look?"

"I'd say so. But that's a hell of a lot of trucks and who's going to risk ruining a consignment of chilled product when there's no refrigerated examination facility? Also, a lot of NATO stuff is refrigerated. That doesn't get touched. If it was my job on the line I wouldn't go near it. Trouble is here, they wouldn't just lose their job."

"Yeah, right bro. OK, good work. Nice theory. Write it up and I'll include it in the weekly report. But here's the thing, are we saying that the pharmaceutical products held in the J'bad Customs warehouse are awaiting reconsolidating?"

"Yes."

"So, someone at the J'Bad ICD is in on it?"

"They must be. The Customs guys probably don't even know they are involved. The three blokes that turned up for the cargo examination, maybe they didn't know what was going on either. Just sent along to watch the goods. So, either they'd never been checked before or they were the nominated stooges. Whatever the setup today, that's why they're not too bothered about the warehouse not being refrigerated. The stuff in there is of no value, it's the use to which it will be put that is of value."

"Shee-it bro. That's some theory. But like we've said before, nothin' in Afghanistan is what it seems to be."

"True. But here's something else that occurred to me: the jingle truck was carrying a load of old shite. Pots and pans. Plastic chairs. Small amounts of low-value junk. And amongst all that is a two hundred kilo load of high-value temperature sensitive goods. All that old shite was a cover load for the displaced cargo from the main cover load. Get it?" I could tell as I was explaining it that Len had already arrived at the same conclusion.

"Yeah. I got it bro. They couldn't just move the two hundred kilos of antibiotic cream, it would stand out too much. Shee-it, they could get that in a taxi. That is some theory. But, can ya prove it?"

"I could but I'd need a lot of help."

"Hmm. Well if ya write it up good, someone in Karrbul might take notice," Len switched on the kettle for tea. "Just one thing stands out here, that is, why would Khairfullah lead us to it? Is he trying to see how smart we are or, is he trying to hit the bad guys without showing his hand?"

"We'll probably never know. We also need to be super careful now. We've got gangster Khan thinking BMTF is all dimwits. We should keep it that way," I said.

"Too right bro," from the pack, Len dealt teabags into our cups. "Dya think ya could devise a strategy around this cargo examination? Kind of a *going forward* thing?"

"Definitely, it'll draw on a number of Customs elements: suspect load targeting and selection, intelligence gathering, surveillance and investigation techniques. Maybe some training for the Customs guys. It'll be heavily reliant on interrogation of ASYCUDA. Wow! It's sounding better all the time."

"ASYCUDA? That's the Customs database, right?" said Len sarcastically, he knew damn well what it was. He'd nominated me Team Subject Matter Expert at Torkham.

"Yes, all those hours spent sat in the main Customs office may not have been wasted after all. It's an acronym so the guys in HQ will love it. Stands for: Automated System for Customs Data. My experience with it comes from my time in the Congo. It's a United Nations computer program, UNCTAD to be precise. It's supposed to facilitate trade as well as enable governments to account for tax. I didn't see much evidence of either in the Congo. It's possible to interrogate it but the ASYCUDA lad at J'bad ICD isn't too keen to share it with me. I think he thinks I know more about it than him. I don't. I can do some basic stuff but I don't know the cheats."

"Cheats?" that got Len's attention.

"Yes, the Congolese Douane knew all the cheats. They routinely altered data after goods were cleared. More specifically, they changed duty payments after clearance when they thought we weren't looking and skimmed off the proceeds. Sometimes it was done by request from importers who would share the loot, but most of the time it was down to the Customs officers. They all got some."

"That's funny man," Len used a spoon to squeeze his tea bag. "How much d'ya reckon the government lost 'cause of it?"

"I couldn't say. Impossible to even guess. The whole system is corrupt. At Lubumbashi, which is in Katanga Province, the Customs guys saw swindling the government as their personal duty. I guess they had to. I watched them unload three big mail sacks from the back of a pickup truck one morning. One hundred and fifty kilos. It was their salary, in Congolese Francs. Almost worthless. Smells like used toilet paper."

"No shit," said Len. We laughed.

"Yeah, plenty of shit. I had to keep the money in a plastic bag so it didn't make my back pocket smell like my crack."

"Woah! Stop right there, bro. Too much information."

"Crazy place. So much money in the economy. Katanga Province is to the Congo what Texas is to the USA: wealthy. Except it's copper not oil.

263

You'll laugh when I say this but I reckon the Afghan Customs are upstanding citizens by comparison with their Congolese counterparts." Len did indeed laugh. "But get this, the Congolese reckoned the Nigerians are worse than them," I smiled. "I had no reason to doubt what they said."

"Yeah well, goes without sayin' goddam Nigerians are congenital crooks. Hey, weren't they parta the jolly old Briddish Empire? They learnt from the best! Ye haha!" Len mocked.

"Just make the bloody tea!" I said. We both laughed.

I checked the Aldabaran email again: "Kermani at Aldabaran says there have been no reports of lost or damaged cargo, so he's saying that Kumar Brothers are pukka. But maybe they subcontracted some of the work and that's where the switch happened. I'll email the Kumars."

"What's pukka?" said Len.

"Oh, sorry. It means proper, the genuine article. It's an old British army expression picked up in India. From Hindi. I bet some of the Afghans use that word. Like lorry. Are you familiar with lorry, Len?"

"Ain't that some Briddish word for one of those quaint little trucks you guys drag yure shidaround in?"

"Yeah that's it," I said scornfully. "Quaint little trucks that produce the same horsepower from an engine half the size without it having to stick out down the road thirty-feet. It means the driver can actually see the front of the vehicle. Is that the sort of truck you mean?"

"Yeah, hahahahaha, that's the kinda truck I meant. Oh, hold on, ya don't make 'em in the UK no more do ya? Heharhaha!"

He'd got me. "Yeah, OK. Point taken. I think there are some manufacturers of small trucks but not the big tractor units like you have in the States. Most of the UK's road haulage fleet is made in Germany."

Kumar Brothers' email arrived the next day. It very briefly confirmed what Kermani at Aldabaran had said, but with one difference: the customer requested a split load. The 350,000 units to Gulf Independent Distribution in the United Arab Emirates, became 300,000 units to Dubai, the other 50,000 units went to a warehouse in Peshāwar owned by a company called Amal Trading. Gulf Independent Distribution filled a customer order locally rather than ship the whole load out to Dubai then send some back. The email-attached copy customer order was from Nabi Habbibi Limited with an address in Peshāwar. Len looked at it over my shoulder.

My pencil pointed to the screen: "But look at the address. See it?"

He did: "Post Office Box number. Where's the business address? No email? Don't look right."

"Exactly! Peshāwar isn't far from here. Fancy a day out?" I joked.

"Yeah right bro!" said Len, with the utmost sarcasm. "We don't have enough ammo to make the trip."

Len's remark made me smile. "I like the way you didn't say no," just below the signature line was a phone number.

"There's a contact number too. I'll ask one of the army interpreters to call it. I bet the Peshwari fella speaks Pashto. It's just one big tribe around here, doesn't matter which side of the Durand Line they're on."

"And say what? Might be an idea to just pass the number upstream and see if some analyst can make anything of it." Len wasn't convinced by his own argument and he could tell by my blank stare, neither was I. "Only kiddin', but block your phone number."

On my way back from the gym, Freddy was heading in the opposite direction. We spoke briefly. He'd be available to play the role: "Sounds like fun man. Just give me the script, I'll act it."

"OK Freddy. I'll write out some questions. What time you available?"

"Anytime man. How about in an hour?"

"An hour sounds good. I'll make the tea."

"No man. You don't need to make tea."

We both laughed. Freddy didn't really rate my British black tea.

At fifteen hundred hours, Freddy sat down with me and Len in the BMTF office. Signal was unusually good. The call connected.

Freddy shouted into the mobile: an angry customer who'd been given this guy's number by someone at Gulf International Distribution. Freddy wanted to know why the Remedian he'd bought hadn't arrived and did the guy have a contact number for the haulier because the delay was unacceptable. The guy's offer to call Freddy back was quickly rejected. Freddy made out he'd spoken to four people already who'd said the same thing but they never called. He wanted a name and phone number as well as this guy's current location. He didn't want to have to drive to Peshāwar to fix this.

Iqbal on the receiving end read out an Afghan phone number used by a guy called Mohammed. It was Mohammed's job to fix things like this. The call ended. I was impressed.

"Really well done Freddy. I don't know what you said, but the way you said it scared the shit out of me."

"Thanks, Mr Gary. That was great fun man," Freddy handed me the pad with his notes. "That guy was an asshole. The guy with this phone," he tapped the number on the sheet, "he won't be so easy. Mohammed's the guy that bought the fifty-thousand but he got Iqbal to take five thousand out and send in a smaller truck. Don't make sense to me. Why'd he do that?"

"Hmm, I think I know why. I'd like to call this Mohammed guy. I'm a bit concerned that some law enforcement agency might be tracking him. Len what do you think?"

"Does law enforcement in this part of the world track anyone for two hundred kilos? Two thousand maybe. I say, go to Mohammed."

"OK, Freddy, here's what you need to say," I wrote some questions on the legal pad. "You feel OK with this?"

Freddy's face was ablaze with fun. "Sure, man. It's not like someone's shootin' at me!"

"Excellent. OK. You're a Customs officer at Torkham. You need to verify a consignment because you can't read the paperwork. Is it one load of fifty-thousand Remedian? And, what is the truck registration? That'll do."

"No problem, man," Freddy made the call. The signal was bad which was good for us, it made the sudden disconnection plausible.

"Fifty-thousand Remedian. One truck. License plate T-1093. Belongs to Abdullah Trucks. He wanted to know if there was a problem with it. I told him there was no problem. It was all OK. He said he needed it in Kabul by tomorrow. I told him that's down to the driver but we're finished with it."

"Brilliant, Freddy. So, gentlemen, we've got five thousand items of Mohammed's load at Jalalabad ICD and he's just told us he's got fifty-thousand in that truck," I pointed to the pad. "What do we make of that?"

Len's eyebrows almost met as he considered the seriousness of the matter: "I reckon we need ta git this upstream to one of the BMTF intell guys, now. Maybe he can make sump'n of it. Great work, Freddy. You'll make a good cop when you get your US visa."

Freddy grinned. "No problem man. Any time," Freddy handed me the phone. "Is this somethin' ta do with the security alert?"

The room brightened briefly. Maybe my pupils dilated. A Eureka moment. I turned to see Len having a similar episode.

Len spoke first: "Ahh, shee-it! Ya know, the kid might be right."

I sat on a water stack. "Hmm. That puts a different complexion on it, doesn't it?"

"Sure does. Coincidence?" Len leaned on the door frame looking sceptical.

"No. Coincidence is an event without apparent causal connection. I'm not going to attempt to rationalise it out of this equation. This is Afghanistan."

My mind was on the Significant Incident Report, the SIR, I was about to write.

Len agreed: "Uhuh! Nothin's quite as it seems."

Freddy spoke. "Hey, guys, I gotta go. We're getting some kebabs delivered from town. You want one? They're real good."

If it had been anyone else but Freddy recommending kebabs from a Jalalabad street stall I'd have said thanks but, no thanks.

"Sounds good. Len, want one?" I said.

"Not for me guys. Watchin' my weight," said Len.

"Here, Freddy, take this," two twenty dollar bills were within his grasp.

"No man. I got this. Be about nineteen hundred," Freddy was heading for the door.

"Freddy, take it. You just earned that."

Freddy grinned, clutched the money and was gone.

Len watched the door slam. "He's a hell of a kid. Make a good American citizen one day."

"Damn right." The contents of the legal pad made it feel more substantial. "Len, I'll write this up while it's still fresh in my mind. Then you'll have it for the weekly report. Maybe call French and let him know there's a SIR on its way to him soon."

"Roger that bro. Including the security alert. I'm on it," Len already had the phone to his ear as he went out the door. I was a good way through writing my report on Word when Len came back into F8. "French is impressed. He says he'll get it to the right people over in DEA. He doesn't have an email for 'em so he'll walk a paper version over to their compound. He don't expect to hear nothin' from DEA. That's just the way they are."

My report included information obtained from our enquiries. It explained how the scenario fitted the profile of a smuggling attempt using a cover load of legitimate cargo and how we strongly suspected that the five thousand items at J'bad ICD were a displaced load that would be reconsolidated with the legitimate load before it was delivered to somewhere in Kabul.

One paragraph proposed an Afghan-led surveillance operation to track the jingle truck with five thousand pieces of Remedian from J'bad. It was highly likely that the jingle truck would meet with truck T-1093 which was suspected of carrying 200 kg of illicit product, could be heroin, possibly guns and explosives. Outcomes would include seizures of illicit material, intelligence gathering, as well as being a good training event.

Our Intell report got cross-referenced with the SIR relating to the security alert.

There was nothing more to be done. Even if there had been more time to prepare for an operation it was unlikely to be successful. It was just a way of letting HQ know we were still out there, observing, advising,

268

reporting. I emailed the report to Len. He sent it upstream. I didn't expect to hear of a result.

French was right. We heard nothing. Maybe a DEA agent made something of it, maybe it was filed. It made no difference to me either way. Six One Zero.

The Big Dish - December 2011 to May 2012

We never had more than three advisors deployed to Jalalabad. It was usually two. For a third of my time on FOB Hughie, BMTF was down to one. Program management wanted six advisors, but it didn't happen. Why we never got the resources was none of my concern but it was probably because a new guy at the Embassy issued his initiative which went in a different direction to the previous guy's initiative. There were contractors in Kabul being paid twice as much as me for sorting this stuff out, let's call it managing. Back in the States, people higher up the chain were paid double that much again for doing whatever it was they did. I just did as I was told, most of the time, and collected the bi-monthly pay-cheque. Bi-monthly was an unfamiliar expression to me until I worked for a US company.

"Hey Len!" I shouted through the partition.

"Wassup bro?" Len was making his third coffee of the morning. It was Friday, our official day off. We were taking it easy. We were getting much better at that.

"Have you had any problem with the internet?"

"No more than usual. Why?"

"I just did a speed-test and the download speed seems to have dropped off quite a bit. I'm going to start monitoring it," another spreadsheet opened.

"Now you mention it, yeah, it was kinda slow last night. I thought it was maybe the weather." Len had a point. If the local conditions changed to something other than scorching hot, the signal became a bit flaky. If we had heavy low cloud the signal couldn't find the antenna.

Within a few hours we had no service. It had started to rain.

Len was on the case: "I'm headin' over to the MWR, git on email to Greg. He's gonna have to git on to the innernet company and fix this. Three thousand dollars a month and it don't frickin' work!"

"OK, I'll keep trying here. Also, I'll push the vac around for a few minutes," I felt the need to clean.

Along with the tin-desks, filing cabinet, 240 Volt microwave cooker that wouldn't work on the 110 Volt supply, was a vacuum cleaner. Like the rest of the stuff, it was a cheap Chinese copy of a real item somewhere in the real world. Like the desks, it too had cost the US taxpayer a fortune.

We let the other guys in our hut use the vac because it was better than just brushing the dust back up into the air with bristles on a stick and the shed spiders couldn't out run its deadly suck. The AC filters would remove more airborne filth until they got blocked and the compressor pipes grew ice and froze solid. Then the maintenance guys would have to come and clean the filters, defrost the unit stood outside in thirty degree heat and the process started all over again.

The vac's brand name made me smile: Penasonic. It may have been a counterfeit with a spelling mistake or a genuine brand trying to capitalise on the similarity of their name to a superior make. One thing was for sure, it was noisy. My noise cancelling ear defenders came in handy.

Dirt that surrendered to the Penasonic got set free out the front door where most of it had originated. Dust evading capture by the inadequate filter, gradually settled on flat surfaces. Then I mopped. What the wet mop didn't pick up I'd get next week.

Then got back to reading my latest book, *Gates of Fire* by Steven Pressfield. One of the specialists we worked with had passed it on to me. The Commandant of the US Marine Corps has it on his reading list. The Battle of Thermopylae is an epic story about Greek heroism. As expected from a story about Ancient Greece, fate and irony are intrinsic to the plot. So too, the military themes of: duty, honour and stoicism.

The first two of those virtues have no place in the contracting world, but stoicism is essential.

F8's door opened. Instinctively touching the Glock on my hip gave me a true sense of security. It remained holstered. Chambered, but holstered. The mud-shedding boot-stomp told me it was Len returned from the MWR with a fresh supply of dust and some good news.

"We're gittin' a new dish!" Len laughed as he spoke.

"Wow! That's good," I was on my feet and in my doorway.

"We gotta get a platform fixed up for it. Gonna have to be on the roof. No further details at present but will be on email, Sunday. Caint do nuttin' today 'cause all the HQ Afghans're off, it bein' a Friday. But the issue's been reported up the chain," Len sat at his desk. "When we get the specifications we can arrange with SFC Mueller to get a carpenter to make the platform."

"Sounds good. Specifications?" I queried.

"Yeah. Dish size. Greg's talkin' maybe twice as big as this one."

"This one was OK to begin with. Maybe the conditions changed. Satellite was repositioned or the dish just shifted on its base. I do wonder about that Green Meanie cleaning truck. I've seen it get very close to the antenna on the dish. Maybe it made contact on a few occasions and moved it," I said.

"Hey bro, I don't know the answer. Those guys up in Karrbul get paid to fix this kinda thing. HQ knows best. Even when they don't," said Len.

The email arrived on Sunday along with a PDF of the order. ACCL were to supply and install a new satellite dish and modem.

"That can't be right," I said. "Four point two metre diameter?" I did a quick calculation, "That's almost fifteen feet across. The hut's only twenty-four feet wide."

"Yup. I know," confirmed Len forlornly. "It's gonna take some structure to support it, especially in high winds and Karrbul ain't providing the platform. That's why we gotta get with SFC Mueller, A-SAP. Another KLE."

Len explained what we needed. SFC Meuller agreed to the request, then got on the phone to arrange for a local day labourer to make the new dish platform.

The following Tuesday an old Afghan turned up with a handful of tools. His attire complied with the Site Safe workwear requirement for the job he was to undertake: shalwar khameez, waistcoat, pakool and sandals. I got the escort job. Old Chippy began sawing and hammering some four by two. Then he cut shapes from plywood. Within a couple of hours he'd fitted a small structure onto the middle of the hut's apex. It resembled one of those false chimneys, popular on US trailer-park homes. He was happy with his work. Not me. The box he'd created was completely inadequate but despite my best attempt to explain, he didn't get it.

Freddy had stepped outside his hut, interrupting his TV cricket time, to see why the hammering had stopped. He explained to Old Chippy what I'd said.

"Mr Gary, he was just told to make a base for a satellite dish. He's done it before and it's always like this."

"OK Freddy. Thanks. It's not big enough," turning to Old Chippy, I said: "Sir. Thank you for your work but please take it down. For me, it is no good. I need a platform to hold a dish this big ..."

After pacing out the diameter in front of him we all agreed it was very big. Old Chippy said something to Freddy.

"Mr Gary, he says that he can't make something that big because he does not have the wood. He just brought the pieces he was told to bring," Freddy pointed to the structure on the roof.

"OK," I spoke to Old Chippy. "I understand. I will speak with the army and get more wood. Mananna."

Old Chippy climbed back onto the corrugated tin roof and began dismantling his work.

Freddy watched Old Chippy squatting on the roof, clawing nails with difficulty. "What's goin' arn Mr Gary?"

"Our internet has gone wrong. HQ in Kabul is sending us a new dish but it's enormous. So, we need somewhere to put it. It would block this alleyway," I pointed up and down the gravel track where we stood. "There's only one place it can go," my finger pointed upwards.

"Hey, Mr Gary, when you get the new internet, could you help me with something?"

"Of course. What?"

"I'm applying for my SIV but most of the stuff is done on the internet. I need to download documents and that's not allowed in the MWR."

"What's an SIV?" Another abbreviation for my glossary.

"Special Immigrant Visa, it's to live in the US. A lot of the interpreters here are applying for them. They need 'em. If they don't get 'em, they're fucked, man," Freddy already had an American accent, more so than some of the Hispanic soldiers I'd met who were born in the States, the SIV would be a lifeline.

"OK. I need to be with the carpenter until he has done the job so as soon as that is finished maybe we can help you. I need to make sure Len is OK with it. Have you already done some work on the SIV?"

"Some, yeah. But it's difficult. The documents are complicated."

"Yeah, I bet they are. OK. Len's a Border Patrol guy. He will know the regulations. I'm sure he'll be fine. And maybe you can teach me a few Pashto phrases. I'm not happy greeting people with *As salaam Alaikum* because it's a Muslim to Muslim thing and I'm not. If I'm working with Pashtuns, I'd feel happier greeting them in Pashto. Does that make sense?"

"Sure. Hey, Mr Gary, that's good man. Yeah, we can help each other," we shook hands.

Back in F8, Len was enthusiastic about the prospect of helping Freddy and his comrades.

"Hey-ell, why not. We can give 'em two hours a day when we're here, which is most of the time. Use our office to do their stuff. Just don't have more than three at any one time. And not when the other guys are at home. They may not take too kindly to a bunch of Afghans bein' in here."

"Thanks Len. It'll mean a lot to these lads and we never know when we might really need them."

"Too true bro. Yeah, great idea. Pity it can't go on the weekly report. Might be the only positive thing that comes outta this fucked up program."

Old Chippy returned the next day with Young Assistant. That was me and Len tied up with escort duty for several hours. By early afternoon the two local tradesmen had made a sturdy platform traversing the gap between the neighbour's hut and ours. All we needed now was the dish, but in the meantime we could use it as an observation platform to survey the locality. Turned out to be a bad idea. It became clear just how close we were to the Afghan National Army base just the other side of the trees to the rear of F8. The enemy lived less than ten feet away. A casually lobbed grenade, or a couple of guys with AK-47s, climbing through the trees on to the dish platform, would make short work of us. I shouldn't have gone up for a look. Too late now. Stay vigilant.

It was another week before the dish team turned up from Kabul. We went through the cooling off yard and visitor pass routine again. Their truck was several hundred yards away so we helped the two skinny Afghan lads carry the kit into the base. They spent the best part of an hour pondering the parts and instructions while recovering from the exertion. Then they admitted to having no tools with which to assemble the dish.

The De Walt power tools were charged and ready. The hex bolt attachments and small adjustable wrench I'd Amazoned several months earlier would come in handy. We fixed the frame to the platform. Assembling the three pieces of curved aluminium that made the satellite dish was made easier by my Leatherman.

"This isn't four point two metres," I felt compelled to mention it just in case they'd brought the wrong one.

"No Mr Gary, this is two point four metres," Afraheem attached the central support arms and feed horn as he spoke. "Four point two metres is too big."

There was no point telling him that Len and I had worked that out, but I did mention our last communication with HQ. "The email said four point two, would you like to see it?"

'There is no need. This is what we must fit,' Afraheem was right. It was this or nothing. Two point four metres was still pretty big. When assembled it stood over the gap between huts F8 and F10 like a secret service listening station. That troubled me. If people thought there was something special going on in our hut, we might become a target. Invaders always seek to either destroy or control their enemy's communications and we now looked like we were doing some serious communicating.

By seventeen hundred hours, Afraheem and his pal, with our assistance, had the replacement internet system up and running. New modem and all new cable. Six drops, one in each room. The Afghan lads were hopeless with hand tools but when it came to the technical stuff they were wizards. We got Afraheem and his assistant back to their small truck and gave them twenty bucks to get a meal on the way home.

Len was in his room enjoying the new internet service. I was in the BMTF office keeping my promise to Freddy.

"OK. How good are your computer skills?"

"Not great, Mr Gary."

"OK, no problem. You will get to learn office skills. Always useful. If I tell you stuff you already know, sorry. But hopefully most of it will be helpful."

"Hey, no way, Mr Gary, it's all useful. Thanks, man."

"OK. You sit here," as the chair came unstuck from under the metal desk the contents of drawers rattled like paperclips in a biscuit tin. "Here's a pencil and notebook. You may need to write stuff down. I'm thinking passwords, computer tips. Got it?" As Freddy watched the laptop boot up I knew he'd get it. His life depended on it. "Let's treat this as a Train the Trainer session. Have you heard that expression before?"

"Yeah, man. The Army do it all the time. They teach people to teach other people. They call it T3."

"Got it. So, you will learn how to get through the SIV system and then help others. Agreed?" I had a feeling BMTF were about to become popular with the Afghan interpreters but I didn't want to do all the work.

"You got it, man."

"What documents do you have already?" The printer was on standby to scan Freddy's stuff.

"Tashkil and some US Army ID docs."

"Tashkil? That's a list of a person's personal information, like an identity document, right?"

"That's right Mr Gary," said Freddy"

"OK. If you have a passport we need that copied too."

"Right. I'll bring that next time."

The internet was still slow, but stable. Downloading documents was pretty quick. By the end of the two hour session Freddy had an email account; Skype account; his documents scanned and stored on a thumb-drive along with downloaded documents he'd completed. I made space in a filing cabinet for drop folders containing paper documents.

"Do you want to put a phrase or quote on your Skype profile?"

"Sure man. What should I put?"

"People often put phrases or quotes from famous people. For example, I like that," stapled to the wall over the desk was an A4 sheet of paper. "Can you read it?"

"Sure man, it says, 'The enemy is anybody who's going to get you killed, no matter which side he's on.'"

He'd been paying attention. That made me smile. "Do you understand it?"

"Yeah, sure. It means the enemy isn't always shootin' *at* yer. Sometimes he's the guy tellin' ya to do stoopid shit. Is it OK if I use that?"

"I insist. It's from a book called Catch-22. Some of the army guys we work with have read it. Ask them about it. They'll love explaining it to you," we both smiled and shook hands. "We'll do more tomorrow. This is your folder." It dropped into the filing cabinet with the name tag showing. "You have a file on this," I held up the thumb-drive. "And we'll keep it in the bottom of the same drawer. OK?" I slid the drawer shut. "Maybe you should finish your application before starting to help others. It looks very complicated."

Two hours had passed.

"Sure thing Mr Gary. See you tomorrow," he was on his feet and out the door.

I walked up the corridor to Len's door. "Did you hear any of that?"

"Sure did bro. Train the Trainer? Ye haa!" Len was amused. "Pity we can't use it in the weekly reports. I think you're gonna be busy. Let me know if ya need anythin'."

Over the next few days Freddy copied and saved documents in different formats. Added stuff to his computer folder and the bunch of papers in the drawer. He also learned how to name emails and attach documents to be saved in Drafts. That way, if the paper and the electronic folders were lost, he had a backup that he could get to anywhere in the world. I called it Freddy's drop-box. In exchange, Freddy helped me compile a list of useful Pashto phrases which I spoke in the local dialect.

Len got involved with some of Freddy's Department of Homeland Security documents because they used unintelligible phrases. How the US government expected the guys that really needed the SIV to get through the bureaucracy is anybody's guess. Maybe they weren't expected to.

Freddy's file was done. It was ready to go to the US Embassy on his next trip home to Kabul. From my room next to the office Freddy could be heard helping another interpreter get through his SIV application.

Zed was switched on. Like Freddy, Zed didn't really look Afghan. With his light brown curly hair, hazel eyes and broad New York accent, Zed could have been a native of the Bronx. If he'd mimicked an Irish accent while wearing jockey's silks he'd have got by most British Immigration officers. Zed had told me about his time with a platoon of the 173rd Airborne Brigade Combat Team in the Korengal Valley. He's in the National Geographic documentary film *Restrepo*. I've watched it several times.

One of those crazy Afghan ringtones with a jumble of clashing sounds announced an incoming call. Freddy answered in Pashto. A long silence ensued as he listened to someone speak.

A chair slid back urgently. Something hit the floor and plywood panel. The shed shook.

Silence.

Then a loud cry, not of physical pain but of torment and anguish. I was on my feet and into the office. Squatting on the floor near the door, Freddy cried incessantly. Zed was already by Freddy's side speaking quietly in Pashto. I squatted the other side of Freddy, gripping his shoulder.

He spoke falteringly: "My father's dead. …Killed. …Taliban went to his house. Shot him eighteen times. He's dead, man. I fucking hate this country," his head went down to his knees.

Zed shouted: "Shit, man. Shit! Shit!" he was right. It was a shit situation.

My feeble words broke a prolonged silence: "Freddy. I am so very sorry. I can't say anymore than that. Nothing I say can help right now."

Wait.

"Zed, LT is your boss right?"

"Yeah, man. I'll go tell him," Zed was on his feet.

"Good. He must come here. Tell no one else. Wait on what LT says. Hurry up. OK?"

"On it, man," Zed pulled a phone from the pocket in his shalwar kameez and was gone.

"Freddy, is it OK if I sit here next to you?" he sat hunched on the floor, his arms reached over shoulder to shoulder covering his head. I didn't need to see tears to know he was crying. He groaned unintelligibly. As my arm pulled him closer, emotion shook free of his body. Len came to the door of the office. He said nothing. There was nothing to be said. We waited. Five long agonising minutes elapsed before LT arrived. The door of F8 slammed open.

"Freddy!" LT called down the hallway. Len flicked his head to the left: *in here*, then stepped aside. "Hey man. Fucking shit. It's … it's fuckin' *shit*, man. We gotta getcha outa here. You need ta go home, man. Ya wanna go home?"

Freddy didn't speak. Right now, he needed someone to do his thinking for him.

LT was the man: "We'll pack some stuff for you. Just one bag." Freddy rocked back and forth with pain. "Zed. Go pack Freddy a small bag. Not everything. Just enough for three days. Got it?"

"Got it, LT," Zed was gone.

He must have packed many bags in a hurry. Within five minutes he returned with a hold-all. Freddy was unsteadily on his feet. His mind had gone. Elsewhere. LT stared into his face at close range. He'd seen shock

279

too many times. Eyes: fixed on infinity. Mind: repeating the same thoughts, almost finding the answer before remembering the question: *why*?

LT spoke: "Freddy, listen to me. We're gonna get you on a flight to Kabul A-SAP. Ya got that?" Freddy grunted. "Len, Gary, can you guys get Freddy over to Finley Shields for the Molson to Fenty?"

"Sure, LT. We're right on it," said Len. We went to our rooms and got into our gear: the same kit that had made Freddy smile on a previous occasion.

LT pointed at Zed. "You're going with these guys. Stay with Freddy till he gets on Molson. I'll have one of our guys meet Freddy at Fenty as he gets off the heelo. He is not to be left alone. Understood?" LT pulled out his phone.

"Yes, LT. HUAh," Zed, was on overwatch.

Two bottles of water snatched from our stack went into Freddy's hold-all.

"Len, I'll bring the Prado down here to the door," it hit me as I turned to go. "Freddy!" he was sat on the office chair. Numb. Hands on knees, shaking. Squatting in front of him got his attention. "Freddy, *listen to me* my friend. Take your SIV folder. Do you hear me?" he looked up briefly, expressionless. He heard me but I wasn't sure he was listening. "Take your SIV folder. You might not come back here. Got it?" There was no way to be sure he'd *got it*, but discussion wasn't appropriate. "It's going in your bag. You will have loads of stuff to do with your family but if you get a chance, deal with this. It's more important now than ever. Understood?" My eyes bored into his, willing him to understand.

"Yeah, man. Understood," he'd got it. A bulky envelope with Freddy's folder went into the hold-all.

"OK, mate. It's in there. If you need anything else, call me or Len. Got that?" He mumbled inaudibly. "Your father wanted you to get this SIV. This is his way of making it happen. He's with you right now. Right?" Don't ask me where that moment of illumination came from, I'm still not sure I said it. Freddy must have been holding his breath. He let it out and cried. I squeezed his shoulder, once. "OK, I'll get the truck."

Len stood at the office door. "Roger that. See ya in a minute."

The ride through the Afghan Army base to Finley Shields was quiet, emotional and fortunately, uneventful. A eucalyptus tree gave some welcome shade to the Prado as we each hugged Freddy near the flight line.

As I removed my helmet, a dove flapped loudly out of the leaves and branches before landing on my head. Its sharp toes felt like needles gripping my scalp.

"What the fuck, man," shouted Zed, excitedly. "Even the creatures love you."

Having a dove pecking around in my hair was irritating, but its presence seemed propitious and brushing it away, inappropriate.

"Hey, Freddy, he's looking at you, man," said Zed. "Whadda fuck man. I never seen nothing like that before. That's crazy, man."

Zed didn't say it was auspicious, nor did he mention Allah. No one spoke as the dove flew back to the eucalyptus tree.

Freddy carried his bag to the Huey. I didn't expect to see him again.

Two weeks later, a knock on the door of F8 preceded the shout from a familiar voice: "Mr Len, Mr Gary. You here?" Freddy returned.

But it was a different Freddy that met me in the corridor with a handshake and man-hug. On the day he left, strands of grey in his black hair must've gone unnoticed in the rush to get him home. But the fluorescence of F8's lights left no doubt, he'd grown older.

"Hey, Freddy. Come in. I'm just making tea. Want some?"

"Sure, Mr Gary. Is it that toor chai?" he grimaced slightly at the prospect of black tea but accepted the hospitality. "Or, you could use this," he held out a six inch cubed box of Afghan green tea.

"I get it. You never did like my tea," I joked.

"No man. It's not that. PG Tips is OK, man. No milk. No sugar," Freddy sounded different but I couldn't pin-point why.

"I know, you're sweet enough," we both laughed.

A fist thrust a mug into the hallway from behind Len's door. "Hey, if you're makin' tea, count me in guys."

"I'm glad you came back. If you want to talk about your dad, I'm very happy to listen. If you don't, that's OK too. You decide," I said.

"Thanks, man. 'preciate it," his eyes became liquid. "Maybe."

Watching blokes cry gets me down. Making tea meant I didn't have to. The sound of boiling water didn't drown out the dry harshness of Freddy's voice. It wasn't from the filthy arid air of Kabul. Emotional stress had taken something from him. On the surface he looked like the Freddy I'd met in July 2011. Underneath his cool exterior was the crystallised resolve he'd need to cut through to his future, far away from the country he now hated.

"Hey man, I wannid to say thanks for the SIV pack. I got it to the Embassy. You were right about that. Everything you said."

I suddenly felt a sense of immense achievement. "You mean the pack was accepted? No problems?" I shouldn't have sounded surprised but I'd expected issues.

"No problems, Mr Gary. Guy went through it while I was there. I'm in the system."

"Well that has *got* to be good. Any idea how long the system takes?" that phrase always makes me suspicious. Freddy shrugged but he was happy with the result. He looked over to the office.

"Is it OK if I use the computer? I got something on email I gotta print."

"Sure Freddy. Start it up," I heard the laptop boot-up chime. "Any more of your guys want to get started on their SIV?"

"Yeah man. I wannid ta talk to you about that. There's four more doin' the SIV. Can you help them?"

"Freddy, it's down to your recommendation. If you say they are good, then they're good. If a guy comes to me and you tell me he's a problem, he's out. Understand?"

"Mr Gary, they are all top guys. Some of 'em do stoopid shit occasionally but they only hurt themselves, ya know?"

"I know. We all do it. OK Freddy, you plus two more and not when the other guys that live here are in our hut. Yes?" It was agreed. "OK, after you've printed the email, print another copy of the folder you took with you. That is a proven example of what your guys will need. Got it?"

"Yes, Mr Gary, they won't be a problem. I'll make sure of that," he said with authority.

Two hours a day. Twelve hours a week. Forty eight hours a month. No hours on Fridays. No hours when the interpreters were on missions with the army and none when the other residents of F8 were home. No hours during lock-down because of enemy incursions. It was like digging an escape tunnel that no one could know about. It took five months to get the interpreters through the SIV application process. The thumb drive and cabinet eventually held six SIV folders. What they really needed was a lot of luck, something most Muslims don't ascribe to. With an all-knowing god there is no such thing as luck only divine providence, because everything is preordained.

In May 2012 my mother departed this world and my little world on Forward Operating Base Hughie also came to an end. She never knew my job was in Afghanistan. Lying about it eased my conscience because knowing the truth might worry her to death.

As a child, not being truthful with parents was an important part of growing up. Telling the truth about what I got up to risked not being allowed out to play with my pals. Mum thought my new job was in the Middle East which, with hindsight wasn't a very clever thing to say as Iraq was more dangerous than Afghanistan at that time. She was very proud of my new job with an American company, it made her happy, especially opening the foreign payment statements from my bank that arrived every two weeks showing four-figure salary deposits. My success was also hers.

I Skyped her half an hour before she died. Her last words to me were: 'I love you Gary,' said with a sincerity that reminded me of the times I'd sat on her lap as a small boy.

"I love you too, Mum," came out so naturally. I should have said it more often.

BMTF abandoned the J'bad mission while I was out of the country. Someone must have got around to reading the reports. Len had the job of packing everything, including my stuff. There wasn't much.

It was a long time before any news reached me about the interpreters and their SIV applications.

The big dish is probably still there.

Incremental - July 2012

Three days after the murders, Jim Morrey ducked in half to get his huge frame out the hatch of the Embassy Air, Bombardier Dash-8 that had just taxied to a halt at Kandahar Airfield. He pulled his body armour, rifle, hold-all and backpack from the small baggage compartment by the aircraft's tail. In a few strides he traversed the concrete to the Meet & Greet area.

Jim was a mountain of a man whose persona was an even greater presence. If he'd been of Mexican ancestry a macho ego would have complemented his size but that's where Jim was different to many of the other CBP Embassy-based management. Jim's ancestry was Irish but he was American to the core. His military background was French Foreign Legion as a young man. He reckoned it had kept him out of trouble. Jim served in the US Marine Corps for several years before moving on to US Border Patrol then DEA. He'd done things and survived in places where a big ego would have got him killed. That's the difference between ego and strength of character: one is unfounded bravado, the other indomitable humility. The first will often get you into trouble but the second will always get you out. Despite my lack of military background I detected a kindred spirit even though our experiences were very different. I liked Jim the moment we met at the flight-line. Ricco and Chris knew him from times past and they greeted each other, accordingly.

"Hey Jim! Great ta see ya! How long ya with us this time?" said Ricco.

"Two or three days," Jim raised his voice as two Chinooks came into land nearby. We huddled together as the helicopter rotors sandblasted our backs. Unbeknown to me, Jim had been at the ceremony for our comrades. He'd then returned to Kabul to be briefed in person by the Ambassador on the way forward after the tragic event.

"Let's go get corrfee or sump'n," suggested Ricco. Conversation was futile amongst the noise and swirling grit. We followed the direction of Ricco's arm wave over to the Land Cruiser. Chris dropped the tail-gate and opened the armoured inner door. Jim dropped his bags, body armour and rifle in amongst the tow-strap, trolley-jack, First Responder kits, cases of bottled water and other essential equipment that littered the grimy space. Rear door secured, mount up. The rocky track led away from the airfield towards Ghurkas on the gate. ID cards held up to the closed windows confirmed we weren't enemy.

Gurkhas swiftly deployed outside the exit. AK-47s ready to discourage uninvited visitors. Two more Gurkhas rushed the gate from the shade of the guardhouse verandah to support comrades. A Gurkha swinging the gate waved us through. They retained their usual jolly manner throughout the action. Gurkha precision in discipline and movement created a calisthenic display that was a pleasure to watch. Even a civilian like me could appreciate the beauty of their work. Despite being a compound within the secure perimeter of Kandahar Airbase, Gurkhas maintained the same vigilance as they would in the Embassy district of Kabul.

We had just left the US Drug Enforcement Agency compound at KAF.

"NAAFI?" suggested Jim. I was beginning to get a bearing on his accent: definitely not, Noo Yoik.

The Navy, Army and Air Force Institute is a British Forces establishment serving those that serve. At Kandahar the NAAFI had a recreation area and shop about a mile away, not far from the White House. Chris steered us towards it. I was in the back seat with Jim.

"Gary, how ya doin' mate?" he looked me over. Not many Americans use that expression so when he referred to me as mate, it made me smile.

"Yes. I'm OK," it was true. I was OK. But I wasn't in denial about the magnitude of the event.

"That was a fuckin' helluva thing ta happen," he shook his head. His huge right arm stretched out to me. "I'd like to shake the hand of one of the luckiest blokes alive."

That made me smile, not just the gesture, but he called me 'bloke.' His familiarity was reassuring. Jim used a lot of British expressions and I was now thinking, Boston accent? Maybe. His huge hand enveloped mine.

"Have ya bin ter the NAAFI yet?" asked Jim.

"No. No I haven't. I know what it is but not where it is. We haven't got around to it. There's a lot going on and everything is so regimented. That sounds a bit daft, doesn't it?" I shook my head at my foolishness. "Regimented with the military, how could it be anything else?" I said rhetorically. "It seems there are so many things to do here before we actually get to do our job."

"You better believe it," said Jim. "Ricco, how ya gettin' on with the various passes and other BS?"

"Well Jim, as they say in Kaarbul: we're workin' on it!" said Ricco. "The meal cards've changed. They now have a blue stripe rather than a purple stripe," Ricco's description of the new D-FAC admission card process was a preview of one aspect of my future activity: war-zone corporate bureaucracy.

"Damn it," said Jim, "does that mean I can't get in the D-FAC?"

"You'll be OK. Just show your LOA," Ricco was referring to the Letter of Authority, every person connected with the DOD had to have a LOA, "and sign a sheet until you get the new one. Just get to stand in a different line. Lynn's been working on the new cards for the past few days. She should have 'em this afternoon."

"She's a great girl," remarked Jim. Ricco and Chris agreed. They knew her well enough to pass judgement. "She's done a lot of really good work with the Afghan women's program. But I warned her, don't let it break your heart when it all turns to rat shit." Our Land Cruiser turned down a bumpy-dusty track. "It won't be her fault. It won't be the fault of anyone in particular. And that's one of the issues. People want the job done but then forget about the support." We grabbed onto door handles and seats to steady ourselves. "Some of the guys at the Embassy just don't see it as a positive contribution. They just don't get it."

Wind and vehicles drove road dust into the air, dragging visibility down to less than ten yards in the strange light. At an indiscernible T-junction, Chris guessed it was a good place to look left, then right. Other vehicles also moved at two miles an hour which was good, because the

Land Cruiser's gold paint camouflaged it in the gloom. Side-on, from more than twenty feet away, it wasn't there.

Jim continued his briefing: "Whatever you, or I, or anyone does here is incremental. We just build on what the last guy did and hope the next guy adds something to what we've done," Jim looked at me. "Incremental. That's the only way."

I knew exactly what he meant: "Change is constant, except in the time it takes to happen," was my contribution to the conversation.

"JAZUS!" Jim roared. "That is the profoundest thing I've heard in a very long time. Who the fuck said that, Einstein?"

"Well, …I did," I replied.

"DUDE! I knew it. You're the evil genius," Chris shouted as he grinned at me in the rear-view mirror.

From the front seat, Ricco let everyone know: "That settles it. You're writin' the team reports," we all laughed. Chris pulled the Land Cruiser nose-first up to a line of T-walls. As we got out, some of the desert and hot air got in. Jim led the way down a passage formed by Hescos. Thirty paces brought us into a square enclosure. In front, the half-round building arose from the dust. It had the same half-sunken tube-like appearance as the Luxembourg NAAFI, on a sign over the doors welcomed customers. Directly opposite, across a small courtyard, the NAAFI shop sold many British products: PG Tips, Embassy Regal, Cadbury's Dairy Milk, Fisherman's Friends and The Sun newspaper, two days old.

Inside the tubular-shaped building were several large screen TVs with comfy leather sofas arranged in front of them. Booths, created by sight-screens, had comfortable and secluded seats for six people. The cafe sold bacon and egg rolls and mugs of PG Tips. Two teas and two coffees were carried over to a quiet corner so we could talk.

"Ricco, how's the move from the RTC progressing?" Jim asked.

"We'll take a run over there at some point and grab the last bits of gear but we're priddy much done. The Dyncor guys have been great. They helped us move our gear on to the base. They even donated some office space although it may not have been theirs to give."

"That's great Ricco," said Jim. "That wouldn't have happened if we didn't have such a good relationship with them and that's down to you two guys and Lynn." Jim turned to me. "BMTF lived on the RTC outside of KAF. Even before Herat, the Embassy had in mind that RTCs are too dangerous for their personnel so we moved our base onto KAF. It'll actually be a lot better."

"It'll make gettin' ta the airport a helluva lot easier," said Ricco. "We won't have four checkpoints a day to get through. The time saved will mean more time on the job."

"So, the office?" Jim went on. "How'd ya get that?"

"Well, the White House is kind of official. The military know we're there but they ain't worked out we shouldn't be. There's no formal agreement," said Ricco. Jim gave silent approval to BMTF's occupation strategy.

"The TLS is a different story. The guy in charge at KBR, Bruce, is a Marine. He mentioned it to me one day and he had a key."

"So you're squatters?" Jim smiled.

"Yeah. Guess so," said Ricco.

"That's great," said Jim. "Seize territory and hold it. Let's face it, no one knows what the fuck's goin' on here. If they ask you to move, so be it. What is it the Brits say?" said Jim bringing me into the discussion.

Shrugging, I guessed: "Carry on?" we all laughed.

"Carry on," replied Jim. "Ain't that just so?"

"Hey, Jim," said Ricco. "Can you and Gary hang on here for an hour while we go check on some things?"

"Sure thing," replied Jim.

They didn't tell me they were collecting Mark's death certificate.

Jim resumed our conversation. "What's your background?"

My description of thirty-five years in UK Customs, my vehicle search experience, hundreds of detections of drugs and weapons was quickly summarised, as was how my investigation experience helped me after the failure of the Congo job. Jim listened intently.

"It's interesting how we take for granted so many skills until we really need them. I was out of a job and out of luck after the DRC nonsense. Then a friend referred a business acquaintance to me. They had a problem with Customs. Several truck loads of beer had been seized by Customs at Dover and I was able to help them."

"That's good. You're right about skills," Jim paused. "Fancy another cuppa tea?"

"Definitely. I'll get them," I stood.

"No mate. Save our seats. You can get the next one." Within a minute he returned with two mugs of steaming hot water, some sachets of sugar and plastic straws of milk. Setting the tray down on the table he took a small clear plastic bag from his jacket pocket. "I always keep a few of these on me." With that he dropped a bag into each cup. "Irish tea," he grinned.

"I like that idea. I'll get myself a small supply. Probably PG Tips," I said.

"What's your specialty?" Jim asked. He'd probably already checked me out but a résumé only reveals part of the picture.

"Specialty? I guess it's fraud detection and investigation. My most outstanding career achievement was establishing a specialist intelligence network to counter cross-border tax fraud."

What I didn't tell him was that I now know the Department didn't want that particular problem fixed. Somewhere amongst all the UK private-public sector partnerships, a lot of people were happy with massive European Union VAT fraud and I naively thought that my efforts would be commensurately rewarded. Just another of life's disappointments. Maybe I'd tell him some other time.

"I felt I'd gone as far as I could in the Department so decided to get into contracting. It's not an easy life," Jim listened intently. "I have a small consultancy in the UK. Mark and I worked together on a few things. Trouble is, the work's irregular and the government keep moving the goalposts. Also, some of the people that approached us were smugglers."

Jim laughed at that.

"Yes. Makes me smile too," I said. "I did some interesting stuff on the Congo-Zambia border a couple of years back. Identified a massive cross-border smuggling operation. Difficulty there was that the Congolese Douane are part of it and their enforcers are the Congolese Army."

Jim laughed out loud. "That's Africa," he said.

I'd lost count of the number of times I'd heard that expression. It had been the directors' excuse for not paying us.

"I saw similar activity last year when we went to Torkham Gate for a week," I said.

"You were at J'bad for a while with Len Kinder, right?" said Jim.

"That's right," I said cheerfully. "Len's a smashing fella. He taught me a lot. Especially about weapons. I'll always be grateful to him for that."

"You got into some stuff down there at the ICD I recall," Jim must've read the reports that I thought were just filed in the metaphorical round metal can under the desk.

"We did. We could've done better. I guess everyone says that. But it was difficult."

Jim laughed. "Difficult? I followed you two guys with interest when I was back in DC. What was it? Walking around on Soviet ammunition dumps? Dodging VBIEDs? Then there was the attack on FOB Finley Shields. I was actually quite jealous," Jim smirked. He wasn't the sort of bloke to exaggerate. "Then ya had that thing with the Pakistani drug company, right?" He was leading me somewhere. I followed.

"Oh! You heard about that? The CBP guy for our area of operation insisted we were out of our lane but I didn't see it that way. It was fun."

"Hey, he didn't get it. He's a dyed in the wool Border Patrol guy, different mindset. He's back where he belongs," Jim winked.

"Oh! That's good," I sipped tea. "I don't expect to hear anymore about that. Criminal intelligence is unusual in that it has a tendency to defy gravity: most of it flows upstream."

"Ya didn't hear?" before I could confirm my ignorance, Jim went on: "The DEA guys developed that information. Quite a package. No result yet but that's because they're still workin' on it. There's all sorts of connections. Helluvva a network. It was your report that sold it: the description of, what was it? …Displaced Loads. I'd say you gotta kinda sixth sense about Customs stuff."

That made me feel good. "Thanks Jim. I really appreciate that. But it wasn't just me. Len could've nipped that in the bud but he saw the potential. Also, the army interpreter, Freddy, he was brilliant. You know, scratch the surface of anything and there's always something interesting going on underneath."

Jim must have experienced it himself. "It's a special kinda situational awareness. You've got it. How'd ya feel about being here?"

"Here? Kandahar? I'm OK with it," I replied. "In fact it's good. I just need time to observe activity and get to know trading profiles, that sort of thing."

Then he came straight out with it: "Tell me what happened at Herat."

His directness caught me off balance. "All I know for sure is that I'm alive and three of our friends are dead," I took a deep breath, then told Jim my story.

"What made you go outside?" said Jim.

Jim sat in my peripheral vision, watching me review the memory on a blank space across the room. "I'm interested in what it was that caused you to move towards danger."

"I really don't know. Just seemed like the right thing to do at the time. It sounded like an attack but I couldn't work out the scale of the attack. It wasn't a rational decision. Len Kinder and I had done some security training with the Mil at Jalalabad. We were attacked several times. It conditioned me to react in a certain way," I didn't need to explain actions under fire to Jim. "I instinctively knew that some of the lads might need help. I suppose it's what most people would do."

"No mate, yer wrong," said Jim. "It's what some people would do." Jim put his cup on the table and watched me, closely, in the way that detectives study suspects. If I'd given anything away, he didn't jump on it. No case to answer.

"Eric McGoff saved a lot of people that day," I knew that much from my conversation with Eric immediately after the event. The murder weapon had sat between us on a table.

"No doubt about that," replied Jim assertively. "We got him out of here quick. He'd have been a target. Got an award stateside."

"I'm glad he got recognition. Eric was the CBP rep at Jalalabad when Len and I first got there," slowly shaking my head helped compose my thoughts. "We didn't get off to a good start," Jim got to hear from me about the lack of basic preparation for our arrival. "It was disappointing to say the least. No transport, almost no accommodation, poor communications. You name it, we didn't have it and that was because someone hadn't prepared the ground for us. Just thinking about that now, makes me smile. I've learnt a lot in the past year. I now know that doing the actual job is the smallest part *of* the job. It's down to us as advisors to create the conditions in which we are able to function," Jim was paying attention to my every word. "It's not like a normal job where everything is already defined. Where you turn up each day and everything is pretty much where you left it. I think what I'm trying to say is, you're on your own and *you* define the job. In most occupations, the job defines you. Here, if you don't have something, beg, borrow or steal it. You have to prepare your own ground. It's like being told: build a canoe, pick a tree."

Jim smiled. "I like your analogy but I'd also say that you'll find here, when you've built the canoe, someone'll ask: why didn't you do it like this?" we both laughed.

"Yes. I can see that already. Well, this may sound selfish but I'm building my canoe for me until someone tells me otherwise," I'd digressed, "What I wanted to say was, that although Eric didn't do much for us at J'bad, he more than made up for it at Herat when he shot the shooter." Jim silently corroborated my statement as I shared my thoughts. "If Eric hadn't been at Herat, more people would have been killed. After that, Eric went right to the top of my list of seriously good blokes."

"Absolutely," agreed Jim.

I couldn't stop talking: "You know, it's things like that which make me think about people who get the Victoria Cross, for Americans that'd be the Medal of Honor. My point is, none of the guys that get those awards set out to get them. They didn't wake up one morning and think: hey, today I'm going to do something really outstanding and get the highest award that my country can give me. They just set out for a normal day's work in abnormal conditions and end up doing something extraordinary. Do you know what I mean?"

"Sure do," said Jim.

"There are lots of examples from the First World War. Ordinary British soldiers found themselves in unbelievably bad situations where a different course of action, or inaction, would have resulted in ignominious death. Never heard of again. Their names might have made it to a slab of granite somewhere but, you get the idea."

"Ordinary British soldier? I never met one," said Jim. "But go on."

"Right. I didn't mean to devalue them. My point is, they take the initiative or maybe do something out of their lane, something off-plan that no *manager* told them to do and they get away with it. For example: Joe Ordinary, is pinned down in a trench by withering machine gun fire. If he does nothing, he's dead. If he does something, he's dead. Not much of a choice: something or nothing. Not the ideal conditions to make a choice. But he has to choose. Now." My finger stabbed the arm of the chair for emphasis. "At that moment he makes his move. Not a second sooner, or later. He storms a machine gun position. Destroys the gun. Kills half a dozen enemy and takes several prisoners. Saves the lives of his pals so they can die another day. One second either way and, well, who knows? Joe Ordinary is not only not dead. He didn't die doing nothing. He's survived intact. He receives a citation for doing what he knew he had to do," I inhaled deeply. "I feel like I'm not explaining this too well."

Jim made no attempt to shake the frown from his forehead. "No mate. I'm with you. Go on."

"Joe Ordinary deserved that award. He deserved a lot more. But, I think my point is, that kind of," rolling my hands around in front of me helped juggle ideas in the air. "That kind of characteristic is unquantifiable. There are thousands of recruitment experts using all sorts of human resource computer programs to select the right guy for a given job and the fact is, human behaviour is irrational. Sorry Jim, I'm rambling." I smiled.

His eyes just visible over the rim of the mug focussed Jim's attention on me. "Keep going, mate. You've hit a vein."

"OK. Thanks. You're a good listener," I took a deep breath, then exhaled slowly to steady my aim, "I think my point is, look at the recruiting system for a large organisation. Let's say it needs to hire a hundred people. An algorithm sifts ten thousand applications. It interviews one thousand people. It signs up a hundred. Of that hundred, two will be outstanding performers. Twenty-five will be good. Twenty-eight will be average and the other forty-five are just along for the ride." Jim had one of those corner of the mouth wry smiles which told me he'd seen it many times. "What I'm trying to say is, there's no system for identifying top performers in advance. Any person or organisation that thinks it can do that, should take a suitcase full of money to the race track. There's no program that can guarantee perfect selection. And ... and ... I've said enough." My back pushed into the leather Chesterfield as I got off my soapbox.

The long moment before Jim spoke stretched beyond the distance between us. He changed the subject. "You'll go home for a while," he wasn't telling me what to do, but it was a good idea. "Will ya come back?"

That question had been rolling around inside my head since the murders. I was just recovering from near bankruptcy, getting divorced and had a load of family commitments including another son to support through another level of education and now I had to deal with the repatriation of my friend. Like I said earlier, no one goes to Afghanistan for their own benefit. Desperation would bring me back but this was not the time for confessions.

"Yes," I was glad he'd asked. "I'll come back, if that's OK with everyone."

Jim smiled. "*OK*? Glad to have you," he said enthusiastically.

"I'm not about to pretend that the Herat attack hasn't affected me. It has," my gaze drifted back to the blank space that helped me compose my thoughts. No distractions. "I don't have dreams about it and I don't think about it every waking moment. That doesn't mean I'm some super hard-case, unaffected by events," I brought my focus back to Jim. "I'm sure you've had many similar, but worse, experiences. But, you know, stress is something that often has a positive influence. Too many people see it as a negative factor," I sipped tea.

"Yeah?" Jim prompted me to expand my thoughts. "Is this about to be another revelation like in the car," that made me feel good: he hadn't just *heard* me describe my change theory, he'd actually been listening and thought it worth remembering.

"Possibly," I smiled. "Plants experience stress in different forms; wind, heat, dehydration, infestation, loads more things. My point is that plants thrive and grow stronger with the aid of some stress and yet the same conditions kill others. Have you ever noticed how in a forest, the bigger trees are surrounded by smaller trees? That's partly down to the protection provided by those at the perimeter. It's a hierarchy. Apply that same principle to humans."

Jim spun tea dregs around in his cup. "I think you got something there. Get the right people around you, you'll reach a higher level," Jim had his own, similar, theory. "Athletes and soldiers train by stressing themselves, physically and mentally. I guess that's part of the selection process you talked about. Finding the people who have the attributes is one thing. Gettin' them to use them, that's about leadership and management," he understood. "You should definitely come back here. The right person here would do well."

"I will. I've thought about what Mark would do if I'd been killed. He would have said, *carry on,*" Jim smiled at my very British expression. "In UK Customs we didn't lose many colleagues by murder. Drink? Yes. Or some other form of ill health brought about by the conditions. My point is that Mark will achieve the objectives he set for the benefit of his family. His girls will do well. Crazy thing is, if he'd died while working in his own country, his family would have been impoverished. Now that, would have really pissed Mark off."

Jim reclined in his seat. "I think you've got it worked out, mate. Like you say, use the experience, good and bad, to your advantage," he swallowed the last of his tea. "Just remember. Incremental!"

Repatriation - July & August 2012

Someone at FedCor head office in Florida, the people Mark and I worked for, had been on the ball. The email in my InBox came from Sergei who worked for a company called Tangere, based in Valetta. Sergei would be dealing with Mark's repatriation and we needed to talk. Urgent. The number on his signature line connected me immediately.

"Good morning Sir. My name is Gary Wilshaw, calling from ..." I didn't finish my introduction.

"Gary," Sergei sounded genuinely pleased to hear from me. His accent was difficult to place. Just because someone is based in Malta, doesn't make them Maltese. "Thank you for calling. I am *very* sorry about what happened to your friend. It must have been a terrible experience for you too. I can't begin to imagine it."

"Thanks Sergei. Yes, it was a terrible thing. How much do you know about what happened?"

"Only that Mark was a friend of yours and you were with him when he was shot," it wasn't quite correct but it had been close enough at the time and it didn't feel right to quibble about the details now.

"Pretty much," I said. "What do you do?" I'd checked out the company's website after receipt of the email but maybe there was an update.

"I work for a company that provides logistical services to non-governmental organisations, aid agencies mostly. But right now, my job is to get Mark home. You will accompany him. Are you still OK with that?"

"Yes. That'd be really good. I do know his family so I'll be a familiar face to them."

"That's what I thought," Sergei was very reassuring. "I won't go into too much detail because I'm sure you have other things to think about but, briefly, Mark has to be embalmed before he can travel on a commercial airliner. It's a health and safety requirement."

"Yes. I understand that. Human remains. They need a health certificate."

"Right!" he sounded relieved that no explanation was necessary. "So, I have arranged for an embalmer from a funeral company in New Delhi to fly to Kandahar and prepare Mark for his flight home. Then, the same plane will take you and Mark to New Delhi where you'll both get a British Airways flight to London, Heathrow."

"OK. New Delhi?" it seemed odd to me there wasn't one closer.

"Yes. Unfortunately it's the nearest reliable service. Embalming is just not done in Afghanistan. It's a cultural thing. Also, Afghans don't get flown *out* of the country for burial elsewhere." That didn't surprise me. He'd obviously checked it out. "I considered getting you both back via Kabul but that would mean three hops through Islamic countries instead of one. Kandahar, Kabul then Dubai with the final hop to London. Messy. Then there's the issue of movement on the ground in Islamic countries. And the time involved. Too many opportunities for error and exploitation. Simpler just to move once." It made sense. Especially in this heat. New Delhi is only around three hours by air from Kandahar.

"OK, sounds good," I said. "I spoke with some Royal Airforce guys the other day in the hope that Mark could get on one of their flights to Brize Norton or somewhere, but they don't do that sort of thing for civilians." I'd been very disappointed with the RAF response but Mark, like me, was a despicable contractor. We had to take care of ourselves. That's why we were paid the six-figure salaries.

"Don't waste your time with the RAF. They can barely take care of their own. You will both be in good hands. I promise," Sergei's sincerity had me convinced. "I'm just awaiting an email from the funeral company. I need to check credentials with the airline. Then I'll let you know when it all happens. Will you be able to meet the embalmer when he arrives at Kandahar Airport?"

"I'm at Kandahar now. Will he arrive at the civilian airport or the military airfield?" I asked.

"Oh, good question. Which is easiest?" I could hear Sergei flicking through papers as we spoke.

"It's the same landing strip. Shared by military and civilian but the morgue is right by the control tower which is on the military site. I'm about two hundred metres away from it right now."

"That's good, so you can meet the flight crew and the embalmer?"

"Yes. Definitely. Not a problem," I assured him.

"OK. I'll let them know. If I give you the flight number or call-sign, will you be able to track it from there?"

"Yes. There's a screen in the arrivals office next door. I know the terminal manager," I'd have to have a word with Bruce or Sabrina and ask them to keep an eye open for it.

"OK. Well I think that's about all we need to know for now," Sergei paused, like he was about to ask an awkward question. "Tell me, what do you do out there?" We went on to talk for around fifteen minutes about our respective jobs. I told him what I was supposed to do. I didn't mention that I'd had very little opportunity to do it. His other phone rang. "Oh! I must go. We'll talk again, soon." Call ended.

Skype got me through to a mobile phone at the British Embassy in Kabul. It was eleven-hundred hours on the third day after the murder when the distant phone was answered on the fifth tone. "British Embassy, Kabul. Good morning!" This fella's accent was north London. More Harrow than Enfield.

"Good morning Sir," I tried not to sound too cheerful but in truth, getting through gave me a good feeling. It wouldn't last long. "My name is Gary Wilshaw. I need to report the death of a British citizen here in Afghanistan."

There was a moment's delay while the guy got his act together.

"I need to record some details. Sorry, your name is Gary ...?"

I spelled it phonetically: "W I L S H A W," with special emphasis on the L.

"Where are you calling from?"

"Kandahar."

"Kandahar? ...Afghanistan?" he made me wonder how many Kandahars there are.

"Yes. What's your name, sir?"

"My name?" the question surprised him. "Whetherall. Charles Wettherall."

I repeated his name and made a note.

"Name of the deceased?" said Charles.

"Mark David Butler."

"British citizen?"

"Yes."

"British passport holder?"

"Yes."

"Passport number?" said Charles, like he didn't expect me to know.

"Three, zero, eight, two, four, two, eight, three, eight."

"Date of Birth?"

"Twelfth of April 1966."

"Place of Birth?"

"Hold on," documents got shuffled around until Mark's passport photo page was on top, "Canterbury."

"Date of death?"

"Twenty-second of July 2012."

"Place of death?"

"Herat."

"Herat?"

"Yes. Herat. Afghanistan."

"Cause of death?"

"Murdered."

"But what was the actual cause of death?"

"He was shot to death by an Afghan Border Police office."

"What does the death cert say about cause of death."

I shifted paper again. "Penetrating trauma - GSW. I guess GSW is gunshot wound."

"Relationship to the deceased?"

"He's married. His wife lives in the UK."

"No. Your relationship to the deceased," he said dead-pan.

"Oh, err, friend."

"Has a death certificate been issued?"

"Yes."

"Is a copy available for the authorities?"

"Yes. I have it here. I'm looking at it."

"Have the remains been repatriated to the UK?"

"No. Actually, that's why I'm calling. Can you give me any advice or guidance on that?"

His advice was no longer required, Sergei was taking care of things, but I thought I'd ask anyway.

"The British Embassy doesn't get involved in the repatriation process. That's for the deceased's representatives to arrange."

"OK. But Mark was a former UK civil servant and Territorial Army officer working on a US government funded project here. Is there no assistance available from the Foreign and Commonwealth Office?"

"He will most likely have some form of occupational insurance policy to cover this event. I can't say anymore on that subject," said Charles.

"So, the short answer is, no?"

"I'm sorry about your friend but the Embassy would only get involved if the person was in difficulty with the authorities in Afghanistan and even then there are exceptions."

"In difficulty? Ah, I see, once you're dead you're not in difficulty," I wished I hadn't said that. I also wished I hadn't called the Embassy. Pointless. "What do you actually do here?" I wasn't that interested but he'd wasted my time so I felt entitled to waste his.

"I record information which is passed down the line to the agencies that need the info. Coroner's office mostly."

"Statistics. There can't be more than a handful of British civilian deaths in Afghanistan each year," I said as my patience began to wane.

"Contractors mostly. Private security. Many don't get reported to the Embassy," he said.

"Really? No wonder. You know, when I read news reports about the Foreign and Commonwealth Office supporting families of dead Brits in the Costa Del Sol, I actually believed they did something. But now I think about it, I've never read anything similar about Afghanistan. So, if some drunk falls off a hotel balcony, his kin gets more assistance than a lad doing his bit for Operation Enduring Freedom," I was even more convinced that civil servants regarded contractors with contempt born of jealousy.

He inhaled sharply. "I'm sorry you feel that way. We do what we can. It's never enough." I'd had enough of this but, he had more questions. "How long have you been in Afghanistan?"

"Just over a year."

"Have you registered with the Embassy?" Was he now touting for business?

"Registered? Why?" I hoped he could sense my irritation.

"So that the UK authorities know you are here."

"And how would that help me?" With hindsight I should have said: well they weren't bloody well interested in me when I was unemployed.

"Well, if you had any problems here, the Embassy might be able to assist you."

"What, like, if I'm dead, they'd get me home?" I said sarcastically.

"Hmm. That's not quite what I meant but," he nimbly changed subject, "what are you doing here?" Now he was trying to empathise.

"I'm training the Afghan Customs and Border Police. I used to be a UK civil servant, like you," I felt the need to remind him why we were having this conversation. "So did my friend."

"Hmm. I do understand. How long do you have to stay?"

"As long as I like. I have an open-ended contract. How about you?"

"Oh no. I'm off at the end of August. Done my time here."

He made it sound like a chore but he didn't fool me. He was getting overseas allowances and expenses. His quality of life at the Embassy would be better than at home in London. Swimming pools, weekend barbecues with full bar at UK prices. It wouldn't all be tax-free but still nice work if you can get it.

"So, are we done?" I said bluntly.

"Err, yes," he sounded like he would have liked to continue the conversation but I really didn't have time for him. If he couldn't help, he was a hindrance.

"Good because I have to call a funeral service provider to see if he can get my friend home." My lying might make him feel guilty.

"Oh, yes. Of course. I'm sorry I can't be of more help."
I didn't comment further, just hung up. We'd never communicate again so there was no need for the usual pleasantries.

All calls made and received relating to Mark's repatriation were in my notebook along with the meetings with other agencies: Tangere, RAF, Copenhagen Group Mortuary Services, emails to his wife, brother, UK funeral director. By the third day I had several pages of notes just in case program management thought I was skiving. Then the long awaited email from Sergei arrived. The embalmer would arrive from New Delhi in the morning, Friday 27th July, by chartered plane. He'd prepare Mark for the journey. We'd both be on the same plane back to New Delhi that evening.

"Hey! Great work," said Ricco. "I don't mean to sound triumphal about it but you've stuck at it every day for, what, eighteen hours in this office working across different time zones. Ya did well my friend," when Ricco put it like that, an achievement-rush made me feel good. It had been difficult in many ways, especially the *wait*. The pressure was off. Then one of those random thoughts came out of nowhere.

"Ricco!" I shouted. "I'll need a departure stamp in my passport. Someone in India or the UK might get a bit difficult over that." It was a petty bureaucratic box to tick given the circumstances but it was best dealt with now rather than in India. Getting into the UK would be no problem. It never is.

"Goddamit! Good point," sat in his chair, he thought it over until Chris came up with a solution.

"Dude, let's go over and see the ABP Colonel," said Chris. "He's the go-to guy for passports. If it costs us fifty bucks, what the hell? It's urgent right." Chris anticipated the need to bribe the Colonel. Anti-corruption was a BMTF mission but expediency always has a price. Time is money the world over.

"OK. Let's try it," said Ricco. "Give me your passport," he brought his hand up to his forehead. "Oh nooo!" The last time I heard him say that he'd accidentally deleted a file on his laptop. "Don't tell me, ya passport's in Karrbul?"

I was already retrieving it from a rucksack pocket as he spoke. It was a stroke of luck that it was with me.

"You know, I nearly left it with HQ like everyone else but my visa is valid until December so it won't need to be renewed until my next leave." Ricco took it.

Usually passports were kept by BMTF HQ so they could get new visas at the Afghan Ministry of Interior in Kabul. It enabled one of the interpreters to earn a few extra bucks by standing in line instead of the highly paid contractors.

"Do you want some baksheesh?" I said.

"It's OK. I got a coupla hundred here. Anyway, he owes us for the tools we got 'im. I might ask him if his guys have used 'em already," Ricco smirked.

"They'll be stored in a safe place." Chris's deadpan response barely concealed his suspicion that they may have been misappropriated.

Ricco and Chris went and the office became quiet except for the sound of jet engines and helicopters. Relaxing in the faux-leather executive chair with my feet on the desk, the aural landscape receded into the distance as I dozed.

"SUCCESS!" Announced Ricco, bursting into the room. He hadn't shouted, it was just my half-awake brain exaggerating the sound. I was on my feet immediately but must have appeared to be still asleep. "Oh, sorry, did we wake you?" said Ricco affably.

"Yes, you did. I was gone there for a while." Two hours had elapsed and my legs were numb. Picking a bottle of water from the fridge helped me steady myself. "Want one?" Ricco and Chris accepted my offering.

"Here it is my friend," Ricco held out my passport open at the page bearing the Kandahar International Airport rectangular departure stamp, dated 28 July 2012, two days' time. "You won't see many of those in BMTF passports," he joked. I pondered the poignancy of that indelible mark.

It didn't occur to me that the date in my passport was the twenty-eighth. Saturday.

Friday in Kandahar was usually day off. But not when you have a body to be embalmed and a flight to India without a visa or travel documents. Alone in the Taliban Last Stand I was thinking about how my life had changed. How I had caused that change and whether the reward would be worth the risk. This lifestyle: sleeping with guns, washing with strangers, eating with thousands of fellow diners of different nationalities, driving armoured vehicles through the desert, pretending to be friends with people who would receive heavenly rewards for killing me, it's not normal behaviour. Previous normal was waking to the shriek of seagulls rising on thermals above my home by the sea in England. Current normal is the jet-scream of Tornados vectored to destroy a desiccated dirt compound in Talibanistan. There was a gentle knock on the office door just before it opened.

Sabrina smiled as she leaned into the room: "Hi Gary," her voice was like mint julep on a hot afternoon in Georgia: cool, sweet, intoxicating.

"Good morning Sabrina, what have I done to deserve this pleasure?" We shook hands.

Her smile said: keep the compliments coming. But when she spoke it came out as: "Yure plane has arrived. It's taxiing to the ramp now."

The dirty-faced vignette of the office clock showed 09:10.

"Thank you for letting me know. Is it OK if I go out to greet the crew and passenger?"

"Shure. Go ahead. Bruce is oh-ready out they-er," Sabrina's smile had a contented permanence. Her magnetism defied resistance. She glanced down. I was still holding her hand.

"Oh! Sorry!" I lied. I let go but retained my smile, "I was distracted."

305

She laughed widely. Then her lips resumed the natural, full, black-girl pout that so many white girls crave. When I'd first seen Sabrina from ten yards away I thought her imperfections had eluded me. When I got a good look at her from less than a metre, I realised she didn't have any.

Earplugs in. Wyley-X eye-pro on. Out into the mid-morning sun. A hundred yards away the single-engined plane was taxiing to park. Bruce waved me over. "Hey, Sabrina told you. OK. I'll leave you to it."

"Thanks Bruce. Much appreciated."

The motor stuttered to a halt as a flight officer deployed a small gangway. He waved nonchalantly. We shook hands.

"Good morning sir! Welcome to Kandahar! My name is Gary. How are you?"

"Very well sir! My name is Sanj. First Officer. Do you wish to come aboard?" he didn't sound Indian. South African maybe, but not much. Slight tan. The confines of the cabin kept him hunched over, impossible to gauge his height.

"Only if you need me onboard," it looked a bit cramped.

"No. Not necessary, but we might need a hand moving the coffin," he looked to his left.

Sticking my head into the cabin my face was no more than two feet away from an aluminium box, lashed down with cargo straps where seats had been removed.

"Ah. OK. I'll get a vehicle to move it."

"That would be very good, sir" he smiled and moved out of the way so the passenger could alight. We shook hands.

"Good morning, sir. I'm Gary. Thank you for coming all this way."

This guy was definitely Indian. He had the body shape of a Rusholme restaurateur with the dark skin of the dentist who had painlessly pulled my wisdom teeth.

"Good morning," he hesitated, "Gary?" he pronounced my name with a little uncertainty, smiled and continued. "Thank you. Sergei said you would meet us. My name is Gupta. Thank you."

To me it wasn't so hot but Gupta was already sweating. Maybe he didn't travel well. The eye-side of his spectacles appeared to be covered in spray, which his tissue quickly removed.

"Do you have any bags?" there was a wheel-along carry-on case on the ground next to him.

"This is all," he pulled it closer.

"OK. We need to go into that building," I pointed at the TLS. "Are you OK to walk or do you need a ride?" he looked like he needed a ride.

"No, no, I can walk. I need to walk after the flight," he was very clear about that.

"OK. Just one moment," I put my head inside the plane and spoke into the cockpit. "Hello, Mr Sanj, sir?"

"Yes. Hello." came the reply. Sanj got up and struggled into the enclosed space behind his seat.

"Mr Gupta and I will go now to do the business. Is there anything I can get you?"

"No, no. We have everything here. We cannot leave the aircraft. So, we came prepared," he smiled.

"OK. I thought that might be the case. If you need water or food or anything else, just call me on this number," I handed him a business card.

"Thank you sir," he was genuinely appreciative.

Sanj clambered back into his seat. The Captain was also in the cockpit somewhere. They carried on with their post-flight checks. Gupta and I walked to the TLS. He was relieved to sit in the air conditioned office.

Gupta's heart rate appeared to be returning to normal as I explained: "The mortuary is just around the corner but I'll drive you there soon. The road is quite dangerous. Lots of big trucks," I said, eyeing him with some concern. He didn't look well. The prospect of a dead mortician in a rodent infested office really worried me.

"Cup of tea?" I suggested.

"I beg your pardon sir?" he sounded surprised. Did he think I said, glass of formaldehyde? Holding up the box of teabags put him at ease.

"Oh, yes, please sir. A cup of tea would be very good," he cheered up.

Steam drifted lazily from the kettle.

Transport: the spare key was on the hook which meant the other key was probably with the car.

"I need to call my colleagues to get our pickup truck to the plane. Please excuse me a moment. If you hear any alarms or sirens, just stay here. You'll be fine," Gupta cleaned his spectacles, again. I went out the main entrance and checked across the road as well as in the adjacent car park to see if the truck had been left nearby. No sign.

Speed-dial connected me with Ricco. He answered on the third tone. "Hey Gary. What's up my friend?"

"Hi Ricco. I need one of the pickups to move a casket to the mortuary. Any idea where I might find one?"

"Yeah! There's one over at the White House. Chris is there now. Call him. He'll bring it over."

"OK. Will do. Thanks," I called Chris.

"Dude, how's it goin'?"

"Hi Chris. Yeah it's goin'. I need a pickup to move a casket to the mortuary. Do you have one over there?"

"Sure man. I'll drive it over. Where are you?"

"I'm at the TLS office but ideally I need the truck by a single-engined plane on India Ramp. What do you think? Fifteen minutes?"

I knew he'd have to get to the flight-line ECP, clear the vehicle entry with the MPs, check the vehicle tyres for foreign objects and debris, that's FOD, then drive slowly to the plane. Easy if there are no other aircraft movements.

"OK dude. See you at the plane at ... ten hundred," we hung up. I got back to the office just as the kettle clicked-off. Teabags liberated from the D-FAC landed in two mugs.

"I hope you like Tetley tea," I smiled at Gupta. He was looking a lot better. The colour had returned to his face and he was no longer moist.

"Ahh! Tetley? I do like Tetley. Made by an Indian company from India tea! The very best of British," we both laughed.

"Only the best," I held up a jar containing sugar. "Do you have tea with milk and sugar?"

"Not usually Mr Gary, but today two sugars would be very good," he smiled as he surveyed the room. "So, this is where you work?" he must have expected better.

"This is our office. We work at the civilian airport with the Afghan Customs and Border Police," he accepted the tea. "It's enough for us. We're out doing things most of the time. My friend will be at the aircraft at ten o'clock. He'll have a truck so I suggest you wait here while we get the coffin and then we'll come back for you when it's loaded. The mortuary is just around the corner but we can drive there, airside. Is that OK?"

"Yes. Very good," he sipped tea.

"How long will the, err, …how long will it take you to complete your work?" I said.

"Four hours, maybe five, we will be in New Delhi by this evening," he was reassuringly confident.

"Have you been to Afghanistan before?"

He smiled. "No, it is a new experience for me," he said, but it came out sounding like: never to be repeated.

"It's very good of you to come all this way to help," I checked my phone. Nine-fifty. "I must go to the plane. Do you need to use the internet?"

"No, I'm fine. I am happy to sit quietly," Gupta smiled contentedly.

"OK, I'll be back in about twenty minutes," Boonie hat and eye-pro on. I went.

Out on the searingly hot concrete of India Ramp, Chris approached the plane in one of our soft-sided Toyota HiLux pickup trucks. There were thousands of them on KAF. There were thousands more, brand new and unused, in parking lots around Kabul. They were always there, easily seen when arriving or leaving by plane. Any colour you like just so long as it's white. Ours didn't have Afghan registration plates and weren't armoured so never went off base.

I called for permission to come aboard through the open hatch of the plane. Sanj had stretched out on one of the passenger seats but was immediately on his feet.

"Yes. Please, come aboard," he smiled.

"We have the truck for the casket. How do we get it out this door?" It seemed to me to be like one of those Chinese puzzles where it can obviously be done but there's a secret move that makes it happen.

"With great dexterity," laughed Sanj. The Captain forced his way out of the cockpit and into the passenger compartment.

"Hello," he raised his open palm to me and Chris.

Sanj introduced us. "This is Captain Ravi," we shook hands.

With a few twists and turns, the large metal box bumped out of the plane and onto the back of the pickup. Chris and I drove to the TLS. Gupta had recovered his composure and was reading a mortician's manual. We got him to the mortuary services building by ten forty-five.

The Danish guys who met us at the door were very respectful. They took Gupta and the box into their care. We could expect a call in maybe four hours.

"Chris. I need to go to our room and pack a few things then get back to TLS."

"Sure thing dude"

It was fourteen-thirty when I got a call from the Danish guy at Copenhagen Group. Mark and Gupta were good to go. Chris and Ricco accompanied me to the mortuary. Along with two Danish lads we carefully placed Mark's casket on the flat-bed of the HiLux. The mortuary manager handed me a small plastic bag tied in a knot.

"Some of Mr Butler's personal effects," I graciously received the small bundle. Mark's watch and wedding ring, maybe. "He arrived with those. Nothing more."

It was a slow dignified drive to India Ramp for Chris, Ricco, Gupta and me. We ensured the Union Flag was tucked in around Mark. This time, I was confident Mark would get on the plane.

Sat in the truck, Gupta leaned over and spoke quietly: "Mr Gary, your friend, did you say he was shot?"

"Yes. He was shot. I heard he was mobile after being shot. He was alive, but very close to death when we got him to the emergency room. Why?"

"Hmm. His injuries. They looked like more than bullet wounds."

"He was definitely shot. Surgical wounds, maybe?" I'd had no previous thoughts on the matter. Now, I imagined the team of military surgeons doing whatever was necessary to save Mark: franticly cutting, slicing, swabbing and stitching to keep Mark alive. My explanation seemed to satisfy Gupta. For me, my thoughts created a false memory of something I didn't witness, but it is no less vivid than if I'd been in the Emergency Room.

Getting the casket into the plane was not as easy as getting it out. Just when I began to wonder if it was the same box, the plane seemed to suck it in like a whale swallowing a fish. The folded Union flag of the United Kingdom was placed on the box. Time to say farewell to Ricco and Chris. If my promise to return hadn't sounded convincing, they didn't say.

The plane gathered speed along the runway. Gaps in the concrete slapped faster and faster against the tyres until gravity defying wings lifted us skywards. Out the window to my right I saw the small mortuary building. Flag at half-mast.

Wheels up.

Kandahar Airfield was soon behind us as we climbed steeply. The single propeller in front of the cockpit window tirelessly beat a flightpath eastward. Pilot and co-pilot busily consulted iPads. Not playing computer games but checking course, direction and speed with navigation aids.

Gupta was already asleep.

The aircraft safety instructions told me:

Piper M350 Variation. In event of emergency, exit the door.

Fairly straightforward.

My phone's clock said 16:00. We flew towards the night. I began to doze.

The engine pitch must have changed because something startled me awake. Mountains not too far below us glowed golden with Himalayan sunlight. Sanj squeezed through to the passenger compartment passing me on his way to the rear of the plane. A few moments later he returned carrying bottled water and a small container of mixed fruit, in-flight catering: simple, but very refreshing.

An hour later, we touched down in New Delhi. As soon as the plane stopped moving and the door opened, the humidity washed over me like a warm wet wave. Very different to Kandahar's arid air. Grabbing my bags, I looked for shade. Two airport workers were in attendance. Unlike their Kandaharan counterparts, they were smartly dressed and quickly sat on the ground under the wing.

"Good afternoon gentlemen. Is it OK for me to sit here?" I said. It was my intention to sit whether they liked it or not but it does no harm to pretend to be polite.

The young lad eyed me suspiciously. "Yes, sir. Please sit."

Two bottles of water came out of my hold-all as I sat crosslegged between my baggage. My two acquaintances declined the offer. Another India-Afghanistan contrast. The young lad stared as I drank, taking in my boots, trousers and shirt.

"Are you a soldier?" He asked. It was a good guess. My work clothes did have a uniform look about them: Tru-Spec rip-stop contractor khaki pants and Blackhawk rip-stop khaki shirt. The boots were my favourite, Nike SFBs. I have Hobbit feet and most combat-style footwear has a narrow profile. I had some very expensive Lowa boots and Blackhawk boots but they caused Athlete's Foot. I tried a number of remedies with varying degrees of slow success. Lying on my bunk one day considering the problem, the solution came to me in a flash of inspiration. Or, maybe I should say, a flush of urination: the anti-bacterial properties of pee. So, last thing at night and first thing in the morning, for three days, I urinated on the infected area. In the morning it got showered off. At night it didn't. The skin was completely fixed in four days. The boots went to a Nigerian lad working in the Cambridge D-FAC. He was so happy they were in the original boxes. I can't imagine how he'd have squashed his feet into my size elevens. He probably sold them.

"No sir. I'm not a soldier," I said. "I'm here to take my friend home. He died. He's in there." I turned towards the plane's open hatch.
The young lad sat upright craning his neck, following my gaze towards the door. There was nothing to see.

"How did he die?" he said, matter-of-factly.

"He was shot by a policeman in Afghanistan," was the easiest way for me to explain it.

"Why did a policeman shoot your friend?" said Young Lad, eyeing me suspiciously like I must have been part of some criminal activity.

"My name is Gary. What is your name?"

"My name sir? Deepak."

"Deepak. OK Deepak, if you can bring us some tea I will tell you the story. What do you think?" from my shirt pocket came a damp twenty dollar bill.

"No, no, no, sir! No money. I will fetch tea," he was off like a Himalayan hare.

Within ten minutes he was back at his place in the shade with a flask, three cups and a small dish of sugar on a tray. The old guy looked at me and smiled. His wink towards Deepak confirmed: *he's a good lad!* Old Guy moved closer.

"Are you sitting comfortably?" I said, in traditional raconteur style. We each had a cup of tea. They sat attentively. "Then I shall begin ..."

Heads rocked in awe, shock and sympathy as they took in every word. Tongues tutted at my description of working in England and Africa. Their dark eyes seemed to look right inside me, anticipating my words. When I got to the part about Mark on the gurney, they were clearly moved by my description. So was I.

Diurnal progress threatened to expose us to the sun's rays. We moved to the other side of the wing's shadow and contemplatively drank tea.

Deepak broke the silence. "I will be a manager here in a few years."

"Yes, I believe you," I said. "I never heard young Afghan men talk much about aspirations."

Old Guy's head swayed supportively. Despite saying nothing the whole time, his presence made a silent contribution to the discourse.

"I have two sisters. They will be nurses," said Deepak.

"Really? That's very impressive. You know, nurses can get jobs all over the world."

Old Guy smiled.

Two hours passed, evening advanced. Gupta returned.

"Ahh, Gupta. I have been in such good company that I forgot all about you. I do apologise," I said. The airport lights began to brighten the surroundings as sunlight faded.

"I am glad they looked after you," Gupta said something in Hindi to Deepak. Old Guy became more animated. Whatever it was, he approved.

"Mr Gary. Deepak will take you to the terminal building. You are on British Airways to London but you must go now. You have no visa but I told them there just was not time to get visa and also it was too dangerous to try to get visa in Afghanistan. Everything is ready for you but you are a transit passenger so must go from here directly to the gate. Deepak will stay with you. You must go *now*. Hurry up."

Hurry up.

Gupta was sweating again. Stress related maybe.

"OK, let's go." Backpack over one shoulder hold-all over the other, I shook Old Guy's hand. He gripped it, prayer-like, between both of his palms, silently wishing me well.

"Mr Gary. Allow me to carry your bag," Deepak offered sincerely.

"Deepak, I do appreciate your offer but I always carry my own bag," Old Guy smiled. He understood: this was my burden, no one else's.

It took fifteen minutes to walk briskly around the apron to a double door just below the jet-bridge of one of the terminal gates. As we approached the entrance, it opened to reveal two giants in Customs uniform. Standing well over six feet tall, their official turbans gave them a

314

fearsome appearance. Their heads moved in that typically Indian way of expressing sympathy. Holding out my hand to the one on my right, he grasped it firmly in a gesture of friendship and professional courtesy.

"Good evening sir, thank you very much for your assistance," I said.

Neither spoke. What could they say? Their collective demeanour implied it was no trouble. Deepak and I maintained their steady pace up stairs and through doors. The external darkness of approaching night turned the internal surface of the terminal windows into mirrors. I caught a glimpse of myself flanked by my escorts as we walked along an empty corridor. The other side of another door and we began to see more people.

"You have a beautiful airport," I commented. The place was spotlessly clean and well maintained. One of the Customs officers smiled with pride. "It looks like a good place to work." For me, his silence was tacit agreement.

Approaching Check-in, the young lady behind the desk looked very business-like in her British Airways uniform. She was expecting me. I shook hands with the Customs officers. They turned and were gone.

"Good evening sir. May I have your passport, please?" she held out her hand, flicked open the biometric page and busily entered data into a computer, speaking as she worked. "You are on the London Heathrow flight. You have an Economy Plus seat so you have two carry-on bags. No hold luggage," she tore labels from a desktop machine. "Do you have any restricted items? Liquids, scissors, canisters?"

"No. Only ..." I stopped myself. The Blackhawk knife that had saved me from disaster at Jalalabad was on my person. It wouldn't get through security. "Just a moment I must check," I felt in the side pocket of my trousers and surreptitiously removed the knife. Slipping it into Deepak's hand, I said: "For you," he was surprised, then grateful. He couldn't possibly know it was a $150 Blackhawk but there is something about an American made knife, like all the tools made in that country, it exudes quality and reliability.

"That knife saved my life. Take good care of it," he glanced at it briefly, smiled, then slid it into his pocket. "All clear," I said to the British

Airways lady. She swiftly handed me two tags for my bags along with a boarding card in my passport.

"You must hurry. Security is doing final checks," she smiled sympathetically. "I'm very sorry about your friend," it seemed like everyone had been briefed.

Deepak and I walked briskly to the final security check. "Mr Gary. You are here," he smiled.

"Thank you Deepak. You have been an excellent facilitator. Maybe if I come back to India in a few years time, you will be the airport director."

As we shook hands I tried to slip him the damp $20 bill from earlier.

"No!" He stepped backwards, his integrity insulted. "Please. I am happy to help you," his expression changed to gratitude as he tapped the Blackhawk in his pocket. "I will always not forget you."

"Goodbye my friend," our grip released. A clerk checked my travel documents. In the time taken to pocket my ticket and re-shoulder bags, Deepak was gone.

Progress through the scanners was quick. My bags were on the bench for final inspection. The aviation security officer pulled the small plastic wrapped bundle from my holdall. I'd forgotten about it. There was little to be gained by questioning me in Hindi but his gestures were plain enough as he held it out for all to see: What is this?

"Ah. OK. It belongs ...," I hesitated, "belonged to my friend. He was killed in Afghanistan. I go home with him."

He got some of it, but by now other passengers at the bench were paying attention. Someone must have rubbed a magic lamp because a beautiful slender young woman was instantly at my side. She was no more than twenty-four years of age. Her Home Counties English accent was a significant clue to her background. She had a level of intelligence no amount of money can buy but also, a humility that too many Oxford students forget to pack after graduation.

"May I help you?" she said, softly.

"Yes, please, Miss. That is very kind of you."

"He wants to know, what is it?"

"Yes, of course," I said, talking directly to the officer while allowing time for the young lady to translate. "I think it contains a watch and a wedding ring and maybe an item of clothing... It was given to me by the mortuary officer at Kandahar Airbase." In my peripheral vision I could see at least half a dozen passengers were listening to the Hindi version. My abridged account of the story had everyone's attention. "I can open it for you if you wish."

When the young lady had finished speaking, the officer shook his head. It wouldn't be necessary to open the bundle. Maybe it's a cultural characteristic related to the personal effects of the deceased, or, perhaps my compelling explanation was sufficient to satisfy his curiosity.

The young lady was travelling alone. We sat together at the gate before boarding commenced. Anita had visited family somewhere up-country from New Delhi and was now returning to her home in Hertfordshire. I had a feeling she was a law graduate, which was confirmed when she mentioned taking up a job with a firm of lawyers in London. As we talked, more passengers were paying attention to us. The story was spreading.

The PA announced the call for Economy-Plus passengers.

"Oh. That's me," I was reluctant to leave her.

"I'm slumming it behind the curtain," she said light-heartedly. We both laughed.

"Thank you very much for your help earlier," Anita's gracious silence imparted it was no trouble. "I wish you good luck in your work. I have a feeling you'll do very well," we both smiled. "Oh, and if there's anything you would like from the on-board shop, send me the bill."

She laughed. "Thank you very much. I have everything here," Anita held up a bag of snacks and fruit. We shook hands. Her eyes stared through mine. I just knew she could read my mind. She will make a very good lawyer.

As the plane carried me back to the UK, a conversation with Mark a little over a year earlier flashed into my mind. We'd discussed the future. I didn't have a plan, they don't work for me, I'd proven that too many times.

317

But I knew Mark did: "How long do you think you'll stick this out?" I'd said.

Prophetically, Mark replied: "Till the end."

Glossary

3BSTB	Third Brigade Special Troops Battalion
ABP	Afghan Border Police
ACP	Afghan Customs Police
ACD	Afghan Customs Department
AK-47	Kalashnikov assault rifle 7.62mm calibre
AKA	Also Known As. Pronounced: *Ay Kay Ay*
ANA	Afghan National Army
A-O	Area of Operation
APO	American Post Office
A-SAP	As Soon As Possible. Pronounced: *Ay Sap*
ASAFP	As Soon As Fucking Possible. Pronounced: *Ay ess ay eff pee*
ASYCUDA	**A**utomated **SY**stem for **CU**stoms **DA**ta. Pronounced: *Ass Eee Kuda*
ANSF	Afghan National Security Forces
ASF	Afghan Security Forces
BCP	Border Crossing Point
BMTF	Border Management Task Force
BS	Bull Shit: exaggerated or completely fictitious claims or statements
Black top	Metalled road. Tarmac.
CASEVAC	**Cas**ualty **Evac**uation. Pronounced *Cassy Vack*
CBP	Customs & Border Protection. An agency of US Homeland Security
CENTRIXS	Combined Enterprise Regional Information Exchange System. A classified data network for email, instant messaging. Pronounced: *Sen Trix*.
CHU[s]	Containerised Housing Unit[s]. Pronounced: *chews*
CLS	Cheese Like Substance. Sliced yellow dairy fat often found atop burgers.
COMKAF	Commander Kandahar Airfield. Pronounced: *Com Kaff*
Condition Orange	*Cooper Code Stage 3.* Specific alert mindset as described by Jeff Cooper
Carhartt	US clothing manufacturer
DC	District of Columbia. Contracted version of Washington DC, Capital of USA. Pronounced: *Dee See*.
DEA	Drug Enforcement Agency [USA]. Pronounced: *Dee Eee Ay*
D-FAC	Dining Facility. Pronounced: *Dee Fack*

DOD	Department of Defense: pronounced: *Dee Oh Dee*
DRC	Democratic Republic of Congo
Dimp[s]	British colloquialism: extinguished cigarette butt[s].
Dooley	Pickup truck with dual wheels [four on same axle]
Downrange	A location distant from current or starting point
DynCor	A US corporation with numerous DOD contracts
ECP	Entry Control Point: Gate to a compound/base.
EyePro	Eye Protection, ie ballistic sunglasses. eg. Oakleys, WyleyX
FOB	Forward Operating Base: a military base
Farangay	Foreigner [Pashto word of Persian origin]
Five Elevens	Tactical trousers [5.11] like cargo pants but better - much better
Fobbit	Non-combatant inhabitant of a military base. Eg. contractors, maintenance crews, civil servants
FNG	Fuckin' New Guy[s]
GM	Green Meanie: a portable chemical toilet [PortaPotty]. See also: PDC
Gorilla Box	Baggage trunk used by military and contractor personnel
Ground truth sion plans	The reality of a situation as opposed to intelligence reports and mis-
HQ	Headquarters
ICD	Inland Customs Depot
IED	Improvised Explosive Device
ISO	Tank International Standards Organisation container for carrying liquids in bulk. Pronounced: *I so*
HESCO	Blast-defence barrier invented by Jimi Heselden [UK]. Pronounced: *Hess Co*
HIIDE	Handheld Interagency Identity Detection Equipment. Pronounced: *Hide*
HUA	Heard. Acknowledged. Understood: US Marine Corps battle cry. Usually shouted as Hooo arrr. Army & Navy has similar.
J'Bad	Jalalabad, Nangarhar Province, Afghanistan. Pronounced: *Jay bad*
JAF	Jalalabad Airfield. Pronounced: *Jaff*
J-DOC	Joint Defense Operations Center. Pronounced: *Jay Dock*
J-RACC	Joint Regional Afghan Command Center. Pronounced: *Jay Rack*
K9	Canine trained for security or detection service
KAF	Kandahar Airfield. Pronounced: *Kaff*
KBR	Kellogg, Brown and Root Limited. Operational support company

KDH	Kandahar International Airport
KIA	Killed In Action
KAI-A	Kabul International Airport - US Air Force Base. Pronounced: *Ky yah*
KLE	Key Leader Engagements [meetings with movers & shakers]
LOA	Letter of Authority: DOD authority for access to specified privileges. Pronounced: *Ell Oh Ay.*
LN	Local National[s]. A person of the occupied territory
M6	Model 6 rifle. Semi-automatic, ie. single trigger-pull shot with auto-eject & reload 5.56mm calibre.
MOLLE	**MO**dular **L**ightweight **L**oad-carrying **E**quipment. AKA body armour. Pronounced: *Molly*
ML	Military Liaison
M-RAP	Mine Resistant Ambush Protected: armoured vehicle. Pronounced: *EmmRap*
MRE	Meal Ready to Eat. Vacuum packed rations.
MWR	Morale, Welfare and Recreation: a building set aside for recreational purposes
Mananna	Pashto: Thank you. Pronounced: Ma - nanna.
Murican	Dialectic pronunciation of the word, American
NATO	North Atlantic Treaty Organisation. Pronounced: *Nay Toe*
NDS	National Directorate of Security: Afghan secret service
NIPR	Non-Classified Internet Protocol Router Network. Pronounced: *Nipper*
NTK	Need To Know: restricted access to classified information.
OEF-A	Operation Enduring Freedom - Afghanistan. U.S. government codename for the Global War on Terrorism.
OGA	Other Government Agency[ies]
OGL	Old Guys Leaving: resignations or dismissals
OIC	Officer In Charge. Pronounced: *Oh I See*
Oakleys	Eye protection manufactured by Oakley: exceeds US Military's requirement MIL SPEC MIL-PRF 32432 [Sun glasses].
Outside the wire	Not on a military base. In the territory of Afghanistan.
PDC	Pre-Dump Check: ensuring GM has the necessary supplies before use
PX	Post Exchange: originally US frontier fort based trading posts, now on-base shops. Pronounced: *Pee Ex*
RTB	Return To Base
RTC	Regional Training Center

SFC	Sergeant First Class
SIPR	Secret Internet Protocol Router Network. Pronounced: *Sipper*
SIR	Significant Incident Report: a written description of an event [rocket attack/serious injury]. Pronounced: *Ess I Are*
SIV	Special Immigrant Visa: US citizenship for TCNs who served the USA
Sangar	A small protected structure built on the ground, for observation or shooting
Six One Zero	Contract pay rate: $610 per day [£400]
Slightly mangled	Damaged but repairable: humans but also, vehicles and other equipment
SOP	Standard Operating Procedure[s]
SSN	Social Security Number
TBC	To Be Confirmed
TCN	Third Country National: a person not representative of their own or any other government. Pronounced: *Tee See En*
TLS	Taliban Last Stand: a building originally part of the civilian airport complex, then a Taliban stronghold before being captured by US Special Forces and becoming COMKAF HQ
T-Wall	Blast protection barrier. Inverted T shape. Solid reinforced concrete. Various sizes
UNOPS	United Nations Office for Project Services. Pronounced: *You Nops*
VBIED	Vehicle Borne Improvised Explosive Device. Pronounced: *Vee Bid*

Printed in Great Britain
by Amazon